BLOODY BLOODY BAKERSFIELD

BLOODY BAKERSFIELD BOOK 2

BLOODY BLOODY BAKERSFIELD

BLOODY BAKERSFIELD BOOK 2

CHRISTIAN H. SMITH

PERMUTED
PRESS

A PERMUTED PRESS BOOK

ISBN: 978-1-68261-687-1

Bloody Bloody Bakersfield:
Bloody Bakersfield Book 2
© 2018 by Christian H. Smith
All Rights Reserved

Cover art by Quincy Alivio

PERMUTED
PRESS

Permuted Press, LLC
New York • Nashville
permutedpress.com

Published in the United States of America

Contents

MONDAY

CHAPTER 1

LINDA HANSARD, A good Christian woman, had not been with a man since her husband died twelve years ago. In all that time, she'd never even entertained the thought of being with anyone else. So why now? Why was she dreaming about the tall, handsome man with the third eye in the center of his forehead?

She had thought herself beyond such fancies, had supposed that that part of her had dried up and shriveled to nothing after her change of life, but for three days in a row Linda had awoken with a warm nostalgic heaviness just below the pit of her belly. She remembered little of the dreams themselves. Just flashes, really. The tall man, standing half-seen in the shadows of her lonely widow's bedroom. His gaze heavy upon her body, third eye glinting red like a ruby catching the moonlight, while she lay in bed with the blankets kicked away. Wearing not the flannel nightgown she'd fallen asleep in, but some flimsy, filmy thing. If she was wearing anything at all. Linda's dream body was that of the lithe and willowy young woman she'd once been. A fitting object for such a gaze. Much of the disappointment of waking came from finding herself sunk once again into the sturdy, stocky frame of an old lady who'd worked on a farm all her life.

Prior to today, Linda hadn't been able to recall the strange man doing anything in the dreams other than watching her. His mere presence in the room had been enough to trouble her sleep. But seeing the cut on her thumb this morning had brought one of the dreams back in disturbing detail.

She'd cut herself while chopping up a chicken for soup last Thursday. The knife had slipped, and the blade had bitten a deep slash at the base of her thumb. She'd bled like a geyser. Linda knew she probably should have gone in to get the wound stitched, but she was of a generation that dealt with minor injuries at home. She cleaned the cut and bound it with gauze and tape. When she took the bandage off to knead some bread this morning, the sight of the black crescent moon scab dredged a memory from the deeper waters of last night's sleep.

In the dream that Linda recalled, the strange man had crouched naked on her belly. Gently taking her hand, he'd lifted the injured thumb to his lips. The man licked and sucked at the wound, dissolving the scab with insistent probing kisses. When her blood flowed fresh again, he drank it with little slurping gulps.

That was the sort of thing that would be absolutely disgusting in real life, something perverts would get up to, but in the dream it had felt... nice. Warm and shivery, almost like, instead of her wounded thumb, he was licking her womanly parts.

Forrest had never once deigned to do her that particular favor in the thirty-odd years they'd been married, but Linda had a boyfriend in high school who'd been a regular maniac for that depraved brand of suckling. Devan Hooper was his name, a skinny, not-quite-handsome boy with crazy unkempt hair who loved nothing in the world more than lapping her up and down like the edge of an ice cream sandwich. Of course, that was back before Linda was Saved, in her wild, long-repented-for youth. Still, she remembered the sensation with a guilty fondness.

Pastor Tuttle would probably call the dream sinful. In his oft-stated view, any sexual activity other than a man lying atop his lawfully wedded wife was to be condemned. If asked, he would no doubt counsel her to pray to Jesus for protection from her demonic night visitor. But Linda was not about to confide such a thing to the pastor, nor to any of the ladies of the Church of the Shepherd Women's Council, of which Linda had been a member for twenty years, and the treasurer for five. It was nobody's business but her own. A woman couldn't be faulted for what she dreamed. It was just in her head, anyway. Just an old lady's lovely nighttime secret, never to be spoken of in the daylight.

She hoped he would come again tonight.

Linda didn't think much more about her dream man as she went about her morning chores. Her head was filled only with the mundane concerns of maintaining the farmyard. There was a lot to do. Not as much as there once had been, true. In the years since Forrest passed, she'd gradually leased out most of her acreage and sold off all the horses and cows. There was still a sizable garden, though, as well as chickens and a few pigs. More than enough to keep an old woman occupied, especially since her good-for-nothing grandson wasn't about to lift a finger to help. She even had to pay a boy from town to come in and mow the big front lawn.

Linda worked most of the morning in the garden. Watering and weeding, turning the compost, staking the tomatoes and pinching out the suckers, getting the bush beans in and drizzling the corn silk with mineral oil to keep the ear-worms out. By the time she was done, the sun was well up in the sky and the air was already thick and humid. It was going to be a sweltering afternoon. Linda was grateful to duck out of the sun into the relative cool of the shaded chicken coop.

She collected the eggs, fed and watered the clucking birds and then raked out their droppings to put on the compost pile. Then the pigs. She slopped the beasts and checked in on the piglets. One of the sows had birthed a litter on Friday and it had been a difficult farrowing. Linda had to manually intervene, reaching right up in there to pull the pink things out one by one, a task she hadn't had to perform since she was in 4-H. Of the eight in the litter, six had been born dead. The two survivors appeared healthy, though. They were nursing heartily at their mother, who appeared none the worse for her tribulation.

Then, looking down, Linda saw something on one of the nursing piglets. A red mark, or something, on its forehead. Linda leaned in close, squinting to see. She let out a sharp gasp when she saw what it was. One gloved hand went to her mouth.

Not a mark. An eye. The piglet had a third eye in the center of its forehead. Just like...

No. That was impossible. The young pig, as if sensing Linda's gaze, turned from its mother's teat to face her. It seemed to smile, in that way that piglets had, its two black eyes looking up at her with perfect baby animal blankness. The third eye was clearly visible, not really red but an albino pink. It moved independently of the two normal eyes, narrowing as it regarded Linda, glinting with what appeared to be a malicious intelligence.

The pig winked its third eye at her. Just like the man did in her dreams.

He was there in the barn with her. She knew it. His presence was suddenly as palpable as a scent, cutting through the hog stink. He was standing right behind her, close enough that she would hear him breathing if she were to hold her own breath. His gaze fell cold upon the back of her neck, so cold that every hair on her body stood on end. What was enticing in the darkness of her dreams was terrifying in the hard light of day, where such things simply could not be.

"Oh, Jesus. Please..." She began to mutter a prayer, but the words caught in her throat. How dare she call upon the Lord *now*? She should have begun every day this weekend praying to Jesus to keep the man away, but for three mornings in a row, she had denied her Lord. Foolishly thinking he would allow her this indulgence or, even stupider, thinking God couldn't see into her dreams. Instead of fortifying her heart with prayer against evil and temptation, she'd accepted the man into her bed just like a young harlot would. To call upon Jesus' protection now would be the height of hypocrisy. She imagined Jesus refusing her entreaty, shaking his head sadly and leaving her alone with the wages of her sin. For her lust and her foolishness, she deserved nothing more.

Linda forced herself to turn around, slowly, to face what she'd called up from Hell.

There was no one there.

Of course there wasn't. Linda let out a short, barking laugh that was almost a sound of relief, except she wasn't relieved. Not at all. Linda looked back down at the piglet. It had resumed feeding, but Linda could clearly see that its forehead was unblemished. There was no third eye. Of course there wasn't. What did it mean that she'd seen it there? Was she cracking up? Losing her marbles? Going senile?

Linda stepped out of the barn, feeling chilled to the bone despite the muggy heat. Again, she tried to pray. She tried to recall the Psalm about walking through the valley of the shadow of death, but the words were all flibbertigibby in her head. The one phrase she could recall, "I shall fear no evil," was a clear lie because she was very, very afraid.

Walking up the path that led from the barn back to the house, she caught a flash of red light from an upstairs window. In the periphery of her vision, it looked like the beam from one of those laser pointers the kids liked to play with.

That, or a glowing red eye.

Linda Hansard resolutely looked down at the ground between her feet. She would not, could not, look at the upstairs window in her own house. Because *he* would be standing there, looking down at her from the very room where Forrest had taken his own life. She knew the man would be brazenly naked in the daylight, his skin gray and his head bald. Though her recollections of the man upon waking were usually vague at best, Linda now pictured him vividly. Tall and stoic, with a square jaw and a lean, muscular body. Handsome features, but with skin gray as the grave and without a hair on his body. In that moment, Linda could even recall what his penis looked like. Stout and blunt and heavy, the head broad and triangular, like that of the copperhead her daddy had shot in the hen house when she was a little girl. Linda shuddered as she recalled, no forgetting it now, all the ways she'd taken that venomous thing into her body. In every way a woman could submit to a man. If she looked up now, she would see it. Either dangling between his strong legs or pointed out the window at her, straight as an arrow.

Nope.

She turned on her heel and briskly walked away from the house, out to the garage. The car keys were in her pocket, thank Jesus. Though she must look like a fright and smell like pigs besides, she'd go into town. Several of the ladies from the church's Women's Council spent their mornings drinking coffee at Jett's Diner. Linda usually didn't attend these informal meetings. All the ladies ever seemed to do was gripe about their husbands and gossip with acid-tinged old lady's envy about the younger women in the congregation. But she'd sit with them today, endure their complaints with a smile. Drink coffee no matter what it did to her stomach. Someone would almost certainly have brought a Bible she could borrow and Linda craved the Good Word now. Maybe after a couple of hours in the real, normal world, emboldening her heart with Jesus' words, Linda could come home. Maybe then she would see how silly she'd been to be afraid. Maybe then she could face walking alone into her own house.

Or maybe she'd never come back.

Either way, leaving right this moment seemed like the only sane choice she could possibly make. She unlocked the driver's side door and slid behind the wheel of her twenty-year-old Lincoln Town Car.

He's in the back seat.

No. He was in the barn or in the house or nowhere at all, just a figment of her imagination. But he wasn't in the car. She didn't hear him breathing behind her, didn't smell the dry autumn leaf scent that he carried with him. If she looked in the rear-view mirror, she would *not* see his red eye and too-familiar grin.

Linda slammed the door. She started the engine and backed out of the drive without turning around or even glancing in the mirror. Relying on decades of sense memory to guide her out onto the road without ending up in the ditch or taking out the mailbox, praying that no cars were coming. She wrenched the car into drive, spraying gravel as she launched up the road that would take her into town.

How many times had she driven this road in her life? Thousands, easily. But today the familiar landmarks looked strange and sinister. Just a half mile up County Road 6, she passed the red barn that had stood on Fred Anderson's land since before Linda was born. The old man had faithfully maintained the barn, re-painting it every year until he died, but Fred's miserable drunk of a son, Steve, had let the structure crumble into rot and ruin. To Linda's dazed eyes, the faded maroon paint flaking away from the weathered wood looked like long-dried spatters of blood. As if the barnyard had been the scene of a forgotten axe massacre.

A few miles past the Anderson place stood Bob Reynold's farm, with the big corn silo where Ray Hook had died back in '90. Seventeen years old, working the farm as a summer job, the boy had gone into the silo to clear out the wet clumps of grain clogging the auger. The corn collapsed beneath him and sucked him in like quicksand. Linda was friends with Bob's wife Nicole, who'd told her that, when they finally managed to pull the corpse out, the boy's jaw had been snapped right off his face by the weight of the grain that had buried him. Linda's morbid frame of mind cast this image up as vividly as if she'd witnessed it herself yesterday instead of hearing about it second-hand twenty-five years ago.

Then, just coming into town, she drove past the tall water tower with the town mascot, King Chip, painted on the side. The king was a crowned and smiling cow dropping who stood beside the motto "Cow Chip Capitol of Illinois." (Graffiti artists, thinking themselves clever, altered this to read "*Bullshit* Capitol" on a semi-annual basis.) King Chip was a tongue-in-cheek advertisement for the annual Sweetcorn Festival, which hosted the largest chip toss in the state. Today, as never before, Linda was stricken by the obscenity of being greeted at the edge of town by a leering turd. The cartoon piece of dung looked diabolical to Linda's eye. As if the seemingly innocent logo had a hidden, satanic symbolism. Lord of Shit, Prince of Flies.

Linda drove on, hands tight on the wheel, foot growing heavy on the gas.

The man leaned forward, over her shoulder. His animal breath was hot on the skin of her neck, the smell both foul and enticing. He made a sound somewhere between a growl and a moan, so low Linda didn't hear it with her ears as much as feel the vibrations against her throat. She knew his lips were peeled back from his clenched teeth, close enough to bite.

Linda, he whispered with a beastly, guttural rasp.

"No," she gasped in reply.

His calloused right hand, coarse as the pads of a dog's feet, clutched her throat in a momentary grasp, too gentle to be called choking, and yet too rough to be a caress. The hand slid from her throat, down into her work shirt, the buttons parting like water beneath his touch. His fingers brushed a sandpaper graze against her skin. Linda's sagging old lady's breast was somehow transmuted under his rough groping hand into a young woman's pert flesh. Her nipple stiffened as he rolled it between the raspy pads of his forefinger and thumb.

Linda, he whispered again.

"No," she pleaded.

His lips grazed the side of her neck, just below the earlobe, tongue flittering snake-like against the tender skin there. Linda tilted her head, baring her throat. She cried out when his sharp teeth pricked her flesh in a quick, nipping love bite.

His other hand, the one not fondling her breast, pressed over Linda's face, closing for a few breathless seconds over her nose and mouth. Two fingers penetrated her lips. His skin tasted like wood smoke and salt. Like copper and dirt. Like dried blood. Linda gagged at first, but there was something wickedly enticing about the taste. The man's digits pressed insistently against her tongue until Linda, of her own volition, sucked them.

The hand upon her breast now reached down between her legs. Linda parted her naked thighs to allow him up inside her short skirt. In some part of her mind, she knew that she was actually wearing the faded work jeans she'd put on this morning. In Linda's fevered reverie, though, she imagined that she had on the same little mini she'd worn that last time she snuck out to meet Devan Hopper. The very night before he shipped out to get himself killed in Vietnam, he'd driven her out to Lake Kenney and laid her down on a blanket beneath the summer stars. Lapped at her sopping wet girly thing until she was worked up enough to let him do anything else he wanted, too. And today, just like that night, Linda had left the house without any underpants on. Bared to the three-eyed man's ungentle probing.

Linda lay across the front seat, forgetting all about the steering wheel and the pedals and all the bothersome mechanics of driving. Forgetting the road and the town and her Lord and all her earthly concerns, she opened herself to the three-eyed man. His glowing red eye turned a piercing blue as he crawled on top of her, and then flared red again. For a few moments, he stared down at her, his third eye flashing back and forth between the two brilliant colors. Then he thrust into her. His copperhead slipped inside as if creeping through the furrow between two ridges of plowed earth.

Linda, he whispered one final time.

"Yes," she replied. "Oh my God, yes."

Deputy Bryant Morris was hurrying to get into Bakersfield before the shift change at Jett's Diner. Iris Wilson owned the place and worked lunches, while her daughter Alyssa waited the breakfast tables, and damn if Bryant wasn't sweet on them both. If someone held a gun to his head, he might have expressed a slight preference for Alyssa's slender youthful body and bright girlish smile, but he also harbored a deep fondness for Iris's more mature voluptuousness. (He thought of her as more mature, though at forty-something, she was Bryant's junior by at least ten years.) But why should he have to choose? If he got there right at 10:30, he could place his biscuits-and-gravy order with Alyssa and watch her cute, skinny little rear end in those tight black pants she always wore. Then he'd stick around to enjoy Iris, whose waitress blouse seemed to be missing a few crucial buttons, leaning way over his table every time she refilled his coffee.

Both mother and daughter were masters of the art of waitress flirtation, and Bryant tipped them appropriately for this vital service. He wasn't sure how much cash he'd left on his favorite corner table over the years, but Iris liked to joke that he'd entirely financed last winter's re-upholstering of the booths.

He was running late today, though, thanks to those damned kids. School was going to be out for the summer in just one week, but apparently driving out to the dump to shoot at gulls and rats couldn't wait that long. Personally, Bryant didn't give a squat what they did out there. Pest control was damn near a community service as far as he was concerned. But Justin Noonin, who managed the dump for the county, had called the Sheriff's Department to report that the kids were drinking, too. Even Bryant had to concede that young kids plus booze plus firearms could only add up to trouble. So he hauled his ass all the way out the county dump to break up the shooting party. Here he was a bit surprised to find that three of the six kids were girls.

Bryant wondered what the hell the world was coming to. He could almost understand ditching your morning classes to go shooting with your buddies, but when he was that age he could have thought of plenty of things he'd rather do with his girlfriend on a warm spring morning than hanging out at the smelly dump blowing a bunch of birds and rodents to hell.

The kids were smoking dope as well as drinking, if their bloodshot eyes were any indicator. Bryant could have run them in on either the weed or the underage drinking. Not to mention, it was illegal to discharge a firearm on county property without written permission, and not one of them was old enough to possess a handgun like the .22 they were playing with. But the mere consideration of the mound of paperwork involved in writing up six juvenile arrests was enough to give him a migraine. So he just doled out verbal warnings, told them to knock the shit off and clear out of the dump so he could go eat his brunch in peace.

That should have been enough, but Gemma Gordon, predictably, appeared to be the ringleader among the kids. Her mom was a lawyer, and that apparently made her think she was a lawyer, too. Gemma went off on a righteous stoner's rant about police harassment and Second Amendment rights and God knows what the hell else. Then she started waving the gun around in a manner that a more easily alarmed police officer could have interpreted as threatening. For a minute there, Bryant was afraid he was actually going to have to cuff the silly little bitch, but her boyfriend, Luke Simmons, finally got it through her weed-addled skull that they were getting off easy here.

After finally sending the kids packing at a little after 10:15, Bryant knew he would only make it to Jett's in time to see Alyssa if he really booked it heading into town. It would take no time at all if he could turn on the lights and siren, but Bryant already had a couple of citations on his record for unnecessary use. So he kept his speed just above the limit and hoped for the best.

He almost made it. Jett's was in sight, two blocks ahead, just past the town square on Main and Mulberry, when Bryant pulled behind a car that was weaving erratically.

At first Bryant thought it was just some goddamned idiot, drunk at ten in the morning. He let out an irritated sigh at the prospect of the lengthy DUI stop and breathalyzer test standing between him and his two favorite waitresses. By now, he was actually hungry, too. But then he recognized the car and his irritation turned to concern.

It was Linda Hansard's old Lincoln. Bryant knew her. She'd been close friends with his Aunt Shirley before she passed. Both of them were pretty hardcore Church of the Shepherd ladies, so he seriously doubted Linda was drunk. Bryant was afraid that maybe she'd had a stroke or a heart attack or something. He hit the red-and-blues just as Linda's car drifted across the left lane and hopped the sidewalk. The big Lincoln rolled to the edge of the square and came to a stop against a hydrant. Fortunately, she was moving too slow to take it out. There was no oncoming traffic. No pedestrians, either. A few young mothers across the park, their kids playing on the playground, turned to watch as Bryant pulled up behind the idling vehicle.

Bryant called in the stop, and told dispatch to stand by in case he needed an ambulance. Then he got out and approached Linda's car with several jogging steps. He peered through the driver's side window. What he saw there both baffled and horrified him.

Linda was lying down across the front seat, her feet not even on the pedals. Her eyes were wide open and darting around crazily. Linda's clothes were disheveled, work shirt all the way unbuttoned to reveal her plain white old woman's brassiere. That was creepy enough, but what really struck Bryant as hideously awful was that Linda's right hand was thrust down the front of her blue jeans and she was...touching herself. Bucking her hips as her arm moved spasmodically up and down.

Bryant, as he supposed all police did, had always entertained a few traffic-stop-related sexual fantasies. The young woman who would do "anything" to get out of a ticket was a well-worn favorite. Of course, nothing of the sort had ever actually happened. Bryant doubted he would accept such an offer should one be made in reality. He was, at heart, a good cop. (Not so incorruptible, though, that he didn't occasionally take into account friendly flirtation or "accidental" exposure of cleavage when deciding whether or not to write up a citation for a pretty young lady). He'd never even imagined coming across a woman who'd pulled off the road to masturbate, but if made a list of every woman in the county who he wouldn't mind catching in such a position, old Linda Hansard would have been way down at the bottom.

Having no real idea how to handle the situation, he rapped on her window. Linda appeared to be lost in the throes of delirium and didn't respond. If anything, her hand began to work more furiously. He heard her moaning even through the closed window.

"Mrs. Hansard?" he called. "Are you all right?"

No reply, no indication that she'd even heard him.

Not really wanting to, Bryant reached for the door handle. He pulled the door open and almost gagged on the smell that wafted out. It was mostly that hog scent that clung to the pig farmers no matter what they did to wash it off, but it was mixed with blood and a musky sex smell, almost overpowering in its strength. Under all this was another scent, strange and prickling to Bryant's nose. Like freshly raked leaves in the fall.

He let out a little cough and took a staggering step backwards.

"Mrs. Hansard?" he said again, hand going up involuntarily to cover his nose. Still no reaction other than the obscene pelvic thrusting, which seemed to be aimed in his direction now.

Bryant didn't want to touch her, but he grabbed one ankle, giving it a little shake. Linda's leg pressed against his hand, writhing sensually beneath his palm. Bryant let go as if he'd touched a live wire.

"Mrs. Hansard!" Louder now. "Snap out of it, ma'am."

She looked up at him for a second, her gaze seeming to focus on a spot in the center of his forehead. But then her eyes resumed the crazy loop-de-loops they were making in their sockets. Looking above him, beside him, *through* him.

"Come on, Linda," he pleaded. "Stop doing that, okay?"

Maybe it was hearing her first name, or maybe it was the desperation in Bryant's voice, but Linda did respond to that. She sat bolt upright, with an alarming suddenness. Bryant was reminded of a vampire rising from a coffin in some old movie he once saw.

Her gaze settled for a moment on the same spot on his forehead before flitting away again, like an agitated insect.

"No," Bryant thought he heard her say.

"What?"

"No." Her voice was distant and detached, like something you'd hear between bursts of static from a far-away radio station. A bit slurred and sleepy, too. She pulled her right hand from her pants. It was covered with blood.

*That can't be...*Bryant was too rattled to form coherent sentences in his own head. *Surely she's too old to...*

She lunged from the car, clutching for the deputy's face with her bloodied hand. Bryant reeled backwards, stumbling over his feet and falling to his ass onto the grassy ground. He reached for his gun, a senseless reaction, but he had not even extracted it from the holster when the old woman fell upon him.

"Yes," Linda Hansard growled, her voice now a snarling come-on. "Oh my God, yes."

And then, as lover's play, she thrust her bloody hand into the deputy's gaping mouth.

FRIDAY

CHAPTER 2

T HE TOWN CREPT up on him.

Every time Mark Davies had imagined this homecoming—and for the past few weeks he had imagined little else—it was always with REM's "Don't Go Back to Rockville" sounding a cautionary note on the soundtrack. Anticipating the poignant bursts of anti-nostalgia from the once-familiar landmarks he would see on the way into town, he had mentally rehearsed cynical observations he could make about the eternal stagnation of small Midwestern towns. But Mark had accomplished his long-dreaded re-entry in the same somnambulant auto-pilot mode that had marked the last couple of hundred miles of this journey. Three consecutive states of cornfields had induced a deep road hypnosis. By the time he was even aware of having arrived, he was already breezing past the infamous cow shit water tower. Bakersfield had no more blipped his radar than Riverton, or Lake Fork, or Mt. Pulaski. And his CD player had crapped out back in Missouri, so Michael Stipe couldn't warn him against wasting another year.

Thirty years old, all his worldly possessions fitting into a Subaru hatchback with room to spare, this return to his childhood home marked the breaking of a vow—an actual, spoken vow—Mark had made to himself never to come back. But when falling through space, the gravity of home is near to inescapable.

And here to greet him as he fell back to earth was old King Turd of Bullshit Mountain, a bit faded with age, but otherwise just as Mark remembered. The towering pink water tower had been an embarrassment to him growing up here. It was such an obvious symbol of the redneck cluelessness of the place. Mark was surprised, though, to feel a real fondness for the massive eyesore upon seeing it in the flesh after all these years.

He'd actually written the tower into a scene in his first novel, *Blood World*. The young vampire Henry, not yet aware of his new powers, is pursued by a rogue gang of teenage vampire hunters. To get away from them, Henry scales the cow shit water tower. His tormentors follow him up the ladder, shooting up at him with BB guns loaded with silver pellets. Cornered at the top, Henry dives off the tower, choosing suicide over death at the hands of his enemies. This is when he learns he can fly.

Many of Mark's early readers had questioned the plausibility of the water tower. Flying vampires they accepted without question, but that a town would choose a smiling piece of shit as its mascot was just too far-fetched.

Blood World had been published four years ago, followed quickly by two sequels. Mark had been foolish enough at the time to believe that a three-book deal with a small press publisher would be the first step in a journey that would lead to, if not fame and riches, at least to a modest level of notice and financial reward. Alas, it had not quite worked out that way. The first book sold reasonably well, but *Blood World War* moved only about half as many copies. As for *Blood World's End*… Mark was glad that one had only been released as an e-book. Otherwise, there would probably be a landfill named after him somewhere.

The failure of his writing career (it seemed pathetic to ascribe such a lofty word as "career" to his feeble literary attempt) coincided with the far more devastating failure of his marriage. Missy, literally his childhood sweetheart, had finally reached the lifetime threshold of his bullshit she would endure. She'd left him for someone better, and then moved back home, taking their son Ben with her.

This had preceded the longest, darkest year of Mark's life. No longer a writer and yet congenitally unsuited to any job requiring a nametag or uniform, Mark's lack of education or experience left him with few other viable options. He subsisted in those lean, lonely months on his increasingly laughable royalty checks and the charity of his mother. This charity, like Missy's patience, turned out to have its limits.

His mom cut him off, but with the final offer that if he would come back home, she would bankroll the move. Not only that, she would get him a job. Not with the company she worked for, thankfully. Mark retained enough self-respect to know that working for Malovo Agricultural Development's ethanol plant—even with the cushy office position his mother could probably score for him—would be like taking a job with Satan, Prince of Darkness. Instead, she got him a gig as a kind of caretaker at some farmhouse outside of town.

The choice being between that and shift leader at the Denver McDonald's, Mark had decided to take her up on the offer. It wouldn't be so bad. At least he'd be near Ben.

Instead of continuing up Route 54, which would turn into Main Street as it passed through the town proper, Mark turned left onto County Road 6, for his appointment with the guy who owned the house.

He used to drive down this stretch of road a lot when he was a kid. Cruising around country roads was as close to freedom as a teenager could get in a town like this. Notably, Mark had lost his virginity somewhere out here. He and Missy had been each other's firsts. Their defining act of love had been accomplished probably less than a mile where Mark was right now, on some farmer's access road between two cornfields. Sweating buckets in the sweltering August mug, mosquitoes biting their bared skin, fumbling and awkward and over way too quickly. But wonderful. That's how it was done around here. Find an isolated spot and get as freaky as you can in the backseat of a Hyundai.

He rubbed his watering eyes. They hadn't yet adjusted to the flat, distant horizon in every direction. Nothing like the Colorado mountain landscapes he'd come to love. The sky was too far away here, the air thick and muggy compared to the thin dry air he'd grown accustomed to in Denver. Everything that had once been so intimately familiar as to be beneath notice when he'd grown up here was now strange and unpleasant. He wondered if there was a word in the English language to describe this dismaying anti-nostalgia. The French probably had a phrase for it.

Mark came upon the old crumbling barn that was his final landmark, and turned off onto yet another anonymous country road. The house was less than a mile up. The man he was supposed to meet, Sam Hansard, waved him into the drive as he pulled in.

Sam was a big guy, Mark's age or maybe a little younger, copiously bearded. Dressed like a biker in a sleeveless denim jacket covered with grimy leather patches, but the goofy grin and the overall softness of his face ruined any tough-guy image he might have been trying to convey. At a glance, he reminded Mark of a mastiff that would lick a burglar in the face.

"Hey there," the guy hailed Mark as he rolled to a stop.

Mark got out of the car, the silence of the dead engine loud in his ears after so many rumbling miles, his legs unsteady on the motionless ground. He was very aware that he looked and probably smelled like he'd been in his car for the past twenty hours. In fact, in that time he'd only stepped out of the vehicle to fuel up and relieve himself at gas stations across the Midwest. All his meals since yesterday had been drive-through cheeseburgers, and his only sleep had been a few hours of restless driver's seat shut-eye at a truck stop somewhere in east Kansas. The big guy didn't seem to mind, though. He grabbed Mark's hand in one of his huge paws and gave him a firm, slightly moist, handshake.

"You must be Sam." Mark forced himself not to wipe his dampened hand on his jeans.

"Yup," Sam said. "Hi, Mark."

He grinned and nodded at Mark for a few awkward seconds.

"Hi," Mark said, uncertainly.

"You don't remember me, do you?"

"I, uh, sorry. No. What, ah..." Mark drew a blank, though it might have just been a case of his brain being too road-dazed to make the connection.

"That's cool." Sam's disappointment was quite evident on his face. "We went to school together, but I was a freshman when you were a senior."

"Oh, yeah. I think I..." Mark squinted twelve years and about fifty pounds off the guy and had a fleeting memory of someone standing in front of a locker. But that was all.

"It's okay. We didn't hang out or anything," Sam said. "But you did invite me to that crazy Halloween party you threw, where you buried that sock monkey out in the corn field."

That clicked. It had been Mark's last monkey party, and his biggest. There'd been at least forty kids out in that field, all in costume. Mark now remembered that Sam's had been quite elaborate, with a jack o'lantern mask and long-fingered gloves.

"Pumpkinhead," Mark said.

Sam's grin burst through his beard like the sun emerging from a dark cloud. "That's right! You were the only one who'd even seen that movie. Nobody else had any idea who the hell I was supposed to be."

"Do kids still do that on Halloween? Bury the monkey?" Mark asked. He'd often wondered if the tradition had continued after he left, though he hadn't expected the subject to come up literally in the first five minutes of arriving back in town.

Sam shrugged. "Greg Trott did it every year I was in high school. After that, I don't know. But that field, where we always buried it? That's a golf course now."

"A golf course, really?"

"Yeah. When they built the Malovo plant here, all the execs moved into that new Lawndale Manor subdivision. I guess those guys couldn't hack living in a place with no golf. They even plowed over the creek across the tracks, for the back nine."

"The creek, too? Jesus."

This struck a chord deep within Mark, and not just because the wild magical places of his youth had been transformed into landscaped and sprinkler-riddled greens for the pleasure of rich men. He'd grown up believing that burying the monkey every year on Halloween had been a compact with the dark forces flowing beneath the surface of the town, a way of keeping things in balance. What would happen now that that compact was broken?

Probably nothing, he thought.

What Mark had once taken as an article of faith seemed distant and childish now. His memories concerning the Monkey and the Snowman were suspect, the experience tangled up with his nightmares for so long that he doubted he could extract the truth from the dreams. It was easy to imagine now that whatever power might have existed in those hallowed places had been negated by the cold adult force of property development. Two centuries ago, they'd cleared the wilderness, evicted the Indians and killed off all the wolves and the bears. Now the same blind march of progress had wiped away the monkey graveyard and plowed over the Snowman's killing grounds. For a fucking golf course.

He wondered what the work crews had thought when they'd dug up dozens of sock monkeys, along with a century's worth of sacrificial Halloween candy.

"You all right?" Sam asked.

"Sorry. Spacing out there. I've been on the road for a long time."

"You drove the whole way from Seattle, right?"

"Denver."

"I knew it was one of those places." Sam conflated everything west of the Mississippi River with a wave of his hand. "Can I ask you something, though? Why come back *here*? I mean, a famous writer like you."

Mark had to laugh. "Famous?"

"Well, yeah. You're famous around here, anyway. Hometown boy makes it big and all that. I've read all your books."

"Really? Thank you."

"Dude, they're awesome. I don't really go in for that romancy *Twilight* shit. I like how your vampires are, you know, real fucking monsters."

"That's really kind of you to say that. I do appreciate it. But those books weren't exactly *New York Times* bestsellers to start with and they're moving even slower now that vampires aren't quite so trendy anymore. Everybody's into zombies now."

"Zombies are cool, too, but I still like vampires." Sam hissed, baring his teeth and hooking his fingers into claws. The gesture was goofily endearing. That was the moment Mark realized he liked this guy a lot.

"Sad truth is, I'm broke," Mark said. "That's why I'm back home. Plus my ex and my son live here now, so it's good to be near them."

"Your ex is Michelle Delany, right? I see her around sometimes. She's, ah..." Sam dropped his voice to a confidential whisper. "*Married to a lady.*"

"I did know that, actually."

"Of course you did, duh." Sam tugged his beard in a gesture of embarrassment. "Come on, I'll tell you about the job."

Sam led Mark down a path that led from the driveway down between a big aluminum-sided barn and a few smaller equipment sheds. The out-buildings were all relatively modern-looking compared to the house, which overlooked the property from a rise too slight to be called a hill. It was a big place, built in a time when "family planning" meant having room enough for the half-dozen or more kids a man would bless his wife with. Mouths to feed, but also hands to work the land that grew that food. Like a lot of big old houses, this one seemed to possess a weary consciousness. Those window eyes had looked out upon this acreage for a century or more, the house weathering generations of life and death until it came to have a life of its own.

"All right, here's the deal," Sam said. "My grandma had been living up here by herself for about twelve years. She did all right taking care of the place, but she was an old lady and was starting to let some things slide. Then she went and had her...thing."

"My mom told me about that," Mark said. "How's she doing?"

"I don't know, dude." Sam shook his head. "The doctors don't even know. It's like she had a total psychotic break and now she's catatonic most of the time. Sometimes she talks and walks around, but it's like she's not even *there*, you know? Nothing she says makes any sense. And her eyes..." Sam made a few crazy fluttering eye rolls. "Anyway, they're not even sure if she's going to recover. So this place is pretty much mine now, not that I even *want* it. If she doesn't wake up, I'm going to sell the place, but I can't in the shape that it's in right now. That's where you come in."

"Right."

"So clean up the grounds. Clear out all that brush over there. Prune the trees. Keep the grass mowed. Gram had a kid come out and do that just last week, and we're in the middle of a drought, so you probably won't have to deal with that one for a while. Then there's the garden." Sam looked out on the rows of corn and potatoes and cabbage, everything in full bloom, and shook his head. "She really loved that garden, but I don't want to mess with it. Seems a waste to just tear it up, so I'll leave that up to you. If you want to eat any of that stuff, it's yours. I already sold off the pigs and the chickens, because I'm sure you don't want to deal with that shit."

"What about the house? My mom said that's going to need some work, too."

"Yeah." Sam squinted up at the structure. "The house is..." his voice trailed off.

"The house is what?"

Sam shook his head and looked Mark in the eye again. "Well, the roof needs shingles and the whole thing could use a coat of paint. Plus, your mom said you're pretty good with plumbing and electrical stuff."

"I can manage," Mark hedged. "Pretty good" was a bit of an oversell on his mom's part.

"The house still has all the original pipes and wiring, and it's more than a hundred years old, so that's all going to need some work. Plus, I don't know, I think some of the floors are probably in bad shape and I'm sure there's a lot of trash inside. Gram was kind of a hoarder."

"You want to take me inside and show me around?"

Sam bit his lip and gave Mark a strange sideways look. "Should be pretty obvious what needs to be done. Anyway, I'll let you use the pick-up to haul stuff to the dump. If you need supplies or anything, just make a list and I'll do a run to the Home Depot in Lincoln."

"Okay," Mark said, wondering about the none-too-graceful changing of the subject.

"Oh, there's one other thing I should tell you about. See that shed over there with the windows taped over? You don't need to go in there."

"Why not?"

"Well, uh," Sam flashed a chagrined half-smile. "All right. I'm just going to trust you to be cool about this. I'm setting up some lights in there to grow some weed. I'm not like a dealer or anything. Just personal use. I just didn't want you to stumble on it and, you know, call the cops or whatever."

"Hey, I don't care," Mark said. "I used to smoke a fair amount of that stuff myself."

"Used to?"

"Yeah, I gave it up."

"Dude, you lived in Colorado." Again, he favored Mark with a confidential whisper. "*Stuff's legal there.*"

"I actually knew that, too," Mark said. "It just caused some problems in my life."

"Huh," Sam said, pondering the strange concept of voluntary marijuana abstinence. "So are you interested? In the job, I mean."

"Definitely."

"That's awesome." Sam grinned. "I was hoping you'd say yes, because I really like you. I think you're cool."

"Thanks."

"Hey, um, do you think maybe you'd want to go out sometime and get some beers or something? Or maybe just come over to my house. We'll hang out and see if we hit it off, you know and...God, this is coming out sounding gay, isn't it?"

"Not...overly."

"Because I'm not. Gay. Not that I'm homophobic, like a lot of people around here. I'm totally cool with it. It's just not my..." Mark was surprised to see he was actually blushing. "Man, why is this so *awkward*? Look, here's the deal. I'm sure you remember how boring this town is. Almost everybody I knew in high school moved away except the fucking losers. I guess that makes me a loser too, right? But I just thought it would be cool to have somebody to talk to. Not like, you know, *sharing our feelings* or anything like that. Just, you know..."

"Sam." Mark cut off his babbling. "I'd love to hang out sometime. Sounds fun."

"Really?" Sam grinned again. "How about tonight? Come over to my place. I'll get some beer and, oh God, do you drink beer? I know you said you didn't smoke weed anymore, but..."

"I still drink beer sometimes," Mark said, though that was also on his list of things that had caused problems in his life. "But tonight I'm probably just going to crash out."

"Well, come over any time you want. It's not like you need an engraved invitation or anything. I live in the apartment above the bank downtown, and I'm always home. If you see the lights on, just come on up."

"Or you could come over here tomorrow night," Mark offered. "Show me the stuff that needs to be done in the house. *I'll* buy the beer."

Sam blanched visibly at that, just as he had the other time Mark had asked him to show him around the house. "Yeah, um, no. I don't really..."

"Why don't you want to go into the house?"

Sam was blushing again. He took a deep breath. "All right. Before you make your final decision, and we shake on it and everything, there's one more thing I should tell you. I'm sure you'll think I'm crazy or full of shit, but if I didn't tell you I'd feel like I was giving you the job under false pretenses."

"What, is it haunted?"

Sam barked nervous laughter. "You probably don't believe in that kind of thing."

"I've seen some crazy shit in my life, Sam. I do believe. What happened to you in there?"

Sam leaned back a little and squinted down at Mark, as if trying to determine if he was putting him on. He took another deep breath. "Okay. I moved in there with my grandparents when I was ten, after my dad and my mom both died."

"How'd they die?"

"My dad was a deputy. He got shot by a drunk driver he pulled over. Mom was pregnant when it happened, but there was some kind of complication. She went into labor early, and then both she and the baby died. Would have been my little sister. So I lost both my parents within a couple months of each other."

"Jesus. I'm so sorry."

"It's all right. That was a long time ago. Anyway, strange things started happening as soon as I moved in here. My Gameboy disappeared from my bedroom the very first night I slept there. I tore the house up looking for that thing. I mean, I just lost both my parents. That Gameboy was the one thing I had that gave me a little bit of happiness, you know."

"Did you ever find it?"

"Yep. A week later. In the loft of the barn."

"No shit?"

"No lie, dude. And that was just the first thing. Sometimes I heard this little girl...crying in the attic right above my bedroom at night. Lots of other stuff, too. Shadows that shouldn't have been there. Sounds, weird smells. Plus, fucked up dreams almost every night."

"Wow."

"The psychiatrist I was seeing said it was post-traumatic stress from my parents dying, and I actually believed that for a while. Gram just thought I wasn't praying to Jesus hard enough. She'd lived in that house since she was a little girl and she never had anything like that happen to her. But my Grandpa..." All the good humor was gone from Sam's face, replaced by a deathly pallor. Despite the thick beard, he looked like a terrified child. "He believed me. He saw shit, too. He said there was a man in big heavy boots who walked up and down the hall at night, scratching his fingernails along the wall. And there were rooms in that house he just wouldn't go into. Like that front upstairs bedroom."

Sam pointed back at the house without turning around to look, his mouth drawn in a straight-line grimace of dread. Suddenly, Mark didn't want to look up there, either. "He said that he heard people whispering in there sometimes, and that he recognized their voices. He said it was his brother and a girl he used to know. They both died when he was a kid. Grandpa said that he was afraid to listen to the words they were saying because he thought they were calling him. Telling him to follow them. Maybe they were, because that was the room he hung himself in."

"No."

Sam nodded. "I found him. I was fifteen. There was a hole knocked out of the plaster in the ceiling. He stood on a chair and tied the rope around a rafter. When I saw him, I ran out of the house. I haven't been back inside since. Literally, not once. I lived at a friend's house until I graduated and then I got my own place."

"My God, Sam."

"Yeah." Sam wiped away a tear. "So I'm sorry I didn't tell you all that up front. If you don't want the job anymore, I'll understand."

"Of course I still want the job. I believe everything you told me, Sam. But I'm not afraid. Actually, I'm fascinated by that sort of thing."

Sam looked at him like he was a madman.

"So, am I hired, or what?" Mark smiled, to reassure him.

Sam nodded thoughtfully. His eyes were drawn back up to the house. "Tell you what. Spend the night here tonight. If you still want the job in the morning, it's yours. If not, no hard feelings. I'll totally understand."

"Deal."

Mark stuck out his hand and Sam shook it, his palm even moister than it had been before. He looked Mark in the eye. "I just hope you make it through the night."

CHAPTER 3

"So HE TITLED the essay 'Hunting for Peasants with My Dad.'" Lana Blair-Delany breathed a bit heavily, keeping up the brisk pace Michelle was setting. "Of course, I assumed that was a typo, but he kept up the same spelling through the whole piece. 'Our dog Perry flushes the peasants out of the bushes so me and my dad can shoot them.' And 'I use a 16 gauge to shoot peasants, but Dad likes his 20 gauge better.' So I'm thinking maybe this kid really is the son of some feudal landowner who's into hunting humans."

Michelle smiled over at her wife to show she was listening, and then glanced back to check on Ben. The boy had lagged almost a full block behind, and was gazing with curiosity at something on the ground. He bent to pick it up, and Michelle saw that it was a snake skin.

"Ben!" she called. "Put that down!"

"Aw, Mom," he called back. "Can't I keep it? I think it's from a rattler."

"There are no rattlesnakes around here. Now come on, keep up."

Ben frowned. Even from this distance, Michelle could tell by his expression that he was debating whether or not to just stuff the nasty thing into his pocket in defiance of his mother. He'd inherited a propensity for dragging home creepy totems (and for defying her) from his father. But Ben must have decided that the skin wasn't worth the fight. He dropped it back to the ground and ran to catch up.

"I gave the kid a C minus," Lana went on, as they resumed their power walking. "And that was *damn* generous. But he came up to me and protested the grade, saying it wasn't his fault the spell checker didn't catch that."

"That's funny," Michelle said, though that sounded flat even to her own ears.

Lana frowned. "You all right?"

"Yeah, sorry. I'm just a little distracted."

"Your idiot ex-husband isn't worth the anxiety, in my opinion."

"It's not that," Michelle said. "Well, not *just* that. It's just...it's strange sometimes, being back home."

"We've been here nine months," Lana said. "I thought you'd be immune to the nostalgia bombs by now."

"I think the weather change has something to do with it," Michelle said. "The feeling hit me really hard when we picked Ben up at the school. You know they haven't changed anything inside from when I went there? Same floors, same walls, everything. Going inside, I remembered how the water from the drinking fountain tasted kind of bleachy and rusty, but really good and cold. And the weird fruity smell of the pink liquid soap in the bathrooms. And how loud the fans always were around this time of the year because there's no air conditioning."

"Sounds miserable." Lana pulled her sweaty t-shirt away from her skin. She was still acclimating to the humidity.

"No," Michelle said. "It's mostly happy associations. That last-week-of-school feeling. The kids out of their minds, excited for summer. But it's poignant, too, because it reminds me of Jess and Toby, my friends who died, and..." She felt herself tearing up and forced out a laugh. "God *damn*, what is wrong with me?"

Michelle wiped her eyes, wondering if the weather change was really what had triggered her emotions. She'd been feeling an undefinable distress all week, even before it got hot.

"It's all right," Lana said, taking her hand.

Michelle accepted her wife's hand, but she did glance around as she always did to see who might be watching. Most people here were surprisingly accepting, but it was still a very small town. There were occasional hard looks and overheard comments from Church of the Shepherd people when they went shopping at the new County Market. Plus a nasty near-confrontation with a couple of old racist farmers when Lana had made the mistake of going to Wolfy's liquor store to buy a bottle of wine for their anniversary. By not only marrying a woman, but a black woman, Michelle had presented a doubly offensive affront to certain elements of the town.

Financial necessity had driven them back home. Back in Denver, Michelle had been a certified professional midwife, but she was still in the early stages of trying to get her practice up and running when Lana had been laid off from her teaching job. This had been a devastating blow. Lana was the primary breadwinner. Then Michelle's sister Jen had mentioned that Mrs. Carruth, who'd taught English at Bakersfield High approximately since Abe Lincoln was still in school, was finally retiring. Almost on a whim, Lana had applied online for the open position and was hired after a phone interview. Only after they'd moved back home did Michelle learn that her Colorado certification was not recognized in Illinois. In fact, attending a home birth as a midwife, without a doctor present, was a felony in this state.

This was unbelievable to Michelle. In order to practice here, she'd have to become a certified nurse midwife, which meant she'd first have to become an RN. That was at least two more years of school and who knew how many thousands of dollars, and even then she could only attend a home birth if a doctor signed off on it. All for the most natural thing in the world, a process women had assisted other women with since the beginning of human history.

Michelle had thought she might be able to teach a childbirth class somewhere, or maybe get a job as a women's health counselor at a shelter. She'd been looking, but no positions seemed to be open anywhere. Still, even with Michelle out of work, they were still bringing in more money here than they had in Denver. And the living was definitely cheaper.

Their house was in sight now. Mark was up there waiting for them, leaning against his dusty car in their driveway.

"Daddy!" Ben called, forgetting in his excitement that he had abandoned such childish forms of address in favor of the more mature-sounding "Mom" and "Dad."

Ben ran to his father and Mark leaned down to hug his son. Michelle raised a hand in a decidedly restrained greeting. Mark stood up when they came close, greeting them with a smile, keeping one hand on his son's shoulder.

"Mark," Lana said. "How was your drive?"

"Long," Mark said. He looked over at Michelle with the pained look he always seemed to favor her with since the divorce, as if lamenting that he'd never see her naked again. "Hi, Missy. You look good."

Mark was the only one who still used her childhood nickname. She hadn't been able to break him of the habit in their four years of marriage, and she'd given up trying.

"Thanks," she replied coolly. She wasn't sure why the mere sight of her ex was so rankling to her now. She'd done a lot of work to shed her anger towards him, and prided herself on being able to think of Mark without bitterness—when he wasn't around. Right here in front of her was a different story.

"You want to come inside?" Lana offered. "I just brewed a jug of sun tea."

"That sounds real good, Lana. Thanks."

Michelle flashed Lana a frown as Ben led his father into the house, and received a shrug in return. Michelle supposed she was right. It was only polite to ask Mark inside. Michelle was going to have to get used to seeing his face sooner or later.

Lana poured out the iced tea and the four of them sat civilly enough in the living room for a while. Ben burbled happily about all that had happened in the six weeks since he'd gone out to visit his dad over Spring Break. Ben being Ben, this consisted mostly of an accounting of the Pokemon cards he'd recently acquired. (Michelle held out hope that Ben would grow out of his Pokemon phase as quickly as he'd worked through his mania for pro wrestling.)

"So, Mark," Lana probed. "Michelle told me you'll be working as, what, a caretaker? At Linda Hansard's farm."

"Something like that, yeah," Mark said. "Her grandson Sam is running the place now. He just hired me."

"I think I know Sam Hansard. Big guy, dresses like a biker, but looks like a big puppy?"

Mark laughed. "That's him, all right. Real nice guy."

"Did he say how his grandma was doing?"

"He said she's still in her fugue state, or whatever it is. I guess the doctors haven't figured out what's wrong with her yet."

Lana clucked her tongue and shook her head sadly.

"But here's something interesting." Mark turned to his son. "Sam told me that the house is haunted."

That definitely perked Ben up. "Really?"

"Yeah. I believe him, too. He's so freaked out he won't even go inside the place."

"Wow. Can I come over and check it out?"

"Well, you're going to be staying with me there for half the week from now on."

"I'm going to bring my kit."

One of their shared father and son obsessions was watching all those ghost-hunting reality shows, with the shaky night vision camera work and the people always exclaiming "Oh my God, what was that?" before every commercial break. Their favorite was *Into the Unknown with Elsa West*. For Christmas last year, Mark had bought Ben the show's officially licensed "Digital Paranormal Investigation Kit." The kit included such quasi-scientific tools as an Electromagnetic Field Detector, an Electronic Voice Phenomena recorder and an Ecto-Spectrum Camera, whatever that was.

Ben had taken his paranormal investigation hobby very seriously. He skulked around the attic and the basement, and had insisted that Michelle and Lana take him to every cemetery in a twenty-mile radius. So far, the most compelling evidence his "field research" had yielded was a brief EVP clip—recorded at an old graveyard north of town—that Ben was convinced was more than just suggestive rustling in the microphone. Michelle had to concede that it almost did sound like someone whispering the word "Waterloo," though Lana said that to her it sounded more like "Where's my shoe?" Napoleon's ghost, perhaps, or maybe just some anonymous barefoot spirit.

"Let me stay there a few nights first," Mark said with apparent seriousness. "Make sure it's safe."

Ben's eyes went wide as he nodded. "Be careful, Dad."

Lana and Michelle exchanged a look. A quick smile from the former and a slight roll of eyes from the latter, the communication imparted and received via the deep intimacy between them. *Aw, they're cute,* Lana said with her smile. *Try being married to that,* Michelle replied with her eyes.

Still, it wasn't too bad. Michelle didn't say much during the conversation, but she did manage to restrain herself from openly glaring at her ex. Mark wasn't being *too* obnoxious, and Ben was so obviously overjoyed to see his father that Michelle didn't want to deflate his happiness. But when Lana went into the kitchen to take a phone call about the end of school picnic she was helping to organize, and Ben ran off to use the bathroom, Mark and Michelle were left alone together.

Silence hung between them. Awkward but, for Michelle anyway, bearable, until Mark managed to infuriate her without speaking a word. Sitting in the easy chair directly diagonal to her position on the loveseat, he leaned forward to set his empty glass on the table. Then the asshole *sniffed* her.

That was one of his weird kinks. He was into pheromones. Back when they were married, he was always begging her not to wear deodorant or, weirder still, to stop shaving her armpits. Harmless enough fetishes to indulge your lover in, but things she had gladly left behind when their relationship had soured. And to presume that he still had the right to smell her just because she was all sweaty from walking to the school and back was every bit as invasive as if he'd peeked through her window while she was undressing.

"Did you just *smell* me?"

"What? No."

"You did. You just leaned forward and smelled me."

Mark held his hands up and barked laughter. "Sorry for breathing in your vicinity."

"You weren't 'breathing in my vicinity.' You were inhaling my scent."

"All right, fine." Mark let out a sigh. "I smelled you. But it was involuntary, okay? I can't turn off my body's natural reactions to your body just because you woke up one morning and decided you don't like dick anymore."

"Decided that I don't like..." Michelle half-rose from her seat, then sat back down hard again, her anger flaring like someone had kicked over a hornet's nest in her head. Nobody on earth had the ability to piss her off like the man now sitting across from her. "You honestly believe that's why we're not together?"

"Isn't it?" Mark challenged. "You left me for a woman."

"I did. But, and I know this is hard for you to wrap your head around, that has nothing to do with your dick."

Out of the corner of her eye, Michelle saw Ben walking into the room, only to be steered immediately into the kitchen by Lana. *Good.* Michelle didn't want her son to see this.

"What then?" Mark had the desperate, childish look on his face that had always irritated her to no end. Like a naughty little boy who had no idea why he was in so much trouble.

"Really? You want to hash this all out? Again?"

"No. But you're the one who went off on me for something my nose did."

"That's so typical." Michelle bit her lip and inhaled a sharp draw of breath. "I'm just curious. Why do you think I'm with Lana and not with you?"

"Because of that girl at the ScareCon in Portland, I know. But I told you, that was a stupid mistake. And it's not like you never..."

"No. Slutty fan-girl was just the last straw. Over that last year we were married, you had two modes, Mark. You were either depressed or you were stoned."

"That's not fair."

"Sorry, you're right. I forgot. Sometimes you were drunk. I guess that's three modes."

"I haven't been drunk *or* stoned in almost a year."

"Good," Michelle said, though she suspected he was exaggerating his sobriety by at least a few months. "I'm happy for you. But you know how nice it is to have a conversation with someone about something other than *their* insecurities and *their* self-absorption? Lana and I take care of *each other's* emotional needs. It's mutual, goes back and forth. That is such a relief after four years of playing wet nurse to a borderline bi-polar, man-child pothead."

Mark endured her tirade with his typical puppy-that-just-pissed-the-rug sheepishness. It was his classic strategy during every fight they'd ever had. He would infuriate her into blowing her top, and then just stand there looking sorry until Michelle felt like a bitch for being so mean. And she almost fell into that same trap again, almost backed off. She might have actually broken down and apologized had she not seen the slight flaring of his nostrils.

"You just smelled me again!"

"Sorry. I didn't mean to..."

"Jesus!"

Thankfully, her cell phone rang right at that moment. Grateful for the distraction, Michelle scooped the phone up from the coffee table. Her sister was calling, probably to bitch some more about Gary, the latest loser she was dating. Even listening to that was preferable to butting heads with Mark in re-enactment of an emotional loop she thought she'd broken free of.

"Hi, Jen."

"Chelle?" Jennifer's voice came through the line drenched in raw panic. "Oh my God."

Hearing the fear in her sister's voice, it hit Michelle that this was what had been nagging at her. The distress she'd been feeling hadn't been sparked by the weather change or even by Mark's reappearance in her life. She been anticipating this, whatever Jen was about to say.

"What's wrong?" Michelle said. "Is it James?"

Mark looked up at her and gave her a questioning frown. He'd always been fond of his nephew. Lana and Ben emerged from the kitchen, too, drawn by the alarm in Michelle's voice.

"Yes. He..." Jennifer gasped and let out a couple of hiccuping sobs. Michelle could tell by the sound coming through the line that she was outdoors. "He had another one of his...attacks. He's going up the..." The rest was lost, either because of the shitty reception or because Jen was crying so hard.

"Going up the what?" A vivid image flashed into Michelle's head, of the town water tower with the stupid cow chip painted on it.

"He's climbing the water tower!" Jen cried, with pure maternal terror.

"Oh, no."

"Is Mark with you?"

"Yeah, he's here. Why?" Michelle gave Mark a hard look, which he returned with a curious tilt of his head.

"Bring him down here, please. I think Ben's acting out the scene from Mark's book." Then Jen broke down into sobs. After a few seconds of this, the line went dead.

"Jen? Jen?" Michelle slapped the phone against her forehead in frustration.

"What happened?" Lana asked.

Michelle looked up at her ex-husband. "Your nephew, and number one fan, has been having bouts of sleepwalking recently. And now it looks like he's sleepwalking right through the flying vampire scene from your stupid-ass book."

CHAPTER 4

NATHANIAL BATES, SHERIFF of Logan County, pulled into the alley behind Barry Tuttle's house around three in the afternoon, driving his private vehicle. He was visiting Pastor Tuttle not in his capacity as a law enforcement officer, but as a concerned friend and business associate.

Nate rolled his big F-150 to a stop, eyeballing the back of the house, and the backs of the neighbor's houses as well. It was early enough that most of the neighbors were still at work, and Nate knew for a fact that Barry's wife, Eve, was over at the church, organizing the weekend bake sale. Good. He wanted this to be a private chat.

Inside his glove compartment was a ring of keys. Nate sorted through them until he found the one labeled PD, for 'Pastor Dipshit.' He'd learned the key trick from his father, who'd been Sheriff here back in the sixties and seventies. Every time Nate came across a key, he'd make a copy for himself. People were always leaving spares in stupidly obvious places. The pastor, just for example, kept his beneath the "As for Me and My House, We Will Serve the Lord" welcome mat right on his front porch. Nate had duplicated the key with the cutter in his basement (confiscated from some dumb-ass burglary suspect) a few years back, when he first went into business with Tuttle. He'd never had a call to use it until today.

Nate debated bringing the Glock that he also kept in the glove box, but decided against it. He did grab his handcuffs, though. That was how he rated the seriousness of the talk he had to have here. Serious enough for the cuffs, but not yet quite enough for the gun. Hopefully it wouldn't come to that.

Nate looked around one more time to see if he was being observed, and then he let himself into the pastor's back yard gate. Halfway up the path that led to the house, he stopped for a moment to look at the half-asleep bear in the dog kennel.

Pastor Tuttle had long dreamed of opening a "Christian Wildlife Park" in Bakersfield, and had held fundraisers towards this end for years. He already had several enclosures built in the big field behind the church, but most of the cages stood empty for now. Tuttle's unimpressive menagerie boasted one red-and-green parrot, a largish python and a "hybrid wolf" that was at least three quarters German shepherd. The mangy black bear, "retired" from the circus that had sold it to the pastor, had been the most exotic animal in the collection. Barry was forced to keep it at home, though, after the cranky old beast bit a kid. Or gummed him, more likely. The sad creature had some serious dental issues.

The bear wasn't much of a watch animal. Lying flat on its back, it watched Nate cross the yard with a deep apathy. The bear snorted once in Nate's direction, spraying snot through the bars, and then rolled over on its side.

Technically, the pastor wasn't licensed to keep "exotic pets" at home, but Nate looked the other way on this issue as an unspoken part of their business arrangement. That might provide a useful bit of leverage, Nate thought as he looked at the pathetic bear in its too-small cage. The poor beast would probably be better off being put down, anyway. It was something to consider. Nodding to himself, he walked up to the house and unlocked the door.

The house was quiet when Nate slipped inside. Barry wasn't in the kitchen or the living room. The television and most of the lights were off. For a minute, Nate thought that maybe he'd miscalculated and the pastor wasn't home after all. He was about to look in the garage and see if Barry's Caddy was there when he heard the water running in the bathroom.

Silently, Nate pushed open the bathroom door. Stepping into the cloud of steam, he could just make out the pastor's silhouette through the translucent curtain. Barry was hunched over, his back to Nate, left hand working torpidly at his crotch. Nate smirked. Jerking off in the shower.

Nate knew Barry was probably casting some of the younger men from his congregation in whatever mental porn was playing in his head. Nate didn't give much of a shit on a personal level—truth be told, he'd stuck his dick in some curious places through the years—but he considered it a good business practice to be aware of his associate's proclivities, considering how Barry's flock would react if they ever found out.

For a few moments, Sheriff Bates just stood there as the other man worked on himself. Barry was muttering something as he wanked it, the words sleepy and syrupy in his mouth. Sounded like he was saying "Hazy waves lit up the whole durn sky, but my ring keeps the rays outta my head."

Nate was mildly curious as to what kind of twisted sex fantasy might contain dialogue like that, but he was growing impatient. He yanked the shower curtain open like his first name was Norman instead of Nate.

The pastor snapped out of his auto-erotic daze really quickly. He turned and let out a scream that would have made Janet Leigh proud. Barry's hand flew up from his sudsy crotch and he stumbled back, almost slipping and falling on his ass.

"In all the years we've known each other, Barry, I never noticed you were a lefty. It's funny how you just don't pick up on things like that."

Barry flushed scarlet to the faded roots of his luxurious blond hair. He made some kind of sputtering, gasping reply.

"Unless you're jerking it with your off hand. I do that sometimes. Gives it kind of a different feel. Good to shake things up sometimes, you know."

"Wh-wh-wh..." Barry stuttered.

"So which is it? Left or right?"

"What are you doing here, Nate?"

"Answer the question. Are you left-handed or right-handed?"

"Left. What..."

Nate brought the cuffs up in a quick flash of silver, clamping one to Barry's right wrist and the other to the shower head. He got pretty wet doing it, but that couldn't be helped.

"See what kind of friend I am? I left your left hand free so you can finish up. I know blue balls hurt like a bitch."

"What are you talking about?"

Barry didn't seem to be processing the situation very well. He seemed more confused than frightened. That was too bad. Nate wanted him scared.

Nate sighed. "I want you to finish jerkin' it so your full attention will be on what I have to say and not how bad you wanna nut."

"For Pete's sake, Nate." Barry's soap-slicked prick had deflated to a sad little wilt. "I ain't gonna do that."

"You sure? Well, maybe we ought to cool you off a little."

Nate cranked the faucet all the way over to cold. Barry let out a yelp when the icy water doused him. He performed an awkward side-step that caused him to slip on the soapy porcelain. He would've fallen into the tub had his cuffed wrist not kept him upright.

"Careful there," Nate chuckled. "You don't want to hurt nothin'." He eased the water back up to a comfortable warmth.

"What the heck are you doing here?"

"Really? You got no idea?"

"I swear to God, Nate. I..."

This time Nate twisted the faucet the other way. The water turned instantly scalding. Barry screamed loud enough that Nate would have been concerned, had he not already made sure the neighbors weren't home.

"Wow. That heats up real quick." Nate pulled it back down to a moderate temperature. "You got one of those tankless water heaters? I've been thinking about getting one of those. Mara takes these *epic* showers and I gotta get up at like four in the morning if I want any hot water at all."

"Please, Nate."

"Don't fuck with me, Barry. You know why I'm here, right?"

Barry closed his eyes and nodded.

"I want to hear you say it," Nate said. "So I know we're on the same page."

"Because of the break-in."

"Break-in? Is that what it was? All I know is that I had about fourteen thousand dollars of my shit go missing. You're telling me there was a break-in?"

"Yes. Somebody broke a window in the church basement and took it all."

"Huh. Well, that's *real* interesting. And you didn't think this was important enough to tell me about?"

"I was hoping we could get everything back without getting you involved. I know you got enough on your plate."

"That's certainly true, Barry. But tell me, how's that working out? Getting my shit back? Because here's what I don't get. The only people who knew about the shipment were you, me, and some of your people. Did you take the drugs?"

"Of course not!"

"Well, I sure as hell didn't take them. So who's that leave?"

"It's not my people. I swear to God."

"Swearing to God? That's a big deal for a man of faith like you, huh?"

"Yes! I would never say those words lightly. My people are solid, Nate. I trust them with my life."

"So what's your theory, then? Did thirty bricks of heroin just evaporate? Grow legs and walk away? Maybe it was some of those goats you got for your petting zoo. I know those fuckers'll eat anything."

"I don't know who took the stuff, but I'll find out. I sw…I promise. I got as much to lose from this as you do."

"No," Nate said. "Not quite as much."

He looked his partner over and performed some calculations in his head. Working with Barry provided an easy solution to many problems. For one thing, the Church of the Shepherd's "Loaves and Fishes International" non-profit charity was the best money-laundering scheme Nate had ever seen. Hell, it was like an ATM that never ran dry. The church was also a valuable cover for all manner of operations related to the flow of product. Warehousing, packaging, a fleet of innocuously churchy-looking vans for transportation. Plus, the pastor had an inner circle of congregants utterly devoted him, who bought that whole "all things serve the Lord, who works in mysterious ways, so it's better not to ask too many questions" line. But Tuttle had at least some inkling of how much Nate relied upon him. That was the problem. Sometimes this knowledge went to his head.

Barry was a pusillanimous little shit, weak and easy to push around. But Nate was beginning to wonder if this wasn't in fact a brilliant passive aggressive defense mechanism. Making himself into an easily manipulated puppet as part of his overall strategy of becoming essential to the operation. Nate didn't like relying so heavily on any one man, especially a flaky little creep like Barry. Working with somebody so indispensable naturally led his mind to considerations of how this person could be dispensed with.

"Will you *say* something, Nate?" Barry cried. Nate realized he had been staring at him silently for a full minute or two.

Nate looked at the sad little naked man before him and felt the rage rising like bile to the back of his throat. Barry was a dandified rooster with a two-hundred dollar haircut and an all-over tan from the booth in his basement. The douchebag actually had his own private tanning booth. Even the pastor's stupid little dripping prick pissed him off. Nate personally knew of six boys who'd served time kneeling and slobbering over that wang dang doodle. Most of them were at least barely legal, but Tom Peters hadn't been more than sixteen the first time the pastor had his wicked way with him. Perversion Nate could stomach, but what he could not abide was hypocrisy. And Barry took to the altar every Sunday to condemn America for slipping into moral decline. Fuck him and his righteous bullshit.

"Come on, Nate. You're scaring me."

"What are you going to do?" Nate cast his eyes down and forced himself to breathe. His temples were pounding like they sometimes did before he lost control of his anger. He did not want that to happen. Not yet, anyway. "What's your plan?"

"Well, I, ah..." Pastor Tuttle stood up straight, in as casual and serious a pose as a naked man could achieve with one wrist cuffed to a shower head. "I got my boys out asking around, you know? Seeing if anybody is selling the stuff who's not one of your usual..."

"Why don't you do what your bumper sticker says?" Nate interrupted.

"What?"

"You've got that bumper sticker on your car. On your *Cadillac*. 'What Would Jesus Do?' So, tell me, what *would* Jesus do if somebody broke into his basement and stole a bunch of heroin that belonged to his business partner? Is that the sort of hypothetical moral quandary you're supposed to imagine Jesus facing?"

"I don't—"

"Here's what I don't get about you, Barry. I could almost understand if all the Jesus talk was just a shill. You know, bullshit to feed the rubes. But you believe that shit, don't you?"

"Of course I believe, Nate."

"So how do you reconcile your goddamn evil behavior with your so-called faith, pastor? Most folks rationalize and compartmentalize heinous petty shit they do on a daily basis. But you're a drug dealer and a fucking pedophile."

"I'm not a—"

"You're not a pedophile?"

"No! Those young men weren't children. They were spiritually lost seekers. I was just trying to help them find their way back to—"

"Oh, spare me. And I suppose all that dirty drug money you're taking is okay because you're helping folks get into Heaven, right?"

"You gotta look at the big picture. The ends can justify the means, you know. Sometimes Jesus asks us to do things that seem wrong, but it all serves the—"

"Oh, that is such *horseshit!*"

Nate rammed his fist into the pastor's wet, flabby side, just below the ribcage. For a moment all he saw was the veins swelling and pulsing bright red in his eyes. Nate wanted to tear this fucker to pieces, chew his goddamn throat out, rip off his stupid bo diddly and feed it to the fucking bear. He had to step back and take several deep breaths before he lost it completely.

The pastor slumped over, dangling by the cuffs from the shower head with all his weight now, and let out a wheezing gasp. When he tilted his head back up in Nate's direction, there was something wrong with his eyes. They darted around, making crazy circles around the room. Nate wondered if maybe the pastor had knocked his head back against the tiles when he hit him. That'd be real cute if he gave the shithead a concussion.

"She's from the same planet the serpent is from," Barry said, lending further credence to the concussion diagnosis. "But I got this ring to protect me."

"What the fuck?" Nate said.

"That thing is not my wife," Barry insisted. "My ring filters the rays and the haze around her eyes so's I can see the flies."

Nate cranked the water all the way cold again. That seemed to snap Barry out of it. He bolted back awake, his eyes settling on Nate and blinking with confusion for a few seconds.

"Huh, what?"

"Thought I lost you for a second there, buddy."

Barry looked up at his cuffed wrist and seemed surprised by the sight. "What's going on, Nate? How did I get..."

Nate's cell phone emitted the little whistling tone that meant he had an incoming text. He looked down and saw it was from Deputy Crawford at Dispatch. "Teen boy climbing Bakersfield water tower—prob suicide—units in route."

"Shit," Nate swore. Just what he wanted to deal with on his day off.

Barry was looking at him curiously, for all appearances still trying to puzzle out how he'd ended up cuffed to his shower.

"I got some business to attend to, Barry. So I'm going to cut this meeting short. But you're on top of our little situation, right?"

"Situation?"

"Jesus. Really?"

"Oh, yeah. The break-in. I'm on it, Nate. I'll get the stuff back."

"You got the weekend, Barry. If we're not square again by Monday, you and I are going to have a real problem."

"Okay."

Nate reached up and unlocked the cuffs. He shook the water off and slipped them into his back pocket.

"Oh, and Barry? Maybe you ought to have a doctor take a look at your head. Concussions are nothing to mess around with."

Barry frowned at that. Nate left him there gaping like an idiot.

CHAPTER 5

THEY SET OFF in silence, the once-familiar town rolling by outside the passenger window. Missy's car was an almost new Honda Civic, much cleaner and nicer than any vehicle she and Mark had owned together when they were married. The radio was tuned to the classic rock station from Springfield, a thin sliver of band-width on a dial otherwise devoted to shit-kicker country and vitreous right-wing talk. "Midnight Rider" by the Allman Brothers played at a near-subliminal volume. Had there been another time in another life when Mark had driven on this same stretch of road with this same woman while this very same song had played on the radio? He was sure there had been, but he could not bring the memory to the fore.

They'd left Ben at home with Lana. The boy looked up to his cousin James like an older brother. If the worst were to happen, Mark didn't want Ben there to witness it. The worst, in this case, being James falling to his death, an image that sprang too easily to Mark's mind every time he closed his eyes.

Missy whispered something, so low that Mark thought at first she was singing along with the radio. Then she repeated herself, a little louder. He still wasn't hearing her right, though. It almost sounded like she said: "I'm sorry, Mark."

"What?"

"For what I said back at the house. I'm sorry."

"You're apologizing?"

"I wasn't being fair. I know this hasn't been easy for you."

"Wow."

"I mean, you were a lousy husband, but..."

"Is this still part of the apology?"

45

"Let me finish. You were a lousy husband, but you've always been a good father. Whatever other problems I have with you, I've never doubted how much you care about Ben. No matter what happens between us, we'll always share that."

"Of course."

"So I'm glad you're here. For him."

"Thank you."

Missy sighed. "I wanted to say that because I don't want you thinking about me or us or whatever. I want you totally focused on what you can do to help James."

"I am, okay? I'm really worried."

Mark had always liked James. He was a good kid. Bright, funny, and industrious, if a bit lonely and withdrawn. Mark had always suspected that James was probably gay, but so far he hadn't come home with either a boyfriend *or* a girlfriend as far as Mark knew (though he had been out of the loop of Delany family gossip for months now). Mark himself hadn't grown up gay, but he'd definitely been an outsider as a teen. That was a tough road to walk in Bakersfield. The town had little tolerance for non-conformity, and this was doubly true at the high school level. Mark and James had always had that point of identification between them.

"So he's been sleepwalking?" Mark asked.

"Jen said it's been happening all week. She caught him in the fridge one night, eating a jar of mayonnaise with his bare hands."

"Ugh."

"And then, just two nights ago, he got into her car like he was going to go for a drive. He didn't have the keys, but he managed to slip it out of gear and roll out into the street."

"That's scary."

"It's been getting worse, and it's not just happening at night anymore. Jen said it's almost like narcolepsy. She'll be in the middle of a conversation with him, and then he'll just slip into a trance or something. They had an appointment with a doctor, but now..."

Missy sniffed. Mark looked over and saw tears gleaming in her eyes.

"He'll be all right," he said. He wanted to put his hand on her arm to reassure her, but he knew that his touch no longer soothed her. More likely it would have the opposite effect.

"James told Jen that whenever he's having a spell, he has really vivid dreams. Always about Henry, the vampire from your books. He says Henry comes to him, and wants to turn him into a vampire, too."

"Oh, God."

James had always been Mark's number one fan. The kid even had a vampire fiction blog, "Pain in the Neck," with a fairly respectable online following. Here James had once ranked his Uncle's *Blood World* series as #3 on his list of "Top Ten Greatest Vampire Stories of All Time." Behind *Dracula* and *'Salem's Lot*, obviously, but ahead of Anne Rice's *Vampire Chronicles*. This was considerably higher in the pantheon than Mark would have placed himself.

"Mark, in that first book, Henry jumps off the water tower and flies away."

Mark felt his heart clench. "I know."

"Whatever happens," Missy said. "It's not your fault."

They had arrived. Missy pulled into the gravel lot beside the little playground at the base of the tower. Two Logan County deputy's cruisers and a few unmarked vehicles were already in the lot, as was the fire department's big ladder truck. The ladder was extended up towards the water tower, though this appeared to be a symbolic gesture. It didn't even reach halfway up to the bell-shaped reservoir. There was no ambulance yet, and this worried Mark. The nearest ambulance service was in Lincoln, fifteen miles away. Even if they were already in route, they might not make it in time if something happened.

Missy was pulling into the lot when the deputy cordoning off the area with yellow caution tape stepped in front of the car.

"Back it up, folks," he called, waving them off.

Before Missy could begin to explain who they were and why they were there, Jennifer came running over.

"You let them in!" she yelled at the deputy. "I called them here!"

Mark had never seen his former sister-in-law looking so ragged. Jennifer had always been prone to melodrama, tending to escalate the slightest problem into a full-blown emotional crisis. Now that something legitimately terrifying was happening, she had gone over the top into the realm of pure panic. Her face was pale with shock, eyes open wide enough to see the whites all around, hair hanging down in sweaty strings.

The deputy nodded grimly and motioned for Missy to pull into an out-of-the-way spot. Jennifer ran over and fell sobbing into Missy's arms as soon as she stepped out of the car.

Shielding his eyes from the sun with one hand, Mark looked up at the tower. At first, he couldn't see James and felt a jolt of terror that they'd arrived too late. But then he made out the small dark figure against the sun-faded pink side of the high tower, directly below and to the right of King Chip the smiling turd. James was sitting on the ledge encircling the reservoir tank. He was too far up for Mark to see his face, so there was no telling what his expression might be.

"Help him, please," Jennifer begged. Mark turned his eyes down from the tower and saw that Jen was appealing directly to him.

Mark had never really gotten along with Jennifer. She'd made her opinion clear from the start that her sister marrying Mark could only end in disaster. Since this dire prophecy had actually come to pass, she'd treated Mark with a gloating "told you so" satisfaction. Still, she'd always tolerated James's devotion to his uncle. As a single mom, she seemed to recognize the importance of having an adult male role model, even as sorry an excuse for one as Mark was.

Now she was just a mother terrified for her son, desperate for help from whatever quarter it might come. Mark wanted to help, of course, but now that he was here, he didn't know what the hell he was supposed to *do*.

Two figures were approaching. One, Mark saw with dismay, was Sheriff Bates. He'd had a few run-ins with the man when he was a teenager, most notably a weed bust when he was seventeen. He was such a prototypical small town fascist that Mark had immortalized him in print. The overweight redneck Sheriff Castor Gates in the first *Blood World* book was a thinly veiled parody.

Bates was out of uniform today, wearing a polo shirt and knee-length jean shorts that were noticeably damp, as if he'd doused himself with a garden hose in an attempt to cool off before coming over here. The civilian clothes, even wet, did little to diminish his air of implacable authority. He gave a curt nod in Mark's direction, but otherwise gave no sign of having recognized him.

The other figure was even more troubling. It was Mark's mother.

She walked briskly towards them, traversing the gravel lot in her heels with no apparent difficulty. She had on one of her Hillary Clinton pantsuits, but somehow managed to look cool while everyone else assembled in the lot was wilting in the summer heat. Mark imagined that his mom had filed some kind of injunction against her sweat glands to prevent them from disclosing confidential information about her levels of stress and discomfort.

"I need an ETA on that crane." She was looking right at Mark as she demanded this information, and he felt a stab of guilt for not knowing what she was talking about. Then he saw the Bluetooth earpiece she was wearing.

"That's unacceptable," she said, pressing the device close to her ear. "No. There's no time to arrange a police escort. You need to get that equipment to me. Now."

Mark empathized with whomever was on the other end of the line. God knows he'd heard that tone of expectation in his mother's voice enough times over the years. He knew well the crushing feeling of failing to meet that expectation. His mother was of a mindset that she could bend reality to suit her will. If you were enlisted to aid her in this pursuit, then you sure as hell better start twisting time and space to give her what she wanted.

She clicked off the connection with a tap of her finger and looked up at her son, whom she had not seen in person for months.

"What are you doing here?" were her first words to him.

Mark thought he could ask her the same. As the beloved uncle of the kid who'd climbed the tower, he at least a tenuous connection to the scene. As the Community Relations Director for Malovo Agricultural Development, he wasn't sure what her function here was. Of course, he didn't attempt to say anything as cheeky as that.

"I asked him to be here," Jennifer said. "He and James are very close."

Gillian Hudson cast her eyes from her son to the distressed mother and only then turned on her warm, professional smile.

"Hello, Jennifer," she said. "I want to tell you what's happening. The local fire department doesn't have equipment capable of reaching James." She waved her hand up at the fire fighter in the bucket atop the fully extended ladder, who was looking up at James with impotent concentration. "But Malovo has a crane that will reach. It's on its way here now, along with personnel trained in tower rescue procedures. We can drop two men down, who will fasten a harness onto James and lower him to safety."

"Thank you," Jen sobbed.

"We're a part of this community," Mark's mom said. "When someone in this community is in danger, we will do everything in our power to help."

Now Mark understood. It was a PR thing. The most cynical part of him suspected that the crane would arrive at about the same time as the TV news vans from Springfield, so there would be adequate media coverage of the beneficence of the Malovo Corporation.

He looked out over the yellow-tape barricade. There were no news vehicles yet, but there were more than a dozen lookey-loos, most of them pointing cellphone cameras up at the tower. One of two future *YouTube* classics would be recorded here. Either "Daring Water Tower Rescue" or "Teen Boy Falls to His Death." No points for guessing which one would garner the most hits.

"Subject's on the move," Sheriff Bates announced.

They all craned to look. James had stood up. He looked out onto the crowd below for a few moments and then walked across the ledge encircling the big tank. He came to the second ladder, which led up to access the hatches and vents on top. As they all watched breathlessly, James began to climb.

"Oh, God," Jen moaned. "Someone go up there and help him."

Jen and Missy held each other tight. Mark's mother stood off to the side. All three women were looking at Mark with a very clear expectation.

Mark closed his eyes and took a deep breath. "I'll go," he said.

He'd actually climbed the tower once before, back in his teen punk days. He and his miscreant buddy Emmett Grady had scaled the ladder to graffiti the side of the tank. Full of adolescent bravado, both of them young and stupid and stoned, it had seemed a hilarious prank. Right now, though, the prospect of climbing up there didn't seem so goddamn funny.

Sheriff Bates didn't think so, either. "I can't let you go up there, son," he said. "I won't be responsible for two civilians on the tower. One of my deputies can—"

"No!" Jen cried. "They'll scare him. He'll think they're the vampire hunters. It has to be Mark." Jen broke free of Missy's embrace and grabbed Mark's arm. "Go up there. Be Henry. He'll listen to you if you're Henry."

Mark nodded weakly. The sheriff scowled. Mark was sure that Jen's words had been just irritating nonsense to his ears.

"Mr. Davies, if you try to climb that tower, I will arrest you. Again."

So he did remember who Mark was. Mark could only hope that the guy didn't read vampire novels.

Mark's mother tapped the screen on her phone. She frowned at what she read there.

"The crane's still nine minutes out," she said. "We could use somebody up there, talking to James. Let Mark go."

She'd addressed that last bit directly to the sheriff. There was an odd moment then, as Bates squinted over at Mark's mother, trying to stare her down, as if to ask "who the hell's in charge here?" Then, answering his own unspoken question, he acquiesced.

"Fine," he said to Mark. "Go."

Mark's mother and the Delany sisters were prodding him on with their eyes. He realized with a petulant start that his safety was of secondary importance to all three of them. At least Missy had the good grace to say, "Be careful, Mark."

Mark glanced up at the tower, reeling towards the heavens, and had a revelatory flash of understanding of just how tall the fucking thing really was. For a second, he regretted volunteering so hastily. Then he thought of James, and thought of James falling. That got his ass moving. He felt cold all over despite the heat. Everything seemed to be simultaneously in slow motion and moving way too fast.

A chain-link fence, erected to bar access to vandals and suicides, encircled the weed-choked base of the tower. Mark saw that someone had removed the padlock from the gate. A member of the new generation of graffiti artists had probably cut the lock off with bolt-cutters. That's how Mark and Emmett had gotten inside, twelve years ago.

Mark wished he was high right now, as he'd been that night. Just a hit to soothe him. To slow his racing heart, to ease the terror-nausea, to keep the fear at bay. But he was hopelessly straight and all alone. He would even have welcomed the company of Emmett Grady and his donkey-bray laughter right now, just so he wouldn't have to climb this damned thing himself.

The bottom rung of the ladder was high enough off the ground that Mark could reach it when he lifted his arms over his head. Exhaling his misgivings, he grabbed the rung. The weight of his body resisted the separation from the earth as he struggled to pull himself up, reminding Mark of the existence of that stone bitch, gravity. As his muscles strained, he was afraid that he wouldn't be able to do it, that his stab at valor would be undone by his own physical weakness. He hadn't done a chin-up since tenth-grade gym class, and even then he'd never been able to do more than one.

Somehow he managed to throw one sweaty hand up to the second rung. And then his opposite hand. He hung there for a moment, and then moved slowly up, hand over hand, until he could get his feet on the bottom rung.

The climbing was easier once he could use his legs to push himself up, but the temperature seemed to have shot up by about twenty degrees. Sweat poured down his body in a sweaty waterfall. The other time Mark had climbed up here, it had been at night and was much cooler. Also dark enough so he hadn't been able to see the ground receding beneath him, which was a vertiginous vexation to him now.

What the hell was he thinking, coming up here?

Mark continued to climb, rung by rung. Shouldn't he at least be up to the ledge by now? He looked up and was relieved to see that it was not so far above him. Maybe ten more rungs. This relief was immediately crushed by a resurgence of fear. His grip on the ladder seemed hopelessly insecure. Hands and feet still gripped their respective rungs, but in Mark's mind seemed to slipping. His strained muscles had turned to cooked noodles, rapidly losing the strength to continue. Would he be able to climb back down when this was over?

Jesus, just keep moving. Nine rungs, eight, seven...

An eternal minute later, Mark pulled himself up onto the narrow railing. Fighting the impulse to collapse onto his back, he stood. Here on the platform, his footing seemed less assured than it had on the ladder. He stood on shaking legs in reeling space, the thin railing a cruel joke that would do nothing to arrest his fall. He clutched it with one hand, his other palm pressing against the sun-warmed metal of the big reservoir tank. Only with both hands braced did he dare to look down at the earth.

No news vans yet, but an ambulance had arrived. Mark was also relieved to see the crane pulling into the lot, towed by a big rig truck. The spectators parted to allow for its arrival, most of them still pointing their camera-phones up in his direction. Whether he lived or died, he would probably be a viral Internet star after this. Just what he'd always wanted.

Mark took a deep breath and walked unsteadily along the ledge, forcing himself to look neither up nor down. He paused briefly when he came even with King Chip. Seen up close like this, the drawing seemed even cruder than it had from down below. Mark wondered what half-talented artist the town had commissioned to draw this monstrosity. Was that the sort of thing you'd include in your portfolio when you were looking for other work? Drawing a literal piece of shit on a town's water tower seemed a dubious thing to list on a resume.

The sneering chunk of feces had a decidedly malevolent cast to it now, as if recognizing Mark. *You're the fucker who painted a dooby in my mouth that one time, aren't you?* Chippy seemed to say. *It's going to be hilarious when you fall.*

Mark patted the king with a sardonic fondness.

"That'll do, turd," he said aloud, and then immediately regretted speaking. The hollow echo of his voice resounding against the tank was ghostly and thin, as if he were dead already.

He came to the second ladder and, not giving himself time to consider the prospect, continued to climb. This ladder seemed more stable than the other one had. The rungs were bolted to the side of the tank rather than hanging down into empty space. But Mark was tired. His legs ached from the strain and each rung presented a real physical obstacle to be overcome. Maybe it was his imagination, but the wind seemed to have picked up, too. It buffeted around him, messing with his balance and playing tricks with his hearing. The sound he heard could have been screaming from below—the crowd crying out as James fell—or it could have been a demonic whisper, advising him to see what would happen if he just let go.

Again the panic threatened to overwhelm him. Mark closed his watering eyes for a moment, but not seeing was immeasurably worse than seeing and so he opened them again. He forced his awareness of his position relative to the distant earth to the back of his mind. Up, he climbed. Up and up.

And then he came to the top.

There was no railing on top of the tower, not even the illusion of safety. Just three-hundred-and-sixty degrees of panoramic acrophobia. The top of the structure rose in a dome-like slope. Directly before Mark was a large access tank and, crowning the big tank, a circular vent.

James sat in stillness atop the vent, his back to Mark, gazing out upon the level distance.

Mark had enjoyed rock climbing in Colorado. Nothing serious with ropes or equipment, just scrambling by hand. He'd never been afraid of heights out there. Quite the opposite. Perching in high mountain places, gazing out onto wondrous vistas, had always soothed his soul. There was nothing soothing about this treacherous man-made structure, though. Instead of mountains there was nothing but a vast cornfield ocean. The cultivated land stretched perfectly flat towards every horizon. Mark was exposed to the sky on a curvilinear metal cloud. Isolated upon this perilous sliver, just him and the boy he had come to save.

A monstrous roar floated up from the ground. Mark looked down and saw that the sound was coming from the crane. The diesel engine belched black smoke as the mast and the jib came slowly erect, the massive portable structure rising towards his place in the sky.

Too terrified to stand, Mark crept like an insect up the sloping rise of the big tank. It was all too easy to imagine sliding back down, right over the edge into screaming death, but he scuttled to the apex, until he was on his hands and knees behind James. His nephew's unmistakable white-blond hair seemed even paler in the glaring sun.

"James," Mark said, his voice insignificant beneath the wind.

His nephew did not respond, did not turn or give any acknowledgement that he had heard. Mark didn't want to touch him, didn't want to make any motion that would upset whatever delicate balance of forces was keeping them both rooted atop the high structure. He crawled around in front of James, so he could see his face.

James's eyes, blue as an ocean horizon, were open, but he didn't seem to see Mark. Nor were they fixed onto the sprawling landscape. Rather, his pupils flicked around, back and forth, up and down, describing complex geometric patterns. This gave Mark a real jolt, because he recognized that look. Rapid eye movements, like those of a dreamer, but with open lids. It looked like the kid was tripping on Neiro.

Jesus, is that shit even around anymore?

"James," he said again, louder. He snapped his fingers before the boy's face. James seemed to focus on him for a second before his eyes resumed their darting spirals.

"Henry?" The name was slurry in James's mouth.

Mark hesitated only a moment. "Yes, it's me. Henry."

"What are you doing here?" James asked. His eyes tried to fix on Mark, but vibrated with a weird stuttering tic.

"I came to help you, James."

James frowned. "I thought you were with Ryanna, down on the human res."

That was a scene from the first novel. Mark struggled to recall his own plot points. It was surprisingly difficult at this altitude.

"That was last night," he managed. "We passed the blueprints for the Malcolm City stockyards to the human resistance."

"Oh." James nodded. "I thought that was tonight. Time's moving so strangely now."

"Yeah, it is." Mark couldn't deny the truth in that statement. "Listen, James. Why did you come up here?"

"They're chasing me." James spoke with sudden urgency, as if he'd just remembered.

Mark kept his voice even. "There's nobody up here but you and me."

"No. The hunters. They have silver pellets in their guns."

"They're gone, James. They left. Now why don't you come with me back down..."

"I can feel your blood inside me." James got to his feet.

"Please, James. Sit down, okay?"

James stood straight up atop the vent, stretching his arms wide. "It makes me feel strong. I can fly now."

"No, James." Panic rose in Mark's chest. "The turning is not yet complete. You're not ready to..."

"There they are now!"

The crane burst into view over the edge of the tank, like the sun rising over the horizon. Two men with helmets, safety goggles and bright orange safety vests rode the crane arm as it rose. At the sight of them, James staggered back on his feet.

Then he fell.

By pure reflex, Mark dove after his nephew. He managed to grab the cuff of James's right jean-leg in his left fist, but James's falling weight pulled him forward. They slid down the sloping dome, Mark on his belly and James on his back, plunging together towards the abyss.

Mark closed his eyes just before James went over the edge. Something caught his own leg at that moment, arresting the fatal plunge.

"Are you all right, sir?" a deep voice boomed behind him.

Mark looked back. One of the rescuers, attached to the crane by ropes and harness, had dropped down and grabbed his legs. He was a black guy, with the cocky athletic look that all these emergency rescue guys seemed to possess.

"Do you have a good grip on the kid?" the man called.

"Not really." James's denim cuff was slipping from Mark's fingers.

"Try to hold tight."

The second rescuer, a white guy, rappelled down beside Mark. He walked down the slope and tried to grab James by the shoulders. James let out a little yelp and squirmed to get away. Mark's grip slipped even more. He was barely holding on by his fingernails now.

"James!" he yelled. "They're here to help you!"

"Don't let them take me, Henry! You know what they'll do to me!"

James gave a panicked thrashing kick, wrenching his cuff free from Mark's grasp.

"No!"

Gravity snatched James. He slipped back towards the open sky, and would have gone over the edge had the rescuer not grabbed the scruff of his neck in one gloved hand.

"You got him, Lou?" called the man holding Mark's legs.

"My grip's not solid," Lou called back. James was still struggling, but seemed to be losing the will to fight.

"I'm going to let go of you, sir," the man behind Mark said. "Hold on, okay?"

When the man released Mark, he scrambled back up to the vent and held on for dear life.

The man who had grabbed Mark now walked down to help his buddy with James, who appeared to be completely unconscious now. Working together, the two rescuers managed to pull the unresisting boy to his feet and sandwich him between them. One of the men slid a spare harness over James's head, and the other guy bound James's limp body between them with a complex arrangement of knots.

Once they had James secured, the man who had grabbed Mark looked him in the eye.

"Are you all right?" he asked.

"Once the adrenaline wears off, I'm going to have a heart attack," Mark said. "Other than that, I'm fine."

The man smiled at him. "What's your name?"

"Mark."

"I'm Will."

"Thanks for saving my life, Will," Mark said. "I'd shake your hand if I wasn't terrified to let go of this vent."

Will chuckled at that. "Listen, Mark. This kid's alive because of you. If you hadn't been up here, he would have bolted when he saw us and probably would've gone off the side. So feel good about that."

"Maybe I will once my feet are back on the ground. I don't suppose there's room for me in that harness."

"Sorry." Will shrugged an apology. "Tandem rescue. Standard procedure for an unconscious victim."

"I was afraid you were going to say that."

"Sit tight up here, okay? We'll come back as soon as we get the kid to the ground."

The other guy, Lou, gave a hand signal to the operator in the crane's cab. With a roar of the engine, Will and Lou rose into the sky with James nestled intimately between them. Mark watched as the trio swung out into the open air. They sank towards the ground as the crane slowly retracted.

Mark sat there for a while, his limbs aching from the strain. The prospect of sitting on top of the world rapidly lost its questionable appeal, and he decided to just go down the way he'd come up. Mark crab-walked slowly back down to the ladder and began the long vertical descent to the earth far below.

In his wildest imaginings, this was not how he'd pictured his first day back.

CHAPTER 6

FATHER BENTLEY OF St. Joseph's Church set off from his little parish house for a walk across the neighborhood at a little after half past four. This was in itself not unusual, certainly nothing to arouse the concern of his neighbors. They were quite used to seeing the old priest strolling about in all sorts of weather, though he typically ventured out in the later evening. Those who knew the man intimately were aware that his twilight excursions were a way of clearing his head after a day's work. Afterwards, he could drop off to sleep untroubled, his limbs tired from the pleasant exertion of a brisk stroll.

Today's walk, besides being earlier than his usual schedule, was also different in that Father Bentley was already asleep.

Only a few people witnessed the priest walking down the street, and not one among them had any inkling that he was sleepwalking. Neil Brooks, outside watering his lawn, was a bit miffed that the good father did not return his wave of greeting. But only a bit. He knew that Bentley could get lost in his thoughts, sometimes to the point of being insensitive to his surroundings. This was certainly true today, to a much greater degree than usual.

Though Father Bentley's eyes were open, they darted with the quick motions of a dreamer. They did not register the sun-drenched subdivision sidewalk or the browning, drought-ravaged lawns or the pleasant family dwellings he walked past. His dreaming eyes instead looked out upon the darkness of a moonless night. A chill mist clung to the empty countryside standing in place of the houses all around him. The actual temperature hovered at around ninety degrees and was quite humid, but the priest shivered in his thin shirt. His dreaming mind had cast him out in a dreary winter midnight.

A small creature scurried on the dark path ahead of Father Bentley. The strange beast was covered entirely in white fur, with wide, cat-like eyes set in a small rodent face and erect ears like those of an immature rabbit. The animal walked upright, with the wobbly gait of a human toddler. At its throat was a red jewel that shone in the darkness. The creature turned around at regular intervals so the jewel's red flash could serve as a beacon to keep Bentley on the path. The red stone reminded him of a ruby necklace his mother had worn. Its presence at the animal's throat brought him to understand that his mother's spirit was somehow present in the curious beast. This is why he followed it into the gloom.

In Father Bentley's dreaming mind, he was sixteen years old. The awareness of the rest of his long life had fallen away. He wasn't a priest. He was just a young boy whose mother had died of cancer less than a year previously. The grief of his youth was a still-fresh wound, but his heart lit with joy at the thought that something of his mother's essence was contained within this creature he now followed. The animal wanted to show him something, and this was a mission of some urgency. The creature scurried faster, and Bentley picked up his own pace to keep up. If any of his neighbors had been watching, they might have thought it strange that the old man was half-jogging now in the summer heat. But no one saw.

The creature came to a mound of stones and scampered up the side. The slight rise seemed to grow steeper as Bentley followed, until he was climbing up a vertical rock wall. Straight up he climbed, so sheer an ascent that even his young limbs strained at the task.

Outside of Bentley's dreaming fancy, the rock wall was in fact the side of the house owned by Mr. Bill Potter, the school teacher. That Father Bentley was able to scale Potter's house can be laid to the happy coincidence that Potter had propped a ladder there more than a week prior. He'd erected the ladder to clean out his gutters, a supposedly annual project that he had neglected for nearly a decade. True to form, Potter had just begun the work when his mind had become distracted by some other concern. He'd left the ladder standing with every intention of returning to the gutters at some point in the future but, as it was propped against the side of the house that he never saw, he had quite forgotten it was there.

Father Bentley reached the top of the ladder and climbed onto the roof. His sleeping eyes fell upon, but did not perceive, Potter's chimney. In its place he saw his mother's grave. Carved upon the tall stone were the words "Rachel Bentley, Beloved Wife and Mother, 1926–1961." Before the stone, the grave itself was an open hole in the ground.

The white creature with the ruby throat was nowhere to be seen. Bentley understood with nightmare dread that it had fallen into the open grave. He scaled the rise of the burial mound and peered into the dark hole.

He saw a flash of dim white light at the bottom, like the reflection of starlight upon water's surface. Had there been some terrible mistake? Instead of burial in hallowed ground, had his mother been tossed into this deep well? With faulty but irrefutable dream logic, this supposition became a dread certainty. And with this realization came an even more horrible truth. His mother was still alive down there, suffering.

He tried to call to her, tried to form the simple word "Mom," but in the way of dreams, Father Bentley's voice caught in his throat and he could not make a sound.

He thought he heard something. A weak cry, echoing from the depths of the well. His mother's voice? Speaking his name? Did he hear a thin, pleading voice cry out "Michael?"

He leaned further into the hole to listen. Deep down inside, he saw another gleam of light. This one red. His mother's ruby necklace, which had been buried with her, caught the reflection of light from above. It was her. She was down there.

Father Bentley leaned forward just a bit more, slipping past balance's tipping point. He fell slowly. His dream body elongated as it dropped into the deep hole, stretching like elastic with the falling motion. His mind slipped, too, from the dream state into deeper waters of sleep where he knew nothing.

Bill Potter, meanwhile, was just settling in for a quiet evening at home. Alone but for the company of his old black Lab, Iggy, he was of a melancholic disposition this afternoon. The end of the school year often brought this mood upon him. The feeling was more acute this time, as this was to be his last year teaching. Retirement, a state long dreamed of and long striven towards, would be a reality in one week's time. Such a milestone naturally inclined a man to rumination, but Potter did not want to wallow in such a gloomy state. He just wanted to kick back and "chillax," as one of his students might say. To enjoy his last true weekend before his life became *all* weekend, unbroken by any intervening week.

So it was towards the goal of chillaxation that Potter stuffed a moist, clumpy and aromatic bud into the bowl of his pipe. He struck a long match and puffed the green matter to bright orange life as he leaned back in his well-worn easy chair. Dope smoking was an indulgence of his youth he had returned to in late middle age. Mara would never have tolerated such foolishness, but they had been divorced now for almost as long as they'd been married. There was no one to judge Potter for his marginal decadence except Iggy. The dog, lying on the floor across the room, did roll his rheumy old eyes towards his master and emit a sigh that might have contained a note of disapproval. But what the hell did he know? He was a dog.

As he filled first his lungs, and then his living room, with intoxicating smoke, Potter's mood instantly lightened. He reached into the basket on the side table, where he kept a confusing array of remote controls. Each was linked to some component of his television. There was one for the set itself, one to control the cable box, one for the Blu-Ray, one for the sound system and a few of obsolete utility Potter was afraid to throw away, just in case they might prove to have some unforeseen future application. The remote he finally selected controlled the streaming player box. This remarkable device, a Christmas gift from his oldest daughter, was capable of calling up any of thousands of movies and TV episodes. From this veritable galaxy of entertainment options, Potter summoned another foolish diversion from his younger days that he had developed a new-found appreciation for in his supposed maturity. The top slot in his favorites queue was currently occupied by the classic *Gilligan's Island*.

Potter sat right back to hear the tale of the fateful trip, cashing out his bowl and filling it anew. The Gilligan experience definitely improved with the increase of THC in one's bloodstream. The herb not only fostered an aesthetic appreciation for the simplistic slapstick and vivid primary color palate, it also bestowed a warm, hazy nostalgia upon the program.

Potter remembered watching this particular episode when it had first aired, on the big Zenith that was his family's first color set. He'd been in the last year of high school, crammed on the old couch with his big brother Pat and their three little sisters. It was the one where a Soviet spy who, by astounding coincidence, looks exactly like Gilligan, lands on the island. The odds of such a thing happening in reality had to be beyond astronomical, but the appearance of one or another of the castaway's doppelgängers was a fairly regular occurrence on the island. This was far from the most egregious lapse of logic in the rules governing Gilligan's universe. The show's cheerful, unabashed stupidity was a big part of its charm.

The primary appeal for Potter as a teenager, though, had been the archetypal feminine duality presented by Mary Ann and Ginger. Revisiting the program more than four decades later, this still held true. At various stages in his life, he might have favored either the glamour of the curvaceous movie star or the homier appeal of the Kansas farm girl. But at his current venerable age, Potter was merely glad fate had stranded them both on this particular desert isle.

His own prurience caused him a small amount of shame. Potter had always prided himself on being progressive-minded. He would even have gone so far as to consider himself a feminist. From this angle, *Gilligan* was inexcusable. The show's sexual politics had been regressive even when it had aired back in the *Mad Men* days. The women on the island were relegated to domestic duties, cooking and cleaning for the men. Their costumes were improbably revealing; low-cut, curve-hugging gowns for Ginger; crop-tops and short-shorts for Mary Ann. Both women were unapologetically presented as eye candy for the male audience. But oh, what candy. Potter's secret heart of hearts yearned for the simpler bygone days when a television show could just put beautiful women in skimpy clothes without consideration of exploitation or correctness. He was an aging single man at home alone, who could fault him for such an innocuous (if voyeuristic) pleasure?

Iggy let out a short growl and flashed his master an alarmed look.

"Shut up," Potter growled right back. *Stupid dog.*

Something was stirring inside him, evoked by a number of factors. The healthy robust sexuality of the young Ms. Wells and Ms. Louise, the invigorating effect of the THC and the remembrance of his own youthful vitality all conspired to elicit an interesting reaction inside his lazy-day sweatpants. A rising, as it were. This being an increasingly uncommon spontaneous event in his advanced age, Potter felt he would be remiss if he did not take advantage.

He slid an exploratory hand past the draw-string waistband. Just testing the waters at this point, weighing the fleeting pleasure of the act under contemplation against the shame and emptiness he often felt upon its completion. Self-pollution, like marijuana and silly sixties sitcoms, was yet another young man's diversion Potter found himself engaging in more and more in these latter days.

Across the room, Iggy got to his feet. The growling turned to a short bark.

Potter closed his eyes, willfully ignoring the dog. Such condemnation seemed a tad hypocritical from a beast who spent so much of his own leisure time licking his balls.

Potter had not quite decided to proceed, though the lower half of him was eager to begin. Grasping the familiar flesh, if not yet actively caressing, he heard a sound that stopped him cold.

A sneeze.

Not a dog's sneeze, either. A man's sneeze. Guilty hand withdrawing, Potter looked over towards the fireplace, from where the sneeze had seemed to originate.

A man's head was hanging upside-down from the open chimney flue. What's more, Potter recognized the man. It was Father Bentley, the priest at the church he attended (most) Sundays. Father Bentley's face was covered with soot, his eyes half-open and fluttering, his mouth pressed into a scowl.

The last thing a stoned Catholic man wishes to see upon touching himself with the intent of onanism is a priest dangling from his chimney. The man to whom Potter had confessed many sins had seemingly dropped in to witness one for himself.

Potter would have almost certainly discounted this vision as a hallucination induced by weed and masturbatory shame had it not been for Iggy's mad barking. The dog apparently found the sight of a priest's inverted head in the fireplace as disturbing as his master did. Even with the corroboration of his freaked-out dog, the occurrence was so strange that Potter could not immediately accept it. He stared at Father Bentley's head for a full minute, trying to convince himself that he wasn't really seeing what he thought he was seeing. Iggy was going nuts the whole time, though, a stubborn rebuke to his denial.

Father Bentley sneezed again, loudly, the expulsion sending a puff of ash into the air above the hearth. The audio from the television, Gilligan's antics still playing, forgotten in the background, responded with an incongruous laugh-track stinger.

Potter finally worked up the courage to go over to the fireplace and have a closer look.

"Father?" he said.

The priest did not respond. His eyes fluttered again and then closed. The head leaned back, jaws gaping open, and a buzzing sound emerged. Bentley was snoring. He was asleep, though God alone knew how he had come to sleep in Potter's fireplace. The snore was cut short when Father Bentley inhaled more ash, which elicited another sneeze.

"Father Bentley?"

Potter considered slapping the priest's cheek to try to rouse him, but thought better of it. Instead, he just touched the man's cheek, more as a final confirmation of his reality than anything else. Bentley was quite warm to the touch, possibly feverish. But real, definitely real. Potter was at least reassured that he wasn't losing his mind.

Deputy Bryant Morris was losing his mind.

He was home by himself in the little house he shared with his daughter. Sally worked the evening shift at Inspiration Fitness on Fridays. They had on-site child care there, so Derek had gone in with her. Bryant was grateful for this. He could not have handled watching his high-spirited toddler grandson tonight. He could barely tolerate his own company.

Even though he brushed his teeth constantly and had gone through four bottles of mouthwash in as many days, he couldn't cleanse his tongue of the strange metallic tang he'd tasted ever since Linda Hansard had stuck her bloody hand in his mouth. Even worse than that was the nagging, gnawing feeling that he'd had the same taste in his mouth before.

Bryant had started doing the dishes—he liked to help Sally with the housework as much as he could—but he was too agitated to stay on even such a simple task. Too worked up. He couldn't put his finger on what exactly was wrong. The taste in his mouth was part of it, but there was also an indefinable sense of mounting discomfort, like he wanted to crawl out of his own skin.

At first, he'd thought that maybe he was just cold. He turned off the air conditioner, but the outside air was so swampy he had to turn it right back on again. Besides, only his body was cold. His forehead was pouring sweat, like he had one of those crazy fevers that gave you chills at the same time. The only thermometer he could find in the house was the one Sally used on Derek, an officially licensed SpongeBob SquarePants product. Bryant felt damn silly jamming the bright yellow cartoon character into his mouth. It didn't do anything to clarify matters, either. According to SpongeBob's precise digital readout, Bryant's temperature was 98.5. Just below normal. Whatever the hell that meant.

He had the radio on while he was doing dishes. WBIL's evening shift DJ called himself Johnny Six-Pack and delivered fake redneck patter between the Brad Paisley and Lady Antebellum records. Usually Bryant found him pretty entertaining, but there was something grating about the guy's voice tonight. Like Bryant recognized it from somewhere.

"Howdy, folks. Johnny Six-Pack here on WBIL. That spells 'weeble,' but I ain't like one of them little toys, because when I wobble, I fall right on my well-padded butt. 'Specially if it's happy hour over at Wolfy's."

Bryant knew, of course, that Johnny Six-Pack was really John Turner's kid Ed, but that wasn't why the voice seemed familiar. It reminded Bryant of something that had happened to him, or maybe something from a movie he'd seen that had stuck in his craw for some reason. Somehow too, though this didn't make any kind of sense, he was sure that whatever the voice reminded him of was connected to the almost-familiar coppery blood taste in his mouth.

"We got some Blake Shelton comin' up and I know I got a Cole Swindell record around here someplace, but first, you ever have one of them dreams where you're back in high school and you're standin' up in front of the class, but you forgot to put your durned britches on?"

Bryant couldn't put his finger on what was bugging him about the voice, but it was disturbing enough that he just turned the radio off.

Without the music, though, the rattling and the roaring of the air conditioner was loud and irritating. Even worse, it seemed like Bryant could still hear the Johnny Six-Pack voice going on under the sound, whispering words he couldn't quite make out. Thinking that maybe somebody was playing a radio outside the window, Bryant turned the air conditioner off again. The silence was even worse. The voice was still there, the words still too low to hear, but now Bryant knew for sure that it was just in his head. He couldn't stand the stifling air or the quiet so he turned the air on yet again.

He went into the bathroom to pee, and stood before the toilet for a whole minute before realizing he really didn't have to go. The pressure building inside him wasn't coming from his bladder. He didn't know what the hell it was. Washing his hands at the sink, he caught his reflection in the mirror. He looked bad. Pale and stricken. As white as...

(snow)

No. Not like snow. Jesus. More gray than white, anyway. Like...

(like a dead girl's face covered with snow)

God damn. Cool it with that shit.

(snow that ain't really snow)

"Shut up," Bryant said out loud. Talking to himself was bad, but it seemed to silence Johnny Fuckin' Six-Pack. At least for the moment.

He tried to grin reassuringly at his own reflection but, strange thing, it seemed like there was a slight lag before the reflection grinned back. Like that old movie gag where two men faced each other, one pretending to be the other's reflection by mimicking his actions. Wasn't so funny when it happened for real.

Bryant pulled the mirror open and grabbed the bottle of Listerine from the medicine cabinet. The bad taste in his mouth was getting worse. It almost tasted...

(like snow that ain't really snow)

"Jesus, shut the fuck up," Bryant snarled. He knocked back a capful of the astringent amber, swishing it around until his mouth was numb. He spat it out and rinsed the sink, then put the bottle back in the cabinet. He didn't close the mirror door, though. In every horror movie he'd ever seen, closing a mirror like that always revealed some monster standing behind you. Bryant wasn't going to tempt fate like that. Not tonight.

He went back into the living room and flopped down on the couch. Turned the TV on. He needed something to distract him, at least until Sally came home. He flipped around stupid reality crap until he found an old John Wayne western on the classic movie channel. It was the one where Wayne's niece gets captured by Indians and he spends the rest of the movie searching for her. Bryant couldn't remember the title. He'd seen the movie a long time ago, and remembered having liked it. Normally, a good old western would be just the ticket to keep his mind off the discontent he was feeling and Johnny Six-Pack and the...

(fuckin' snow)

...rest of it. But there was a scene in the movie where John Wayne comes across a Comanche corpse. He shoots out the dead man's eyes so the Indian can't enter the spirit land, destined instead to "wander forever between the winds."

What the fuck was that? Bryant didn't remember that part. John Wayne was supposed to be the hero and yet here he was desecrating a corpse? Jesus. Bryant couldn't abide that. It reminded him of the...

(snow)

Fine. Goddamn fine. Bryant allowed the memory, long suppressed, into the front of his mind. It was obviously eating at him, although he didn't know why it should come back to him now, tonight, after all this time.

Twenty-odd years ago, early on Christmas morning, Bryant had been part of the search party looking for a girl named Lori Wallace, reported missing by her parents just a few hours before. This was two months after another teen girl named Paula Tate had been murdered, and so everyone feared the worst. The sheriff, it had been Jane Gray back then, had called in every single deputy in the force, at one o'clock on Christmas morning.

Bryant had gone alone, on a pure hunch, down to the creek that used to run beside the railroad tracks, where the Lawndale golf course was now. He found Lori there just before dawn. A pretty, young dark-haired girl, naked in the freezing cold, pale skin blue in the rising light. No visible wounds, but her throat was bruised and swollen. The fucker had strangled her.

Lori's face and parts of her body, her breasts and her crotch, were covered with what appeared to be a light dusting of snow. This was strange because there hadn't even been a snowfall yet that year. Without thinking,

Bryant had brushed the stuff from the girl's face so he could close her eyes. It didn't seem right that snow should be caked over her open eyes like that.

Poor Lori Wallace was the first corpse Bryant had ever seen outside of a funeral home. Her face had been fixed with the most awful expression. A blank kind of terror, which was etched indelibly into Bryant's mind. Whenever he thought of his own death (and thoughts of this sort came to him more and more frequently in the years following his discovery of Lori's body) the memory of the dead girl's face always came to him. It looked like she'd come to a dismaying realization in her final moments, an ultimate disappointment. The sight shook him to his core. Bryant tried to be a faithful man, but the look on Lori Wallace's petrified face made him fear that the promise of a glorious reward beyond death might be the cruelest lie ever told.

The medical examiner's report came back a few days later, revealing that the white flaky substance covering Lori's body wasn't snow. It was frozen semen. More than a gallon of the stuff, all from one man, presumably the killer. He must have been saving it for months, freezing it, shaving it like ice into snowy flakes so he could pour it over the girl in a final insult. Who could even conceive of something like that? It was so fucking obscene.

That was why they'd started calling the killer the Snowman within the sheriff's department. The name had leaked to the press, but not the reason for it. Some things are just too terrible for public consumption.

Worse, Bryant had touched it. With no gloves on. He still remembered the queer sticky feeling of the flakes under his fingers. And now he recalled, though he hadn't thought of it in years, how he'd smoked a cigarette while he was waiting for the sheriff and the coroner and the crime scene people to arrive. He still smoked back then. Lifting the cigarette to his lips, with that stuff still on his fingers, he'd noticed an odd metallic taste on his lips. Like aluminum shavings. Then afterwards, after he found out what the stuff really was, he'd conveniently crammed that memory into a deep dark hole. He remembered it now, though. It finally clicked.

The taste was the same as that of Linda Hansard's blood.

Bryant felt sick. Physically ill. He dashed back into the bathroom and knelt, retching, before the toilet, but was unable to purge himself. What was inside him would not come out.

Then something else clicked, too. He remembered where he had heard the voice before.

Kneeling beside the body, wiping the snow that was not snow from Lori's dead glazed eyes, a voice had spoken in Bryant's head.

(fuck her)

An alien voice, thick with rural twang that Bryant had somehow understood to be a put-on, someone mocking ignorant country boys like him.

(Go on now, boy. Ain't nobody watchin'. You know you wanna. Just look at them fine young titties. And that fuzzy little pussy's so tight you wouldn't fuckin' believe it.)

Shaken by the voice in his head, Bryant stood up and staggered backwards. Called in what he had found and lit a cigarette with shaking hands. Touched his tongue to his lips and swallowed the tiny flakes of the killer's seed. That's how it had got inside him. It had been in there for decades now, lying dormant, until that woman's blood had re-awoken it.

Bryant stood on weak legs. He wished he had a drink, or about twelve, but there was no booze in the house. Sally was in AA, though it had been her late husband Ed who'd been the drunk. Out of respect for her, Bryant did whatever little drinking he did anymore down at Wolfy's. He couldn't imagine going down there tonight, though. Couldn't imagine any kind of human company, not with this taste in his mouth and this voice in his head.

He splashed cool water on his face and had another hit of Listerine. Considered swallowing the stuff for the alcohol content, but just spat it into the sink instead. He put the bottle back in the cabinet and, without thinking, closed the mirror door.

A snowman stared back out at him from the mirror. With jagged white teeth and two burning lumps of coal for eyes. And, as if someone had gotten their Christmas songs mixed up, a bright red light for a nose. Frosty the Red-Nosed Killer Snowman. Bryant screamed at his aberrant reflection and the Snowman screamed back.

He awoke with a jolt on his couch, the scream stuck in his throat, face dripping with sweat. He'd fallen asleep at some point.

On the television, the movie was coming to an end. John Wayne carried the rescued girl (was that Natalie Wood?) back to her family. The camera looked out from the dark interior of the cabin, Wayne framed by the open door. The hero watched the happy homecoming, but could not participate. Isolated from civilization, forever shunned, he turned away to walk back into the wilderness. The door closed and the end titles came up on the dark black screen.

Bryant sat up on the couch, trying to sort out in his head where reality had ended and the dream had begun. Had he really tasted the Snowman's frozen seeds or was that a false, dream memory? Had he really heard the Snowman's whispering voice in his head?

He couldn't sort it out. He had no idea what was real and what was not. He still felt like he wanted to crawl out of his skin, though. There was an emptiness inside him, but at the same time a growing pressure that needed to be relieved. It was almost like a horniness, too, though that didn't quite convey the feeling, either. More like he wanted to...

(kill)

No. Not that. He just wanted to...

(wrap my hands around some little monkey fucker's throat)

No. He just wanted to go to sleep and wake up sane again. That's all.

(Monkey never dies unless you kill the fuckin thing)

He looked over at the clock. It was just after seven. Sally didn't get off until eleven o'clock. The prospect of those four hours with only the company of his own sickening thoughts...

(monkey never dies)

...was horrifying, but now Bryant was afraid of his daughter and grandson coming home.

('less you kill it)

He didn't know how much longer he could trust himself around them.

CHAPTER 7

THE FEW MINUTES following his descent from the water tower had to count among the happiest moments Mark had known for years. Limbs jittery from the unnatural exertion, adrenal glands utterly depleted, he dropped to the blessed, grassy earth to the sound of applause from the onlookers behind the police barricade. This was nowhere as gratifying for him as the sight of his ex-wife and his mother waiting for him. Smiling at him.

Missy ran over and threw her arms around him, with a warmth he hadn't felt from her in years. He'd managed to suppress how much he missed touching her, but the sudden embrace brought all that back in a rush of physical and emotional sensation. She smelled great, too.

"Thank you," she whispered in his ear.

Then, Missy let him go and his mother had a turn. It had been more than a year since his wife had touched him, but it had been at least a decade since he'd hugged his mom. Her embrace was cooler and more restrained than Missy's, naturally, but none the less remarkable.

"I'm very proud of you, Mark," she said.

Mark had managed to please the two women in his life whose approval he most craved. He had to force back a grin, to show the proper concern.

"How's James?" he asked.

"He was unconscious when they took him away," Missy said. "Jennifer went with him to the hospital. They wouldn't let me ride in the ambulance, but I'm going over there later. She said she'd call as soon as she knew anything."

Mark nodded, and then did permit himself a small grin. It was returned with a slight eye roll and head shake from Missy, a gesture of hers that he hadn't seen in ages. Indulgent, bemused exasperation. As if she knew exactly what he was feeling and found it both predictable and amusing. His heart ached a little to see it again.

They lingered for a few minutes at the base of the tower. Mark shook hands with Lou and Will, the tower rescue guys who'd saved him, the real heroes here. There was even some congratulatory back-slapping from a few of the deputies on the scene. Sheriff Bates didn't deign to approach, but he did give a firm nod from across the lot that Mark took to be a show of grudging approval.

Still no news vans, though, which was surprising. This was the kind of story that local media outlets ate for breakfast. As gratifying as Mark found all this attention, he had no desire to show up on the evening news. Best to leave now, while he still could.

Missy seemed to be on the same wavelength. "Come on," she said. "I'll drive you home."

Walking with her over to the car, Mark fought a powerful urge to take her hand. It would just feel so natural, slipping his hand into hers as he'd done thousands of times since they were kids. He was afraid, though, of how she'd react. He knew he was floating inside a very thin bubble right now.

"I have to tell you something," he said as Missy was driving out of the lot. "When I was up there with James, I noticed that his eyes were darting around. Rapid eye movement. Like he was tripping on Neiro."

And then, just like that, the bubble popped.

Missy stomped the brake. "Did you give him some of that shit?"

Mark, still pulling his seatbelt on, flew forward and nearly smacked his head on the dash.

"No! I haven't even seen the stuff in years," he said. "Anyway, you really think I would do that to James?"

"I don't know, Mark," Missy snarled. She took two deep breaths and started driving again. "No, I guess you probably wouldn't. I'm sorry."

"Give me some fucking credit. I care about James like I care about Ben."

"I said I was sorry." Missy bit her lip. "You really think he was on Neiro?"

"If he was, it would have to be a massive dose. For him to disassociate completely and do something like climbing a water tower because he thought he was a flying vampire."

"When you were on that stuff, you almost crashed my scooter into the Dairy Queen drive-through."

"I was hot and I wanted some ice cream."

"You were naked!"

"So, I was *really* hot. But I wasn't delusional. But I was still aware of my surroundings. I knew who I was. James was acting like he had a complete break with reality."

"He doesn't do drugs, though," Missy said. "He doesn't even drink."

"Not that we know of," Mark said. "Maybe he was just really good at hiding it."

"I don't buy it. Not James."

"Maybe somebody dosed him."

"If that happened, there's only one place it could have come from."

"Shaner." Mark nodded.

"Does he still live in Springfield?"

"I don't know."

"You don't know? You were his favorite customer."

"Yeah, well, he's not exactly the stay-in-touch-on-Facebook type. He could be in prison, for all I know. Or dead, even."

"He might still be living in that same house, though," Missy said. "I'll go over there tomorrow and have a talk with the guy."

"You don't even know him. I'll go."

"We'll both go. Early tomorrow. First thing."

"Okay." Mark smiled. He felt a strange lightness inside, as if Missy had consented to go on a date with him, rather than into a potential confrontation with his former dealer.

"Hey, on the seat behind you, there's something Jen gave me," Missy said. "She wanted you to look at it."

Mark turned around and found a large drawing pad on the back seat.

"Those are all drawings James has done since he started having his attacks," Missy said.

Mark opened the pad and found page after page of colored pencil sketches. All were portraits of Henry the vampire. One showed Henry in the aftermath of the key battle scene in *Blood World War*, weeping bloody tears as he walked through the red-stained snow where so many of his friends, both human and vampire, had fallen. Another had Henry shaving with a straight razor, in a shattered mirror, only his glowing red eyes and the bloodied shaving cream visible in the reflection. (That was a scene from a short story Mark had written for a vampire anthology, titled *Blood is Murder*.) The largest and most detailed of the drawings showed Henry standing atop the water tower, in the anguished moment just before he took flight.

James was a very talented amateur artist. His style was unpolished, perhaps a bit flat, but he was so young. If the kid went to art school and received some real instruction, he could easily become good enough to find work as an illustrator or graphic artist.

Consideration of his nephew's future brought a sharp pang to Mark's heart. He hoped to God the kid was all right.

Flipping through the pages, Mark noticed an odd detail that didn't come from any of his books. In every picture James had drawn, Henry's heart was glowing with a radiant red light, visible even through his skin and clothes. Like something from a religious icon.

"What do you think the glowing heart means?" Mark asked.

"Isn't that something from your books?"

"No. Did you even..." Mark looked over at her. "You never really read them, did you?"

"I...looked through them."

"That's just...great. Really. I mean, no wonder I'm a failure. I couldn't even get my own wife to read my stuff."

"Really? You want to do this now? You think now is the appropriate time to have this conversation again?"

Mark sighed. The good feeling he'd got from Missy after coming down from the tower had evaporated completely, leaving only the familiar bitterness.

"The glowing heart was *not* in my books," Mark said, shrugging off his hurt the best he could. "It almost looks like a religious icon. The Sacred Heart of Mary, or whatever you call it."

"The Sacred Heart of Jesus," Missy corrected. "It's the Immaculate Heart of Mary."

"How do you know that?"

"Lana's Catholic."

"Really?" Mark had to laugh.

"Why is that funny?"

"I just imagine the sisterhood of black Catholic lesbians to be a pretty exclusive club."

"You're such an ass."

"So, are you going to convert?"

"No, but the artwork and a lot of the rituals are really beautiful."

"Just as long as you keep our son away from the priests."

They'd pulled into her driveway now. Missy lurched to a stop with another slam of the brakes. "You drive me crazy! Here, I was thinking that maybe you'd finally grown up a little, but then you had to go and fuck it up."

"*I* fucked it up?"

"Yeah, you did."

She jumped out of the car and slammed the door. Mark slipped out of the passenger seat as she stalked up to her house. He was just going to get back into his own car and drive home, if he could call his new place of employment that. Then Ben came running out of the house, followed closely by Lana.

"Dad!" Ben gave his father a running-start hug that nearly knocked him off his feet. Mark hugged his son back, in self-defense. "You saved James's life!"

"How did you hear about that already?"

"People are posting videos to the Internet left and right," Lana said. "We must have watched half a dozen of them. You're going to be a local celebrity."

"Great."

"You're a hero, Dad."

"No, I..." Mark started to demur, but then decided to just accept it. His son's admiration was almost enough to make up for his ex-wife's scorn. "I'm just happy James is safe."

Lana slipped her arm around Missy's waist. Missy slid in close, leaning her head on the other woman's shoulder in an easy, intimate gesture. Missy obviously drew comfort from her wife. The stress lines on her forehead just melted away. Had there ever been a time when she'd responded to his touch like that? All Mark could remember now were the times she'd pulled away. His heart ached to see her fit so naturally with someone else.

"I'm going to go now," he said to his son. "We'll get together tomorrow and hang out."

"Can we go to Allen Park?" Ben asked. "They have a fountain there now."

"Sure, whatever you want to do."

"Don't forget what we're doing in the morning," Missy said. Her voice was, if not warm exactly, at least not icy cold anymore. "I'll pick you up early. Eight o'clock. Be ready."

"Yes, ma'am." Mark released his son, gave his ex-wife an ironic salute, and then got into his car and drove away.

Mark didn't feel like going back to the possibly haunted, definitely lonely, farmhouse just yet. He was too nerve-wracked from his adventure atop the water tower, and from his frustrating conversation with Missy afterwards. So instead, he drove over to the town square, intending to walk around a little. To clear his head and to glean whatever nostalgia he could.

The shadows were growing longer as the sun sank down, and downtown was tinted a poignant dusky orange. Mark was surprised by all the things that had changed, and he was also surprised by all the things that had not. Grady's Feed Store stood as it always had, impervious to time, exactly as it had appeared back in the nineties. Or the seventies, for that matter. Probably even the fifties. Ditto Jett's Diner. Wolfy's Tavern, next door to Wolfy's Package Liquors, had added a big neon sign advertising video gaming, but was otherwise exactly the same. A Discount Tobacco shop was in the space where the K-9 Kollege Dog Training Academy used to be. Many of the other businesses Mark remembered from his youth had folded without replacement. Coney Island Cones, the closest the town had ever had to a teenage hangout, was gone. So was the Martial Arts Academy, where Mark had taken precisely two lessons as a kid. The United Methodist Church endured, though, an island of faith in this little lake of commerce.

After a few wandering moments, lost in memory, Mark found himself standing before the Community Bank of Bakersfield. The lights were on in the little apartment above the bank. Sam Hansard was at home. Though

Mark had not come here by conscious design, the thought of friendly human companionship held a warm allure. He pressed the little button on the intercom beside the bank entrance.

"Yeah?" Sam's voice crackled through the speaker.

"Hey, Sam. It's Mark Davies. Just wondering if you wanted to..."

"Hell, yeah. Come on up!"

The door unlocked with a buzz. Mark stepped into a dim, narrow stairwell flooded with loud country music and aromatic pot smoke. The door at the top of the stairs popped open.

"Mark!" Sam's bearded grin wafted out upon a cloud. "Holy crap, man. You're all over my Facebook page. You sure know how to make a splash with your homecoming."

"Yeah, I didn't really plan it that way."

"Come in, come in."

Sam held the door while Mark stepped into the hazy living room. A bong still simmering on the coffee table was the obvious source of the miasma.

"Sorry about the..." Sam batted at the clouds to disperse them. "Here, lemme just crack a window."

"It's fine," Mark said. "Doesn't bother me." In fact, his mouth was watering. The accumulated tension of the cross-country drive, the terror of the water tower climb and all the frustrating ex-wife bullshit hung from his shoulders like heavy bags. A few drags of the water-cooled smoke would fill the bags with helium and allow them to just float away.

If he offers, I'll say yes.

But Sam scooped up the bong and the loose weed on the metal tray and made it all disappear into a hall closet. He sprayed air freshener that banished the tantalizing smoke in favor of cloying artificial flowers.

"Sit down, sit down," Sam said.

The radio was still blaring. Mark's knowledge of contemporary country was limited, but he believed the artist to be Blake Shelton. Sam eased the volume down.

"You want something to drink?" he asked. "I'm out of beer, but I have... water. Milk's been in the fridge for a while, but it might be okay. I really need to go to the store."

"I'm fine, Sam. Thanks."

"Good." Sam smiled and settled into a weary-looking chair that groaned under his weight. Mark sat on the blanket-draped couch. "So is that kid all right?"

"I don't know. The ambulance took him away before I even climbed down from the tower. He was unconscious."

"Do you know him? Or are you just like Batman, coming along to rescue anyone who's in trouble?"

"He's my nephew," Mark said. "Missy's sister's kid."

"I know him a little bit," Sam said. "He mowed gram's lawn a few times. Seems like a nice kid. I hope he's all right."

"Wait. He mowed your grandmother's lawn?"

"Yeah. He had his own riding mower. Why?"

"Sam, James climbed the tower because he had some kind of break with reality. Just like you grandmother did."

"Really? Do you think they're...How could they be related?"

"I don't know, but that's a pretty wild coincidence, isn't it?"

"Yeah, maybe..." Sam appeared to lapse into contemplation for a second, but then he leapt to his feet. "Oh shit, my cake!"

He ran to the kitchen area and threw the oven door open. Thrusting his hand into an oven mitt, he pulled out a slightly smoking pan.

"It's okay, just a little burnt around the edges," he assessed. He flashed Mark a sheepish grin. "Yeah, I baked a cake. Just a Betty Crocker mix. You like Funfetti? I got that cream cheese frosting, too."

Mark barely heard him. "You said something before, about your grandma's eyes."

Sam came back and sat down on his chair. "They dart around, all twitchy-like." He gave a little demonstration.

"Rapid eye movements," Mark said. "Like people do when they're asleep and dreaming. James was doing that, too. It's also a side effect of this drug I took a few times when I was younger. Neiro."

"I've never even heard of that."

"It was a designer hallucinogen. I knew the chemist who created it."

"Damn. Sounds like you really knew how to party."

"The drug puts you into a kind of dream state, but you're still awake," Mark said. "Your grandmother and my nephew both had breakdowns that look just like heavy Neiro trips."

Sam frowned and shook his head. "I don't know. Gram was Church of the Shepherd, hardcore. She never even drank. I can't see her taking some fancy club drug."

"James didn't do drugs, either. But maybe somebody dosed them with it. And he mowed her lawn, so that means they had a connection."

"I wouldn't read too much into that. This is Bakersfield, population sixty-five hundred. *Everybody's* connected somehow."

Mark nodded. There was something here, just out of his reach. It was like someone was slowly dropping jigsaw puzzle pieces on a table in front of him. Linda Hansard, James, Neiro, vampires with glowing red hearts. If he wasn't so goddamn tired, maybe he could start putting the pieces together by shape and color, assembling the borders and working his way in. But his weary brain balked at the task. He should just go out to the farmhouse and get some sleep, look at it all with fresh eyes in the morning. Maybe drive around for a while first. He did his best thinking when he was driving.

"Listen, Sam. I really should get—"

"Wait." Sam jumped to his feet again and went over to the radio to crank the volume a little. "Listen to this."

"Hey there, home fries. This here's Johnny Six-Pack on WBIL. Bakersfield, Illinois' number one-and-only country-fried radio." The rural twang of the DJ's voice was amped to a cartoonish level. "That was Sam Hunt, talkin' about breaking up in a small town. And we all know how awkward that can be."

"Do you know who that is?" Sam grinned. "Ed Turner!"

"Who?" Mark said.

"Shit, you wouldn't know him. He was a year behind me in school. Kind of a weird kid, but he could do any voice in the world. He's like the guy who did all the Bugs Bunny voices."

"Mel Blanc."

"Right, right. Like a hometown Mel Blanc. I don't even like country that much, but I listen just for him. He's hilarious."

"We got some Darius Rucker comin' up," the DJ riffed. "Maybe if you're real good, I'll throw in some Kelsea Ballerini in there, too. Dang, she's purdy. But first, you ever have one of them dreams where it's your birthday and everybody's singing and you blow out your candles? And then you dig into your cake and it tastes kinda strange and sticks in your teeth funny. Then you wake up and realize you're just passed out face down in a urinal and that little cake's not there no more. Lemme tell ya, that ain't good."

Sam laughed out loud at that, but Mark just smiled. He had never been a fan of redneck comedy, having seen too much of the real thing in his life to find it particularly funny. He was about to stand up to leave again when the intercom buzzed.

"Yeah?" Sam said into the little speaker on the wall.

"Mr. Sam, this is Bill. Wondering if I could come in and have a—"

"Hell yeah, come on up!"

"You know who *that* is?" Sam said as he buzzed the new visitor in. "Bill Potter!"

"Bill Potter, the teacher?"

"The one and only."

"Oh my God. Really?"

Mr. Potter's English classes had been a rare bright spot in Mark's troubled and depressing four-year slog through the grim institution known as Bakersfield High School. Potter had been the first adult to take his writing seriously, the first to actually encourage his creativity. He'd learned more from the man than from all of his other teachers combined.

Sam opened the door and Potter stepped into the apartment, hair gone completely gray, but just as frizzed and unruly as Mark remembered. He'd always thought Potter looked more like a cartoon mad-scientist than a small-town English teacher.

Potter didn't at first notice Mark sitting on the couch. "Sam, my man," he said. "Hate to trouble you, but would you perhaps have a quarter ounce of your finest you might be willing to part with?"

"You already smoked up the bag I sold you on Tuesday?"

"I had to dispose of that, unfortunately."

"Why?"

"I'll tell you all about it," Potter said. "But can I have an emergency refill? I have a very real need of its medicinal properties tonight."

"Sure, sure," Sam said. "Come on in. Hey, look who's here."

Potter saw Mark had given him a comical double take.

"Mark Davies, as I live and breathe. You in town on a visit?"

Mark hopped up to shake his hand. "Long visit, let's say."

"He's going to be working for me," Sam put in. "At my Gram's house."

"Moving back?" Potter's lively eyes examined Mark's as he pumped his hand. "I always thought you'd be one to make good your escape."

"Yeah, well. Best laid plans and all that."

"Ain't that the bitter truth?"

"Sit down, guys," Sam said. "I'll go grab your stuff, Bill."

"You know, I always wanted to tell you how much I enjoyed your books, Mark," Bill said as they sat on Sam's ragged couch. "I'm not typically a fan of the horror genre, but your novels have a real emotional depth. A sense of humor, too. Humor's important."

Mark felt his face flush with the praise. "Yeah, well, I learned from the best."

Potter had published a novel, too, back in the eighties. *Graveyard Grove* was a Faulkner-esque tale about a farm family in a small Illinois town, embroiled in a local scandal when the oldest brother is accused of murdering the mayor's son. Mark was one of the very few of Potter's students to whom he'd shown the book, probably because of the high levels of sex and violence. The sister's rape scene, in particular, had been graphic and indelible.

Sam returned with a tightly rolled plastic baggy. Potter swapped it for a couple of bills and ran the baggy under his nose with an appraising sniff.

"Quality herbage as always," he said. "Far superior to that mediocre shake those gangster Barber boys peddle in town." He turned to Mark. "Do you partake?"

"Well, actually..."

"Mark quit smoking the stuff," Sam put in. "He said it caused some problems in his life."

"Admirable." Potter nodded. "It is better to face reality unfiltered. That being said, do you mind if we..."

"Go right ahead," Mark said. He would have liked to smoke up with his old teacher, but it was probably for the best that he didn't. He would have regretted it afterwards.

Sam produced papers from a drawer and Potter rolled a fat one with the practiced grace of a man who had been performing the task for many decades. Bill sparked the joint and passed it to Sam. Mark contented himself with inhaling their exhalations.

"So, Mark," Potter said. "How are you enjoying your homecoming?"

"I just got in this afternoon," Mark said. "And it has been one of the craziest days of my crazy life."

"Ha!" Potter barked smoke. "I want to hear that story, Mark. I really do. But let me tell you mine first. I bet I have you beat for the title of craziest day ever."

"I doubt that," Mark said. "But go ahead."

"Well, not two hours ago, my house was full of representatives from both the sheriff's and the fire department. That's why I had to divest myself of my pharmaceuticals. Given my history with our fine sheriff, I thought it prudent to flush my stash before they arrived."

"Why were they all at your house?"

"I requested their help, to remove a priest from my fireplace."

"What?"

"You heard me right. Father Bentley, the priest over at St. Joe's, for some reason took it into his head to climb a ladder onto my roof and dive headfirst down my chimney. He was unconscious when the fire department finally managed to extract him. I suspect he was in some sort of fugue state."

Mark and Sam exchanged an astonished look.

"This may seem like a strange question," Mark said. "But do you happen to know who mows his lawn?"

"That is a *very* strange question," Bill said, "and one I have no answer for."

"Hold on, I'll explain in a second." Mark pulled out his phone and dialed up Jennifer, hoping she was in area of the hospital that allowed phone calls. After two rings, Missy answered.

"Mark, hi," she said.

"Hi," he said back. "You're at the hospital with Jen?"

"Yeah, I just got here."

"How's James?"

"Still unconscious. They're going to run a CAT scan and some other tests."

"They think he might have brain damage?"

"Well, that's what they're trying to determine."

"Listen, can I talk to Jen? I have to ask her some questions. About James."

"They gave her a sedative. She's kind of out of it. What do you need to know?"

"Okay, so James was making money mowing people's lawns?"

"I think so, yeah."

"He mowed Linda Hansard's yard, right?"

"I don't know. Did he?"

Mark sighed. "Can you just put Jen on?"

"What's this about?"

"Please, Missy."

"Fine. Jesus. Just a second."

Some shuffling on the other end and Jen came on.

"Hi, Mark," she said dreamily. Mark guessed Xanax.

"I'm so sorry, Jen, but I need to ask you about James's lawn mowing business."

"Yeah. I lent him the money to buy him the mower last summer. He made enough to pay me back within a month. He was always so responsible. He was saving the money for college. He's going to graduate next year and..." She trailed off. Light sobbing came through the line.

"I know he mowed Linda Hansard's lawn," Mark prodded. "But what about..." Mark looked to Bill. "What's the priest's name?"

"Father Bentley," Bill provided.

"What about Father Bentley, the priest?"

"Yeah," Jen replied, her voice spacey.

"James mowed his lawn, really?"

"Just at the parish house. They had a landscaping service for the church grounds."

"Who else?" Mark asked.

"Why? What's this all about?"

Across the room, forgotten, the radio station was returning from the commercial break. "Howdy, home girls and boys. Johnny Six-Pack here again on WBIL. Bakersfield's Billy-boy radio 98.5."

"I can't explain right now. I just need to know. Who else did James do mowing for?"

"He has a day planner on his iPad. I can look it up and call you back when I get home."

"Just off the top of your head, Jen. Whoever you can think of." Mark snapped his fingers and pantomimed a request to Sam for something to write on.

"We got some really great countries coming up for you." Had Mark, Sam or Bill been paying the slightest bit of attention, they might have noticed how the DJ's drawl had slowed to a low drone. "But first, you ever have one of those dreams where Jesus Christ hisself descends from the clear blue sky?"

"Pastor Tuttle, I think, from the Church of the Shepherd."

Sam handed Mark a dull, stubby pencil and an envelope containing his electric bill. Mark wrote Pastor Tuttle's name on the back.

"You know they got time machines now," Johnny Six-Pack intoned. "Them machines make windows in the clouds. Yer only s'posed to look through 'em, but if you break the glass, you can reach right in there and grab folks from days gone by. Just don't cut yourself or you'll be bleeding out through the centuries."

"Who else, Jen? Can you give me another name?"

"Somebuddy opened up one of them time windows on our boy Jesus. The bastards snatched Him up and out and then they dropped him down into the here and now. I seen him with my own two lies. His palms were glowin' like bright red Christmas lights."

"Uh..." Jen was fading. Mark could hear it in her voice. "The disc jockey guy, what's his name? Ed something?"

Mark looked up at the radio. "Ed Turner?"

"Yeah. That's it."

"He can't see me no more," the DJ lamented. "They got me stuffed way down here in the dark. Jesus' glowin' red hands could light my path if He only knew where to find me."

Johnny Six-Pack's bizarre monologue finally registered with Mark. Sam and Bill were hearing it, too, each of them wearing stony expressions of alarm.

"What's all this about, Mark?" Jen asked.

"I'll tell you later. Sorry. Gotta go." Mark disconnected the call.

"You gotta light a signal fire," Johnny Six-Pack cried. "A light in the darkness so Jesus knows where y'are."

"Where's the radio station?" Mark asked.

"Just a couple blocks from here," Sam said.

"Let's go."

"He's comin' for me," the disc jockey sobbed with wonder and joy. "Oh, Jesus. He's comin' for me right now."

CHAPTER 8

MARK SAW THE column of smoke rising into the twilit sky as soon as he descended from Sam's apartment. Wailing sirens were already echoing between the downtown buildings. Somebody else must have seen the smoke, or heard Johnny Six-Pack's alarming rant, and put in the 911 call. The firehouse was less than two blocks from the WBIL studios, and the first of the trucks had already arrived on the scene before he and his two companions had made it even halfway down there.

"The fire guys are already there," Sam panted. The short dash had winded him. "The sheriff's probably coming, too. We don't need to go down there."

"I have to see," Mark said. "Maybe I can talk to somebody, tell them what's going on."

"Dude, I'm high as hell and I got a cake to frost," Sam said.

"Go back inside, Sam. I'll be fine."

"No, goddamn it."

"So, let me get this straight," Bill said, walking briskly to keep up with Mark's half-jog. "Sam's grandmother, your nephew, Father Bentley and now Eddie Turner all somehow got dosed with the same drug?"

"I don't know," Mark said. "Maybe. There are too many similarities, and they're all connected via James. It can't all be coincidental."

Mark stepped up his pace, leaving Bill and Sam a bit behind, and reached the corner of Mulberry and Archer. The radio studio was on the block just ahead, thick black smoke billowing from the front doors. The big ladder truck, the same vehicle that had been at the water tower earlier, was just now pulling up, sirens screaming. The crew in the smaller truck that was already on the scene had tapped the hydrant. The gutters ran with the spillover as two volunteer fire guys in coats and helmets carried the taut house into the front entrance.

Curious onlookers were stepping out of the other businesses on the block. A few patrons of Wolfy's Tavern had wandered outside, carrying their beer bottles in blatant defiance of village open container ordinances. Old-timers wearing farmer caps stepped out of Grady's Feed Store, followed by Gerald Grady himself.

One firefighter came over to push back the small crowd. Mark recognized him as one of the Johnson brothers, who had both been a few years ahead of him in school. He wasn't sure if it was Paul or Frank.

"All right, folks. Stand back," Paul-or-Frank Johnson said. "It's under control. Just a small fire." The wind shifted as he spoke, blowing the black smoke right into the faces of the onlookers, filling the street with an eye-stinging fog.

Mark went over to him. "Hey, listen," he coughed. "I need to talk to whoever's in charge here. I think I know why the DJ started the fire."

Johnson frowned. "How do you know the DJ started the fire?"

"We were listening to the radio and he started ranting about..." Mark realized as he spoke how crazy this all sounded. "Listen, isn't there somebody in charge I can talk to?"

Bill and Sam caught up then.

"Frankie Johnson," Bill hailed the firefighter. "Thank you again for helping pull Father Bentley out of my chimney."

"Oh, hi Mr. Potter," Frank said. "What's going on here?"

"It's a bit much to explain, Frank. Is Chief Haywood about?"

"The Chief's over in Mt. Pulaski, doing a training exercise. Missed out on the busiest day we've had in years. Three calls, including the one out at your place. The sheriff's going to be here pretty soon, though. I guess you can talk to him."

Bill's face fell at that. "No. That's quite all right. We'll just head on back home and make some phone calls in the morning."

Another fire fighter was pulling somebody from the station, holding him under the arms and dragging him out the front door.

"Is that Ed Turner?" Mark asked Sam.

"Yeah, that's him."

"Ed!" Mark called, rushing past Frank Johnson. "Ed Turner!"

"Hey, you can't go over there!" Johnson shouted.

The firefighter set Turner down on the curb. Another rescuer rushed over with an oxygen tank and slipped a mask on over Ed's face. Mark got close enough to get a good look, and thought for a moment that there had to be a mistake. He knew it was a fool's game trying to guess how a person looked based solely on his voice, but Ed Turner was thin and pale with long, stringy black hair. He looked like a goth kid dressed as Professor Snape for Halloween, not a redneck disc jockey.

"Ed!" Mark called, running over. Turner didn't look up when his name was called, but the largest of the assembled firemen intercepted Mark, putting up a hand to block him.

"Get back across the street," he said, voice rippling with masculine authority.

"I need to talk to Mr. Turner," Mark said.

"Sir, I'm going to have to insist that you stand back and let us do our jobs here."

"Ed," Mark called again. "My name is Mark Davies. I need to ask you some questions about what you were saying on the air."

Turner's eyes twitched and rolled. His voice was muffled by the mask he wore, but he was clearly in Johnny Six-Pack mode. "He ain't comin' now. Jesus ain't comin'. They got him blocked. He can't get through."

"I think you might have been drugged," Mark said. "Do you have any idea how that might have happened?"

The big firefighter grabbed Mark's arm, hard.

"I'm not asking, sir. You need to get back. Now."

Ed Turner tore the mask from his face. "They're going to seal us in here where Jesus can't get to us! They're gonna trap us inside so the sickness can spread!"

"Sickness?" Mark called. "What sickness?"

But the burly fireman's friend now had Mark by the other arm. They pulled him back, away from the raving man. The two firefighters half-carried Mark across the street and tossed him down onto the sidewalk.

Bill helped him to his feet as the firemen returned to their duties.

"No luck?" Bill said.

"Why won't anyone listen to me?"

A big pick-up roared past, blue dome light flashing on the dashboard, and pulled to a stop beside the fire trucks. Sheriff Bates slid from the driver's seat, still dressed in his civilian clothes. He did not look happy to be there. Scowling, eyes set hard with purpose, he stalked over to talk to the fire crew.

"Low down, wretched son of a bitch." Bill spat upon the ground.

Mark glanced down curiously at the phlegm-splat on the sidewalk. "So I'm sensing some bad blood between you and the sheriff."

"Mara divorced me the year after you graduated," Bill said. "Then she married that black-hearted snake. It would've been bad enough for her to move on with a decent fellow, but she picked *him*. Nate Bates is a bully and a crook. A corrupt, violent, rage-filled monster."

"Wow. You really hate the guy."

"Not as much as he hates me."

Over across the street, Bates was talking to the firefighters who'd escorted Mark from the scene. One of the guys pointed right at Mark. Bates looked over and flashed a pained grin.

"He's coming over here," Sam whispered.

"Shit," Bill said. "I've still got that bag in my pocket."

"Just be cool," Mark said.

"Well, goddamn," Bates called as he crossed the street towards them. "If it ain't Larry, Moe and Curly."

"Sheriff Bates," Mark said. "I need to tell you something."

"Nah, that's giving you clowns too much credit," Bates mused. "You're more like three wannabe Shemps."

"That's real funny, sheriff." Mark grinned and forced a little laugh. "Listen, though. I think there's a connection between..."

"Did you know it's my day off?" Bates stepped in front of Mark, leaning right down into his face. Close enough for Mark to surmise that he'd had a tuna sandwich for lunch. "Then twice now, I get called in to deal with some weird crap and find your punk-ass already on the scene. My least favorite author."

Mark forced himself not to back up, to just endure the fishy smell and the violation of his personal space. "You've, ah, read my..."

"Sheriff Castor Gates?" he said. "Rhymes with 'masturbates?' That's really fuckin' clever, guy. You know, those 'Bates' cracks stopped being funny for me in the third fuckin' grade. The only thing that pisses me off more is Andy Griffith jokes. And, hell, you threw a couple of those in there, too."

"I do appreciate honest feedback, thanks."

"Not to mention, you painted me as a stereotypical redneck fascist."

"Any similarity is purely coincidental, I swear," Mark said.

"Horseshit. Now Steve Nabors told me you were interfering with the firefighters while they were in the line of duty. You know I can arrest you for that? And your Mama's not here to get you out of it."

"I'm sorry about that," he said, meeting the sheriff's pointed eyes. "But listen, please. My nephew up on the tower, Father Bentley in Mr. Potter's chimney and now Ed Turner setting the fire. I think they're all connected."

"And I suppose you got some half-assed pothead theory to tie it all together. Something the three of you cooked up over bong hits?"

"I'm not under any kind of influence right now."

"Don't lie to me, son. I've got a structure fire half a block away, wind blowing smoke right in my face, and you three *still* smell like the back of Willie Nelson's tour bus."

"Come on, Mark," Potter said. "He's not going to listen to what you have to say."

"Oh, hey Bill. Tell me, are you just smoking dope with these kids, or are you getting into the heavy stuff tonight? Mara told me about your little," Bates made two quick sniffs, "habit."

"I haven't done that in years," Bill said.

Bates chuckled. "You ain't done *her* in years, neither. Speakin' of which, you'll be happy to know she's having real orgasms now. Yeah, she told me that in all the years she was with you, she never got off once. Turns out she just needs a real man-sized cock up in her and that bitch is a *screamer*. I tell you, our neighbors must hate us. Especially when I stick my little finger up her ass when she's right on the edge. Ah, man, she just goes off like a..."

Bill's lunge at Bates certainly would have connected had Mark and Sam not grabbed him and pulled him back.

"Anytime you want to tussle, Bill. I'm ready." The sheriff's eyes gleamed with good cheer. "Hell, I'll even take off my badge so we can go it man-to-man."

"Leave him alone!" Sam cried.

"Samuel Hansard." Bates turned on Sam now. "Your daddy was a good deputy. Wouldn't he be ashamed to see what a fat, lazy stoner slob you turned out to be? Every time I see you, you're stoned to the goddamn gills, but you never buy from anybody in town. So lemme guess. You got a little grow closet set up in your apartment, right? Maybe a high pressure sodium lamp on a timer? Using soil now, but you been shopping around for a hydroponic system. What do you got up there now, ten plants or twelve?"

Sam gaped. His jaw dropped open and he went pale behind his beard. If he was attempting to act cool, he was failing miserably.

"Just a heads up," Bates said. "Bakersfield Elementary is three blocks south of your place. That means you're officially inside a Drug-Free School Zone. Double penalties, man. Kind of herbage you're holding, that's Intent to Distribute right there. You could be looking at twenty years."

Sam gulped and swallowed. Sweat beaded on his forehead.

"Judge Guthrie over in Lincoln is a good buddy of mine. He'll write me up a probable cause warrant if I just buy him a drink and ask real nice. Maybe I'll be paying you a visit sometime soon. What do you got to say to that, boy?"

Sam opened his mouth as if to answer, but snapped it shut again. A second later, a reply of sorts did come, in the form of a loud, juicy-sounding splat.

"Did you just *fart*?"

"Sorry."

"Son of a bitch."

"I can't help it," Sam cried miserably. "It happens when I'm scared."

A low rumble followed, a sound like thunder across the prairie. The smell hit at the same moment. The noxious sulfurous reek was unmistakable even with the smoke blowing all around.

"Jesus Christ, boy." The sheriff cringed, waving his hand in front of his face. "What the fuck have you been eating?"

"Sorry," Sam said again, clutching his belly.

"Smells like a skunk crawled up your ass to die."

The third blast of flatulence erupted from Sam's nethers, this one an almost tuneful wah-wah sound. Like a trumpeter working a mute.

"Go. Just get the fuck out of here." The sheriff retreated, hand over his nose, and stalked back over to the fire crew.

The three of them stood there for a few moments, breathing through their mouths.

"That's a very effective defense mechanism you have there, Sam," Mark finally said.

"I'm so sorry, guys."

"Got rid of the bastard," Bill noted.

"We should clear out of here before he changes his mind and comes back," Mark said.

"He knew exactly what I have," Sam said as they walked back towards his place. "Down to the kind of lamp. I'm going to have to break it all down and haul the stuff out to Gram's house, keep it in the shed."

"Don't do it tonight," Mark said. "He might be watching. I'll help you, tomorrow."

"Yeah, okay." Sam looked utterly miserable. "All I wanted to do tonight was eat my cake and watch about five hours of *The Walking Dead* on Netflix."

"I'm so sorry, Sam," Mark said.

"Whatever. It's not your fault." He put his head down and shuffled off to his front door. "Listen, guys. I'm just going to back upstairs. Thanks for coming over and all."

"Good night, Sam," Bill said. "And don't be so downhearted. I've been on the good sheriff's shitlist for the better part of a decade, and I'm still a free man."

"Yeah, thanks." Sam nodded glumly. "See you guys later."

Sam disappeared up his stairwell, leaving Bill and Mark out on the sidewalk.

"Come with me over to Wolfy's for a couple beers, Mark," Bill said. "I'm buying."

"Thanks, but I'll take a rain check," Mark said. "Twenty hours in a car followed by the weirdest day in my life kind of beat me down. I'm going to go slip into a nice warm coma."

"Another time, then," Bill smiled. "It's truly good to see you again, Mark. I'm glad you're back home."

"Honestly, I'm not sure how glad I am to be here," Mark said. "But it's good to see you, too. Goodnight, Bill."

Mark turned his back on the still-burning building and walked back to his car.

The weariness hit Mark hard as he drove out to the farmhouse. Bone-deep exhaustion that precluded all thought. He didn't think about James, or about the mysterious rash of sleepwalking incidents. He didn't think about the fact that he'd somehow already got on the bad side of a potentially very dangerous man. He didn't think about Missy, or his mother, or any of the thousand other things from his past that had been lying in wait for him here. The sole focus of his concentration was making it back to the Hansard farmhouse without nodding off at the wheel.

He'd forgotten how fast it got dark out here. Even with the high-beams on, the cone of light cast by his headlights seemed in danger of collapsing under the dark-matter mass of country night. The bugs were thick as a fog, kamikaze streaks of light terminating with moist little splats on his windshield. Blasting the wiper fluid only smeared the dead bug fug.

The corn was tall on both sides of the car, forming the walls of a long, green corridor. Mark kept his eyes fixed forward. He knew it was too easy to be hypnotized by the rows as they blurred past, too easy to imagine things watching from behind them.

Mark was afraid he'd miss the turn-off in the dark, but he found the first left past the barn easily enough. His rear tires kicked dust up from the gravel road, his tail-lights reflecting cherry-red in the trailing cloud. The house was less than a mile up the road. His new home.

Mark pulled into the drive and killed the engine. It was a clear night, but the moon had not yet risen. He wished he'd thought to leave the porch light on when he'd been up here earlier, or at least remembered to keep fresh batteries in the flashlight in his glovebox. The only light Mark had as he walked up to the house came from the stars, which were surprisingly bright. He could just make out the light-colored bricks of the walkway beneath his feet. The house itself was a dim blue silhouette.

A city dweller for years, Mark had forgotten how many stars were visible this far from a sizable town. He even made out a hazy band of light arcing across the sky that he recognized as the Milky Way. It brought to his mind a summer night much like this one. He and Missy had driven out to Lake Kenney, ostensibly to watch the Perseids meteor shower. Of course, they gave up on stargazing after about five minutes. Their young bodies had held such fascination for one another that all the celestial wonder of the heavens could not hope to compete. Mark remembered lying on his back on the blanket, looking up at Missy moving above him, and seeing the Milky Way fringe her hair like the lace of a veil. The spiral arm of a vast galaxy, a billion stars and billions of worlds, was mere decoration about his beloved's head.

Damn. He had to stop. Memories like that no longer led him anywhere good.

He dug in his pocket for the house keys and fumbled at the lock for several seconds before he managed to get in. The darkness inside the house was absolute, no starlight penetrating in here. Mark remembered from his brief foray inside earlier in the day that the entryway opened up onto the kitchen to the left, with another door to the right that led down into the basement. Mark blindly stepped into the kitchen and groped at the unfamiliar walls, searching for the light switch. He couldn't seem to find it. In the dark, he remembered that Sam's grandfather had hung himself just upstairs. Recalling the wide-eyed sincerity of Sam's terror, he felt his own fear rising inside him.

Mark had seen a hanged man before. When he was just a kid, he and his best friend Jess had discovered Jess's brother's suicide. Mark had never forgotten how Boone Tate had looked hanging in the garage. Eyes open and bloody red, tongue swollen right out of his mouth. Did Sam's grandfather look like that when Sam had found him? Would he look like that now, sitting at the table with the noose still around his neck, waiting for Mark when he turned on the light?

Mark finally found the switch, but hesitated for a moment before flipping it. Which was worse, the uncertainty of not knowing what was in the dark, or turning on the light and having your worst fears confirmed?

Quit being a pussy.

Mark flipped the switch. The overhead lights revealed only a homey-looking country kitchen, nothing more.

Mark breathed a sigh of relief. The rest of the house was still dark, though. Would he have to go through this same routine with every room he stepped into? He forced himself to walk, not run, as he made his way up the steps to the upstairs hallway, hitting every light switch he passed on the way.

The first bedroom at the top of the stairs had been Linda Hansard's. There was a big king-sized bed with a down comforter in there, but Mark had detected a faint, distasteful old lady smell to the room. Plus, there was something decidedly creepy about the thought of sleeping in the bed of someone who had so recently lost their mind. Instead, Mark decided to sleep in the room that he guessed had been Sam's when he was a teenager.

The bed was twin-sized, with a mattress that sagged in the middle, but the sheets smelled fresh enough that they might have been changed sometime in the last month or so. The room retained a hint of Sam's presence. Though Mark had only known the big guy for a few hours, it was still comforting to feel that he was close by.

Mark pulled off his jeans. He turned off the bedroom lamp, but left the hallway light on. He fell into bed in his t-shirt and underwear, twisting the unfamiliar pillow in search of comfortable support for his head.

As soon as he closed his eyes, Mark saw a vivid picture in his head. Words written in dripping blood on the yellow wallpaper in the hallway right outside his room. "THY WILL BE DEAD." He saw this so clearly, he didn't want to open his eyes for fear the vision would be real.

He forced himself to look, though. The wallpaper he could see from where he was lying was faded and stained with age, but was definitely free of bloody writing. Of course it was.

Just frayed nerves, he told himself. Perfectly understandable at the raggedy-ass end of a long, stressful day. He was exhausted in mind and body. This was just his brain coughing up the preamble to a nightmare. Mark rolled over so he was facing the wall. He closed his eyes again.

Now he saw a man hanging from the ceiling in the bedroom across the hall. Though Mark had no idea what Sam's grandfather looked like, he had no doubt that was who he was seeing now. A tall, thin man in his mid-sixties, long legs swaying beneath him. He wore horn-rimmed glasses over his bulging eyes, and his face was bristly with white stubble. The chair he'd stood on lay on its side, kicked away. There was another detail, too, something Mark had noticed years before when he'd seen Boone. The front of the dead man's corduroy pants was damp with moisture, bulging with a cadaver's priapism. Mark recalled reading somewhere that this phenomena was known as "angel lust."

"Shit," Mark swore, opening his eyes again.

Now there was a sound. A cold, chilling weeping that sounded like a girl or a young woman. It seemed to be coming from above the ceiling. He knew there was attic space up there. The sound faded when Mark sat up, but he heard it quite clearly when he laid his head back down on the pillow.

It went on like that for a few minutes. When he closed his eyes, he would see some lurid vision. When he opened them, he would hear a chilling sound coming from somewhere in the house. Eyes closed and he saw an elderly woman lying in bed while a gray-skinned naked man with a glowing red jewel in the center of his forehead lapped blood from a cut on her hand. Eyes open and he heard chanting from the basement and heavy footsteps in the hall.

Mark sat up in bed. "All right, listen. Just shit-can the nightmare slideshow, okay? And turn off the Halloween sound effects record while you're at it. I'm trying to get some fucking sleep here. I promise tomorrow I'll be properly terrified by all your spooky shenanigans, but right now I'm just too goddamn tired."

He stopped and listened. Blessed silence. Mark lay back down.

"Oh, and by the way, it's '*thou* will be dead,' not 'thy.' Second person subjective. One thing I can't fucking stand, it's a ghost with bad grammar."

Mark closed his eyes, and was untroubled by any further visions. Within a minute, he was fast asleep.

CHAPTER 9

IT WAS FULLY dark by the time Sheriff Bates finally left the scene of the fire, and by then he was beat. Crazy fucking day and he still had some personal business in town. When he left his house early in the afternoon, he'd thought he would have plenty of time to attend to things and still be home for dinner. Of course, he hadn't planned for a water tower suicide attempt and a live-broadcast arson on the same day. Whole damn town was losing their shit.

He stopped at the red light at Main and Mulberry. A right turn would take him home, where Mara had probably already put his dinner in the fridge and opened a bottle of sweet red wine to catch up on her episodes of *Scandal*. Going straight through would take him west of town, to the home of another of his local business associates. This would be a more pleasant call than the one he'd made earlier to Pastor Dipshit, but honestly, it could wait until tomorrow.

Right, microwaved leftovers and a buzzed wife. Straight, Suzy Barber and her sons.

The light turned green and his hands on the steering wheel made the choice for him. Nate pulled straight through the light and cruised past the town square. Suzy Barber it was.

"Phone," he said out loud.

There was a ping from the dashboard and a chipper female voice replied, "Phone."

"Call Mara," he said.

"Hey, Nate," came Mara's voice after three rings. By her warm slur, Bates estimated two episodes and three glasses. "You coming home?"

"'Fraid not, honey," Bates said. "It's been nuts down here. Looks like I'm going to have to escort the Turner kid into Springfield for a psych eval."

"It's your day off," Mara protested, though without much vigor.

"Yeah, well, you know how that goes."

"Are you coming home tonight at all?"

"Probably not. I'm dead on my feet. If this runs too late, I'll just crash at Charlie's place, come back in the morning." Charlie McMurtry was a master sergeant with the state police and a good buddy. Nate seriously doubted Mara would call Charlie to verify the story, but Charlie would cover for him if she did. The two cops had a gentleman's agreement. Nate had fielded similar calls from Charlie's wife on more than one occasion.

"Okay," Mara murmured. "Better that than driving all the way home tired."

"Right," Nate said. "Oh, by the way, I ran into your deadbeat ex at the radio fire."

"What was he doing there?"

"That's a damn good question. I think he was buying weed off Sam Hansard. They were down there with that Mark Davies punk, all three high as fuckin' hoot-owls. I should've turned out their pockets and run 'em all in."

"Oh, leave Bill alone. He's harmless."

"So you keep saying. I can only turn my head so many times, though."

"I know."

Nate could tell by the silent pause that she was itching to get back to her show.

"I'll let you go, honey," he said. "See you tomorrow."

"Love you."

"You too."

Bates hung up and tossed the phone onto the passenger seat. He accelerated out of town.

The Barber compound was about two miles up the road. It was a big place, large enough that four of Suzy's six living sons still lived at home, along with assorted skanky girlfriends and more illegitimate grandkids than Nate could ever hope to keep track of. It had been a clean, modern-looking place when originally built, but fifteen years of housing the Barber family had gradually transformed the structure into a white-trash palace. Dirty kid's toys, knocked-over lawn ornaments and straight-up garbage littered the brown, patchy lawn. A desiccated garden hose lay like a dead snake in essentially the same position it had occupied for years. Burned-out Christmas lights from many seasons past dangled from one rotted awning. John Barber had kept up the maintenance back before his accident, but that was six years ago.

Nate tried the doorbell before remembering that it hadn't worked the last time he was here. When something broke at the Barber place, it tended to stay broken.

Billy Barber answered the door when Nate knocked instead. At nineteen, he was Suzy's youngest. The burn scars on his face, results of a bad car crash that had also killed his brother Ed, made him look older.

"Hey, sheriff," Billy said.

"Hi, Billy. Your mama home?"

"Yeah, she's here. Come on in."

Nate stepped inside. On the couch, right next to the front door, one of the Barber boy's baby mamas was breast-feeding a diapered infant. Titty hanging right out there, without even a blanket for cover. The girl, who looked to be even younger than Billy, was watching the reality show playing on the big flat-screen across the room with a no doubt stoned concentration. On the chair opposite the couch, Jesse Barber watched her tit with the same dazed focus, like he was hoping to get the next turn.

"I'll get Mom for you," Billy said.

He left Nate standing next to the shelf that displayed Suzy's collection of porcelain dolls. Suzy doted on those goddamn things like they were the daughters she never had, but Nate hated the very sight of them. The dolls had been dead-eyed abominations on the day they'd been taken out of the box, in Nate's opinion, but the scars they bore from two generations of abuse at the hands of Suzy's kids and grandkids had made them positively nightmarish. Some were missing eyes or limbs. Others had been cracked and haphazardly glued back together. A few on the bottom shelf bore burns from the electrical fire that had destroyed the Barber's previous house. Suzy couldn't bring herself to throw any of the creep-shows away, no matter how disfigured. Nate didn't know how anybody managed to sleep with the skin-crawling things in the house.

"Nate, honey!" Suzy came out of her bedroom dressed in purple sweatpants and a Rolling Stones t-shirt. She'd once been pretty damned attractive, in a trashy kind of way, back when Nate had first known her back in high school. Bearing seven of John Barber's had taken its toll on her body, though. She bore scars too, just like her dolls. This was another by-product of her more than thirty years of marriage. "I thought you were going to come by earlier."

He went to her and accepted her customary hug-and-a-cheek-kiss greeting. "Sorry about that, Suze. I had to deal with a fire at the radio station."

"Yeah, we heard Johnny Six-Pack talkin' all kinds of crazy about Jesus, and then the radio just went dead."

"Full moon or somethin'."

"Anyways, come on back. I got a couple things for you."

Nate followed her back into her bedroom and she closed the door behind them. John was parked in a corner in his wheelchair, a smoldering cigarette butt jutting from his mouth.

"You done with that, sweetie?" Suzy asked her husband.

"Urgh," John Barber replied, moving his head in the half-nod that was the extent of his muscular abilities. His eyes fixed on Nate and narrowed. "Ulp."

Suzy took the butt from his mouth and stubbed it out in an overflowing ashtray. Then she opened her top dresser drawer and pulled out a plastic grocery bag stuffed with money. The Barber boys weren't big on neatly stacking and bundling their bills, so Nate had to estimate by weight. Felt heavy.

"Good week?" he asked.

"I don't know whose idea it was to put blue food color in the crystal, but tweakers go nuts for that shit. They think they're on that TV show. You got any more of that?"

"I will in a couple days. Send JJ by the church on Tuesday. I should have some by then."

Suzy's eternally devoted sons were Nate's exclusive local distributors. Their territory covered all of rural Logan, Sangamon and Christian counties, pretty much everything between Springfield and Decatur. They were hard workers and good earners. Useful as muscle, too, whenever Nate needed it. Their mother kept them in line and managed their money. Made sure they always paid on time, and gave them holy hell if they ever started dipping too heavily into their own supply. It was a pretty sweet arrangement. Nate had inherited the Barber family franchise from John, who used to be Tony fuckin' Soprano of the tri-counties before he went and had his little accident.

"Oh, I got something else for you, too," Suzy said. "Little early for Christmas, but I know you got a birthday comin' up."

She reached under the bed and pulled out a shoe box. Inside was a small package tightly wrapped in cellophane, with a slight vinegar smell and a little cartoon horse sticker on top. It was one of his missing bricks.

"Where did you get this?"

"Some east-side nigger sold it to JJ over in Springfield."

"Who?"

"JJ didn't know him. Sure as hell wasn't one of his guys."

"Urn!" John called from the corner. "Urk!"

"Hold on, honey." Suzy put another cigarette in her husband's mouth and lit it for him. The paralyzed man started puffing smoke like a diesel locomotive.

"JJ's seeing a colored girl over there." Suzy clucked maternal disapproval. "This clown came over to him as he was leaving her place. Just assumed that a white man in that neighborhood had to be there buying drugs. That racist or what?"

"The guy didn't know who JJ was?" Every real player in Springfield knew John Junior on sight. They called him "The Candyman."

"Dumb fucker didn't know shit," Suzy said. "He started out trying to sell JJ a little gram bag, but JJ could tell something was off about the guy. So he let on that he wanted to buy some real weight. This guy took him right over to his place."

"His actual house?"

"Yeah, I told you he was grade-A stupid. Anyway, the guy dusts up a joint with some of the H and asks JJ if he wants to get high. JJ goes along, just puffing smoke without breathing it in, thinking he can get this guy talking."

"Did it work?"

"Heh, get this. The guy was a faggot. All JJ had to do was bat his baby blues and the cocksucker told him his whole life story. Turns out, small world, he's got a white boyfriend who lives right here in Bakersfield. You know Jacob Norrell?"

"Pasty-face, pansy-ass kid, one of Duane Norrell's sons?"

"That's him. And here's the good part. Turns out Jacob was having a little gay affair with a certain pastor you might also know."

"No shit."

"Yep. So these two criminal masterminds got it in their heads to blackmail your good buddy Barry Tuttle. Said they'd tell the whole congregation about the butt-fuckery if Barry didn't pay them off. But I guess he didn't have the money, because instead he gave them..."

"My fucking drugs."

"Bingo."

For a minute, Nate could only stand there grinning and nodding like a fool. He was literally seeing red, the blood beating in his eyes. Then he took a deep breath. This wasn't so bad, really. At least now he had confirmation of what he'd only suspected before. And justification for the move he'd already been considering.

"Barry's got to go." Saying it out loud was like a load off his chest.

"You want my boys to pay him a visit?" Suzy gave him a sideways look, with a little flicker of a smile that brought to his mind how good she'd looked when she was young.

"Nah, Suze. That's something I gotta do myself. I would appreciate it, though, if they'd go over to this queerboy's house and collect whatever's left of my heroin."

"Absolutely, Nate. JJ wanted me to ask you, though, what you want him to do with the guy. The nigger faggot made a pass at him. Put a hand on his leg." Suzy made a face and shook her head. "JJ can't abide that kind of incursion onto his personal space. He wants your permission first, though."

"He's got it, then." Nate nodded. "But if he's going to do that, he better take care of Jacob Norrell, too."

"Yeah, that's what we already figured. Damn shame, really. Duane Norrell's a good old boy. Must break his heart that his son turned out that way."

She gave Nate another look, a slight tilt of the head and a shift in the focus of her eyes. Nate couldn't say for sure what the look was meant to convey. Maybe she was acknowledging the gravity of the three judgments they'd just passed together. Or maybe she was just horny.

"Ull," John said. "Gahh."

"You done with that already?" Suzy went over and pulled the ash-dripping butt out of John's mouth. "I keep feeding the son of a bitch cigarettes, but he ain't got cancer yet."

She turned back to Nate. "You got to go home, or can you stick around for a while?"

"Mara thinks I'm spending the night in Springfield."

"Well." There was no chance of misinterpreting the meaning of her smile this time. Nate felt the hot rage-blood draining from his head, to flush the lower regions of his body with a different kind of heat. "All right, then. Come over here."

Nate stepped across the room. Suzy knelt before him and undid his belt. He looked over at John Barber and saw the hatred burning like hard little coals in the other man's eyes.

"Look at that, honey," Suzy said to her husband as she freed Nate from his suddenly very confining pants. "He's nice and hard and ready for me. Didn't even have to take no pills like you used to. You know what else, too?" She gave Nate's little man a quick suckling kiss that made him gasp. "Clean. Mmm."

She rolled her eyes up at Nate. "John used to hardly never take a shower," she told him between slurps. "Mmm. Motherfucker was rank and nasty. But you, Nate..." Her mouth was full for a few seconds. "Sweet and musky, like a man ought to taste. Oh, I love it."

Then she stopped talking altogether. Nate grinned over at his former business associate, who could only say "Blaughh, youllk," in response. Drool ran down his chin in a slimy flow.

John Barber used to be big shit. He'd been in the game long before Nate got into it. For a few years after Nate opened up shop, the two men existed in the uneasy symbiotic dance of enemies who each recognized that working together was more beneficial than eliminating the other guy. Nate had contacts with Chicago street gangs that opened up supply chains John had never had access to before, and John had distribution channels established that were far easier for Nate than building up his own from scratch. Still, Nate had always hated the son of a bitch and he knew the feeling was more than mutual.

Barber was a crude, belligerent hothead, and his own family suffered the worst of his rage. He had raised his boys with a heavy hand, and beaten the shit out of his wife on a regular basis. Nate considered any man who beat women and children to be something less than a man. But what could he do when he had so much of his business tangled up with the guy?

Nate knew Suzy from way back. They'd even gone out a few times in high school. Nothing serious. Suzy was a good-time gal back then. Most of the guys in their class had had at least a couple go-rounds with her before John knocked her up junior year, thus claiming her for life. Nate felt bad for her, but kept his distance out of respect for his partnership with her husband. They never even fucked around before the accident.

It was at one of John's Fourth of July cook-outs. He always went all out for these bashes. Invited his labor union buddies, his whole extended family and just about everybody in the tri-counties who had any kind of juice. Steaks on the grill, full tended bar and a bigger fireworks show than the one the village put on. He'd been hosting these parties annually for more than twenty years, but this was destined to be his last.

Barber was drunk, of course. Coked up, too. His always volatile temper became dangerously hair-trigger with this particular mix of chemicals. What set him off this last time was seeing somebody at the party using one of his "good" steak knives. Of course, people had to cut their meat with something. Suzy had set out the cutlery not knowing that John had ordered a set of high-end knives imported from Germany that cost him almost two thousand dollars. That was just like the guy. He was always buying needlessly extravagant shit. He thought it somehow made him sophisticated, when he'd never be anything but a white trash gangster.

The classy motherfucker started laying into his wife, calling her a "fat cow" and a "dumb cunt" right there in front of the guests. Everybody at the party was tied to John Barber with various combinations of blood, greed, and fear. Nobody said shit, even when he dragged Suzy into the house by her hair. They all just kept eating his steaks and drinking his booze, nobody meeting anyone else's eyes, even though they all heard him banging her around inside. Nobody moved, even when she started screaming.

Finally, Nate decided it would have to be him. He kicked in the front door. Suzy was on her hands and knees in the front hall, blood pouring from her face. John stood above her, raging. He gave her a brutal kick to the stomach before Nate could get over to him. Nate grabbed John with one hand on the back of his neck, the other on his belt, and dragged him away from the woman on the floor.

John spun on him, all his rage re-focusing on Nate. Barber had eighty, maybe a hundred pounds on him, but most of that was flab. Nate also had the advantage of not being fucked up on booze and cocaine. Still, a fat, drugged-up raging bull was still damn dangerous. Nate swung before John could react. His fist connected to the big man's ribs and it was like punching a side of beef.

John swung back, but Nate rushed in close, dodging the blow. John gave him a shove to push him away and Nate, off balance, flew back into the shelf with Suzy's dolls. The shelf collapsed and Nate fell to the floor in a pile of the fucking things. It was like getting tossed into a nest of spiders.

John loomed above Nate, ready to stomp the shit out of him. Nate leapt to his feet screaming. He launched himself at John's massive gut. Here pure blind luck proved to be on Nate's side. Directly across the hallway was the door that led down to the basement. One of John's sons had just gone down there to bring up a crate of liquor, and he had failed to close the door behind him. John fell back through the open doorway and flew down the stairs. Halfway to the bottom, his head cracked through a rotted step. John performed an awkward backwards half-flip, legs flying up into the air, before coming to a rest on the basement floor.

Nate looked down the stairs and saw John lying in a broken pile, neck and head at an unsettling angle to the rest of his body. The sight made Nate cringe, even though he knew it meant John Barber wasn't going to be a problem for him ever again.

The tough bastard lived, destined to spend the rest of his life eating through a straw and shitting into a bag, propped in the corners of rooms while the people he had once terrified now paid him all the attention due a potted plant. If you could call that living.

It all worked out pretty good for Nate, though. The state police investigated, but Suzy's testimony and that of dozens of other witnesses made it clear that his actions had been entirely justified. Nate was cleared of any wrong-doing, and was even lionized to a degree in the press for coming to the rescue of a battered wife. He thought he might have some problems with John's sons, tough boys who'd been raised to believe in blood loyalty and vendettas, but lucky for him the Barber boys hated their dad even more than he did. If any of them had harbored any thoughts of revenge, they'd been laid to rest by Suzy, who had a long talk with her sons about the future of the family business.

She laid out her plan to Nate less than a week after the accident, while John was still in the hospital, letting a machine do his breathing for him. Hers was a much better arrangement for everyone involved than the way things had worked under her asshole husband. That night also marked the first time she showed her gratitude in the other way, too.

Suze released Nate from her highly experienced mouth and grinned up at him. Then she stood and yanked the Stones shirt off over head, unhooked her huge white bra and let the purple sweatpants drop to the floor. She slid her big old panties off and tossed them wadded into her husband's face.

The sight of Suzy Barber naked was not quite the glorious spectacle it had once been, but then Nate knew he was probably looking pretty gray and saggy himself, these days. Besides, he had to admit the real turn-on came from cuckolding his vanquished enemy while he had to sit there and watch. Sometimes, when Nate was in bed with Mara at home, he imagined Bill Potter helpless in a corner of the room. That *really* got him going.

Nate stripped off his own clothes and flashed John a wink.

"Urll," John said, his whole face quaking. "Hurrarrgh."

He looked pissed, but for all Nate knew he was getting off on this, too. God knows he wasn't getting off any other kind of way.

Suzy bent over the bed, fat ass sticking up in the air so Nate could plow her from behind, the way she liked it best. Nate leaned in and went to work while Suzy moaned and screamed and her husband gurgled.

Within a few minutes, Nate had worked up a sweat and his heart was pounding from the exertion. He couldn't do this all night like he used to when he was a younger man. He was ready to bring things to their natural conclusion when Suzy let out a strange, dragging moan. "Ooh," like a record slowing down.

"There she is," she said in a sleepy whisper.

"Who?" Nate panted.

"My new dolly." Suzy's voice was spacy and far away between her cries of pleasure. "See her standing over there? Ah. She's a walker. Oh. And a talker. Uh. A walky-talker."

"Oh God." Nate looked up. For one strange second he did think he saw something move in the corner of the room, but he was too close to stop. "Oh shit, Suzy."

"See how her belly button lights up? Um. It's a ninny, not an Audi."

"Jesus, Suzy. Shut up. I'm gonna—"

"She's watching us, Nate. Yes. She sees what we're doin'. Oh God, yes."

"Ah Jesus!" Nate's yelp was not quite manly as he launched himself into the void.

Nate rolled over and collapsed on the bed, utterly spent. The long, weird-ass day caught up with him all at once. He sank like a stone into sleep, not even hearing the nonsense the naked woman burbled beside him.

CHAPTER 10

THAT EVENING, AFTER the Chili Prayer Supper and the Youth Outreach Weekend Concert, Eve Tuttle and her husband, Pastor Barry, retired to their home for a little bit of TV together time. Eve still hadn't quite adjusted to Jimmy Fallon hosting *The Tonight Show*—she'd *adored* Jay Leno—but it was still nice to have a good laugh before bed.

Husband and wife sat in separate chairs before the big flat screen, side table between them. Barry seemed distracted, not even chuckling at Fallon playing Pictionary with Bryan Cranston and Vera Farmiga. He had his Bible open on his lap before him. That wasn't unusual. He often read the good book while he was watching television, being a more devoted student of God's word than any other man Eve had ever known. What was a *little* strange, though, was that Barry had set his high school class ring down on the page and was dragging it over the lines of text, like the ring was some kind of reading lens.

Eve wasn't too concerned with her husband's behavior. He was full of quirks like that, which she on balance found endearing. It was only natural, she thought, for such an intelligent and creative man to have his little eccentricities.

The show went to commercial and Eve took a deep breath, steeling herself. There was something she'd had on her mind for a while. She'd been putting off bringing it up because she wasn't sure how Barry would react. Now was as good a time as any.

"Honey," She nudged the volume down a few notches with the remote. "I was talking to Janine Hauger the other day. You know she's on the school board, right? Well she was telling me, on the QT of course, that Terry Mackey's health is not so good. It's his heart, poor man. We'll keep him in our prayers, of course, but Janine told me he probably isn't going to run for re-election in the fall." Deep breath. "It was *her* suggestion that I consider running for his seat."

Eve paused for a reaction here, but none came. She looked over at her husband. He was spinning the ring between his thumb and forefinger and nodding thoughtfully, mulling over what she'd said.

"I think I stand a pretty good chance of winning," Eve continued. "Especially if I start laying the groundwork for a campaign pretty soon. If I won, we'd have me, Janine, and Evangeline Blunt all on the board. That's one seat short of a voting majority, but with three of us from the church, we could start to have a real say. In text books, in the curriculum, in hiring. You said yourself, the schools here are a mess. Especially the high school."

"Mmm," Barry agreed.

"I mean, the health class is finally teaching abstinence as the best option, but not the *only* option. They bring *condoms* into the classroom, for Pete's sake. And don't get me started on the English department. Bill Potter's finally retiring, thank God, but he's tapped that Lana Delany woman to take over the department when he leaves. An *open* lesbian, not even with the decency to be in the closet about it in front of the kids." She shook her head. "Imagine what *her* reading list will look like. If I'm on the board, I can help fix some of these problems."

Barry didn't say anything. He just kept twirling his ring. Eve started to get a bad feeling, like he didn't really like the idea. Barry had firm ideas about the role a pastor's wife should play in her husband's ministry. Maybe she was overstepping her bounds.

"It's just a thought, Barry. You think it over. I'll do whatever you say is best."

At that, Barry finally turned and looked at her. His whole face was scrunched up like Popeye the Sailor, the ring set like a monocle in one squinting eye socket. He leered at her, his one open eye rolling around like crazy. Mocking her.

"You could just say no." Tears came to Eve's eyes. "Even if you think it's a ridiculous idea, you don't have to be *rude* about it."

The invisible rays bombarding the earth penetrated the very walls of Barry's house. They filled the air with a haze that obscured everything, a gauzy veil laid over everything he saw. But God had given Barry a filter. The blue jewel of the ring blocked the rays. Kept them out of his head. Peering through the band, Barry saw things as they really were. As they always had been.

The ring had originally belonged to another boy. Senior year, Barry and Mike Trent had exchanged their class rings as a token of their affection for each other. Both rings had blue stones, so no one had noticed when they'd traded. It was a thrilling secret shared just between them. Wearing one another's tokens so boldly was like hiding in plain sight.

Mike was long gone. He'd moved away years ago. Barry wondered, though, if he had also discovered the power the rings held. Was Mike, wherever he was now, at this moment peering through *Barry's* old class ring, and seeing the awful truth of how the world looked beneath the hazy rays? Did he have a wife, too? And was he now seeing her true form, as Barry was finally seeing Eve's?

Her name was apt, for just like the bitch who had brought God's disfavor upon Adam and all of Adam's children, Barry's Eve had tried to corrupt him with the taint of her sin. Barry shuddered to think of the times he had lain with her, doing what he thought was his duty as a husband, not knowing what she really was.

With the obscuring rays filtered out, he saw the gaping maw that lay beneath the mask of her face. Set just above this repugnant fleshy hole was what looked like a bright red jewel. The jewel flashed with slow, irregular pulses of light, as if receiving signals from her home world.

Barry knew that this thing that called itself his wife had been beamed down, as all women were, from the same planet out in space that was the source of the rays. Female spirits rode the waves of radiation across the universe like spores on the wind. They settled to earth and penetrated the souls of poor little baby boys still in the womb, causing their little man parts to shrivel and fall off before they were even born. These castrated fetuses matured into atrocities like the one seated across from him. The hazy space rays concealed their true nature from all but those chosen few to whom God had given eyes to see.

Barry knew all this because he'd read it in his Bible. The *true* Bible. Perhaps the greatest crime the alien monsters had perpetrated upon mankind was perverting the word of God. The rays superimposed the pages of the Bible, scrambling the words and twisting their meaning. Barry's miracle ring had allowed him to see through all that. He had deciphered the *true* word. Through the ring, Barry had read the truth about what went down in the garden. He now knew that the serpent who had conspired with Eve to bring about the fall of man had descended from that same distant star. Barry now understood, too, how God's laws had been twisted to serve the alien agenda. A man lying with a man, just for one example, was *not* an abomination, as the alien would have everyone believe. The true abomination was woman. For all souls began as male and were only feminized by the hazy rays. Only men were pure beings, free of the corrupting taint of vaginal sin.

Barry's eyes were finally wide open.

Running the ring over the words on the page, he came across a passage that was almost the same in both the veiled and the clarified versions. Exodus 22:18. *Thou shalt not suffer a witch to live.* The words were identical in both, but in the true version he read through the ring, they were in bold red print and underlined. Just as he read them, the Eve-thing beside him started talking. Or made the sounds that passed for speech from that pestilent hole. When Barry was seeing the true world through his ring, the words she spewed just sounded like moist smacking, punctuated with little farting queefs. Still, he had to pretend he understood, had to nod and make little affirming comments so she wouldn't catch on that he knew what she really was.

But then Barry made a mistake. He looked right at her with the ring set in his eye and, for one fatal second, could not conceal his fear and repulsion. That was enough. She saw that he saw. She knew that he knew. If he hadn't had the ring to protect him, there was no telling what might have happened. But, thank you Jesus, he did have the ring.

He glanced back down at the page and read the passage again. The words had changed, as they sometimes did. Barry had learned that the

Bible he saw through his ring was a live, direct connection to the mind of God. Sometimes God had a particularly urgent message to convey.

Now the passage read: "Thou shalt not suffer a *bitch* to live."

The meaning was clear enough to him.

"Why are you looking at me like that, Barry?" Eve had thought he was just mocking her, ridiculing her vain, foolish aspirations. But something was seriously wrong. It was like Barry wasn't there at all.

His head lolled around and his one open eye rolled and darted behind the ring. He opened his mouth to speak, but all that came out was a syrupy mumble: "Thoushalnt suffitch tulve."

"What did you say?"

Eve was getting alarmed. Barry had been acting especially odd for the past couple of days. Talking to himself, taking naps at odd times, showering for hours on end. She'd put it down to stress. He had a lot of responsibilities. But he was scaring her now. What if he was having a seizure or a stroke or something?

Barry lurched from his seat and shuffled out of the room. He walked with the shambling, off-kilter gait of a zombie on a TV show. The ring was still affixed in his eye socket.

"Where are you going?"

Eve followed him into the kitchen. He didn't even bother turning on the light. He just stopped in the middle of the dark room, head bowed like he was looking at a spot on the floor. Eve hit the light switch, but Barry didn't move or even glance up.

"What's wrong, Barry?" she said. "Talk to me."

He grinned down at the floor, lips moving. She heard him mutter something that sounded like: "Hazy razy daisy."

"You're scaring me."

"Crazy waves of grace." Barry looked up suddenly, as if remembering something urgent. He walked over to the knife rack on the counter, and pulled out the big meat cleaver.

"What are you doing, honey?" Eve's voice came out as a squeak.

Barry turned around, his face a perfect mask of madness. Crazed grin, one eye closed and the other flipping around in its socket behind the ring. He raised the cleaver. The manic Cheshire grin grew wider as he stepped towards her. "Your hazy rays don't work on me no more."

"What are you talking about?"

"A man must *cleave* to his wife!"

Barry leapt at her. Eve turned as she screamed. She took two running steps into the hallway before he caught her. The blade sank into her left shoulder, slicing through nightgown and bra-strap, splitting skin and muscle and tendon, catching in the bone. There was no pain, really, just a hot splash of blood down her back. Eve's legs gave out. She fell to her knees, and then flat on her face.

Barry stood above her, planting one foot in the small of her back. He grasped the cleaver handle firmly and pulled the blade from Eve's shoulder. The removal was much more painful than the entry had been. Despite this, Eve managed to roll over onto her back. She looked up at her husband and something snapped inside her. She'd granted this man years of denial and countless silently forgiven transgressions. She'd defended him from rumors and accusations and had turned blind eyes and deaf ears to things he'd done because she'd been raised to believe that this was an unspoken tenant of the covenant of marriage. But in her dying moments, Eve Tuttle would have no more of any of that. It all came out of her at once.

"You're a liar and a pervert!" she screamed. "And a criminal! I knew all along, you son of a bitch! I know about the boys, about the drugs. I know why you never touch me. I know why we never had children. You monster. You...filthy *fucker*!"

Barry swung his arm with a madman's strength. In his ring-filtered vision, the cleaver shattered the blinking red jewel above the monster's putrid orifice. In reality, he drove the blade between his wife's eyes, directly above the bridge of her nose, with enough force to crack through her skull and into her soft brain. Like hacking into a melon.

Eve Tuttle went out like a light. Her final defiance was forever fixed in her eyes.

SATURDAY

CHAPTER 11

Driving out to the Hansard farmhouse the next morning, Michelle kept coming across little harbingers of death. A bloated raccoon corpse just past the County Road 6 turnoff. A big black snake bisected by a tire track a couple of miles out. Two rabbits and a possum along the way, as well as a few unidentifiable gory fur pancakes. And finally, just before she turned off the hardtop for the gravel road, a dead dog. A cute little Benji-looking mutt, somebody's farm dog that had wandered out into the road and was just now being noticed as missing by soon-to-be heartbroken kids.

This probably wasn't all that unusual. Michelle didn't doubt that on any given morning, the roads around Bakersfield were littered with the previous night's roadkill harvest. The dead wildlife (and not-so-wildlife, in the case of the dog) wasn't necessarily a portent of anything, but Michelle's notice of the animal carnage did reflect her state of mind. She was seeing omens everywhere she looked. This only fed the sense of mounting dread that had been building inside her for days.

There had been no change in James's condition, and no explanation yet for his behavior yesterday or for the coma he had slipped into afterwards. Jen had wanted to spend the night at the hospital, and Michelle had been ready to stay there with her, but the doctor had sent them both home. A rather severe woman named Dr. Carroll was overseeing James's case, and she had been brusque in her insistence that they not stay overnight. Almost rude.

"Your presence here serves no purpose," Carroll had said. "And is in fact, distracting. We will do everything we can for James. The best thing you can do for him is to go home and get some rest."

Michelle couldn't shake the feeling that the doctor knew more than she was telling them, especially considering what Mark had told her on the phone. At least three other people in town had suffered similar attacks, and they were all people whose lawns James had mowed. Mark thought that maybe they'd all been exposed to that drug he used to take. Michelle hadn't mentioned Neiro to Dr. Carroll. It sounded so crazy and far-fetched. Hopefully their visit to Mark's old dealer would yield some answers, though Michelle had her doubts.

Pulling into the Hansard driveway, Michelle's already bare nerves grew even more frayed. The big yellow farmhouse radiated menace so potent that her chest grew tighter as she pulled up to it. She'd read of people who could pick up radio broadcasts with the braces on their teeth if they were close enough to the tower. This was like that, except the house was broadcasting festering madness. Hatred and misery and death. So much death. Michelle wondered how many people had died inside the house and the answer came...

(twenty-three)

...from somewhere outside her mind. She did not doubt that that the number was perfectly accurate. Twenty-three human beings had lost their lives inside that structure during the hundred or more years it had stood, and most of the deaths had been violent. Murders and suicides and horrifying accidents. She knew that, if she were to probe any deeper, she would be able to see every one of them vividly in her head. The house wanted her to see, like a kid proud of his toys.

(or is it twenty-four now?)

The teasing voice emanating from the house gave Michelle a start. She'd talked to Mark just a few minutes ago, giving him a call to make sure he was awake and also to give him the update about James. He'd sounded fine, if a little groggy. But what if, after hanging up with her, he'd found the gun Linda Hansard kept in her nightstand drawer? What if he'd slid it into his mouth and pulled the trigger?

Why was she seeing that so clearly? How could she even know where the old lady kept her gun?

Michelle got out of her car and hurried up the brick path that led to the front door. She had the distinct sensation of being watched from one of the upstairs windows. It was strong enough to be undeniable, as was the sense that whatever was watching her was taunting her.

(he's your ex-ex-husband now)

She remembered the darkest days of her first marriage. Mark's already morbid sense of humor grew positively macabre when he was in the depths of his depression. He would make grim jokes about Kurt Cobain and Sylvia Plath. ("Not Hemingway, though," he'd said once. "I'm nowhere near that fucking good.") To his credit, Mark had never said anything like that in front of Ben, but he knew how that talk scared her. That was the point. What if whatever was inside the house had got inside him, whispering to him, clouding his mind and seducing him? What if he'd finally made good on one of his veiled threats?

She reached the front door and looked inside. Mark was in the kitchen, going through the cabinets. She knocked on the door, feeling a surge of relief at the sight of her ex-husband. He smiled up at her, and came over to let her inside.

"Morning," he said. "Can you believe there's no coffee in this house? I know the lady who lived here was really religious, but who doesn't have coffee? There's not even any of that instant crap. Anyway, come inside."

Michelle followed him into the house, fighting an urge to give him a relieved hug. He'd certainly take *that* the wrong way. Despite her relief at seeing him unhurt, her dread multiplied as soon as she stepped over the threshold. The pressure on her heart felt like what she imagined deep sea divers experienced when the weight of the water compressed their organs.

"You *slept* here?" she said.

"I know, right?" Mark laughed. "Sam wasn't kidding about this place. It's like Little Amityville House on the Prairie."

Michelle clutched her chest. "How can you even stand to be in here?"

He gave her a sideways look. "What are you feeling?"

"That whatever's in this house does *not* want me to be here."

"I don't really get that," Mark said. "But it was putting on a hell of a show last night. Crazy pictures in my head, weird sounds."

"And you stayed anyway?"

"I was so tired even the fuckin' ghosts couldn't get me out of bed. Besides, it stopped when I asked it to."

"You asked it to stop and it did?"

"The spirits are very obliging around here."

"Ben is *not* staying in this house."

Mark's smile dropped from his face. "We have joint custody now. You can't stop me from seeing my son."

"I don't want to stop you from seeing him. I'm just saying he can't come here."

"Where do you expect me to spend my half of the week?"

"I don't care. Just not here. You can stay in the guest bedroom at my house."

"That wouldn't be awkward at all."

"How about your mom's place, then?"

"Great idea. *So* much better. I'd rather camp out in the woods three nights a week." Mark shook his head. "Look, I work here now. I *live* here. I don't know what you expect me to do."

"We'll talk about it later, okay? Can we just go do what we're going to do? I really want to get away from this house."

"Fine. I want to get some coffee first, though. Maybe some breakfast. There are eggs in the fridge, but I don't know how long they've been in there."

"I wouldn't even eat food that's been in this house."

"Seriously? Haunted eggs?"

"Come on. We can stop at Mel-O-Cream in town."

"Mel-O-Cream?" Mark lit up. "Oh my God, I forgot all about Mel-O-Cream. Do they still have those raspberry bismarks with the white frosting?"

"Yes, and they're still disgusting."

"You mean disgustingly delicious."

Shaking her head, Michelle held the door open for her ex. Though her every instinct was telling her to bolt and run, she walked casually out to the car with him, not daring to look back at the house. They were half a mile up the road before she could breathe normally again.

Mark drained the last of his coffee and wiped his mouth in case there were any traces of frosting or jelly on his face, which might have diminished the air of seriousness he was trying to project here. From the outside, Shaner's house was exactly as he remembered it. A spacious, immaculately maintained old white house on a pleasant, tree-lined residential street in a historic Springfield neighborhood. It looked more like the family home of a prosperous attorney than the abode of a drug dealer. Mark remembered Shaner telling him that the house had once been a funeral home, and that his basement laboratory used to be the embalming room. That seemed entirely appropriate.

Missy's t-shirt hiked up a little just as she was unbuckling her seatbelt. Mark, hating himself for being so helpless to resist, glanced down and caught a glimpse of her briefly exposed midriff. He was a bit surprised to see ink staining those few square inches of toned flesh that he had once loved to kiss. A blue dolphin peeked out from her jeans.

"That's new," he said.

Missy followed his gaze and pointedly pulled her shirt down. "Yeah, Lana and I got those done at the same time."

"Matching dolphin tattoos? That's...nice." He had tried to convince Missy to get matching tattoos for years, ever since they both turned eighteen. She'd always told him that she didn't feel a connection with any image strongly enough to want it permanently etched into her skin. Turns out she just didn't feel a strong enough connection to *him*.

"Are you ready to do this, or what?" Missy said.

"Yeah." Mark let it go. He was getting used to letting go of a lot of things.

They walked together up the sloping walkway to the porch stairs. Mark rang the doorbell. For a minute or so, nobody answered. He was about to ring the bell a second time when a woman answered the door.

She wasn't very tall, but was quite intense-looking. Pale skin and straight black hair, dark sunglasses and blood-red lipstick. Her white blouse was unbuttoned enough to display the amply-filled black leather bra she wore underneath. She looked exactly like the way Mark had pictured the character of Hayley, the domineering vampire executive in *Blood World*. Mark half-seriously wondered if he should ask for her headshot in the remote chance that there would ever be a movie version.

"Can I help you?" the woman said, with an appropriately vampirish coldness.

"We're looking for Shaner," Mark said. "Does he live here anymore?"

"Who are you?"

"I'm an old friend."

"Friend?" The word came out like a foreign term she wasn't certain how to pronounce.

"An old customer," Mark clarified.

The woman nodded, almost imperceptibly. "Shaner no longer exists."

"He's dead?"

"In a way."

The woman was inscrutable behind her dark glasses. Mark looked to Missy, but she seemed as nonplussed as he was.

"I'm sorry," Mark said. "I'm not sure what you mean by that."

"*Shana* lives here now."

"Shana?" Mark said. "You mean he's, uh, had a..."

"She's transitioned?" Missy supplied.

The bright red lips pulled into a grin, revealing perfectly white teeth that Mark was a bit surprised were not fanged. "She's *metamorphosed*."

Mark hadn't expected that, but at least they were getting somewhere now. "Okay, that's cool. I'm Mark Davies. This is Missy, ah, Michelle. He'll remember us."

"She." This came out as a hiss.

"Right, sorry. *She'll* remember us."

The woman removed her sunglasses. Her eyes were a startlingly vivid green, and contained a predatory glint. She didn't meet Mark's eye, but seemed rather to be scanning his throat for the best place to sink her teeth. It was a little unnerving.

"Shana is entirely devoted to freelance research and development now. If you're looking to *score*," this word also came out like she'd never spoken it aloud, only read it on a page, "you'll have to go somewhere else."

"We don't want to buy anything. We just want to ask her a few questions."

"Questions?" The woman's flat Midwestern accent slipped a bit, revealing something much more exotic underneath. "What questions?"

"Look," Missy said, her patience obviously worn thin. "My nephew almost died while he was on some of the poison Shana used to peddle. We're trying to figure out how that might have happened. If she's not willing to help us with that, we'll have to go to the police."

"We do not respond to threats, Missy Michelle." This came out in an undisguised eastern European accent. Polish or Hungarian or something.

"Nobody's threatening anything," Mark said. "Listen, um, I didn't catch your name."

"Because I did not give it." The woman scowled. "My name is Cassandra."

"Okay, good. We're just concerned, Cassandra. And if someone out there is using *Shana's* creation in an irresponsible way, I would think that she would be concerned, too."

Cassandra slipped her sunglasses back on. With them, both her cool demeanor and her American accent were restored.

"Wait here," she said. She retreated inside, slamming the door behind her.

Mark and Missy exchanged a glance.

"What the hell was that?" he said.

"I don't know, but Vampira, Mistress of the Night is starting to piss me off."

As they waited on the porch, Mark noticed a small glass circle set above just above the door. He had no doubt it was a camera. He looked up at the electronic eye and tried to imagine the strange man he had once known, now an even stranger woman, watching from somewhere inside the house.

Cassandra returned a few minutes later.

"Come inside," she said.

Mark and Missy followed her into the house, down a long central hallway. The entryway and front rooms were brightly lit and tastefully furnished, but this part of the house was a façade. The lights grew dimmer and the furnishings more sparse the further back they walked.

"Shana has consented to speak with Mark and Mark only," Cassandra said as she led them into the barren gloom. "Missy Michelle will wait in another room with me."

Missy didn't look very pleased with that, but she said "Fine, whatever."

Cassandra stopped walking and turned to face Mark. "Shana is waiting in the room at the end of the hall, behind the red door. She's asked me to prepare you before you enter."

"Prepare me for what?"

"Shana was severely burned and badly disfigured in an industrial accident. Her appearance can be unsettling. So she will be present in the room, but will be seated behind a curtain. She will speak to you through a video interface. Do not approach the curtain." Cassandra removed her glasses again, as if to emphasize the seriousness of this point. "Even if she requests that you do so."

"Okay...thank you, Cassandra."

"Do not thank me. I advised her against speaking with you. You have fifteen minutes. I will be watching the time."

Mark looked to Missy, who gave him an encouraging nod, then he took a deep breath and stepped through the red door.

The room was cold. Mark could almost see his breath. The only source of light was a single window, fogged over with condensation. The diffused sunlight dispensed a bright white glare, but most of the room was in shadow. Only gradually did the furnishings become visible to Mark's slowly adjusting eyes. He saw a large wooden desk, antique in design, with a chair set before it. A computer monitor was set on the desk, facing out towards him. Bookcases lined the walls, filled with duty-looking leather volumes. One corner of the room, as Cassandra had indicated, was partitioned off by a red curtain hanging from the ceiling.

"Hello?" Mark said, taking a seat.

A woman's face appeared on the monitor as soon as he sat down. Brown eyes, short blonde hair and smooth skin. Too smooth, in fact, with the lifeless eyes of a computer generated image deep into the uncanny valley. The face was nondescript to the point of being generic, containing all the personality of a police composite sketch. Behind the CG woman's head was a swirling, psychedelic backdrop that reminded Mark of the old Max Headroom show.

"Mark Davies, my favorite guinea pig. Welcome."

Mark heard the words spoken twice. The voice originated as a grating snarl from behind the curtain and was echoed half a second later from the monitor's speakers, where it was filtered into a clipped, robotic feminine purr.

"Um, hi," Mark said. He tried to look directly into the little camera above the monitor, but couldn't resist a peek over at the partition, behind which he saw shadowy movement.

"Pay no attention to the woman behind the curtain."

Shana laughed at her own joke, a grinding, "heh heh heh" chuckle from behind the curtain, followed half a beat later by a barking electronic, "ha ha ha" from the speakers.

"I was sorry to hear about your accident," Mark said.

"It was not precisely an accident." Shana's avatar shrugged. "It was the greatest thing that ever happened to me. It has liberated me in ways you could never understand."

"Right. Okay, then congratulations, I guess." Mark nodded. "And you're Shan-*a* now. That's new."

"My genitalia were damaged in the fire." The bright, chipper voice was entirely inappropriate to the atrocity it described. "I had the choice of living as a eunuch or as a woman. I chose to be a woman. Though, in a way, I now transcend binary concepts of gender."

"That must be very exciting for you," Mark said. "But I take it we don't have a lot of time, so I'll just get right to it. I need to ask you some questions about Neiro."

"Neiro." The voice gained the simulacrum of warm fondness, as if speaking the name of a beloved child. "The primary distillation."

"Yeah," Mark said. "My nephew, James, climbed to the top of the Bakersfield water tower yesterday because he believed he could fly. We got him down safely, but he was having rapid eye movements, and I recognized that as a side effect of Neiro."

"If he was so severely delusional, then he was not in possession of the lucidity that was Neiro's most characteristic effect," Shana noted. As she spoke, the face on the screen slowly shifted. It was swelling up, becoming fuller.

"True," Mark conceded. "But there are at least three other people in town who've had similar episodes, or attacks or whatever you want to call them. And they all had personal contact with James. Maybe there's a derivative of the drug floating around, somebody out there trying to imitate your work."

"Unlikely," Shana said. The face on the screen was aging as well as fleshing out. Wrinkles appeared and the hair lost its color. The voice shifted to match the face, growing both huskier and more brittle. An old woman now spoke. "The neurochemical pathways I have blazed would be most difficult to reproduce."

"Do you have any idea about what might be happening in Bakersfield?"

The old woman smiled, then her face began a slow morph into yet another form. The wrinkles smoothed and the skin's tint gradually shifted. It was hypnotizing to watch.

"Dreams have characters, just as novels or films do. The dreamer himself plays a role, as an actor does on stage." The shape of her eyes changed and her hair grew black and straight. Shana now appeared on the monitor as a young Japanese woman. "A dreamer may dream he is a child, caring for an old woman. He may dream of sexual relations with a desirous lover, or of a conversation with a long-departed friend. Parents, spouses, and siblings appear most often. However, no matter what face they wear, most dream characters are simply manifestations of the dreamer. Incarnations of the anima or animus. A dream is a hall of mirrors in which all the reflections wear masks."

"I've heard all that before, sure." Mark shook his head and blinked his eyes, trying to clear his head of the mesmerizing effect of the changing face on the screen. "But what does that have to do with James?"

"There are exceptions," Shana continued. The face sprouted a full beard now, becoming that of a hirsute middle-aged man. The voice deepened at the same time, lecturing now like a college professor. "Occasionally— rarely—a figure appears that is external to the dreamer's consciousness. Sometimes these figures are helpful, but more often they are malevolent. These intruding spirits, for lack of a better word, wear masks too. Because dreams are entirely subjective, the dreamer chooses the mask. In traditional cultures, the dreamer would choose a form supplied by their society's prevalent belief structure. Angels or demons, perhaps incubi and succubi. Ghosts or witches or jinn. However, in our modern, fractured and secular culture, the interlopers are just as likely to take on an image borrowed from popular culture as from religious tradition. A vampire, for example or a gray-skinned alien."

"Did you say, vampire?"

"No matter how the dreamer disguises these spirits, they are the same beings. Individuals just perceive them differently." Shana's face now cycled through visages at a dizzying clip, her image as mutable as liquid. Male and female faces, of every age from infancy to the very elderly, every race and skin color imaginable. The voices wavered along with the faces, becoming a discordant babel. "They may share common physical characteristics, but where one person sees the red eye atop the pyramid, another may see the Sacred Heart of Christ."

"Wait," Mark said. His head was reeling. "How did you know about..."

The face abruptly stopped shifting and solidified. Now the face on the monitor was that of Mark's mother.

"Mark," his mother said. "I'm so glad you've returned to the source. It's nice to have you living inside me again."

"You're not my mother." Mark wasn't so certain, though. "Are you?"

"I am a mirror," she replied. "A mirror wearing a mask."

As she spoke these words, Mark realized he was looking at the feed from the camera atop the monitor. It was his own face on the computer screen, moving as he moved. Somehow, though, he was perceiving it as his mother's.

A similar thing had happened to him once before. On his first Neiro trip, in fact. Home alone in the first apartment he and Missy had shared, before Ben was born, Mark had swallowed the dose he'd scored from Shaner. He'd made the mistake of glancing into the bathroom mirror, and had been more than a little freaked out to see his mother's face staring back out at him.

Now, as then, he was struck by the resemblance that others often remarked upon, but which he himself rarely saw. His mother's face and his own had similar structures, high cheekbones and a slender jawline. There was something, too, about the shape of the eyes, though his mother's contained flecks of green while his own were a solid sky-blue.

If I'm looking at my own picture, Mark thought. Does that mean I'm talking to myself?

"Don't worry," his mother said. "You're not losing your mind. Not yet. I want to tell you a secret, though."

"What secret?" Mark felt very strange. A dizzy, spinning sensation in his head.

"Step behind the curtain and I'll whisper it in your ear."

"No." Someone, somewhere, had warned him against doing that very thing. He was almost sure of it.

"Then you may never know."

Mark found himself rising from his seat. He slowly crossed the dreary room and stepped behind the red curtain partition.

Shana sat in a wheelchair behind the curtain. Mark recognized the thin, delicate features of the former man he had known as Shaner. Her head was completely hairless and her skin looked as though it had been melted off and carelessly re-applied, like a remolded candle. Still, there was something indefinably feminine about her molted features. Or maybe that was just the impression Mark got from Shana's ample, and apparently unburned, breasts, heaving forth from a white tank-top.

"Give us a kiss," she said, with the cancerous rasp of a forty-year pack-a-day smoker.

Mark didn't want to, but he did. He leaned in to kiss the blistered lips. Shana moved her mouth against his. Her fluttering tongue tasted like raw meat dipped in a dirty ashtray.

Mark pulled away and Shana whispered a breathy rustle into his ear: "The spies in the sky have eyes on the flies."

Mark awoke with a jolt, back in his chair. The face on the monitor was the generic woman's face that he'd seen at the beginning.

"Are you all right, Mark?" Shana asked through the monitor. "You dozed off for a moment there."

Mark's shock quickly ceded to anger. He jumped to his feet.

"This is bullshit," he said. "I came here to ask you a few simple questions, not for this...mind fuck."

The woman's face on the screen gave a flirtatious tilt. "Aw, you used to like it when I fucked your mind."

"I'm leaving now. Thanks for precisely nothing."

"I've enjoyed our chat. Please come back when you can stay a bit longer."

Mark stormed out of the room. He found Missy waiting in the front room with Cassandra, locked in what looked to be a very long and awkward silence.

"Let's get the fuck out of this bughouse," he said to Missy

Missy nodded eagerly and stood up.

"I trust you found what you came here looking for," Cassandra said.

"No, in fact, I didn't."

"So very sorry," Cassandra said, with the least amount of sincerity humanly possible.

"Come on." Missy tugged his sleeve and led him out of the house.

"Well, that was pointless," Mark said once they were both in the car.

Missy started the engine and pulled away from the house.

"What happened?"

"It got weird."

"*Got* weird? It was weird from the second that bitch opened the door."

"Yeah, well, it got weirder, okay? It was like Dorothy finally got in to see the wizard and found Hannibal Lector instead."

Missy flashed him a look, but did not ask him to elaborate on his pop culture references. "Did you get *any* information?"

"No," Mark said. "Well, maybe. I don't know. It was all very vague and cryptic. I think he hypnotized me or something. I actually dozed off."

"She."

"What?"

"*She* hypnotized you. She's a woman now."

"Sorry for the politically incorrect pronoun. I'm a little rattled."

"It's okay," Missy said. "Because while you were having naptime with your old buddy, I got this."

She unclipped a USB drive from her key chain and handed it to him.

"Cassandra was working on her laptop the whole time she was babysitting me. Then she got a phone call. Whoever was calling, it made her very nervous. She took the phone with her into another room so I couldn't hear her talking, but...she forgot to log out of her computer."

"Really?"

"I plugged in my drive and started grabbing files at random. I dumped as much on there as I could before she came back."

"Wow. You're amazing, you know that?"

Missy flashed him a smile. "When we get home after the hospital, I'll take a look and see if I can find anything interesting."

Mark shook his head, impressed. "You know, if this midwifing thing doesn't work out, you might want to consider a career in corporate espionage."

Missy's phone rang. She pulled it out and glanced at the screen. "It's Lana. Here, will you answer it?"

"What do you want me to say to her?"

"She's probably calling from the hospital, asking where we are," Missy said. "Just tell her we're on the way."

Mark tapped the screen and lifted the phone to his ear. "Hey, Lana. It's Mark."

"Mark?" Lana sounded more stressed than Mark had ever heard her. "Where's Chelle?"

"Driving. We're on the way to the hospital now. Should be there in a few minutes."

"No. Don't go to the hospital. Get back to Bakersfield now. If you still can."

"What does that mean?" Silence from the other end. "Lana? Hello? Are you there?"

The line was dead. Mark's jaw dropped as he looked over at Missy's baffled face.

CHAPTER 12

Though it was only May, Ben knew summer had come to stay and he was glad. Lana and his mom both liked to complain about the swampy heat, but Ben liked it. The heat reminded him of his dad taking him on hikes in the woods. Reminded him of seeing movies at the drive-in; of long, lazy days with no school; of fireworks and of hamburgers cooked on the grill. Of the one family vacation he could recall, flying in a real airplane out to San Diego with his mom and dad when they were still together and splashing in the ocean waves. Nearly everything sweet and good Ben had known in his short life had come from summertime, including his birthday on June tenth. The pleasures found on the other nine pages of the calendar paled in comparison, even with Halloween and Christmas factored in.

Until James had gone up the water tower yesterday, Ben would have said that he didn't have a trouble in the world. Some of his happiness was due to the year's first real blast of summer heat, but mostly it was because his dad had come back here to live. It wasn't any good when he lived far away and Ben could only see him a few times a year. Now everyone he loved lived in the same town. He even held out a small, secret hope that his mom and his dad might get back together. That was a little complicated, though, because now he loved Lana, too.

He couldn't see why his mom couldn't have a husband *and* a wife, anyway. Then they could all live in the same house. This solution was so simple he didn't know why nobody else had thought of it.

But Ben was really worried about James. He hoped with all his heart that his cousin was all right. They were on the way to the hospital to see him right now. Aunt Jen was asleep in the passenger seat. Ben knew the doctors at the hospital had given her a "tranquilizer" because she was so worried about James. The word "tranquil" meant calm and the pills worked really well because Aunt Jen was *way* calm. So calm she'd nodded right out.

"What the hell?" Lana said.

Her voice was sharp and Ben looked up. The road ahead was blocked off by a big army truck parked sideways, uniformed soldiers standing before it. With guns. It was like something you'd expect to see on TV, not in real life.

Ben leaned forward over Lana's seat. "What is that?"

"I don't know, Benny. Sit down."

Lana pulled to a stop and rolled down her window. One of the soldiers came over to the car, a burly-looking man wearing a surgical mask over his mouth and nose.

The soldier leaned down and looked into the car. His eyes above the mask looked back at Ben, and then lingered on Aunt Jen for a moment before focusing on Lana in the driver's seat.

"This area is under a mandatory quarantine," the soldier said to Lana. "Please return to your home, monitor local media and await further instructions."

"Wait, what? Quarantine? What for?"

"It's a temporary emergency health measure," the man said. "You are in no immediate physical danger. Return to your home and turn on the radio to the local station. There will be a broadcast soon that will contain all the information you need to know."

"What's this about?"

"I'm not authorized to discuss the situation with civilians, ma'am. Please, just return to your home."

"This woman here has a son in the hospital in Springfield." Lana pointed over at Jen, who was still conked out. "We need to get her into town so she can see him."

The man looked back over at Aunt Jen. His eyes seemed to linger on her for a few seconds longer this time.

"No exceptions, ma'am," he said. "We've closed all exits. No one in or out."

"On whose authority?" Ben recognized the about to get mad tone in Lana's voice.

"The Center for Disease Control, a federal agency."

"And you are, what, national guard?"

"That's right."

"Second lieutenant, judging by your gold bar there. Lieutenant Graham, right?"

"That is my name."

"Bullshit. I had two brothers and a sister in the army, and you're a half-assed imposter," Lana said. "Not even half-assed. You've got a little goatee beard thing going on under your mask. That is *not* regulation."

"How would you..." The man was getting mad, too. Ben could see it. "That's not..."

"Plus, you're a little heavy to be a soldier."

"You're calling me fat?"

"No, Pillsbury. I'm calling you a fake-ass doughboy. Who do you really work for?"

"Look, bitch..."

Ben didn't like when words like that started flying around. It reminded him of times when his mom and dad used to fight.

"Ah, here we go," Lana said, temper rising. "That's more like it."

"I don't think you understand the situation. I am authorized to use any force necessary to enforce this quarantine."

"Fake-ass threat from a fake-ass doughboy. Bring it on, Stay-Puft."

Ben wanted to tell her to stop. He was really scared now.

"Morgan!" Graham barked to another soldier. "This lady's got a gun in her glove-box!" He lifted his rifle up and pointed it at her.

"No," Ben whimpered, but nobody seemed to hear him.

"So it takes two big men with two big guns to take care of one unarmed black woman?"

The other soldier ran over, also holding his rifle up, and Ben couldn't take it anymore.

"Lana!" he cried. "Stop!"

Lana looked up and met Ben's eyes in the rear-view. This seemed to snap her out of her rage.

"Okay, okay. Sorry," she said to the man. She looked down at the steering wheel, not meeting his eyes anymore. "I'm sorry. Let's cool down, okay?"

The other soldier, the one named Morgan, stood beside Graham. "Problem here?"

Graham lowered his weapon. "No, my mistake." He leaned in close to the window. "Listen to the kid, lady. And get the fuck back from my roadblock."

Lana put the car into reverse and got turned around, but she pulled off onto the shoulder just a little way up the road.

"I'm so sorry, Benny," she said. "I didn't mean to scare you like that. It just makes me mad when a man thinks he can tell you what to do just because he has a gun."

"He was going to shoot you!"

"I didn't think he was really willing to go that far," Lana said. "I was wrong, though. I was so angry, I couldn't see that I really should have been scared. Now hold on, I'm going to call your mom."

She pushed a button on the screen and lifted the phone to her ear as it rang.

"Mark?" she said. "Where's Chelle?" She shook her head. "No. Don't go to the hospital. Get back to Bakersfield now, if you still can. They're barricading all the roads out of town. It's a quarantine. They're…"

Lana frowned. She looked down at her screen. "The line went dead," she said.

At that same moment, Aunt Jen stirred from her nap. She blinked over at Lana, groggy and confused. Then her eyes spun in her head and she looked out the windshield, up at the sky.

"There's a spot of blood on the moon," she said.

But of course there was no moon out. It was daytime.

"Wolfy put his stuff inside my blood." She looked right at Ben for a second before her eyes darted away again. "When I start to change, you have to run, James. I don't want to hurt you, but when the moon's bleeding, Wolfy's gonna wanna *eat*."

At the same time, out on the western edge of town, Sheriff Bates drove his big truck past the invisible line where Mulberry Street turned into County Road 600. He found the barricade less than two miles outside the village limits. Even seeing it with his own eyes, he could hardly believe the federal bastards were doing this *here*, in *his* town.

Billy Barber had awoken him less than twenty minutes before, knocking urgently on his mother's bedroom door. Nate came to beside a naked, snoring Suzy Barber, who didn't even stir at the commotion. John was awake, though, sputtering and gurgling over in his corner. Nate rolled, groaning, out of bed, pulled on his underpants and answered the door in his shorts. Billy told him that he'd just got a call from one of his buddies, saying that government agents were blocking off all the exits out of town, with national guard troops providing the muscle to enforce the order.

At first Nate thought that *had* to be horseshit. But when he tried to get some confirmation, none of his calls would go out. Like the cell towers were down. That sure was hell was ominous. So he pulled his clothes on and booked it the hell out here to see for himself.

An army green Humvee was parked horizontally across the road, blocking half a dozen or so local cars and trucks that were trying to get out of town. At least six national guard troops stood before the barricade, wearing surgical masks and carrying rifles, holding back the few folks who were standing outside their vehicles, looking harried and sweaty. Just beyond the roadblock, suited federal agents of some stripe observed the proceedings from beside several identical Ford Escape Hybrids with government plates.

Bates pulled off onto the shoulder. He drove past the blocked traffic with his passenger tires angled down into the ditch, right up to the barricade.

A masked soldier came running up to the truck, waving his hands for Nate to stop. Not one to be intimidated, Nate kept rolling forward until the soldier had to hop out of the way. One of the guy's buddies came over to help, and started rapping on Nate's window. Actually laying his hand upon Nate's vehicle. Nate was fuming inside, but took his time. He put his truck into park, killed the engine and undid his seatbelt with slow, deliberate motions. Then he furiously shouldered his door open, forcing the soldier to step awkwardly back from the truck.

"Remain in your vehicle, sir!"

"Yeah, fuck that, sonny." Nate stepped down from the cab. He'd had the AC cranked to max cool. The moist heat of the outside air immediately soaked into his chilled skin. Not even nine in the morning and it was almost ninety degrees out here. It was going to be a hot bastard of a day. "What's going on here?"

Two masked soldiers faced Nate now, young twerps both of them. If either was older than twenty-one, Nate would eat his hat.

"This area is under a mandatory quarantine," the taller of the two said. His name patch identified him as "Friel." "You need to return to your home, monitor local media and await further instructions."

"Instructions?" Bates said. "You're gonna come to my county, put up goddamn roadblocks around *my* town and then tell me to await *instructions*? I don't think so, kid. I'm the only motherfucker who gives instructions around here."

The two boys exchanged a sweaty, uncertain look. The shorter kid was named Brown, and he looked like he was on the verge of living up to his name, right in his pants. His gun twitched up. Just slightly, but enough that Bates saw the motion.

"Point that rifle at me, you're going to find about nine inches of barrel in your colon."

"Let's calm down, sir," Friel said. "Who are you?"

"I'm Logan County Sheriff Nathanial motherfuckin' Bates. Get me someone in charge to talk to ASAFP because that sure as shit ain't you."

To his credit, Friel didn't immediately back down. He just nodded thoughtfully. "Do you have any identification?"

Bates was sweaty and disheveled, wearing yesterday's civilian clothes, and he probably smelled like Suzy Barber's pussy and her cheap perfume. He could have gone back into the truck to grab his badge, but fuck that. No way.

"Yeah, I got some identification. My foot in your ass." Bates grinned at the kid. "Now go on. Get your boss over here."

Friel's wounded pride was flaring up, rising to meet Nate's intimidation. "You can't talk to us like that, sir. You need to be civil and respectful, or we will arrest you."

Bates had a good chuckle. "Yeah, that'd be fun. Try to do that, see what happens."

"Just wait here," Brown said, though it was unclear if he was talking to Bates, or to his buddy Friel. "I'll get Agent Cheung."

Only then did Nate turn and realize he had something of an audience. The folks from town standing outside their cars had witnessed the confrontation. That was good. Nate wanted them to see him standing up for their rights.

Old Pete Jones, a farmer from way back, stood close by, in overalls and John Deere cap. "What's happenin', sheriff?" he drawled, cigarette dangling from his lip. From his tone, he could have been asking about the weather, but Bates saw the worried squint to the old timer's eyes.

"I don't know, Pete," Bates said. "But I sure as hell am going to find out."

From Shana's house in Springfield to the southern limits of Bakersfield was about a thirty mile drive. Missy covered that distance in a little more than twenty minutes, which had to be some kind of record. As soon as she hit the two-lane blacktop, she pushed her little Civic to sustained speeds that would have impressed even the most optimistic engineers at Honda, slowing only slightly in deference to speed-trap burgs like Cornland and Lake Fork. The whole way, she had Mark repeatedly go over his brief conversation with Lana.

"Did she say come back to Bakersfield *if* you still can, or *while* you still can?" she said, tilting over onto the narrow gravel shoulder to whip past a sluggish farm truck.

"If." Mark closed his eyes and clenched the grab handle above the door, pondering the reliability of passenger side air bags. "I'm pretty sure she said 'if.'"

"How did she sound? Scared, anxious, what?"

"Anxious, maybe a little peeved," Mark said. "I don't know her tones like you ah, ah, watch out for the..."

Missy wove into the left lane to pass a tractor and very nearly kissed the front grill of a red pick-up in the oncoming lane before veering sharply right again. Though a staunch agnostic, Mark caught himself whispering a quick prayer. Just in case.

Missy laid on the gas, the honking horns of both vehicles receding behind them with a Doppler warble.

"Try to call her again," she said.

"I've tried four times. It just goes to voice mail."

"*Please*, Mark."

Mark dialed the number on Missy's phone and was unsurprised to get the voice mail message again. He'd already tried Jen's number, too, with the same result.

"No luck," he said.

They came upon the road block a few miles outside the city limits. Missy slowed to a stop at the tail end of a line of cars. One by one, they were being turned back by armed soldiers wearing surgical masks. There were also men in dark suits swarming about, wearing more elaborate respirators with air filters built in. Above it all, at least two helicopters hovered noisily.

"Jesus," Mark said. "What the hell is this?"

Answering his question, two soldiers erected a large sign just before the barricade. The small black print was unreadable from this distance, but he could clearly see the bold red letters spelling out *QUARANTINE* and *EXIT OR ENTRY PROHIBITED.*

"Quarantine?" Mark said. "Does that mean James had something contagious?"

"I don't know," Missy said. "But Ben and Lana are inside there. We've got to get in."

"How? They've got it blocked off."

"They can't stop us. I'll ram the barrier if I have to."

"Ram the barrier? Are you crazy? They've got guns."

"I don't care."

"I do!"

The last car in line in front of them turned around and roared away. Missy pulled up to the blockade. One of the suited men wearing a respirator stepped over to the car. He was tall, very focused looking, with small beady eyes and a high forehead. His receding hairline was concealed beneath a comb-over made even more obvious because it was dripping with sweat.

"Let me do the talking," Missy whispered.

"Sure," Mark said. "Because you're clearly the more rational one right now."

The man tapped his ring finger on the driver's side glass. Missy rolled down her window.

"Hi, good morning," the sweaty suited man said, his voice muffled by the mask. "I'm sorry, but this area is under a mandatory quarantine. No entry beyond this point. There's a detour being set up right now on CR400, but I'm afraid you're going to have to turn around."

"But we live here," Missy said. "My wife and my son are in town right now."

"Wife?" This seemed to genuinely confuse him for a second.

"Yes, my wife. Now, please. I understand we won't be able to leave again, but you have to let us in."

"No exceptions. We're containing the spread of a dangerous communicable disease."

"Does this have something to do with the sleepwalking?"

The man's beady eyes narrowed even further. "I'm not authorized to discuss the nature of the contagion. If you have family members within the quarantine zone, a representative from the Centers for Disease Control will be in contact with you to discuss their individual cases. But in the meantime, you must vacate this area."

At that moment, Mark saw, or thought he saw, movement outside the window. Something darted quickly in the air above and in front of the car. It was probably just a horsefly or a bumblebee or some other large flying insect, but something about the object's movement made him think that it wasn't a bug. It seemed, too, that rather than something small and close, what he was seeing was larger and farther away. For some reason, he couldn't say why, it reminded him of what Shana had said to him in his daydream vision:

"The spies in the sky have eyes on the flies."

Whatever that meant. Mark tried to follow the object's path, but it flitted away and he lost it in the sun.

The agent noticed his twitching gaze. "Are you all right, sir?"

Mark was struck with sudden inspiration. "Bats," he muttered.

"What was that?"

Mark turned towards the man, making his eyes dance in their sockets.

"Don't you see the goddamn bats?" he cried. "They're all over the fucking place!"

The agent stepped back, hand going involuntarily to his face mask.

"For God's sake, take shelter, man!" Mark screamed as his eyeballs went into spasms. "Red bats are swarming from the sky!"

Bates was left waiting on the side of the road for five or six minutes, growing more pissed off by the second. The blazing heat certainly didn't help his mood. He kept mopping his brow with his handkerchief. Behind him, at least half a dozen anxious locals had gathered, standing outside their cars, whispering and murmuring. Before him, facing down the citizenry, were the national guard troops with the blue masks on their faces. Friel, the guy Bates had already tangled with, stood with his rifle across his chest, refusing to meet Nate's eye.

Finally, an incongruously cool-looking Asian man in a black suit and a respirator slipped through a small gap built into the fence.

"Sheriff Bates," the guy hailed cheerfully. "You're a hard man to get a hold of."

"And you are..." Bates, out of polite reflex, shook the guy's hand when it was pressed into his.

"Agent Cheung, Centers for Disease Control," he said. "I've been calling you all morning, hoping to coordinate this operation with you, but your phone's been off. Your wife said you were in Springfield with Sgt. McMurtry, but I couldn't raise you there, either."

"I had to come back to town early to attend to some personal business," Bates said, though it pained him to make excuses to this guy. "Now what the hell's all this about?"

"Due to a possible outbreak of a contagion within the city limits of the town, the area is under a mandatory quarantine order until further notice."

"What contagion?"

"Come with me," Cheung said. "I can provide you with some details."

"Why can't we talk here? You got something to hide from these people?"

Cheung's eyes above the respirator didn't even flicker at the challenge. "Please, sheriff." He turned and walked back through the opening in the fence.

Nate flashed a look back at his constituents, to let them know how irritated he was, then he followed the government man past the wooden barricade.

There was a canvas tent set up on the other side. Cheung unzipped the flap and held it open for Bates. "Step into my office."

A rattling AC unit pumped blessedly cool air into the tent, which did indeed seem to be set up as a mobile office. A large-screen computer monitor took up most of a small desk, a satellite map of the town up on the screen. In one corner of the tent was a small refrigerator.

Cheung zipped the flap closed again and pulled off his respirator mask.

"I'm sweating like Val Kilmer's buttcrack in this thing," he said, flashing Bates a grin.

"You sure you want to take that off?" Bates said, not even cracking a smile. He was in no mood for jokes. "What if I'm carrying this bug, whatever the hell it is?"

"Oh, we know what it is. And I've been inoculated." Cheung removed a small plastic device from the little fridge and handed it to Bates. "Here."

"What is this?"

"Nasal spray. Give yourself a blast up each nostril."

Feeling a bit foolish, Bates stuck the little plastic thing up his nose. He depressed the button on the end and inhaled a little aerosol puff. He repeated the motion in the other nostril and tasted a foul trickle in the back of his throat.

"That's both a vaccine and a cure," Cheung noted, holding out a small plastic garbage pail for Bates to deposit the used applicator. "So if you already happen to be infected, the drug will counteract the contagion before the symptoms take hold."

"If you have a cure, why are you quarantining the town?"

"Because this little refrigerator here," Cheung gave the mini-fridge a kick, "contains our entire supply. In fact, most of *our* people haven't been inoculated. We have several labs around the country producing batches of the stuff, but that's going to take time."

"How much time?"

"Days, maybe weeks. We were not prepared for an outbreak on this scale."

"No shit," Bates said. "So what are we dealing with here?"

"It's a neurological disease, highly communicable, though we're not sure of the exact method of transmission. We think it's airborne, but it moves so quickly and the transmission is so erratic that we're just not sure. Those afflicted are prone to spells of narcolepsy. They may appear to be awake, but they're actually asleep and experiencing very vivid dreams. Sleepwalking is very common, along with other parasomnias."

"Is it fatal?"

"No. In the terminal stages, the patient simply slips into a deep, coma-like sleep. But while suffering an attack, the patient can engage in behavior that brings the risk of serious injury. They're quite literally acting out their dreams. Unaware of their surroundings, they may put themselves in dangerous situations."

"Climbing water towers," Bates said. "Diving down chimneys, setting shit on fire."

"Precisely, sheriff. You've already witnessed several of these cases. In some instances, the patient may exhibit violent behavior, but usually their behavior is just bizarre or illogical. Some of them, the fun ones, do really crazy sex stuff. Dreams are funny things."

"So, what is this? A biological weapon? Terrorist attack?"

"There's no evidence to suggest that. If a terrorist organization were to weaponize this disease, don't you think they'd target a major metropolitan area instead of..." He gave a little chuckle. "Mayberry?"

Bates gritted his teeth. "You did not just make a Mayberry crack to me, did you?"

"I'm sorry, sheriff. I didn't mean to—"

"Look, mister."

"Agent, please."

"All right, Agent. Cheung, is it? This ain't Mayberry and I ain't Sheriff Andy whistlin' like an asshole down to the fishing hole, all right? So I don't know if this is some shit that escaped from a government lab or what the hell it is, but I do know that it's your job to clean it up. And it's *my* job to maintain law and order, and to protect the good folks of this county. You need to let me get to my headquarters in Lincoln so we can coordinate and do our jobs together."

"I'm afraid we can't do it that way, sheriff."

"Excuse me, what the hell did you just say?"

"We can't let you leave."

"*Let* me?"

Cheung smiled again, unperturbed. "For one thing, though you're now in no danger of contracting the disease yourself, you might still be a carrier. For another...well, let's just say it's fortuitous in a way that you were in Bakersfield when the fence went up."

"Fortuitous?"

"Yes. Good fortune. Lucky chance."

"I know what fortuitous means, you condescending shit. I just don't know how you could possibly think that trapping me inside here could possibly be a good thing."

"Apologies, sheriff. Allow me to explain. The outbreak has much potential for civil unrest. Not only from the behavior of those afflicted, which will be dangerously unpredictable, but also from the natural reactions of a frightened populace contained against their will. Because of the unique nature of the contagion, the national guard troops the governor has kindly called in to assist us have been instructed to only hold the perimeter. For their own safety, and for yours, we're not allowing them in the town itself. You don't want the guys with the guns to be walking around doing crazy stuff in their sleep. So it *is* fortuitous that we have someone on the inside with a strong hand, capable of keeping order."

Bates just stared back at Cheung for a moment, chewing on what the guy was saying.

"We have temporarily suspended all communications in and out of town, in order to prevent a wider-scale panic. We wish to keep this quiet, for now. But I'll activate your phone, and anyone within the town will be able to receive calls from you."

"But I still can't make calls outside of town?"

"Regrettably, no. You will by necessity have to operate with a high level of autonomy, without any outside command or oversight."

"I only have one deputy who lives in Bakersfield, and he's old as hell. The rest are spread out all over the county. I can't maintain order all by myself."

"Of course, you are authorized to temporarily deputize any citizens you trust to assist you. Text me their numbers and I'll activate their cells as well, so you can communicate. You may even wish to arm them, at your discretion."

Bates nodded slowly.

"So, sheriff. Are you willing to take on this responsibility?"

"Let me ask you something first. You're a Chinese fellow, right?"

"Worse," Cheung smiled. "I'm a Hoosier. Gary, born and raised."

"I don't mean where you grew up. I mean your ancestry. Chinese, right?"

"All four of my grandparents were born in Hong Kong."

"Right," Bates said. "So maybe you'll know something about this. I read this thing about the Chinese word for 'crisis.'"

"You mean that old bit about how the character supposedly combines those for the words 'danger' and 'opportunity'?"

"Yeah. There any truth to that?"

"I don't read Mandarin myself, but it's my understanding that's a misperception."

"Really? I wondered. You read stuff like that on the Internet and you don't know how much of it you can actually trust. So that's not some nugget of ancient Chinese wisdom?"

"I'm afraid not."

"That doesn't make it not true, though," Bates said. "That just means it's modern, American wisdom instead. Hell, to my thinking, that's even better."

"If you say so, sheriff. Do we have your cooperation in this matter?"

"You got it, Cheung. Lock my ass up."

Bates stepped out of the soporific chill of the air-conditioned tent into the invigorating heat, his mind teeming. He slid back past the barricade and looked upon his town in crisis. Here he saw a whole world of opportunity.

Michelle rolled slowly through while Special Agent Combover held the wooden barricade open for them. On the seat beside her, Mark kept up his act.

"Duck, man!" he screamed out the window, rolling his eyes crazily. "Did you see the size of that goddamn animal?"

"Hey," Missy hissed from the side of her mouth. "You're overplaying it."

They were inside, though. The soldiers inside the barrier waved Michelle along. Stopped cars clogged the opposite lane, people from town trying to leave. Several of them stood outside their vehicles, giving her and Mark hard, strange looks as they drove past. Probably wondering why the hell they were coming inside when everybody else was trying to get out.

Lana's little Prius was parked on the shoulder just a few hundred feet up the road. Michelle felt an almost overwhelming relief at the sight. She pulled to a stop and jumped out of the car. Lana ran to her and kissed her with a fervent desperation.

"Oh thank God," Lana said. Her lips were wet, salted with sweat and tears. "How did you get those bastards to let you in?"

"Mark faked an attack."

"I pretended like I was hallucinating." Ben had his arms tight around his father's waist, and Mark embraced his son back. "It was a real stretch for me."

"Thank you," Lana said to him.

He shrugged. "The philistine obviously never read any Hunter S. Thompson, or he would have seen right through it."

"I'm so happy you guys got in," Ben said, burying his face in his father's shirt. "I'm not scared when we're all together."

With one arm around his father, Ben reached out for Michelle with the other. She was still tangled up with Lana, and so Ben pulled all four of them into one huddled embrace. It was a little awkward, but they allowed it to happen for Ben's sake.

A somewhat chunky-looking national guard soldier walked over while they were still clinched. "You all are going to have to get back in your cars and go home. I'm not going to tell you again."

"Back the fuck up, Michelin Man," Lana said, flipping him off. "This is my family here."

The soldier watched them for a moment, confounded by the menage-a-whatever he was witnessing. Then he walked away, shaking his head and muttering.

"Friend of yours?" Mark asked, extricating himself from the group hug.

"We had some words earlier. I'll tell you one thing, these are not real soldiers."

"What are they, then?" Michelle asked.

"Private security contractor, maybe. I don't know. Makes me wonder if this is really a government operation or what the hell it is."

"Maybe it's Malovo," Mark said.

"You think everything's Malovo," said Michelle.

"Yeah, well, they do their share of evil in the world."

"That's true," Lana said. "But Bakersfield's kind of their home base. Don't they have an official 'don't shit where you eat' policy?"

"They even put that on their letterhead," Mark conceded.

A strange wailing came from inside Lana's car, making them all jump. Michelle looked into the vehicle. Jen's head was tilted back, her mouth a perfect circle. She was *howling*.

"Yeah, Chelle," Lana said. "I think Jen's...got it."

Michelle leaned down into the passenger side window. "Jen?"

Jen turned and gave Michelle a vicious warning growl. Her eyes were flitting about in the now-familiar fashion.

"She was saying stuff about blood on the moon," Lana said. "And how Wolfy said she's going to change."

"Ah, Jesus, sis," Michelle said, shaking her head. "Can this day get any *worse?*"

CHAPTER 13

"BY THE AUTHORITY of the Centers for Disease Control and a special executive of the Governor of the State of Illinois, the village of Bakersfield is under a mandatory quarantine order." The statement was delivered by the same text-to-speech robo-voice that made the emergency weather alert announcements and the amber alert notifications. It was the male version of the voice, which Mark supposed was selected because it sounded more authoritative than the female. "In order to contain the spread of a highly communicable, non-fatal disease, exit from or entry into the village borders is hereby forbidden until further notice. Citizens are advised to remain in their homes and monitor this radio station for further information."

WBIL 98.5, which until last night had been Bakersfield's source of modern country and the home of Johnny Six-Pack, now broadcast only this mechanical man's terse proclamation. Over and over again, on a continuous loop punctuated by the shrill warning tone. Mark listened to it half a dozen times before turning the volume almost all the way down.

He was driving Missy's car, Ben sitting next to him in the passenger seat. Missy had gone with Lana in the other car, just ahead up the road, to help with Jen. Mark had last seen his former sister-in-law growling and panting like a rabid beast. Fortunately, she seemed unable to unbuckle her seatbelt with her imagined paws.

Mark looked over at Ben, who was gazing out the window.

"Are you okay?" Mark asked.

"Yeah, Dad," Ben said.

"Are you sure? Because I don't mind telling you, this is all pretty scary to me."

"I was scared before," Ben said. "When that guy pointed his gun at Lana and you and Mom were outside the fence. But it's all right now. I know that whatever happens, you and Mom and Lana will take care of me. I just hope Aunt Jen's okay."

Mark turned back to the road, feeling utterly unworthy of his son's absolute trust. For about the millionth time since becoming a parent, he was struck by the magnitude of his responsibility to this bright, beautiful, perfect little human being who he had somehow helped to create. The most constant of the many fears of Mark's adult life was that he was that he would fail his son on some fundamental level, and screw him up as badly as his own parents had done to him. He just hoped that it wasn't too late, that the damage hadn't already been done.

Mark pulled into the driveway beside Lana. His ruminations about his son's welfare were supplanted by the more immediately pressing concern of what to do about the werewolf in the other car.

"Help us get her into the house!" Missy called to him.

Missy and Lana were struggling to get Jen out of the car. She was totally out of her mind, growling and snapping, literally frothing at the mouth, her darting eyes wild and feral. Mark ran over and grabbed one arm. Jen was burning hot, as if running a dangerously high fever.

Missy tossed Ben the car keys. "Open the door!"

Ben obediently ran ahead and opened the door. Mark took one of Jen's arms and Missy the other, while Lana stood behind, holding tight to Jen's hair in an attempt to restrain her from biting. Together the three of them managed to get the raving woman into the house and over onto the living room couch.

"Ben," Missy said. "There should be an orange prescription bottle in the guest bathroom. It'll say 'Xanax.' Go get it. Hurry."

Ben ran off as Mark and Missy managed to get Jen into a sitting position on the couch. The heat radiating from her was intense, but dry as a desert wind. She wasn't sweating at all.

"The moon is bleeding!" She growled, with a deeper rasp than Christian Bale doing Batman. "Full and red and Wolfy's hairy!"

"Jen!" Missy shouted. "You're dreaming. Snap out of it."

Jen replied with a snarl and an attempt to bite Missy's hand.

Ben came back with the bottle. Lana grabbed it and popped the lid.

"One, you think," she said. "Or two?"

"Two!" Mark and Missy called together.

"How are we going to get these into her?" Mark asked.

"There's some Cheez Whiz in the fridge," Missy said.

"Cheez Whiz?" Mark laughed, still pinning Jen down on the couch. "I thought you guys were organic."

"Now's not the time to..." Missy dodged another snap of Jen's jaws. "Lana, get the damn Cheez Whiz, please."

Lana hurried off into the kitchen and came back a moment later with a big spoonful of the orangey-yellow stuff. She embedded two Xanax into the glob of processed cheese spread.

"Tilt her head back," she said.

Mark put his arm under Jen's chin and Michelle pulled her hair back. Jen let out a little protesting bark. In the brief second her mouth was open, Lana shoveled the spoonful of cheese in. Mark pushed her jaw closed. Jen resisted for a moment, but then swallowed. Her spinning eyes narrowed and settled on Mark.

"Jen." Mark took advantage of her brief attention. "You've just swallowed some pills. They're an infusion of, uh, wolfsbane with a, you know, a...silver leaf coating. It's a temporary cure for lycanthropy. They'll make you sleep for a while and when you wake up, you'll be back in your human form. Understand?"

Jen nodded. "Okay," she said reasonably. "I am feeling pretty sleepy."

With that, she went limp. Mark and Missy released her and allowed her to lay her head on the couch pillow. Within seconds, she was completely out.

"How did you know that would work?" Missy asked, pulling a blanket over her sister.

"It's something I noticed when I was up on the tower with James. People with this thing are very suggestible."

"Jesus." Missy flopped down on a chair. "I can't take much more of this."

She let out a huge exhaling sigh and put her face down in her hands. Mark thought she might be crying, but her eyes were dry when she lifted her head again. Still, she wore a stricken expression that made him want to go to her, to hold her, to whisper soothing words in her ear. He knew this wasn't his place anymore, though. This truth was driven home for him when Lana sat on the arm of Missy's chair. Missy leaned into her wife as

Lana slipped her arm around Missy's shoulders. Lana kissed her, first on the forehead, and then on the lips.

"She'll be all right," Lana whispered.

Missy nodded, and then she did begin to cry a little. She rested her cheek on Lana's chest and allowed herself to be held.

That stung like hell. It was more painful for Mark than watching them make love would have been. He could not think of one instance in all the time they'd been together when he had soothed Missy so easily. In fact, almost every time he'd seen her this upset was because of some dumb-ass thing he'd done. He couldn't be the source of comfort for her when he was usually the root cause of her misery.

"So," he said, in hopes of diverting them from their flagrant nurturing. "We should check out what's on that USB. Maybe we can get some answers about what's going on here."

Lana looked down at Missy. "Do you really think this Shana woman has anything to do with all this?"

"I don't know," Missy said. She grabbed her laptop off the coffee table and powered it up. "But I just thought of something. Cassandra got that phone call that freaked her out so bad at almost the exact time the road blocks went up. That's kind of wild to be a coincidence."

She made several clicks and taps on her device, and then frowned.

"Well, I'm sure this won't come as much of a shock," Missy said, "but the WiFi's out. There's no connection."

"So they shut off the cell phones *and* the Internet," Mark said. "I'd be willing to bet they cut the land lines, too. Whoever's behind this, they don't want us talking to the outside world."

Missy plugged the USB in and clicked the folder to view the contents. "It's a bunch of video files," she said. "Really strange names. 'Insufflation via Rectal Glister.' 'Opal's Ostentiferous Oxters.'" She tapped on one of them and shook her head. "Password protected." She clicked on a few more. "They're *all* password protected."

"There's got to be a way around that," Mark said. "Do you know any good hackers?"

"I do, actually," Lana said.

Missy looked up at her. "Who?"

"A student of mine named Alice Kiernan. Mr. Gaynor, the Computer Sciences teacher, is the official IT guy at the school, but he's kind of an idiot. Whenever anybody has any *real* problems with their computers, they go to her. She's super bright, and I know she does things that aren't... totally legal."

"I like her already," Mark said. "Do you think she'd take a look at this?"

"She loves this kind of stuff."

"Is she the one you were telling me about?" Missy asked. "The girl with cancer?"

"Yeah. She got really sick a few months ago. Came close to dying. She's doing better now, but she can be...intense."

"So how do we get her to do this?" Mark asked. "We can't call her."

"She lives over in the Fox Glen subdivision," Lana said. "I'll take you over to her house."

"Good, let's go." Mark stood up. "I like the idea of doing something, instead of just sitting around, freaking out."

"Hold on," Missy said. "Lana, can I talk to you in the bedroom for a second?"

"Yeah, Chelle."

They went off together, leaving Mark alone with Ben. The boy squinted down at his mother's computer as if he could break into the files with the sheer power of concentration.

"Do you really think there's something in there that can tell us what's happening?"

"I don't know," Mark said. "It's probably kind of a long shot."

"It'd be so cool if we exposed the conspiracy or whatever." Ben looked up at Mark, his eyes lit. "It's like we're detectives."

Mark remembered how he'd felt the same way back when he was a kid, when the Snowman killings had first started. It had been exciting at first, a relief from the normal monotony of daily life. That feeling hadn't lasted long.

Missy returned from the bedroom a couple minutes later. "Mark, come into the kitchen with me. I need to ask you something."

He followed her into the kitchen and she handed him a slip of paper. "What's this?"

"Alice Kiernan's address," Missy said, "and a note from Lana, explaining the situation."

"Why can't Lana just explain it when she gets there?"

"Because you're going to go over there without us for right now," said Missy. "We'll meet up with you later."

"You want me to go over to some teenage girl's house who I don't even know?"

"Take Ben with you. You'll look less like a pervert that way."

"Why aren't you guys coming?"

"Somebody has to stay here and keep an eye on Jen."

"You can do that. Why can't Lana come with us at least? She knows the girl."

"I want Lana to stay here with me. We need to...reconnect."

"Reconnect?"

"This has been an incredibly stressful couple of days. With what happened to James, and now to Jen. And when we were outside the fence, thinking I was going to be separated from Ben and Lana. That *terrified* me. I just need reassurance, you know, of a physical—"

"Oh my God. You want me to clear out of the house with Ben so you can get *laid*?"

"That's putting it bluntly, but basically, yes. Is that a problem for you?"

"Do I need to point out which of us, you or me, needs to get laid *more*?"

"Please, Mark." She grabbed his arm and met his eye. "I need this. I *need* it."

Mark looked at his former wife. Her skin was slightly flushed, her eyes just a bit unfocused. There was also a subtle, evocative change in her scent. These were all signs of her arousal he had once been attuned to with all his senses. He now noticed an obvious looseness beneath her t-shirt, too. An unbroken line of naked shoulder at her collar and two hints of distention through the thin material down where his eyes were no longer allowed to linger. He was pretty sure she'd been wearing a bra before she went back into the bedroom with Lana.

Seeing her like this, knowing that none of it was for him, was like a knife to his heart. That she was asking him so matter-of-factly to step aside, his obsolete yearning not even a factor in her considerations, gave the knife a brutal twist.

"Sure." He smiled. "Fine. Have fun. We'll see you guys later."

"Are you okay?"

"I'm great." Mark stepped into the living room. "Grab that flash drive, Ben. You and I have some detective work to do."

The Church of the Shepherd complex was comprised of several brown brick buildings on a hundred-acre lot just northeast of town. Driving past on Highway 54, it would be very easy to mistake the facilities for a suite of upscale offices, or maybe the campus of a prosperous community college. There were no gaudy crosses on display or anything else to mark the buildings as a place of worship, except for the big sign out front displaying the week's topical message: "You have one new friend request...from Jesus!"

Nate paced the patio as he dialed Mara's phone again. She wasn't picking up. His wife had a bad habit of leaving her cell phone off; damned frustrating when he wanted to get a hold of her. The phone rang four times and then went to voice mail. Nate didn't leave a message, but he did shoot her a text:

Call me when you get this. Love ya.

Nate slipped his phone back into the its little holster on his belt and walked around to the front of the main church building, where there was quite a bit of activity. Congregants were showing up from all over town, gravitating in this hour of crisis to the fellowship of the other members of their flock. Many of the women came bearing casserole dishes and pie pans. He didn't doubt if he lingered among them, he'd hear all the clichéd aphorisms about how decent Christian small town folk always came together in times of trouble. Nate hated that self-serving bullshit. That's why it had needled him so badly when that Agent Cheung had made his stupid Mayberry crack.

Fucking Mayberry. That show was the bane of Nate's life. He'd grown up in this so-called heartland community, back in the supposedly halcyon early sixties, and his dad had actually been the goddamn sheriff. As soon as that show hit the airwaves, kids at school had started calling him Opie. That is, until word got around that this was a good way to get your ass kicked. Nate's feelings on the matter hadn't softened much over the decades.

Politicians and talk radio assholes and country singers loved to evoke that fiction as if Mayberry had been a real place and time that had existed once and could exist again if only people would vote this way or buy that thing or turn back to God or whatever. Nate knew better. Some people chose to remember the past like it was all Aunt Bea baking apple pies in black and white, but they were lying to themselves. Nate remembered what it had really been like.

His daddy, the original Sheriff Bates, had been a fine, upstanding lawman and a devout Christian who attended church without fail every Sunday. Outwardly, he played the Andy Griffith archetype to a tee. A calm and stoic keeper of the peace, loved by the people, handily elected to six terms in office. But Nate remembered overhearing his daddy drinking with his top two deputies once he was ten. The three lawmen cheerfully reminisced about killing some "nigger hobo" who'd made the fatal mistake of passing out drunk in the Lincoln bus station, and then burying the guy in a field out north of Hartsburg. A couple of years after that, Charlie Trott, son of the richest man in Bakersfield, raped Abigail Stevens, whose daddy didn't own shit. So Nate's father went out and paid Abigail and her daddy a visit. Nate didn't know what kind of threats his father had made, but Abigail recanted her story the very next day. Two months later, the whole family moved away for good.

Oh, but Ted Bates had been an incorruptible lawman, who would have been horrified if he'd lived to see how his son made the bulk of his income. At least Nate knew what he was. At least he was no goddamn hypocrite.

Out across the church parking lot, Nate's newly deputized police force had assembled, waiting for him. This improvised force consisted of the six Barber boys and four of Pastor Barry's guys. Bryant Morris, the only deputy actually on the county payroll who lived in town, was nowhere to be found. Nate had made several calls to him already, but he couldn't raise him. Maybe that was for the best. Morris was a bit too soft-hearted, not to mention too damn old, for the kind of police work that this crisis would likely necessitate.

Billy and Chucky Barber, Suzy's two youngest sons, were up on top of Chucky's big Ram truck, trying to attach a full-size red-and-blue police light-bar. God knows where they'd scored the thing, sure as hell wasn't legal for civilian purchase, but they were strapping it precariously to the roof with bungee cords.

With the exception of JJ, who possessed more sense than all his brothers put together, the Barber boys behaved more like they were getting ready for a hunting party than taking on the sacred responsibility to serve and protect their fellow citizens. There was a lot of laughing and horsing around, no doubt exacerbated by the cooler of Budweiser in the bed of Chucky's truck.

All the Barbers were armed, of course. Nate didn't even need to ask. They had all shown up fully strapped, with leather holsters on their belts. He'd requested that Tuttle's Sheep Shackers bring weapons as well, but they were at least more discreet about it. The four well-dressed young men stood beside the Barbers, looking faintly embarrassed by their fellow deputies' rowdiness.

Tom Peters was the leader among them, the closest thing Barry had to a lieutenant. He'd been the Youth Outreach Director for the church for ten years or more, and was also the lead singer of The Young Lions, a Christian rock band that had achieved a small measure of regional fame. A football player in high school, Tom still retained that big, dumb lumbering look. Nate knew that Tom was sharper than he looked, but wasn't *too* smart, either. Just exactly the right amount of smart, in fact. He was loyal and obedient and didn't ask very many questions.

Nate had been thinking about Tom a lot since he'd come to his decision about Barry. Once the pastor was eliminated, Tom would be the logical choice to step up and replace him. Nate would have to handle that transition very delicately, though.

Tom, seeming to sense the sheriff's scrutiny, looked up at him.

"Have you heard from Pastor Barry?" Tom asked. "I thought for sure he'd be down here at the church."

Barry's making himself scarce, Nate thought. I'm sure he's got a pretty good idea what's going to happen next time I see him.

"I haven't talked to him since yesterday," he said. "But I'm going to go by his house in just a bit to check up on him. I'm worried he might have this sickness that's going around."

Tom's eyes went wide at that. "I'll pray for him."

"You do that, son."

"What about the Mayor?" asked Dennis Budd.

Dennis played drums in the Young Lions, and was about as bright as Nate would expect from a drummer in a mid-level Christian rock band.

"What about him?" Nate shot back.

"Well, shouldn't he be here?"

"I'm pretty sure Mayor Sager has gone to ground," Bates said. "Literally."

Buck Sager was a hardcore doomsday prepper who had begun construction on the underground bunker in his back yard on the day Barack Obama was elected. The esteemed Mayor had without a doubt interpreted the town quarantine as the hammer of the long-anticipated Obamaclypse finally coming down. He would emerge from his fully-stocked hidey-hole only when he was confident that the armies of the Antichrist were weak enough to be conquered. Anybody attempting to rouse him before them was apt to get a shotgun to the face.

"It doesn't matter, though," Nate said. "Right now, *I'm* the mayor. I'm also the governor, the president, the CEO, the king and the goddamn Pope. We're on our own here, boys. The national guard is only maintaining the perimeter. They're not allowed to set foot in the town. That means it's up to us to keep order. This sickness that's going around causes people to go out of their minds and do all kinds of crazy shit. And even the healthy people are apt to get a bit buggy when they're trapped in town with no phone and no Internet."

"Now, I know none of y'all are doctors, but here's the deal," Nate went on. "If you come across somebody demonstrating lawless behavior, you've got to make a diagnosis. If you think they're sick and just acting out some crazy dream, take 'em over to the Malovo plant. They're setting up a treatment center in the cafeteria there, with doctors on hand who can take care of folks. However, if they're just looters, rioters, demonstrators, agitators or any other stripe of lawbreaker, I want you to bring 'em back up here. We'll detain them out back, in the animal cages Barry's got set up for his wildlife park."

"Now, when you're apprehending somebody, your personal safety is of the utmost importance," Nate said. "If you feel physically threatened, I hereby authorize you to take whatever measure you deem necessary to defend yourself. If there's any kind of inquest or investigation after this is all over, I will back you up to doomsday defending your actions."

Nate didn't miss the quick grin that passed between Billy and Chucky Barber at that statement. They seemed to like the sound of that a little *too* much.

"Bill, Chuck," Nate said. "You two are staying here at the church, guarding the jail."

"Aw, man," Chucky griped.

"Don't argue with me, son," Bates said, with enough weight to his voice that Chuck didn't press the issue. "Tom and JJ, you two are my chief deputies. I want you guys to find a map and divide the town up into sections. Buddy everybody up in pairs and send them out to patrol. Got it?"

"Got it, sheriff," JJ said.

"Yes, sir," said Tom.

"Okay, I know these are your friends and neighbors," Nate said. "But we have to be strong, to keep everybody safe. Curfew's at eight PM tonight and that is *firm*. *Nobody* out on the streets after that. I want y'all to meet me back up here no later than nine. In the meantime, call my phone with any questions you got. Other than that, I'm trusting you to work on your own. Be careful out there."

Nate turned from his troops and saw Sally Morris, Deputy Bryant's daughter, standing a little way across the parking lot. She was looking over at him like she had something urgent to say. He knew she was hesitant to approach with all the Barber boys present. Sally used to be married to Ed Barber, the son who took most after his father in the "drunk, abusive asshole" department. Lucky for her, Ed drove his car into an oncoming semi one night and saved her the inconvenience of getting a divorce. Since then, she tried to have as little to do with her former in-laws as possible, though that put her in the unenviable position of coming between Suzy Barber and one of her grandbabies.

The kid was with her now, peering shyly around his mother's legs at his outlaw uncles. The Barbers stared right back, though Nate knew they wouldn't do much to harass Sally in his presence. He went over to her.

"Mornin', Sally," he said, tipping his hat.

"Sheriff," she said, her pretty brown eyes quivering with trouble. "I need to talk to you about my dad."

"Where's he at? I've been trying to get a hold of him all morning."

"That's the thing, sheriff. He's...this sickness. He's got it, bad. I came home from work last night and he was out of his head, raving. Saying crazy things about monkeys and snowmen. He kept calling Derek a little monkey and I was afraid...I was afraid he might try to hurt him."

"Where is he now?"

"Chained up in the shed behind our house."

"Chained up?"

"He told me to do it." Sally pulled a sweaty clump of auburn hair away from her face. "He woke up for a little bit this morning. He was himself for a little bit, but he was afraid he'd hurt us when he fell back asleep. We tried to call for help, but the phones were dead. So he made me put...a dog collar on him. I chained my dad up in the shed like a mad dog."

She broke down a little. Nate pulled her into a light embrace and patted her back, very much aware of the Barber boys watching them.

"It's all right, Sally," he said. "You did the right thing."

"I heard on the radio that they have this treatment facility set up. Can you go get him and take him there? Maybe they can help him."

"Of course. We'll take care of him."

She pulled away and looked him in the eye. "It has to be you, not one of..." She glanced over at the Barbers. "...your new deputies."

"I'll see to it personally," Nate said. "I promise. I'm heading that way right now."

She heaved a sigh. "Thank you. So much."

"Don't worry," he said. "Your dad's a good deputy and a good guy. I'll make sure he's taken care of."

Nate considered his next move as he walked over to his truck. The Morris house wasn't too far from Pastor Barry's place. He'd see to Bryant Morris, as promised, but there was one thing he had to take care of first.

Driving his ex-wife's car across town, Mark did his best not to picture the ballet of Sapphic delight he imagined to be playing out back at her house. At this, he failed miserably. He envisioned Missy and Lana's sweaty tryst like something out of a European art film. Stark black and white cinematography filled his head, the two women writhing naked together beneath twisted silk sheets while their lacy bedroom curtains fluttered in the languid summer breeze.

"Hey, that's grandma," Ben said, uttering a word that threw ice water over Mark's guilty erotic daydream.

"What? Where?"

"On the radio."

Ben nudged up the volume. Mark's mother's voice came from the car speakers.

"...Gillian Hudson, Community Relations Director for Malovo Agricultural Development," she was saying, in the slow, deliberate cadence she used for all her public addresses. Her voice was cool and detached, and yet she managed to deliver the obviously prepared statement in a manner that made it sound natural and off the cuff. This was so unlike how Mark remembered her voice at home when he was growing up. Back then, his mom could range from a passive aggressive whisper to a histrionic rant, sometimes within the span of a single sentence. "Like all of you, we at Malovo were shocked this morning to learn of the emergency quarantine placed upon the village of Bakersfield. As you know, many of Malovo's executive team, including myself, have homes within the quarantine zone. We're all in this together. So, as part of our long-standing 'good neighbor' policy, I would like to outline some of the measures we're taking in order to help our community through this temporary crisis."

Mark was coming up on the downtown area now. There were quite a few people about and around the square, more than he would have expected had this been in any way a normal Saturday morning. It was impossible to gauge their mood. Any or all of them could have been sleepwalking, for all he knew.

"First off," his mother continued, "all production at the Malovo Renewable Bioenergy ethanol plant is temporarily suspended. Plant employees will receive full pay for the entirety of the shutdown, so they may stay home and care for their families."

"That's nice of them, isn't it?" Ben said.

"Yeah, I guess," Mark scoffed. As unlikely as it was in reality, he still wasn't convinced that this whole outbreak wasn't Malovo's fault. He didn't know how. A mysterious sleepwalking epidemic seemed an unlikely side effect of ethanol production, but he had a pretty low opinion of their ethical track record.

He wasn't going to say anything like that to Ben, though. To him, his grandmother was just the sweet older lady who bought him the best presents at Christmas, and who had an indoor heated pool at her house. But Gillian Hudson was uniquely well-suited for the job she did for Malovo. She managed to put a positive spin on everything they did. Making Malovo look like beneficent saints to the community that hosted their presence required her to deliver smiling half-truths and straight-faced disinformation. And she was really good at it.

"In addition," she continued. "Malovo is opening an emergency medical facilities in the employee cafeteria at our renewable energy plant. Trained and equipped medical professionals will be available there to care not only for individuals afflicted with the contagious disease, but also for any other..."

"Dad, look out!"

Mark slammed on the brakes as a large shape leapt in front of the car. He missed running over the person by scant inches. It was such a near collision that the man before his bumper slapped his hands down on the hood of the car.

Mark looked up and was surprised to see a familiar bearded face.

"Sam?" he said.

Sam squinted into the windshield. In the span of two seconds, his face cycled through fear, surprise and then relief.

"Mark!" he cried. "Let me in the car!"

A young woman with some kind of shawl wrapped around her was running towards after him. Mark unlocked the doors and Sam dove into the back seat, the whole car rocking with his sudden weight.

"Drive!" he said. "Go! Go!"

Mark hit the gas. The woman in the shawl ran after the car for about half a block, shaking her fist and screaming something he couldn't make out.

"Thank God you came along," Sam said, sitting up in the seat and looking out the back window at the woman as she receded behind them.

"What was that?" Mark asked.

"Fuck, dude. That was fuckin'..." Sam noticed Ben sitting in the front seat. "Sorry."

"It's all right," Mark said. "This is my son, Ben. Ben, this is my new friend Sam. I guess you could say he's my boss."

"Ah, man. Don't call me that," Sam said.

"It's nice to meet you, Sam," Ben said.

"You too, kid." Sam was still trying to catch his breath. "You too."

"So what happened back there?" Mark asked.

"That girl." Sam cocked his thumb back. "That's Alyssa Wilson. She's a waitress over at Jett's Diner. Her mom owns the place." He exhaled sharply. "She was sitting on the sidewalk right outside my place, crying. So I went out to see if I could help her. She told me her baby was sick. I didn't even know she had a kid, but she's holding something in her scarf, and it's squirming around. I didn't know what she thought I could do for her, but I said I'd take a look. Then she opened up her scarf and showed me." Sam's voice broke a little. "It wasn't a baby."

Ben, wide-eyed, turned around in his seat. "What was it?"

"Squirrel."

"What?" Mark said.

"Yeah, man. Fuckin' squirrel. I don't know how she managed to catch the thing, but she had it all wrapped up in her scarf. The squirrel was freaking out, trying to get away. I could see that her, you know, her *breasts*," he whispered this word, perhaps in deference to Ben, "were all bloody, covered with bites and scratches. But she just said 'I think her belly button's infected. See how red it is?' And I said 'Lady, that's not a baby. That's a fuckin' squirrel.'"

Sam shook his head. "She held it out for me and I didn't even want to touch it, so I dropped it on the ground. Of course, the squirrel tears off like a bat out of hell. Alyssa looks up at me and just *screams* 'My baby!

You killed my baby!' And then she starts chasing me. That's when I ran into you."

"Are you all right?" Mark asked.

Sam nodded and then shook his head. There were tears in his eyes.

"Fuckin' squirrel, man!"

CHAPTER 14

"SHERIFF BATES HERE," Nate answered the cell when it rang. The caller ID on his truck's dash informed him that it was Calvin Barber on the line.

"Yeah, sheriff," Calvin's slow drawl came through the speakers. "What's your forty?"

"My what?"

"Where you at?"

"Do you mean what's my *twenty*?"

"Uh, yeah. Me and Jesse are over here in front of the Mobil station on Washington. Are you anywhere close to that?"

"Why the hell are you asking?"

"Well, Bobby Trott wrecked his car over here. Drove it right into an abutment. He's acting kinda strange, and I remembered what you said about how people might have the sickness. We ain't sure if we should take him up to the cages at the Church of the Shepherd, or to one of those treatment places. Could come over here and have a look at him?"

"Fucking useless," Nate muttered.

"What was that?"

"Jesus. Acting strange how?"

"Well, he's walking kinda funny and he says he's got bugs in his pants."

Somebody, presumably Jesse, said something to Calvin that Nate couldn't make out.

"Right," Calvin said. "Jitterbugs. He said he's got jitterbugs in his pants."

"Remember what I said to you about making independent assessments and judgment calls? How I'm entrusting you to operate autonomously? What do *you* think you should do with a guy who says he's got goddamn jitterbugs in his pants?"

"Uh, treatment place?"

"I don't give a shit either way. Just don't fucking call me again."

Nate terminated the call with a jab of his finger, shaking his head. Maybe culling half his force from the Barber clan hadn't been such a brilliant idea after all. He wondered if it was possible that John and Suzy had been first cousins or something. That would explain a lot.

He was pulling into the alley behind Tuttle's place again, just as he had yesterday afternoon. He rolled to a stop and scanned the backs of the houses for activity. Barry's neighbors were either holed up behind closed curtains or they were out wandering the streets, dreaming up crazy shit to do. Either way, they weren't looking out their back windows. That was good.

Nate unlocked the glove compartment. Inside, appropriately enough, was a pair of leather gloves. He slid them on, and then grabbed out two other items. A clear jewel case containing a DVD and a little Beretta he'd found beneath a dead woman's car seat while investigating a fatal wreck out on I-55. He also grabbed the ring that had the keys to the pastor's house. It turned out he didn't need them, though. Walking up to the house, he saw that Barry was in his backyard.

The gate to the dog kennel was hanging wide open and Barry was standing in there, hand-feeding the bear scraps of meat. The bear sat on its haunches, docile as a big dog, patiently gobbling up the little bloody chunks as Barry held them out one by one.

"You sure that's a smart thing to do, Barry?" Nate said. "That's a goddamn wild animal you got there."

Barry didn't even turn around at Nate's voice. "Cleavin'," he mumbled. "Leave it to cleaver. That's a good boy. Yes, sir." He chuckled sleepily. "I don't even need the ring no more. Crazy raisins."

"Barry, what..." Then Nate saw something that stopped him cold.

Eve Tuttle was lying face-down on the piss-stained concrete of the kennel floor, stripped down to her prim church lady underwear. One buttock and thigh was flayed open, laying bare the red meat inside. As Nate watched, horror-stricken, Barry knelt beside his wife. He picked up a knife off the ground and sliced another strip of flesh from Eve's back side. He fed the morsel to the bear, which licked its chops with appreciation.

"Jesus, Barry," Nate gasped. "What the fuck did you do?"

"Oh, hey," Barry finally noticed Nate standing there. His eyes were heavy as he turned to look at him, the lids drooped halfway closed. "Razed the haze there, Natey Batey? Nutter Butter? Nut-n-honey? Heh heh. That stuff's for kids."

"Oh my God." Nate was a man who had seen some serious shit in his life. He had murdered without remorse, many times, but this was too much for him. His head reeled with horror. He almost felt like he was going to throw up. "That's your wife."

"That ain't my wife," Barry said. "That's a Gorgon-bitch from the snake planet."

"Ah, fuck. Barry."

Nate took a step forward. The bear grew skittish upon his approach, and lurched out of its pen. If Nate had been thinking more clearly, he would have put the beast down. What if the thing had a taste for human flesh now? He was still momentarily stupefied, though. Besides, he didn't want to fire the Beretta. The old grey bear loped past him, moving as fast as its arthritic joints would allow. Nate and Barry watched together as the beast made its slow bid for freedom, disappearing down the alley.

"I'm feeling kind of sleepy," Barry said, once the bear was gone. "Mind if I sit down?"

He sat down and leaned back against the chain-link kennel, right beside his wife's mutilated corpse. Nate stood there for a moment, leaning against the fence with his head lowered until he was thinking straight again. Then he knelt down beside Barry.

"I came here to kill you, buddy," Nate said. "I found out how you used my heroin to pay off Jacob Norrell. Did you really think I wasn't going to find out about that?"

"Can't suffer the Gorgon-bitches," Barry said. "Not when they got snakes in their hair."

"You know, you could have come to me. You could have said, 'Look, Nate. I fucked up. I stuck my dick somewhere I shouldn't have and now I got some dumb-ass kid making threats.' I would've taken care of the situation, Barry. I probably would have held it over your head for the rest of your life, but I would have made that problem go away. But no, you had to steal from me. Your friend and partner."

"You know about the snake planet?"

"Just shut up and listen, okay? Here's what I'm going to do for you."

Barry's eyes rolled all the way back into his head and his eyelids fluttered. Nate slapped him across the face.

"Stay with me, buddy. Just for another minute. Here, hold this gun."

He pressed the small pistol into Barry's hand. Barry listlessly lifted the gun up towards Nate's head.

"Don't point that at me," Nate said calmly, pushing Barry's hand aside.

"Sorry. Hey, you seen my ring? I dropped it somewhere. It filters the raisins. Cuts through the haisins."

Nate held up the DVD in his gloved hand for Barry to see. "You know what this is?"

"It's not my ring." Barry lifted the barrel of the gun to his face and used it to scratch his eyelid. "Will it work on my Bible?"

"This is some really nasty kiddie porn, Barry. Stuff with little boys. I found it in the basement of this guy who committed suicide a year or two ago. Hid behind a bookcase. I held on to it, thinking it could come in handy for a situation like this. I wasn't thinking of you specifically, not then." Nate frowned. "I watched...the first couple minutes, just enough to be sure of what I had. I mean to tell you, Barry, it kinda shook me up. In fact, up until about five minutes ago when I found you feeding your wife to a goddamn bear, I would have said it was the most disturbing thing I've ever seen in my life. And I've seen some *shit*. Anyway, I was going to leave this clutched in your dead hand. Wordless confession and all that. Humiliating you even in death, destroying your legacy. But you know what? I changed my mind. I ain't going to do that. For one thing, when they find you beside the butchered corpse of your wife, that'll be enough. For another..." Nate shook his head. "I don't want to use the word respect, Barry, because I don't respect you. At all. But we had a good thing going before you fucked it up. For years. I mean, look what we built together. Now it's all mine. So, maybe it's out of respect for *that*, or maybe it's just my fucked up way of saying thank you, but I'm not going to leave this here. Maybe I'll burn the fuckin' thing. I don't know."

Nate stood up.

"Put the gun in your mouth, Barry," he said. "Pretend it's a dick you want to suck."

Barry took to that suggestion with a little too much relish, licking and slurping at the barrel as he plunged it in and out of his lips.

"Stop that, Jesus," Nate said, disgusted. He took a deep breath. "Pull the trigger, Barry."

Barry nodded. "Muh-huh," he said around his mouthful. For a second, Nate didn't think he was really going to do it. There was a slight hesitation, but then came an explosive concussion. A flash of light and smoke in his former partner's mouth.

Barry slumped over onto his wife's body, shuddering and gurgling. Nate saw that the path of the bullet had been too low. It had gone straight through Barry's throat and exited out the back of his neck. Likely didn't hit his brain at all. Didn't matter, though. He would bleed out within a few minutes.

Barry made awful pitiable burbling noises as his body jerked and kicked. He clutched his wife's naked back, a dying man's final desperate grasp. That's how they would find him.

Nate didn't want to watch. He got back into his truck and pulled out of the alley, heading over to Bryant Morris's place.

The knocking at her door sounded like a man to Alice Kiernan's ear. She couldn't have said why, but there was definitely something manly about the rapping. It wasn't like whoever was out there was banging on the door or anything overtly masculine and aggressive like that. If anything, the knock was cautious and tentative. Maybe a woman would have rung the bell instead of knocking and that's how she'd known. Or maybe it was just a case of daydream fantasy wish fulfillment. How often had she imagined the FedEx driver or the pizza delivery guy at the door when she was home alone, so taken by her beauty that they ravaged her right there on the living room carpet?

Kind of far-fetched, she knew, and a cliché besides, but as a teenage sex fantasy it did the dirty job.

She paused the game of *Call of Duty: Black Ops III* she was playing and clicked open a window showing the feed from the front door camera. She'd installed the cam not because she was some kind of paranoid home security freak or anything like that, but just because she was bored one Sunday afternoon and Gemma Gordon had given her the mini-camera in trade.

There were actually two men at her front porch, and a young kid. One of the men was a dark-haired guy. Older, maybe even thirty, but still kind of good looking. The other was a big, bearded biker type. The kid was about ten and looked familiar, though she couldn't place where she'd seen him before.

She knew her father probably would have advised her against opening the door for two strange men, especially when there was some kind of disease going around that supposedly turned people into psychomaniacs or whatever. But Dad had spent the night in Decatur, maybe because he had a girlfriend there now or maybe just because he didn't want Alice to have to witness another of his benders. Either way, he'd been trapped outside of town when the quarantine came down. That didn't bother Alice in the least. She preferred to be alone. Besides, the two guys weren't likely to double-team her when they had the kid with them.

Too bad. That could be fun.

She edged the volume down on the James Blunt song blaring from the computer speakers, mainly because she was embarrassed to be caught listening to something so cheesy and cornball. Then she put on her wig, popped in her glass eye and answered the door.

There was an awkward moment when she opened the door, but she wasn't going to mollify them by speaking first. She just stared out at her visitors, smacking her gum.

"Hi," the good-looking guy said, flashing a friendly smile. "Um, my name is Mark Davies. This is my friend Sam, and my son Ben. I'm, ah, friends with your English teacher, Lana Blair-Delany. She, uh, well, here. She wrote you this note. This will probably explain it better than I can."

He handed her a slip of paper filled with handwriting she recognized from the red ink notes in the margins of her essays. Alice, becoming intrigued, read:

Alice,

This is Michelle's ex-husband Mark. He's mostly harmless, but he has a USB drive containing several password-protected video files that we think *might* have something to do with the reason the town is being quarantined. We're hoping you might take a look and see if you can open them.

Thanks,

Ms. Blair-Delany

Alice looked up at the guy. "Is this for real?"

"Yeah." He handed her the flash drive. "It might be nothing. It's *probably* nothing, but we won't know until we can see what's really on there."

"Where did you get this?"

"Long story, but I used to know a guy who was a...chemist. He made a drug that caused people to act in a very similar way to how people act who have this sickness. I went over to his house this morning to ask him about it, and he acted very suspicious, to put it mildly."

"So you stole some computer files from him? Wow. That's...cool."

"Do you think you can help?"

"I'll look at it, sure. Come on in."

The two men and the kid followed her into her house.

"So, are your parents at home?" Mark asked.

Alice flopped down on the couch and looked up at him.

"My dad's drunk in Decatur, and my mom bailed on us years ago. So I am home alone with absolutely no adult supervision." She'd attempted to make that come out ironically flirtatious, but it seemed to fall flat. The guy just looked around nervously, as if trying to spot the *Dateline NBC* hidden cameras.

Alice plugged the drive into her laptop, which had more power than her dad's desktop computer, and also had a few programs she'd written herself that would be useful in unlocking whatever was on it.

"So, all the stuff on there's password protected," Mark said. "We weren't able to..."

"Yeah, I got it," Alice said. The files weren't encrypted in any kind of serious way, and her general password cracking program had unlocked them easily. She had a couple more advanced programs she could have used, but these were really basic encryptions. Which, of course, made it doubtful that the files contained anything really top secret.

"You can open them?" the big biker guy, Sam, asked.

"Yeah, easy."

"What are they?" Mark asked.

"Hold on."

She clicked on a file named "Insufflation via Rectal Glister." Her video player window was immediately filled with fleshy motion.

"Porn," she said.

"What, really?" Sam laughed.

"Yeah," said Alice. "I think you just stole this guy's porno stash."

"Great," Mark said. "Well, that was a waste of..."

"Holy crap," Alice exclaimed.

"What?"

"Your buddy's into some weird shit."

On the screen, a naked man was bent over a hospital bed, hairy ass thrust into the air. A woman doctor, her face concealed beneath a surgical mask, parted the man's buttocks with her gloved hands and inserted a tube into his butthole. The tube was connected to what looked like a big antique hookah, which the doctor primed with several pumps of a leather bellows. She was literally pumping smoke up his ass.

Sam leaned over her shoulder to watch. "What the hell is she doing to him?" he cried out, appalled.

Alice tilted her monitor away from the kid, who was craning his neck with curiosity. "Your name's Ben, right?"

Ben guiltily straightened. "Yeah."

"I've got an Xbox in my bedroom," Alice said. "Maybe your dad wants to take you in there and get you set up."

"That's a good idea," Mark said.

He led the kid away down the hall. Alice dragged the slider bar forward, morbidly curious as to where this video was headed.

"Oh my God," Sam gasped. "It's coming out of his *mouth.*"

Alice closed out that video and opened another one at random. "Arachnophilia" contained ultra-high-definition microphotography. Black widow spiders mated in extreme close-up, the image more vivid than life.

"Spider porn," Alice said, appreciatively. "That's different."

She fast-forwarded that one to the inevitable cannibalistic money shot, the female consuming the male.

"Oh my God," Sam the biker gasped. "What the fuh..."

"I hope at least the sex was worth it for the little guy," Alice said.

The video then cut to a couple of praying mantises going at it, to Sam's horrified gasps. Alice was starting to feel nauseous now, though she wasn't sure if it was from the sick-ass videos or from yesterday's chemo session. Either way, she wanted some of her medicine.

"Hey," she said to Sam. "There's a bag of gummy bears on top of the fridge in the kitchen. Would you mind grabbing it for me?"

"Sure."

While he was gone, she opened up another video, entitled "Opal's Ostentiferous Oxters." This one showed a woman, her face digitally blurred out, who had a growth in her armpit that looked like a bird's beak. It even opened and closed and made little chirping noises. Then a man leaned in and started feeding it earthworms. Sam came back in time to see the guy feed the lady's pit-beak a cricket.

"What is *that*?" he cried.

"Pretty fucked up, I would say." Alice took the bag of gummies from him and ate two.

"Can I have some?" Sam asked.

"Sure," Alice said. She gave him a small handful and watched him pop four into his mouth. That seemed like a good dose considering his body weight. "I wouldn't eat any more than that, though. They're pretty potent."

"Potent?"

"They're laced with THC," Alice said. "It's my medicine."

"What, really?"

"Yeah, the chemo makes nauseous as hell, kills my appetite," Alice said. "This is the only thing that helps."

"Shit, I'm sorry. I didn't mean to eat your medicine."

"It's cool. I get more than I need. It's more fun sharing."

There was the customary awkward silence then, the big guy finding it less uncomfortable to watch a mutant girl's armpit beak eat bugs than it was to address her illness.

"So you have, uh..." he finally mumbled.

"Cancer, yeah. Started as a rhabdomyosarcoma behind my left eye, which they had to remove. Then they found some in my ovaries, and they took those out, too. Now I've got it in so many places that they can't cut it all out. Basically, I'm fucked."

"Oh, God. I'm so sorry." He looked utterly stricken, as if he'd known her for years.

"Don't. It's cool. Look, *I'm* sorry. I didn't mean to make you uncomfortable. Here, do you want to watch some more weird-ass porn?"

"I don't know if I'm comfortable with that, either," Sam said. "I mean, you're..."

"Seventeen," Alice said. "And I've seen porn before, trust me. Actually, I like gay porn."

"Really, um..."

"The hetero stuff is all fake-looking Barbie-doll bimbos with plastic tits and no pubes. And the men are ugly. It's gross. But a gorgeous pretty-boy twink getting pounded by some super muscular top? With, like, lots of tattoos. Oof. *That's* hot."

"Yeah, uh..." The big guy was blushing now.

"You know, there are lots of guys out there with a bear fetish. You could probably do pretty well."

"So...Oh hey, Mark!"

The other guy came back into the room just in time to save him.

"Did you find anything interesting?" Mark asked.

"Depends on how you define interesting," Alice said.

She clicked open the next video, titled "A Real Bad Egg." This one started out looking like a more conventional sex vid, with a close-up shot of a vagina. It got weird soon enough, though. The vagina expelled a bright blue Easter egg. Then a red one. Then a green one. No cuts or edits as far as Alice could tell. She wondered how many eggs this chick could possibly have stuffed up inside her.

"I've gotta...take a leak," Sam said after about half a dozen eggs came out. He hurried out of the room.

"You know, you don't have to watch any more of this," Mark said.

"It's all right," Alice said. "It's fascinating, in a twisted kind of way."

She looked up and saw Mark toss a couple gummy bears into his mouth. She was about to say something, when she saw a brief, strange flicker on the video. "Did you see that?"

"See what?" Mark said, popping a few more gummies into his mouth.

"The colors were off for a second there. I think it was just a single frame." She played with the slider bar, trying to find that frame again. "By the way, how many of my bears did you just eat?"

"Oh, sorry," Mark said. "I haven't eat anything since breakfast."

"Yeah, just don't...oh there it is. Do you see that?"

The colors were seriously jacked up in the still image she'd paused, which showed a rainbow-striped egg just beginning to crown. Some of the hues were desaturated, others had the values way too high. The grayscale was flipped, so the blacks were white and vice versa, but the colors remained positive.

"Is that some kind of glitch?" Mark asked.

"The color shifting is too varied to be random or accidental," Alice said, tilting her one eye towards the image. "Someone would have had to have gone in and manipulate the colors, one by one, just on this frame."

"Why?"

"I read an article," Alice said. "You can encode a hidden image based on the color variables between two frames of video."

"Really? Can you *de*code it?"

"Maybe."

She captured the frame and copied it into another program, then toggled back one frame, where the colors were normal. She ran a color analysis comparing the two frames.

Sam came back from the bathroom then, looking a little more at ease.

"I think those gummies are kicking in already," he said.

"What?" said Mark.

Alice stayed focused on the program she was running. There *was* an encoded image, embedded in the color shift between the two frames. She opened it in a new window.

"Yeah, don't eat the gummy bears," Sam advised. "They're laced."

"Laced with *what*?"

"They each have about ten milligrams of THC," Alice said. "Sorry. I didn't see that you were eating them until it was too late."

"How many did you take?" Sam asked.

"I don't know," Mark sounded like he was freaking out a little. "A couple handfuls. Maybe nine or ten."

"Nine or ten, really?" Alice said, impressed.

"Maybe eleven or twelve. I wasn't counting."

"Wow," Alice said. "I never even heard of anybody eating that many at once."

"Oh my God."

"It's okay," Alice said. "You can't OD on pot."

"No, but you can get really fucking high."

"I'm sorry, okay? It's not like I invited you to have some of my prescription medicine. I mean, who just walks into a room and starts eating gummy bears without asking first?"

"Who *doesn't*?" Mark squeaked. "They're delicious!"

"You're going to be fine," Alice said. "In a few hours."

"Oh, Jesus. This isn't happening."

"Dude," Sam said. "It's cool. I'll stay with you through this. I've talked a lot of people through crazy trips. They used to call me Captain Chill."

"I appreciate that, Captain Chill. But with all that's going on, today is *not* the day I want to be doing this."

"Go stick your finger down your throat," Alice advised. "You probably haven't absorbed that much yet."

"That never works for me." Mark shook his head.

"Anyway, you want to see what I found in the file? It's really weird."

She tilted the monitor up so Mark could see what was on the screen. The image she'd recovered was the front page of a really old newspaper, the Bakersfield Beacon, dated November 1, 1920. It had been a negative image, as if scanned from microfilm, but Alice had inverted it back to black-on-white. The banner headline read: 'Bakersfield Nightmare at an End; Scarecrow Found Dead.'

Mark looked down at the screen and his jaw dropped open.

"Oh my God," he said. "Oh, Jesus."

"What?" Alice said.

"Oh *shit*!"

"*What*?" both Alice and Sam said in unison.

"I've seen that before, when I was just a kid. My friend Jess..."

He sat down hard on the couch, and went so pale that Alice worried for a moment that maybe he was overdosing, after all.

"Dude," Sam said. "Are you all right?"

"No. Remember the Snowman murders?"

"Well, yeah," Alice said. "That's why they call this place Bloody Bakersfield. But this article is from, like, the twenties."

"There was another killer back then. They called him the Scarecrow, but it was the same thing as the Snowman. Same methods, same kinds of victims, everything."

"It couldn't be the same guy. There's almost ninety years between."

"Not the same man," Mark said, his voice gone all far away, like he was quoting something from deep memory. "The same devil. Devil gets astride a man and rides him like a horse until somebody puts him down. Then the devil just finds himself another horse to ride. Ninety years ain't nothing to a devil."

"Okay..." Either those gummies were kicking in wicked fast, or the guy was already a little crazed.

"Uh, guys?" Sam said.

"Why is *that* newspaper article hidden in the video?" Mark asked.

"I don't know," said Alice. "But it would have taken a lot of work to set it up. Makes me wonder if there's anything like that on any of the other videos."

"We're going to have to go back through them all." Mark had his hand on his forehead, shaking his head slowly.

"Uh, *guys?*" Sam said again.

"What is it, Sam?"

"Why is there a picture of my Grandma's house?"

He was pointing at the screen. The photo accompanying the article was a grainy picture of a big old farmhouse. The caption underneath read: "The home of Hans Klausen was site of several of the Scarecrow killings."

Mark sat back up off the couch and leaned in close to the monitor. "That can't be...oh my God."

He turned to look at his friend. "Sam, your grandma lived in the Scarecrow's house."

Nate felt great as he rolled across the neighborhood. Buzzed and happy and *up*, like he'd just snorted a line of good coke. Putting Barry down had brought him no pleasure in the moment, but now that it was over, cool relief suffused his veins from his head to his groin. It was like a tremendous weight had been lifted. The best part was, there was no way it would ever be traced back to him.

In the past, whenever Nate had taken care of a business problem by means of elimination, there was always a fear that some tiny forgotten mistake might come back to haunt him. Sometimes he woke up in the middle of the night, remembering some potential snitch or deadbeat slinger or some other obstacle to his financial well-being or freedom that he'd unclogged years ago, buried in a desolate hole or burned up in an abandoned incinerator someplace. Those things came to light sometimes. Nate was always careful, but maybe there was something he'd missed. He knew all those *CSI*, *Bones* and *Cold Case* shows that Mara liked so much were ninety percent made-up TV bullshit, but hell, DNA testing had been science fiction until about twenty years ago. Who knows what they were going to come up with next?

And there were people out there he'd worked with who could tell some very interesting stories about Sheriff Nathanial Bates. Not very many, Nate kept his circle close, but any of the Barber boys, just for example, had the potential to roll over on him if the right pressure was applied. *That* thought had given him plenty of nightmares over the years.

But Barry's death had been clean. No witnesses. The gun, which couldn't be traced to anybody, had been fired by Barry's own hand. His mutilated wife beside him, this crazy sickness coursing through his veins. Nobody would look any further than that.

This epidemic, Nate was beginning to see, could provide cover for lots of loose ends he wanted to tie up. When it was all over, the town that emerged on the other end of this crisis could be a lot more conducive to his interests if he played it right. Bakersfield was like a lump of clay now, and Nate had his hands in the stuff, shaping it to suit him. While this thing was going on, he could do pretty much whatever he wanted as long as he was smart about it.

It might be the greatest opportunity he'd ever been handed.

His truck radio was tuned to WBIL, where that cold cunt, Gillian Hudson, was blathering her PR spiel. That was one string he'd love to sever, but Nate doubted that even this quarantine could provide enough cover for him to pull off a feat like that. Malovo had quietly financed almost his entire campaign last election, with the unspoken implication that if he didn't play ball with them, they would throw their considerable weight behind someone else. Money talked, as loud here as anywhere else.

Just because he was Malovo's lapdog in some respects, that didn't mean he had to listen to their alpha bitch yapping on the radio. He switched the stereo from FM radio to the.mp3 player and clicked around until he managed to queue up some Led Zep. "Immigrant Song." Hell yes. Hard-driving, kick-ass rock and roll. One of the many secrets about Nate that would sink his chances at re-election if it ever got out was that he hated the shit-kicker music that these yokels ate up like fried chicken and potato salad around here. Fuck country. Give him some good old rock and roll any fucking day. He wailed along with Robert Plant, beating his fist on the dash until he remembered the seriousness of the mission he was on now.

Deputy Morris's house was just a short drive from Pastor Barry's. Nate pulled into the drive before the song was even halfway through. He turned down the volume and composed himself for a few moments before stepping out of the truck. Bryant Morris was kind of soft-headed and soft-hearted to be an effective lawman, a real Barney Fife if there ever was one. Not to mention, he'd turn his head and let robbers clear out the bank vault if he saw a pair of legs in a short skirt across the street. Despite all that, Nate liked the guy. The amiable galoot was hard not to like. Plus, Nate had a lot of sympathy for Sally Morris. He took his promise to her seriously. He'd do everything he could to help her dad.

He pulled his Taser from his belt, just in case, and walked around the side of the house to the backyard. The rusty metal shed was over beside the flower garden, which was in glorious full bloom. Probably Sally's doing, Nate thought. Bryant didn't strike him as the green thumb type.

Nate crossed the yard, feeling a slight apprehension creep into his ebullience. He sensed something off here, though he couldn't have said what it was or how he might have known. He debated swapping the Taser for his piece, but shook off his uneasiness. Even if Bryant was out of his head with some disease that made him violent, he was still a flabby old fart two years from retirement. The day Nate couldn't handle him was the day he should hang it up himself.

He grabbed the door latch and pulled it open with a rusty-hinged screech, ready for whatever he might find inside.

There was nothing. The shed was empty. Bryant was gone.

Nate saw the doggy choke collar hanging down in the middle of the small room like a broken metal noose, secured by a chain to the ceiling. He grabbed it and looked it over in the sunlight streaming into the shed from behind him. One of the metal loops was bent way out of shape. Bryant would have had to have half-strangled himself to get it off that way.

Something else, too. The close confines of the metal shed were heavy with fumes from fresh spray paint. It was dark in the shed, but Nate reached up and pulled the chain on a bare bulb hanging next to the chain. Dim forty-watt light illuminated the walls, exposing the words written there in dripping black spray.

Nate frowned, wondering what the hell "MONKEY NEVER DIES" could possibly mean.

CHAPTER 15

Mark's mind was moving a mile a minute, simultaneously mulling a million mad theories. It felt like he was teetering on the verge of understanding, but comprehension was just out of his grasp. Each of the pictures Alice had recovered from the videos on the flash drive was a revelatory piece of the puzzle Mark had been putting together since yesterday. The new images swirled around in the stew bubbling in his head, along with pictures from James's sketchbook and cryptic clues Shana had dropped and his own jangled memories of the Monkey. Mark felt like he could still the frenzied churning of his brain and put all these pieces in order if only he wasn't so goddamn high.

THC had reasserted itself in his brain cells like a rowdy old friend who'd returned to town after years away, and who really wanted to party. This state of mind had once been more comfortable to him than straight, unaffected reality, but was now strange and overwhelming. He'd lost his hard-earned tolerance during his long months of abstinence, and these wondrous gummy bears were potent as hell. Their effects reminded Mark of the first time he ever got stoned, ditching school with Missy while his mom was at work, and how they got absolutely *wrecked* together. Before he got lost within the erotic promise of that particular memory chamber, his mind was off again, returning to wild speculations about the pictures on the flash drive. His brain was a spinning carnival ride, and the carny at the controls was a sadistic fucker.

There was something wrong with his eyes, too. It was like he'd been fitted with goggles coated with a cascading oily film that blurred some objects and rendered others in excruciating magnified detail, the ratio shifting and changing every time he moved his head or blinked.

"Are you all right?" Alice asked. She was driving because she was, by a wide margin, less fucked up than either Mark or Sam.

He struggled to answer her question. English now seemed like a language he'd studied extensively but had never actually spoken. "I'm..." Mark was struck by the homophonic resonance of the words "I" and "eye." That made sense, considering that the subjective ocular camera was the focus of the first person point of view. "...all...RIGHT!"

"Dude, you're high as fuck," Sam said from the back seat.

"No!" Mark protested. "I am...way higher than that. I blew past 'high as fuck' about five minutes ago."

Sam fell back in his seat, laughing. "Oh, man. Gummy bears. Who knew?"

"This isn't funny," Mark insisted.

"Yeah, it is," Alice laughed.

"It is kind of funny, Dad," Ben put in.

Mark looked up. Ben smiled at him in the rearview mirror. It was like the mirror trick at Shana's house all over again. Then he'd seen his mother in his own reflection, and now when Mark looked his son, he saw himself as a boy. During that terrible year of the Snowman and the Monkey and his parent's divorce, Mark had been the exact age Ben was right now. That was the year that had divided Mark's life between a time of innocence and a time of terrible knowing. He hoped and he *prayed* that this year would not provide his son with the same clean demarcation.

Mark's emotions were magnified and distorted, just as his thoughts and his sensory perceptions were. Looking at Ben, he felt so many things at once. A crushing impotence at his inability to shield his son from the terrible things in the world, a rush of pure love, dreadful fear, pride, regret, warmth and an embarrassment that his son should see him in such a state.

"Listen," Mark said. Maybe by speaking out loud, he could get back on track. "We just found out that..."

"What did we find out again?" Sam asked.

"Yeah, I didn't quite get what you were saying before," Alice said.

"We found out," Mark said, "the sickness started at Sam's Scarecrow's house." He suspected this hissing sentence used excessive sibilance, so he strived to rephrase. "The disease originated with..." How did it go again?

Getting a hold on this theory was like trying pick up not-quite-set lime Jello with his bare hands.

Mmm, he thought. *Lime Jello.*

"Oh, man. How am I going to pull this off? Maybe if we don't say anything and just act like normal straight people, they won't notice how stoned we are."

"Seriously?" Alice said. "They're going to notice. You should just be up front about it. It wasn't your fault."

"Yeah, I'm sure she'll buy that." Mark looked out the window. "Shit. We're here. Please, try to be cool, everybody."

The anxious, giggling company emerged in a huddle from the car and made their way up the drive, shushing one another's laughter as they stumbled to the door. Mark attempted to compose himself before he rang the bell. He stood up straight, striving to present as sober a façade as possible.

Lana opened the door and Mark was struck, as never before, by her radiance. She was angelically beautiful, her dark skin luminous with internal golden light. Was that an aura? Was he seeing her aura? Then it struck him that her glow was post-coital.

"Hi," she smiled out at them.

Coital? Mark thought. Is that really a word?

"Why are you looking at me at like that?" she asked.

"Hello, Lana," Mark said, attempting a sane man's normal tone of voice. It sounded in his head like a record player winding down. He tried to nod at her, but it felt as if his head was submerged in a tub of clear syrup. "Is Missy home?"

"She's in the kitchen, cooking." Lana did give him a strange look, but then she smiled at the guests he'd brought with him. "Come on in, guys."

Lana stepped back to allow the four of them to enter the house.

"Hola, Ms. B-D," Alice said.

"Hi, Alice. How are you?"

"Real good."

"And you must be Sam Hansard," Lana smiled.

"Yes, ma'am. It's good to meet you, Miss Beady."

"Lana, please."

Missy emerged from the kitchen, wiping her hands on a dish towel, carrying with her the warm red scent of her lasagna. The tomatoes and oregano and garlic and memories of family meals when he still had a family made Mark's mouth and his eyes water, but the aroma was nothing to how Missy looked. If Lana had appeared radiant to his eyes, his ex-wife blazed with brilliant light. Like a star that had fallen to earth.

"Wow," he said helplessly at the sight of her, grinning like a mad fool.

Missy frowned at the look he was giving her. "What?"

"Nothing, nothing."

"Were you guys able to open the files?"

"Oh, yeah," Mark said. "And Sam's Grandma's Scarecrow started the sickness. I mean, originated the disease."

She squinted at him. "Are you *stoned*?"

"Ah..."

"It's not his fault, ma'am," Alice said. "I have a prescription for medical marijuana because I'm on chemo. I get it in gummy bear form. Mark accidentally ate...a lot of them."

"Accidentally." Missy put the same inflection upon that word that she would lend to the phrase "utter horseshit."

"Yeah," Alice insisted. "The bag was just laying out. He ate some before I could warn him. If anything, it's my fault."

But Missy's piercing blame was still focused with laser intensity upon Mark. "Who just walks into a room and starts eating gummy bears without asking?"

"Why do people keep saying that?" Mark said. "Who *wouldn't* eat from an open bag of gummy bears? They're like congealed chunks of rainbow!"

"I swear to God, if Ben ate even one of those, I'll kick your ass right here."

"I didn't eat any, Mom. I promise." Ben said.

Missy went to her son, angling his head up into the light so she could examine his pupils.

"Dad was being responsible," Ben insisted. "He even sent me out of the room before they started the pornography."

"The *what*?"

"Okay, okay," Mark said. "Calm down. Just give me a second, let me get my head together, and I'll explain everything."

Well aware that everyone in the room was staring at him, Mark closed his eyes and tried to find his center. Surprisingly, the slow-dripping honey coating his synapses now granted him a new clarity and focus. He opened his eyes and began to speak.

"The files you downloaded from Cassandra's computer were short pornographic videos. Very bizarre, very perverse. I'm sure this was meant to throw people off. If anyone was able to unlock the passwords—which Alice did in about four seconds, by the way, this girl is smart as hell—they'd see that it was just the weirdest porn on earth and leave it at that. And I mean, this stuff was crazy. Dogs getting it on with chimpanzees, some guy getting smoke blown up his..."

"Enough, I get the idea," Missy said, holding her hands over Ben's ears.

"Sorry. The porn content was just a diversion, because there were encrypted pictures, embedded in the videos. Something to do with the colors being...um, you can probably explain this part better than I can, Alice."

"Right," she said. Jen was still lying on the couch, completely senseless. Alice sat down on the edge of a couch cushion near her legs and opened her laptop up on the table. "Every one of the videos we looked at had at least one frame where the colors were distorted. Some of them had several. The color distortion was a code. Comparing the distorted frame to the unaltered one just before it gave me the key to unlock embedded image files. I'm sure there are more on there, but I put the ones that we already decoded into a slideshow."

She clicked open the first one, the newspaper article. Michelle and Lana leaned in close to look.

"Remember that?" Mark asked. "Jess found that same page in the newspaper archives."

"Oh my God," Missy said, her hand going to her mouth. "The Scarecrow."

"Recognize the house?"

"Is that..." Missy looked up at Sam. "Is that your grandma's house?"

"Yeah." Sam nodded grimly. "That explains why it's so haunted, right? Some guy killed a bunch of kids there. I guess now at least I know I'm not crazy."

"Wait a minute," Lana said, scanning through the article. "There was *another* serial killer in Bakersfield? Even before the Snowman? What is wrong with this town?"

"That's a whole..." Mark said. "I'll get to that in a minute. Just let me stay focused here for a minute. Can you show the next slide, Alice?"

Alice tapped her screen. The next image was a very old-looking scanned blueprint. Alice zoomed in close on the picture.

"I think this is a site plan for the house," Mark said. "This area highlighted here looks like a boarded-over well. Do you remember seeing anything like that in the basement, Sam?"

"You kidding? I never went into the basement. That place was freaky enough upstairs."

"Anyway, Shana called Neiro the 'primary distillation.' What if it was derived from something Shana extracted from the water in the well?"

"I don't know, Mark," Missy said. "That's kind of sketchy."

"Just let me show you a couple more of these pictures."

"Um, excuse me?" Sam said. "I don't mean to interrupt, but I haven't eaten anything all day and whatever you're cooking in the kitchen smells like heaven on earth. Do you think we could eat while we're doing this?"

"I didn't expect for this to turn into a party," Michelle said, "There's not enough lasagna for everyone. I think I have some ice cream in the freezer, though, if you want to..."

"Ice cream, really?" Sam said. "Ice cream?"

"Yes, ice cream."

"Do you mind if I..."

"Please, go ahead."

"Anyway," Mark said as Sam hurried off into the kitchen, "most of the rest of the pages we found are chemical equations. That stuff that goes right over my head, but I found these doodles and sketches in the margins."

Alice advanced to the next slide.

"Look at this," Mark said, leaning over to tap the screen. "Can you make that bigger?"

Alice zoomed in on a black ink drawing of a raven with a bright red nimbus around its head. Mark worked the scroll bar, showing other drawings on the same page. A monstrous cyclops with one red eye. A bare-breasted angel with a glowing red heart.

"See?" Mark pointed at the angel. "All these archetypal figures share a common element. The red heart, or eye, or jewel. Just like the vampire's glowing heart in James's drawing. I think they're what Shana meant when she was talking about 'intruding spirits.' Figures external to the dreamer's consciousness. She said that they're all the same being, but each dreamer perceives it differently. Everyone puts their own mask on the intruder."

"You're losing me, Mark." Missy said.

"Please, Missy. Just let me.... I'm so close to figuring this out. Just let me finish, okay?"

Sam came back in the room, spooning ice cream straight from the carton. "Oh my God, guys," he said. "You've gotta try this. I mean, you get used to ice cream with all kinds of flavors and swirls and chunks of cookie dough and whatnot, and you forget just how amazing plain vanilla is. Sweet and creamy and..." He slid a spoonful into his mouth and made a near-orgasmic moan of pleasure.

Mark shut out this distraction by force of will. "Okay, so Shaner, Shana, whatever, created this drug that puts you into a dream state, where you're more receptive to seeing these things that are maybe all around us all the time. This sleepwalking sickness has some of the same effects that the drug does, only it's more potent. If Shana derived Neiro from something he extracted from that well, maybe Sam's grandma got exposed to the actual source. The drug gives you a mild version of it, but Sam's grandma got it full blast. Then James caught it from her somehow, and he spread it out to other people in town. Including Jen here."

"Hey, try this," Sam said to Alice, sliding a spoonful of ice cream into her mouth. She had been looking up at Mark, listening to his impromptu spiel, but her one eye went wide when the cream melted on her tongue.

"Holy shit," she said. "You're right. God, you think of vanilla as bland, boring, hetero missionary style, but the flavor's really...subtle and complex. It's like..."

She stopped when she saw how Mark was looking at her.

"Can you guys cool it with the ice cream for just a minute?"

"I'm listening," Alice said.

"Yeah, dude. Keep going," said Sam. "You're making sense to me."

"All right, check this out." Mark tried to regain his thin strand of thought. "What if our minds have natural defenses against demonic possession and things like that? Like we have a *psychic* immune system. Maybe this sickness attacks that, just like AIDS attacks our physical immune system. So people who get this sickness don't have any resistance to spiritual..."

Sam reached over and slid the spoon into Mark's mouth, cutting him off.

"Damn it, Sam. What the...Oh my God." Mark's taste buds were overwhelmed with white, creamy sweetness. Mark was rocked to his heels. "That's fucking amazing," he said around the mouthful of frozen sensual pleasure. It reminded him of breast milk on some deep associative level.

"Right?" Sam said. "Told you."

"Give me that goddamn ice cream," Lana said. "You're done."

Sam regretfully surrendered the carton. Mark had to wait until the sweet cream had completely dripped down his throat before he could continue.

"Look," Mark said. "There are...forces in Bakersfield, just under the surface. The Scarecrow and the Snowman were two men, almost a century apart, but they were possessed by the same spirit. It's reborn in cycles. The only way to counteract it is with the Black Monkey."

"Chelle's told me that story," Lana said. "About how you guys buried a monkey doll out in the woods when you were kids. But you're saying you actually called up a good spirit to fight off the evil spirit?"

"That's not what really happened," Missy half-whispered.

"No," Mark concurred. "It's more like we fought evil with something slightly less evil, or a different kind of evil. The important thing is that the two forces stay balanced. Every so often, they become *un*balanced and that's when someone has to call up the Monkey. Our friend Jess did it when we were kids, and it destroyed him. He sacrificed himself so nobody else had to die."

Missy made a loud scoffing noise, but Mark pressed on: "The kids in this town are supposed to bury a monkey, just a regular grey sock monkey, out in the cornfield every Halloween. That's what keeps things balanced. Do they still do that anymore, Alice?"

"You're asking me?" Alice said.

"Yeah."

"I've never heard of that," she said. "But then, I never get invited to the cool kid parties."

"See?" Mark said. "I don't think anybody's done it since Malovo built their golf course on top of that field. I'm afraid that might have thrown everything out of whack. It might have caused the cycle to come around again, way ahead of schedule."

There was silence in the room for a few seconds, though Mark didn't know if it was from disbelief, or if everyone was just digesting what he'd said.

"Mark," Missy finally said. "I appreciate that you're trying to figure this out, and I'll admit you found some very strange things on that flash drive. But this all reminds me of something you said to me once, back when I was trying to get you to stop smoking pot. You said you needed it for your writing. You remember what you told me then?"

"I said it helped me make connections."

"No, your exact words were: 'connections that aren't necessarily really there.' I can see how intuitive leaps like that can help you plot out vampire novels, but this is real life we're talking about. You've taken a few solid facts and spun them into this wild theory because your brain's been rewired by spiked gummy bears."

"I don't think you're getting it."

"No, I got it. The virus that's going around erodes people's resistance to demonic possession, which is somehow accelerating a centuries-old cycle of unbalanced spiritual forces. That's your theory in a nutshell, right?"

"Yeah."

"Do you know how fucking crazy that sounds?"

"Well, sure. When you say it."

"And I think your memory's fucked up, too. Jess did bury a monkey doll in the ground, but that's not what killed him. The Snowman killed Jess. Then he went home and he killed himself and that's what ended it. Not the stupid Black Monkey."

"Is that really how you remember it?" Mark said.

"Of course," Missy said. "That's how it *happened*."

"We never talked about it, did we?" Mark said. "Not afterwards. It's strange. It's like I locked the memory in a room and then never opened the door. I think the forgetting is built into the thing. But now...I'm starting to remember again."

"You have a very creative imagination, Mark. It's almost a curse with you. But recovered memories are almost always fabrications. That shit got debunked in the eighties."

"I don't think I'm imagining this. Look, maybe you should eat one of the..."

"Oh, I should eat one of the magic gummies? I eat a blue one and everything goes back to normal, or I eat a red one and see how deep the monkey hole goes? See, I can do pop culture references, too."

"Monkey hole," Sam chuckled.

"It doesn't matter, Mark. It doesn't change anything. Your crackpot theory doesn't help us figure out what to do about the fact that my sister's infected with this thing, and she'll probably infect one or all of us, if that hasn't happened already."

Alice, sitting on the couch near Jen's legs, abruptly stood and walked to the other side of the room.

"It doesn't change the fact that we're trapped in this town," Michelle went on. "Or that they're probably not going to let us leave until this thing has burned itself out. Or that a lot of people out there in town are acting out crazy dreams that might end up getting them hurt or even killed. What do you propose we do this new information you've uncovered? Do you think we should go to Sheriff Bates with your theory, so he knows what he's up against?"

"Ah, no. That would be a bad idea."

"Okay, then. Let's just focus on reality and try to figure out what the hell we need to do."

"Which is...what?"

"I don't know." Missy sighed and looked away. She looked very tired all of the sudden.

"We should stick together and wait this out," Lana said decisively. "There's safety in numbers. Why don't you stay with us tonight, Mark? That way you can be close to Ben and help us deal with Jen when she wakes up."

"That's a great idea, Lana," Mark said. "Thanks."

Missy was looking up at Lana, obviously grateful that she was taking charge. That was something else he had never been able to give to his wife. He wasn't exactly a take-charge kind of guy.

"You're welcome to stay too, Sam," Lana said. "You and Mark can sleep in the guest room. Is that okay with you?"

"Can I have some more ice cream later?"

"Whatever. And Alice, we can get you home or you can stay here with us. Whatever you want to do."

"My dad's out of town and I'm by myself over there. Is it okay if I stay with you guys?"

"We would be happy to have you," Lana said. "The more people, the better."

"She can sleep in my room," Ben volunteered. "I can just put my sleeping bag on the floor out here."

"Thank you, Ben," Lana said. "That's very generous of you."

"Yeah, thanks." Alice nodded. "But if I'm going to do that, I need to go back by my house and grab my medicine."

"More gummy bears?"

"Well, yeah. But it's not like I take them *just* for fun. I do need them, unless you want me to spend the whole night with my head in your toilet. And I'm on about ten other meds, too."

"Okay," Lana said. "I'll drive you over there."

"Can I come with you guys?" Ben asked. He was looking up at Lana with obvious respect. Mark felt a jab of realization that she was not only a better spouse than he had ever been, but probably a better parent as well.

"Yeah, Ben. That's fine." Lana grabbed her car keys from the hook by the front door. "Let's go."

Mark watched them walk out the door.

Alice leaned her head against the passenger side window. The glass, chilled by the air conditioning, felt nice and cool against her brow. The vibrations of the vehicle were soothing, too. She closed her eye until the nausea subsided a bit. The gummies were still fighting the good fight against her eternal queasiness, but she felt like she should take one or two more. Or maybe a whole handful, so she could get on the same wavelength as Mark. That guy was a trip.

If this quarantine lasted more than a couple of days, though, she'd run out of medicine. Not just the gummies, either. If she ran out of Oxy, she'd really be screwed. Pain was a constant companion. Right now it was standing back in the shadows, but when the magical opioids were expended, the pain would step into the spotlight to sing a show-stopping solo. And what if the quarantine lasted a week or more, and she couldn't go to the hospital in Springfield to take the poison that kept the cancer at bay? She knew she was fighting a losing battle, knew the tide would eventually overtake her, but the chemo at least bought her some time. How long would she last without it? How long would she want to, if she didn't have pain medication?

Alice made a calm, rational decision. If it came to that, she'd just end it herself. Find a gun somewhere, or pull the old carbon monoxide trick with a car in an enclosed garage. Razor blades in the bathtub if she couldn't get access to a gun or a car. There were lots of ways to do it. She'd plotted her suicide many times before, kept the thought always in the back of her mind. It was comforting, in a way. Death wouldn't make her its bitch. She could check out on her own schedule, any time she liked.

She was feeling good right now, though. Things were actually exciting for a change. Yesterday, she'd been looking at the prospect of yet another long weekend at home with her drunk-ass dad, playing video games to distract herself from her misery and the always looming specter. But now, Dad was gone and her usually boring town had been overtaken by some mystery illness and she'd actually fallen in with some interesting people. Ms. Blair-Delany was easily her favorite teacher at school, even if English was far from her favorite subject. (Being one half of an interracial lesbian couple made Lana exponentially cooler in Alice's estimation.) Then there was this Mark guy, with his wild eyes and crazy theories. Alice didn't know if she believed any of his talk about demonic spirits and whatever, but he was pretty entertaining stoned.

Best of all, she felt like she *belonged*. Most people, her dad included, treated her like some kind of sad freak. But with these guys, she was valued. Unlocking secret messages hidden in bizarre pornos was the kind of shit she was born to do.

Alice suspected that she'd been depressed before, but had simply been too medicated to notice. It felt like she'd been asleep, up until Mark had knocked on her door with the note from her teacher and the flash drive from the shady transgendered chemist. Now she was awake, in a strange, exciting new world. All it had taken to snap her out of her personal funk was a major civic health crisis.

"What are you doing, Ben?" Lana asked, glancing at her stepson in the rear-view.

Alice turned to look. The kid was taking pictures out the window with a little digital camera, though the view out the window wasn't very photogenic. Lana was taking the back way across town, past the lumber yard, and there was nobody even out on the street.

"Just taking some pictures," he said. He held the camera up for Alice. "This is my Ecto-Spectrum camera."

"What's that?" Alice asked.

"It registers a wider band of frequencies," he said, confident in his knowledge. "It can sometimes detect paranormal activity. Ghosts and things. If my dad's right about the spiritual forces in this town, maybe I can get a good picture."

"Yeah, what was that all about?" Alice asked Lana.

Lana shrugged. "Mark and Michelle were kids here when those Snowman, Holiday Killer murders happened. They lost a couple of their very close friends. One of them was a boy named Jess. He was a son of the only African-American family in town."

"Huh," Alice said. "I never really thought of this before, but are you the only black person living in Bakersfield right now?"

"Yeah," Lana gave a strange, sideways smile. "It's just me."

"Is that like really weird for you?" Alice said.

"You have no idea." Lana shook her head. "Anyway, Jess's sister was the first victim of the Snowman. Jess thought that the monkey funeral thing that Mark was talking about was a ritual that could summon a spirit to stop the killer. He convinced Mark and Michelle to help him make this thing and bury it."

"So what really happened?" Alice asked.

"Depends on who you ask. Chelle says Jess was the last victim of the killer, who committed suicide right after. But Mark...you heard what he said."

"What do you think?"

Lana hesitated a moment before answering. "I think...the experience was so traumatic that it's warped both their memories. Chelle doesn't like to talk about it, and when she does, she tells it a little differently every time."

"There's some interesting distortion around that police car," Ben said.

"Do you think there's any truth to what Mark said?" Alice asked.

Lana tilted her head for a second, as if considering, but then she frowned. "No. I don't believe in any of that..."

Ben dropped his camera. "It's coming at us really...Lana, look out!"

The police car rammed them on the rear driver's side. Alice had almost no peripheral vision on her left side. She barely registered the sudden oncoming movement before the jarring crash and metallic screech and the explosive force of the airbag deploying in her face.

She must have blacked out for a second, because there were a few moments of confusion. She was blind for a second, except for a bright red smear on a pale canvas just before her. It took her a second, but she realized it was her own blood. It had exploded from her nose and stained the fabric of the airbag, which was now slowly deflating.

For a moment, she was stunned, not sure what was happening. She heard the rear passenger door being wrenched open, and Ben crying out. She turned to look, but there was blood in her eye. She could just make out a red shadow of a man reaching into the back seat and the frantic motion of Ben struggling. He cried out "No, no!"

Alice couldn't move. Her seatbelt had locked, strapping her tight to the seat. She fumbled for the release, but in her confusion she couldn't find it.

"Got ya, fuckin' Monkey," Alice heard the man in the back seat snarl.

Ben was screaming for help. The man grabbed him.

Alice found the buckle, but either the button didn't work or she didn't have the strength in her hand to press it. She tried to call out, but the breath had been knocked from her chest.

The man pulled Ben, frantically kicking and fighting, out of the back seat.

The seatbelt finally released, freeing Alice, but the man was gone and so was Ben. Alice wiped blood from her eye and twisted in her seat. The tall, burly man tossed the boy into the back seat of the police cruiser. Alice saw the guy lean over Ben and wrap something around him. He was bundling him in a blanket, or something. She couldn't see straight enough to be sure. The blood was still dripping into her eye and everything was woozy and blurry even without that. Facing backwards like this was too disorienting. She turned and looked over at Lana.

Alice's teacher was lying back in her seat, eyes closed. Unconscious, bleeding from somewhere on her head.

"Ms. B-D?" Alice cried, shaking her. "Ms. B-D, wake up!"

The police car slammed into reverse, extricating itself from the collision with shrieking metal and squealing tires and the animal roar of the engine. The cruiser lurched forward, and then sped away up the road.

"Lana!" Alice screamed, tears flushing the blood from her eye. "Wake up, please! Lana! He took Ben! That man took Ben!"

CHAPTER 16

CALVIN AND JESSE Barber were getting the hang of this thing. It wasn't so hard really. A twitchy-eyed motherfucker like rich-boy Bobby Trott was an easy call to make. He was spouting crazy-ass shit and acting like he had bugs in his shorts, so they ran him over to the ethanol plant, where Malovo docs in green scrubs and face masks took charge of him. A dozen such cases were already lying sedated on cots set up in the cafeteria when they dropped Bobby off. It seemed like a real organized operation.

Then there were your standard, run-of-the-mill fuck-ups, like Polly Underwood. A scrawny tweaker bitch with unfortunate, but apt, initials, they'd found her sucking pipe in the alley behind Casey's General Store. She'd bitched and moaned when they busted her dumb ass, protesting that she couldn't get high at home because her mother was acting crazy. According to Polly, her mama had broken all the mirrors in their house and was sticking the shards into her skin, crawling around the house naked and bleeding. Or something like that. Calvin couldn't quite track the whole tweaked-out rant.

Anyway, public intoxication with an illicit substance was exactly the kind of lawbreaking that the sheriff had talked about. Polly had tried to bargain her way out of getting arrested. Said she'd do *anything*. Except Polly Underwood trying to get flirtatious was just gross and kind of sad. There weren't a lot of places in town where Calvin *wouldn't* stick it, but Polly's festering meth mouth was definitely one of them. Plus, she smelled like she hadn't bathed in a week. Jesse, younger and hornier than Calvin, wanted to at least consider her offer, but Cal talked him out of it. He told his brother he'd probably be able to line them up some *quality* tail after curfew.

So instead, they'd confiscated Polly's shit and tossed her in the back of Chucky's Power Wagon. So she wouldn't get any cute ideas about jumping out and trying to escape, they'd driven back to the Church of the Shepherd fast as hell, lights and sirens blaring. It was kind of cool. Calvin had never really considered being a cop before, but giving Polly her rough ride across town, he could see the appeal. Maybe when this was over, he'd talk to the sheriff and see about getting hired on as a deputy for real.

They dropped her off and helped Billy and Chucky wrangled her into one of the animal cages up there. They were already holding old John Perry. Barber brother Max and his partner, a Sheep Shacker named Dennis Budd, had busted Perry for discharging a firearm on the town square. The guy said he was shooting rats, but there weren't any rats that anyone else could see. He might have been a twitchy eyeball case, but it was hard to tell with him. He'd always been a little fucked in the head.

After that, Calvin and Jesse hit the streets again. Before resuming their hunt for crazies and criminals, though, they pulled off onto a neighborhood side road to smoke up some of the crystal they'd confiscated from Polly. It'd give them a good edge. Make them better cops.

Cal took a long hit from the pipe, inhaling the nearly odorless smoke. It was pretty pure stuff, the blue Mexican glass Bates had them running. He knew the blue was just a dye job, to sell the stuff to shitheads who only knew meth from TV, but he couldn't deny that it looked cool and burned clean.

"Oh, shit," Jesse said from the driver's seat. "Ain't that the sheriff's wife?"

Cal waved the smoke from his eyes and looked out the window. There was a lady walking up the sidewalk on the opposite side of the street, dressed in some kind of silky-looking nightgown, carrying what looked like a feather duster. He got a good look at her face when she walked past. It was definitely Mara Bates.

"Yeah, that's her," Cal said. "What the hell's she doing out here?"

"I don't know," Jesse said. "But, damn. Don't you think she's kinda, I mean for a lady her age, kinda hot?"

"I guess so," Calvin allowed. He passed the pipe back to Jesse. "In a rich bitch, cougary kind of way."

"Cougar," Jesse seized on the word, taking a deep hit off the pipe. "That's it. A *classy* cougar. A MILF."

"More like a GILF," Cal laughed. "She's gotta be Mom's age."

"Yeah. Don't that make you wonder?"

"Wonder what?"

"Why is Nate hittin' Mom when he's got *that* at home?"

"Hey, don't be dissin' Mom."

"I ain't. I love Ma, you know that. I'm just sayin'. In terms of...looks."

Calvin had to concede that point. He loved his Mama, too, but she wasn't going to win any pageants anytime soon. "Hey, start the truck. Roll up behind Mrs. Sheriff there, but be cool about it. I want to see where she's going."

Jesse passed the pipe back and slipped the truck into drive. They rolled slowly forward. "It's like when you were going out with Kirstin and you had that side thing going on with Karen Stanton, even though Kirstin was *way* hotter."

"Yeah, well. Kirstin's cute as hell, but sometimes nasty girls will do stuff that the pretty ones won't."

"What kind of stuff?"

"I don't want to get too damn specific, but sex stuff."

"What, like swallowing? Or in the butt?"

"Damn, Jesse. What's your point?"

Jesse looked like he'd just come to a horrible realization. "So you think Nate hooks up with Ma because she does stuff he can't get at home?"

"Hell, I don't want to think about...hold up. Where's she going?"

Mara was opening the gate on a tall wooden fence and slipping into somebody's backyard. They rolled up close enough so Calvin could read the name on the mailbox. It dawned on him whose house it was.

"Holy shit," Calvin said. "I'm calling the sheriff."

"He freaked out last time we called," Jesse said. "Told us not to do it again. He was kind of a dick about it, actually."

"Yeah, well, he's going to want to hear about this."

"Sweet God in Heaven, this is the best lasagna I've ever had in my *life*," Sam said. He shoveled another forkful into his mouth and closed his eyes to savor the taste. "Mmm."

"Glad you like it," Michelle said. She glanced up at the clock. They'd only been gone a little more than fifteen minutes. There was no reason for her to be worried, not yet, but she was. She'd grabbed her phone to call Lana twice already, out of habit, before remembering that there was no service.

"Do you make your own sauce?" Sam asked, shaking his head in utter disbelief. "There's no way this came from a jar."

"I grew the tomatoes in my garden," Michelle said.

"Fresh tomatoes!" Sam exclaimed.

"The herbs are fresh, too. Oregano, rosemary, thyme."

"You're kidding me. That's incredible."

Michelle chewed a fingernail, a habit she thought she'd broken herself of, and did some calculations in her head. Say ten minutes to get across town, maybe another ten or so to gather Alice's medications and whatever else she needed to stay the night, then ten more minutes to get back home. There was no reason to get nervous until they'd been gone for more than half an hour. So why couldn't she shake the feeling that something was terribly wrong?

"What kind of cheese is this?" Sam asked.

Being stuck here at home with Cheech and fucking Chong was doing nothing to soothe her nerves, either. Sam was off in munchy nirvana and she kept catching Mark staring at her with stony fascination.

"What?" she finally said to him.

"I get it," he said.

"Get what?" she said wearily.

"You and Lana. I understand it now. I didn't before but, really, it's so obvious."

"Oh, this should be good."

"I'm serious. She brings out the best in you. That's why you two are so good together. You're a better person when you're with her. You're kinder, more empathetic. More generous and patient. I think, and please don't get offended by this, but I think in some ways, I brought out the *worst* in you. In fact, we probably brought out the worst in each other. I brought out your anger and possessiveness. You brought out my insecurity and selfishness. So I think that you're not only in love with Lana, you're in love with the version of yourself that you become when you're with her." He leaned his head back and laughed. "It makes so much *sense* now."

Michelle looked at him sideways, distracted for just a moment from her anxiety. Mark had always tended to get hyper-verbal when he was high, but usually it just came out as a mish-mash of free-associated fantasy. Now he was spewing something close to emotional honesty. Like he was speaking in insightful tongues.

"You needed pot-laced gummy bears to come to this epiphany?"

"Hey, don't knock any path that leads to enlightenment."

She was still trying to figure out what to say in response to that when the front door burst open. Lana and Alice staggered in together, holding on to each other for support. Both had blood on their clothes.

Michelle stood up, all her anxieties suddenly made real. "Where's Ben?"

"He took him!" Alice sobbed.

"What?" Mark leapt to his feet, too. "What happened?"

"A guy in a cop car," Alice said. "One of the deputies, I think. He rammed our car. He took Ben!"

Michelle went to Lana. There was a swelling cut on one temple, the obvious source of the blood all over her shoulder. "Are you all right?"

"I'm fine," Lana snarled. "Don't worry about me. Just Ben."

"I'm so sorry." Alice seemed utterly distraught. "Ms. B-D got knocked out. I had to drive. I didn't know if I should follow them, but I couldn't see where he went so I just came back here. I'm so sorry."

"It's not your fault, Alice." It felt like Michelle's heart had turned to stone and was sinking into her gut. Panic flooded her head like a rising swarm of locusts blotting out the sun. "You did the right thing."

"What the fuck do we do?" Mark punched himself in the side of the head. "Why am I so fucking high?"

"I'm sorry for that, too," Alice cried.

"Don't," Michelle said. "Just stop that. Sit down. Tell me everything you remember. Everything. Who was this deputy?"

"I don't know his name. I recognized him, though. I see him in town a lot."

"I didn't get a look at him," Lana said, gingerly touching the side of her head. "But Bryant Morris is the only deputy who lives here in town."

"I know Bryant Morris," Sam said. He set his lasagna plate down and wiped saucy chunks from his beard. "He's a good guy. He would never..."

"He might if he was sleepwalking," Michelle said.

"Oh, yeah." Sam went white. "Oh *shit*."

"I gotta come down," Mark cried in anguish, pacing the room. "I gotta think straight."

"Alice," Michelle pressed. "Where did they go?"

"I don't know." The girl was crying. "I think I got knocked out for a second, too. Everything's all jumbled. They just drove off."

"Which direction?"

Alice closed her eyes. The lid covering her left, glass, eye did not close completely, which gave her an off-kilter look for a moment. "North, I think. On Archer Road."

"Okay, do you remember anything else? Anything at all."

She opened her eyes. Her real one locked on Michelle. The glass eye trailed lazily behind. "Gotcha, fuckin' Monkey."

"What?" Michelle said.

Mark came over. "What did you say?"

"Right before he grabbed Ben, the guy said 'Got you, you fuckin' little Monkey.' Or something like that."

"Are you sure?" Mark said. "He called Ben a monkey?"

"Yeah. It reminded me of the stuff you were talking about before."

"Jesus."

"What are we going to do? We can't even call the police." Michelle sat down hard on the couch, right on her sleeping sister's legs. Jen stirred a little, but did not wake. The enormity of what had happened was still rising inside her. Ben was gone. This knowledge, and her helplessness in the face of it, seemed as if it might swallow her whole.

"We're going to get our son back," Mark said with a strange sudden confidence.

"How?" The word emerged from Michelle's throat like a cry of pain. She couldn't see and it took her a moment to realize that this was because her eyes were flooded with tears.

"Because you know where he is."

"What?" Michelle felt cold all over. "I don't..."

"You do. Remember my pathetic book tour? Portland ScareCon? Slutty fan girl?"

"Why would you bring that up now?"

"Because I called you that night and you *knew*. Before I said one word to you, you said 'Did you have fun fucking Juliette Lewis?'"

"Whoa," Sam said. "You had sex with Juliette Lewis?"

"No. I hooked up with a girl wearing that same skimpy chain-mail dress she wore in *Strange Days*."

"That is *hot*." Sam nodded, impressed.

"And she knew." Mark turned back to Michelle. "You *knew*."

"So what, Mark?"

"And you told me that when you and Lana were first dating, you dreamed that her brother lost his leg in Afghanistan. Six days before it actually happened."

"That's true," Lana said, looking at Michelle now with some of the same intensity Mark was. "You did."

"You've been able to do that since we were kids. You *know* things," Mark insisted. "So use that. Where's Ben?"

"That stuff just happens," Michelle said. "I can't make it happen."

"Have you ever tried?"

"Of course I've tried. I tried to guess lottery numbers when we were broke in Denver. It didn't do shit."

"Try now."

"I can't." A fresh wave of panic rolled over her. Ben's voice. His scent. He was gone. Her baby was in danger.

"Fuckin' try," Mark insisted. "For Ben, Missy. For Ben. Please try."

Michelle closed her eyes. She let her body go limp. Lana came to her and put her hand on the back of Michelle's neck. The warm comforting touch penetrated through layers of terror and fresh grief. Michelle reached back and put her hand on top of her wife's. Then she saw something. A color.

"Green," she said.

There was a strange buzzing in her head and verdant light behind her closed lids. She felt like she might pass out, just collapse forward onto the coffee table, but Lana was holding her shoulders now, supporting her. Michelle let herself slip. Green wasn't quite the right word.

"Greens," she amended.

"Greens?" Sam said. "Like spinach?"

"Shhh," Michelle hissed. She closed her eyes tighter. Michelle's breath became rapid, shallow huffs. Green grass laid flawless over rolling terrain, beneath a blazing blue sky streaked with distant white clouds and contrails. The images were coming fast. Sand, like a beach but not a beach. Her pulse raced. Water, cool blue rippling surrounded by tall reedy weeds. The pictures in her head pummeled her with their clarity. A ridge of trees on the horizon. Her heart hammered against her breast. A yellow triangle flag on a pole, emerging from a hole in the ground.

"Easy, baby," Lana soothed. "Breathe."

"No!" She snapped. She almost had it. The tranquil green was a façade, laid over darkness and decay. They'd plowed over the field and the creek. For a game. A game of...

"Golf," she said, opening her eyes. "Golf course."

Mark grinned down at her. "You sure?"

"Yes," Michelle said, her nerves still snapping and crackling like a bare live wire. "He's taking Ben to the golf course."

"Don't think about it, Iggy."

Bill Potter reclined in his pool chair and tilted his head back to release a chimney exhalation. Smoke rose listlessly from his lungs into the torpid sky. The humidity was rising to unbearable levels, driving even the flies to indolence. One lit upon Bill's pale, hairless, blue-veined old man's leg, and gave him a quick, painful bite. He swatted at the insect. The fly took off as lazily as the rising smoke, only to land again on Bill's arm. He blew a little smoke on it, trying to get the little fucker too high to bite.

Iggy leaned forward into the pool, barking at the blue water. He was definitely thinking about it.

"If you jump in there, I'm not pulling you out this time," Bill said, though of course he knew that he would. He couldn't really blame the dog for wanting to cool off. After fourteen summers, though, the dumb beast still hadn't learned how to swim to the steps to get *out* of the pool once he was in. Bill would have to dive in after the panicky, struggling animal and carry his dumb ass out. Half-drowning himself in the process, reeking like wet dog until he could shower the smell off him. Not mention the time he'd have to spend afterwards skimming black hair that would otherwise clog his filter.

Iggy bit at the water, nipping at it like it was an intruder. Bill also knew from bitter experience that the dog would puke if he swallowed too much of the chlorinated water. That was fun to clean up, too.

Bill took another deep draw off the joint. He knew he shouldn't be getting stoned so early in the afternoon, especially with everything that was going on. The town was under quarantine. He should be...what? Attending community meetings? Hoarding supplies at the grocery store? Filling his bathtub with drinking water? Hell, he didn't know. Something other than getting wasted on his back patio, though. But Bill couldn't shake the blues that had been gnawing at him for weeks now. A man, after all, tended to look at his life in terms of milestones. Graduation, marriage, career, kids, grandkids, retirement. And what came after that? Death. That was the next one, logically. The big dirt nap.

Bill had never particularly dreaded his own demise. He looked upon it as a step into the grand mystery, slipping behind the curtain from beyond which no one had ever returned. As a thoughtful, if not precisely devout, Catholic, he believed in Heaven. As a man of inquisitive imagination, he had a bold curiosity, but no fixed idea, of what Heaven might actually be like. So he didn't fear death. What he feared was dying alone.

As a young man, he'd believed that he'd found and married his soul mate. He and Mara had been high school sweethearts, married at twenty. She'd given him four wonderful children. Bill had always supposed that they would grow old together. In this vision of his future, he had always imagined that he would be the first to die, because couldn't bear even the hypothetical pain of being a widower.

In his more self-generous moments, Bill could make himself believe that their ultimate incompatibility had come down to the issue of contentment. Mara had been content to be the wife of a small-town English teacher, a mother and a volunteer librarian. Content to see the rest of the world only through books and television shows. Bill had never been content with anything in his life. He wanted to travel, to create meaningful literature, to never say no to new experience, to learn and to engage and to grow. To live life.

But maybe he was just a philandering jerk who smoked and drank too much, and who had failed to save their baby son. He had been overly fond of wine and weed and, yes, other women. There'd been a few indiscretions. More, even, than the ones she'd found out about. And then, little Donnie. Their son's death had been the mortal blow to their marriage. Bill's ultimate failure. The event that had finally driven her into the arms of that low-down son of a bitch.

Just recently, Bill had been missing his ex-wife intensely. He was an old man turning to rust beside a swimming pool that he kept up only for the two or three weekends a summer that his grandkids came to visit. He never dove in himself except to fish out the stupid dog. Iggy was getting as gray as he was. The old dog would soon be dead, leaving Bill truly alone. That thought brought sudden tears to his eyes. So goddamn maudlin.

He sucked the joint dry and began to roll another. Why not? What the hell else was he going to do with the rest of his long, lonely life?

He was on the verge of lighting his freshly rolled doobie when movement out of the corner of his eye stayed his hand. His back yard gate swung open. Iggy turned from his vacillation concerning the pool water, to bark at the intruder stepping uninvited into the yard.

Bill gave a nervous start, dropping the unlit joint. It rolled off his belly and fell forgotten to the ground. His addled mind scrambled to think of what he could use as a weapon. He could get to the tool shed with ten sprinting steps, but the deadliest implement he had on hand there was probably the garden hoe. He'd look real cute swinging that at an attacker. Then he saw who was slipping through his gate.

Mara.

Bill's ex-wife stepped into his yard, as if summoned by his longing. He blinked over at her, wondering if perhaps he had caught the sickness that invoked waking dreams. She looked as beautiful as any vision his subconscious had ever summoned. Mara was wearing a silk kimono, sashed tight about her waist but hanging provocatively open at the throat. Her long brown hair was down and flowing wild, like his fondest memory of it spilling in luxurious waterfalls over her pillow.

She walked slowly across the lawn, barefoot. Iggy ran towards her, but stopped short. He assumed a low stance and started barking. As if he'd never seen her before.

"Shut up, Iggy!" Bill stood up. "Mara, hi. What are you..."

She looked dazed, glancing about the back yard as if not quite sure of her surroundings. Maybe she was hurt. Maybe that bastard had hit her. Potter had for years entertained the fantasy that Nate was an abusive shithead and that Mara would one day escape from his grasp and return to him, her true husband.

Iggy was going crazy now, growling and barking. Bill gave him a sideways kick and walked over to his former wife.

"Are you all right?" he said.

She looked up at him, and her confusion seemed to coalesce into something else. It looked to Bill like a regal, haughty pride.

"I've been hunting," she said. "With my arrows I have felled two hares and a stag."

"Oh yeah?"

Mara lifted her left hand, in which she held a brown feather duster. She raised it up and, with her right hand, pantomimed pulling a bow string back. She drew a bead on an invisible target across the yard, and then let the arrow fly. The motion was so confident that Potter actually turned his head, as if to watch the path of the imaginary arrow.

"Nice shot," he said, playing along.

"My crescent heart is aglow," said Mara.

She pulled her robe open. Directly between her breasts was a small red birthmark, shaped like a crescent moon. He'd discovered the mark the first time he ever removed her bra, at the age of sixteen. That had been one of the most joyous moments of Bill Potter's young life. Throughout their marriage, the little moon had remained among his two or three favorite parts of her body to kiss. Seeing it again now, her revealing it to him, almost brought him to his knees with the force of remembrance and loss.

The stupid dog wouldn't stop his yapping. He seemed afraid to get too close to Mara, but his warning barks were rising in their ferocity. Bill, dazzled by his former wife's casual exposure, didn't quite hear him anymore.

She walked past him, dropping the feather duster bow, silk robe slipping from her shoulders and falling silently to the concrete. Mara cast a look back at him, either an invitation or a challenge. She stepped naked into the pool.

Bill Potter, helpless as a man in a dream, quickly and awkwardly stripped off his own clothes. He followed the only woman he had ever loved into the cool blue water.

Last time, the Black Monkey had killed the Snowman with his own kitchen knife. This time would be different, though. This time the Snowman had acted first. He'd snatched that little shit right out of his black mama's arms. Wrapped it up tight in a blue plastic tarp and tossed him into the monkey cage.

"Y'ain't gonna make a monkey outta me." The Snowman laughed. That was funny. Funny as hell. Funnier than shit. "Ain't gonna," he cried as he laughed, "make a monkey," he screamed out the words, "outta *me!*"

Raspy plastic rustling from the back seat of the police cruiser. Muffled cries. The Monkey was trying to wriggle free of the baled blue bundle. Didn't matter none. The back of this carriage was partitioned off with wire and glass that wasn't really glass because it wouldn't break even if it took a bullet. It was made for cartin' monkeys like this one. The doors back there only opened from the outside. If that old Monkey got free of the tarp, it could screech and howl all it wanted. Tear up the seats and piss and shit all over the place even, but it couldn't get loose.

Still, it'd be better if it stayed wrapped. That way it'd be easy to just toss the Monkey bundle into the hole. Maybe whack the shit outta it first with a shovel. Then bury it deep in the hallowed fuckin' earth.

The Snowman stomped the brake pedal. The little wrapped-up Monkey flew with a thump into the back of the Snowman's seat. That oughtta stun the fuckin' thing.

The Snowman sat there for a minute in the stopped car. He felt a weird, reeling dislocation as he looked down at the dashboard with all the dials and numbers and needles and things. For a second he didn't even know how to make this fuckin' carriage *go*. But the deputy knew. The deputy could ride this carriage and the Snowman sure as shit was riding the deputy. He just needed to tell him where to go.

"Down by the creek bed," the Snowman said. "Where I do most of my killin'."

Then they were off, the carriage taking off as if it knew right where to go, like a smart horse that knew the way home even if the rider was too drunk to remember. If he buried the fuckin' Monkey deep enough this time, maybe it would stay good and righteously buried. That would end this weary age-old cycle of death and re-birth. Monkey never dies unless you kill it. Then the Snowman could stay alive to kill for a while without worrying about the deviled fuckin' Monkey rising up to spoil his plans. It'd be real good to stay alive and kill for a while. Only first he had to get this Monkey into the goddamn ground.

CHAPTER 17

BATES GOT BACK up to the church at a little past three. Five hours into the quarantine and the calm seemed to be holding. He had seen a few people out on the streets on his journey back from Deputy Morris's house, but no overt weirdness or lawless behavior. Just scared-looking folks giving him nervous waves as he drove past.

The Church of the Shepherd was a hive of activity, though. The huge parking lot was more than half full, people drawn to the comfort of their community and their faith like iron fillings to a magnet. The good people milled in and out, clogging the front entrance, but Nate didn't want to have to talk to those sorry fuckers. He walked around to the back.

Four of the animal cages now housed human prisoners, along with the one occupied by the "hybrid wolf." Chucky Barber had dragged a hose over to the cages, and was spraying down the one female prisoner while his brother Billy watched, laughing his stupid ass off.

"What in the holy fuck are you doing?" Bates demanded.

Chucky turned around with a guilty start, but recovered himself quickly. "I was just giving this one a bath," he said. "She's *stanky*."

The girl shivered despite the heat, hugging herself to cover her wetted-to-transparency clothes. Bates recognized her. Polly Underwood, a brain-fried little meth head. No big deal. John Perry, unofficial village idiot, was sitting in a corner of the pen next to Polly's, head down, hands hanging loose between his legs. Next to him was the glowering Jimbo Morse. Morse had no doubt been hauled in, as he had a hundred times before, for either public drunkenness or using his eternally suffering wife Claire as a punching bag. The last cage held some tie-dye-clad long-haired kid Bates didn't know by name. Four nobodies.

"Sheriff!" Hippie Boy called out. "Hey, sheriff! This is wrongful arrest here. I didn't do anything. I swear."

Billy Barber scoffed at that. "Max and Dennis Budd hauled him in. He was lootin'."

"I wasn't," the kid insisted. "There was nobody working the register at Casey's, but I left money on the counter. More than enough. My girlfriend's kid needed milk."

"And that sixer of Coors was for your girlfriend's kid, too?"

"I paid for it!"

"Tell it to the judge," Chucky snickered.

"I'm innocent, too," Jimbo declared, grasping the chain links in both hands. "I never laid a finger on her."

"You can't hold me like this," Hippie Boy said. "I have a right to a lawyer. These guys aren't even real cops."

"Shut up, both ya," Chucky turned the hose on the two complaining prisoners, drenching them, to renewed protests. Then, for good measure, he hosed down the wolf as well. The canine, at least, seemed to enjoy the spraying. He snapped at the jet of water, drinking it down as the two Barber brothers laughed.

"You two are doing a bang-up job," Bates said. "Keep it up."

He turned around. John Junior was standing behind him, silently watching his brothers with an expression that could have been either amusement or contempt. It was hard to tell with JJ's perma-scowl poker face.

"Sheriff," he greeted. "I got something you should probably come take a look at," said JJ. "In the basement."

Bates followed JJ into the back door of the main church building, past the big kitchen and through a door that JJ unlocked with a key from a ring on his belt. Behind the door was a dimly lit stairwell, leading down into the back basement. This area was only accessible to a select inner circle of the former pastor's followers. It was where the action was.

"So how's your Mama?" Bates asked as they descended the stairs. "I ain't had a chance to talk to her since last night, before all this started."

"Truth is, sheriff, I'm a little worried about her," JJ said, though the tone of his voice was no more expressive than his face. His concern came out flat, deadpan. "When I left the house, she was asleep. I couldn't get her to wake up. It's almost like how she used to act when she was taking those pills, but she's been off them for a while."

"She seemed all right last night," Bates observed. Addressing the topic of his relations with the boy's Mama was a little awkward, even phrased so obliquely.

"After this, do you mind if I go out to the house and check up on her?"

"Of course not. I'll even go out there with you. Now what did you want to show me?"

"Through here."

They'd reached the bottom of the stairs. Down the hall, on the left, was another locked door. Tuttle had used this room for product storage. In fact, it was the very room from which Nate's bricks had gone missing. Appropriately enough, it now housed one of the men responsible for that nefarious disappearance. Jacob Norrell sat on the floor in a corner of the room, cuffed to a pipe on the wall. He was one of those goth-looking kids, with the spiky hair and the earrings and even the eye make-up. Like being a queerboy in a town like this wasn't enough to piss people off on its own, he had to go and make a big production about it. He had on a t-shirt that might have advertised some faggot band, but was now so soaked with blood as to be unreadable. He looked up when Bates stepped into the room. The sight of the sheriff seemed to cause something to break inside him. Nate could almost see the light of hope extinguishing in his eyes.

Sitting at a desk across the room, watching the prisoner, was Tom Peters. A handgun rested on the desk before him. The gun was angled to point at Jacob, but Tom had his arms folded over his chest, as if refusing to touch the weapon out of some unstated principle.

"Hey, Tom," Nate said.

Tom looked up at him. "Sheriff. John said that this is the guy who stole your merchandise. We thought you might want to talk to him."

It hadn't been theft, precisely, but Nate supposed the truth about the matter might be a little much for Tom to readily accept. He let the comment slide.

"I got nothing to say to the punk," Nate said. "I assume you guys asked him where the rest of my product is?"

"He says it's at his boyfriend's house in Springfield," JJ said. "So of course we can't get to it right now."

"You think he's telling the truth?"

"If it was here in town, he would've told us," said JJ.

Nate didn't doubt it. The kid looked like he'd been worked over pretty good.

"So, Jacob," Nate addressed the prisoner. "Does your daddy know you're a blackmailin' little cocksucker?"

"Suck my..." Jacob started, but his defiance broke down into a choking cough. He vomited blood onto the floor.

"Yeah, that's what I thought," Nate said. "Hey, JJ. Can you watch this shithead for a couple minutes? I want to talk to Tom."

"Sure thing, sheriff."

Nate led Tom out into the hall. He put a hand on his shoulder.

"Son, I'm afraid I've got some bad news for you."

Tom's graceless features fell, eyes and mouth drooping like wax melting in the sun. "Pastor Barry?"

"Yes, Tom. He's gone."

Tom closed his eyes and leaned back against the wall. He moved his lips as if mouthing the words to a prayer.

"You all right?" Nate asked.

When he opened his eyes, they were dry. "How?"

"He did it himself. Stuck a gun in his mouth. But, Tom. It looks like he killed Eve, too."

Tom's dull brown eyes flashed a puzzled look. "He killed Mrs. Tuttle?"

"Hacked her up with a knife. I found them both in that kennel in his back yard," Bates said. "The bear was gone. God knows where."

"Why?"

"I'm sure he had this sickness. It makes folks do crazy things. We ain't seen a lot of violence connected with it, but there's just no other explanation."

"Jesus help us," Tom whispered.

"Don't they say that Jesus helps those who help themselves?"

Tom gave him a questioning look at that.

"What are you going to do here, Tom?" Nate asked. "Those folks upstairs, the flock. They're going to need guidance. This is the Church of the Shepherd, right? Well, the shepherd has fallen. Who's going to rise up and take his place?"

"Christ is the shepherd," Tom said.

"So then what was Pastor Barry? Head sheep?"

"The pastor is the shepherd's staff."

"Heh. That sounds like Barry, all right."

Tom frowned up at the sheriff, still looking like he wasn't quite taking all this in. Nate's patience was wearing out.

"Look, Tom. I know what he did to you."

"He didn't..."

"You're not the only one. That asshole in the other room there? Barry was fucking with him, too. That's how he ended losing my merchandise."

"No." Tom's eyes performed a weird evasion, looking away for a second. "He was probably trying to help him, like he helped me."

"Oh, son. Don't go spoutin' that crap to me. The lies he filled your head with."

"That sin was already in my heart, sheriff. Pastor Barry helped me root it out."

"You were, what, sixteen when it happened? A couple months after your little brother was murdered? You turned to Jesus because you were searching for some meaning to this horrible thing that happened to you. Some comfort and strength to get through it. You were vulnerable and that bastard took advantage of you. What he did was unforgivable."

"To cast out sin, you have to confront it. That's the only way you can get pure again."

"You were *raped*, Tom."

"No, you don't understand. I was a sinner and—"

"It wasn't sin. Goddamn it, boy. It was just human weakness and fuckery. Barry was weak and he preyed on you because you were weaker. But he's dead now. His shadow holds no weight on your back. Not no more. So step up. Those folks need a leader. And you're twice the man he ever was."

Tom nodded, uncertainly. Now tears glistened in his eyes.

"And I need you, too."

Tom looked up at Nate and wiped away the tears.

"I had a business arrangement with Barry, and I'm still going to need somebody to manage the resources that he brought to the table. Somebody strong, smart, loyal. Somebody who knows how to keep his mouth shut.

Those are all qualities you have in spades, Tom. Now, I don't know what kind of compensation Barry was providing you with."

"It was fair."

"Just fair?"

"The things I did for him, I didn't do for the money."

"Now, see there, that's another way he was taking advantage of you. Counting on your devotion so he wouldn't have to pay you too goddamn much. But you wouldn't be working for me, Tom. You'd be my partner. You got two kids, right?"

"It'll be three come August. Liz is expecting again."

"I didn't know that. Congratulations. So I don't gotta tell you how damned expensive kids are. Just think of the kind of life you'd like to provide for them. Working together, we can make that happen."

"What about Loaves and Fishes?"

"The charity? Of course, that's vital. You'll still be doing God's work here on earth, and our business will provide you with the resources you need to do that work. You'll be a better steward of those resources than Barry ever was."

"I don't know, sheriff. I gotta think about all this."

"Of course. But if we're going to do this, I'm going to need something from you first."

"What do you need?"

"A demonstration. Of your loyalty, and your willingness to do what needs to be done."

"What do you have in mind?"

Bates cocked his thumb back at the door. "Jacob in there. He's a problem. Not only did he steal from us, but thanks to your *predecessor*, he knows way too much about our operation. He needs to be dealt with."

"You want me to—"

"I want you to show me that you'll be the kind of partner I can depend on."

Tom gulped and nodded slightly. Either he had it or he didn't.

"Now go on in there. Send JJ out. We're going to go out and check up on his mama. Can you have an answer for me by the time we get back?"

"Yes," Tom said. "I'll have an answer for you."

"Good man."

Tom slipped into the room. JJ stepped out a moment later. He and Nate walked up the stairs together.

"Did you just tell Tom to kill Jacob?" JJ asked.

"I implied that might be a move that would benefit him in the long term."

"Implied?" said JJ. "Usually with Tom you got to be a little more direct than that."

"I think he got my drift," Nate said. "You think he'll do it?"

"I don't know. He's a hard dude to read."

"Well, we'll find out one way or the other by the time we get back from your mom's."

Those words were scarcely out of Nate's mouth when his cell rang.

"Shit," he said, seeing who was calling. "It's your idiot brother. No offense to your family, John, but I think your daddy had one good squirt in him and he used it up on you."

Nate tapped the phone. "This better be fucking important."

Calvin spoke quickly and clearly, and Nate could feel his blood pressure rise with every word. "No," he said into the phone. "Don't do a goddamn thing until I get there."

He ended the call and barely restrained himself from dashing the phone down on the steps. "Motherfucker."

"What is it?" JJ asked.

"You're going to have to go check on your mom by yourself," Nate said. "I gotta deal with some son of a bitch trying to fuck my wife."

Nate stormed up the rest of the stairs, so intent in his rage that he didn't even hear the muffled gunshot coming from the room at the end of the hall.

"He's taking Ben to the golf course!" Missy said, the words so inevitable it was as if Mark had heard them a thousand times before, echoing in his head as he awoke from nightmares. Of course, the golf course. Where the green sod had been laid over the monkey graves. Where the earth below had been sanctified by children's blood spilled by the Snowman. Of course that was where the monster was taking his son.

"So what do we do?" Lana asked.

"We go get him," Missy said.

Mark sat down hard, his head reeling. He was still so fucking high. It felt as if he was floating above the scene, his head a helium balloon tied to the real world by the thinnest of tethers. He forced himself—Ben—to keep invoking his son's name—Ben—to keep from drifting away. Ben Ben Ben. Please be all right, Ben. Please be safe, Ben. Mark realized he was doing something akin to praying. Not to God, but to his son. Though addressing his desperate wishes towards either seemed equally futile.

"Right," Lana said.

She disappeared back into the bedroom and came back a few moments later, carrying a gun. Mark had to blink a few times before he realized what was in her hand.

"What the fuck is that?" he said.

"Glock 19. What the fuck do you think it is?" Lana replied.

"I didn't know you guys kept a gun in the house."

"I'm a gay black woman living in a town with men who think it's perfectly acceptable to ask me if my titties give chocolate milk when you squeeze them. Did Chelle tell you about that?"

"No," Mark said.

"That happened a couple months ago, at the liquor store here in town. You think those shitheads don't have guns?"

Mark regarded the black metal in Lana's hand with both dread fascination and an acute awareness of the latent death contained within its chambers. Something of an anomaly in rural America, he had been raised by middle-class liberal parents who had never owned guns. It was difficult for him to conceive of firearms as a thing that existed in the real world, and not just as some fantastical device created as a convenient Deus ex Machina by writers of books and films.

"Lana and I are going," Missy said. "You three stay here and keep an eye on Jen."

"What?" It took a moment to understand that she actually meant to leave him behind. Mark stood up. "No. No fucking way."

"Don't argue with me about this, Mark," Missy said. "You're too goddamn stoned to be anything but a hindrance."

"He's my son," said Mark. "If you want to keep me here, you're going to have to use that thing on me."

"Let him come, Chelle," Lana said. "He's the boy's father."

Missy gritted her teeth. "*Fine.* What the fuck ever. Let's just *go.*"

"Are you two going to be okay here with Jen?" Lana asked Sam and Alice.

"Why?" Sam said. "What's wrong with her?"

"She thinks she's a werewolf," Lana said. "If she wakes up, just..."

"Just what?" Alice said. "Rub her belly and give her a treat?"

"You're going to have to figure it out. We're gone."

Mark followed the two women through the door, out to the car. He was still climbing into the backseat when Missy cranked the engine to life. She peeled out of the drive before Mark had even closed his door. He fumbled at his seatbelt as she accelerated up the quiet neighborhood street. Terrified, yes, but still thankful that Missy was such a speed demon.

He just hoped she'd be fast enough.

Bill Potter's former wife floated weightless in the blue water before his wide open eyes. His glasses had been left on the umbrella table beside the deck chair, and his astigmatic vision was further blurred by the chlorine water. Mara was perfect in his imperfect eyes, the age smoothed from her skin, her flesh unburdened by gravity in this mystic ether. An erotic angel, her long hair floating about her head like a million living tendrils. He hoped that the filtering medium of the pool water had worked the equivalent miracle upon him in her eyes, that he too had been restored to the man he had once been. The man she had once loved.

The sight before him was at once so surreal and so directly torn from the most fervent longings of his heart that he wondered again if he was suffering a waking dream. If so, thank God. May he never wake.

He went to her, moving effortlessly through the water. Bill kissed his former bride. For a long moment it seemed that the breath they held between them might be enough to sustain them, but of course it couldn't. He was not sure if it was she or himself who kicked to the surface, but they broke into the air together. He took a gasping breath of oxygen and then kissed her again. Beneath the water, her smooth legs wrapped around his waist. He slipped inside her easily, her flesh grasping his with surprising warmth under the cool water. They were joined once again, in the sacred union that had summoned four perfect souls into this world. The magical clinch lasted but a moment. Mara arched her back. She pulled him for one instant deep inside her, and then she kicked away backwards through the water.

For a few minutes, they performed a teasing dance. She would allow him to pull close enough for a quick, shallow coupling and then kick away again, leaving him tingling in the cold water. The aquatic ballet reenacted the cycles of attraction and estrangement woven through their entire long marriage.

And then they came to the divorce. The light of sensual play in her eyes faded away and was replaced with shuddering outrage.

"You dare?" she growled. "You dare to gaze upon me as I bathe?"

"Mara?"

"You dare lay hands upon my flesh?"

"What are you…"

She thrust her arm out at him. The heel of her palm drove hard into the bridge of his nose.

Potter staggered backwards, losing his balance and slipping under the water. The blood from his nose seemed to be everywhere at once. A crimson cloud darkened the clear blue water. He broke the surface again with a glugging nasal exclamation of shock.

Mara lunged, flashing tooth and claw. Bill swam backwards, but she darted after him with shark-like brutality. Her teeth sank into his shoulder. Not a playful love bite, but a ferocious predator's strike.

"Yow!" he cried out.

Mara pushed him under again. Bill knew that if he didn't get her off of him, he was going to drown. He wouldn't hit her, though. In all the years they were married, he had never laid a hand upon her and he was not going to start now. He grasped at her instead, pulling her under with him. He clung to his ex-wife in the desperate hope that she would release him before she drowned along with him.

Then, suddenly, she pulled away. There was no longer anything holding Bill under. He couldn't see anything with all the blood in the water, so he broke the surface again.

Mara was a few feet away, struggling with Iggy, who had climbed onto her shoulders and was biting at her hair. The blessed stupid beast had jumped into the water to save his master from the woman attacking him.

"Iggy!" Potter tried to call, but the name came out in a choke of bloody water.

Seeing that the aquatic battle was going to drown his wife and/or his dog, Potter dove over to try to extricate the two. Man, woman and beast struggled for a few minutes, churning the water, until Mara broke free. She swam to the pool stairs and climbed, naked and dripping, out of the water. Bill followed her out and collapsed half-drowned upon the sun-hot concrete.

Then came Iggy. After all these years, he'd finally learned how to use the stairs.

The dog, comically skinny with his dripping fur plastered against his body, tore off running after the woman.

"Iggy, no!" Bill staggered to his feet.

The dog clamped his jaws upon Mara's calf. She screamed and beat her hand back at the dog, trying to shake him off.

Bill picked up the long pool skimmer, resting beside him on the water's edge. He wedged the five-foot pole between Iggy and Mara and pushed the dog away. When Iggy let go of her leg, Mara snarled and lunged after Bill again. Bill swung the skimmer, catching Mara in the chest with the heavy plastic net. Iggy went for Mara again and Bill swatted the dog across the nose to back him off.

The storm door leading down his cellar was open—he'd neglected to close the door behind him after he hauled out his pool chair. With the long aluminum pole, Bill guided Mara back towards the underground stairs. Iggy somehow seemed to catch on to the plan. With threatening barks, he helped Bill force Mara back into the cellar door. Bill prayed that she would not trip down the stairs and break her neck. Someone seemed to be listening to this prayer, at least. Mara retreated backwards into the darkness.

Bill dropped the pool skimmer to the ground with a metallic clank. He ran over and slammed the storm door closed. For a minute, he just stood there before the rattling door behind which he had locked his wife. He was still dripping wet and naked, utterly stunned.

Then, from behind him, he heard another intruder step into his yard.

"Now what the fuck is *this*?" came the all-too-familiar voice of Sheriff Bates.

The gunshot rang out before Bill could even turn around.

Ben drifted out a little. There was something comforting about being wrapped up like this. Bundled, like a baby. His mom had showed him pictures of him when was little, tightly swathed in a blue blanket. "Baby burrito," she called it. That was funny. Though he'd been just an infant and it was too long ago, for a moment he thought he could remember the feeling. Warm and safe in Mommy's arms. Her softness and milk-scent close. Nice. The thought gave him a sleepy smile and he wanted to close his eyes.

No.

Ben forced himself back into the moment, made himself fully awake. He wasn't safe. Not at all. He was on the floor in the back seat of a police car that was being driven by a crazy man. Wrapped up not in a baby blanket but in a blue plastic tarp, so tightly he couldn't move. So tightly he could barely breathe.

He couldn't see anything but blue. The rough plastic smelled like dirt and blood. His own blood, he thought. His car window had shattered when they'd crashed and a flying shard had sliced him across the bridge of the nose. Was he hurt anywhere else? He couldn't say. The rest of his body was numb. He was so disoriented he couldn't even tell if he was lying on his stomach or on his back.

Could he get free? He thought that maybe he could loosen the tarp a little looser if he wriggled around inside of it, but last time he'd tried, the deputy driving the car had heard the scratchy sound the plastic made. He'd slammed on the brakes and sent Ben flying. That's how he'd ended up on the floor instead of on the seat.

For a moment, fear almost overwhelmed him. Ben thought of his mother and father and Lana, and wondered if he would ever see them again. The thought that he might not was worse than any consideration of what the crazy man was going to do to him. The man might kill him and bury him in a hole somewhere and his mom and dad and Lana would never find him and then they'd be sad forever. Ben felt a shuddering cry welling up deep inside him, but he was too tightly bound for it to emerge. A cold, consuming hopelessness chilled him to the very core. If he allowed it to, the fear would freeze him solid and then he wouldn't feel anything at all.

No.

Again, Ben forced himself to come back to what was happening right now. For a few moments, he just focused on breathing. That was hard enough to do with the plastic wrapped so tightly around his chest. Crying would just make it harder. So he just slowly breathed in and out until a strange calm came over him.

He was very aware, very focused. His thoughts were very clear. Again, he wondered about ways he might get free of the tarp. Never mind that even if he did, he would still be trapped in the back seat of the police car, still the prisoner of the crazy man. It was still important to get out of the plastic.

He knew somehow that his mom and dad and Lana were coming for him. He could feel them, getting closer. When he closed his eyes, he could almost *see* them, driving in Mommy's car, tense and quiet and determined. They would catch up soon, but Ben needed to be ready when they got here. He needed to do whatever he could to help himself.

He tried to move his arms. When nothing happened, a horrible thought struck him. Maybe his spine was broken or something and he was paralyzed and that's why he couldn't move. This thought rose up inside him in a fresh tide of panic. He couldn't feel anything below his neck and maybe he never would again. Even if he was rescued, he would spend the rest of his life in a wheelchair, just a helpless head attached to a dead body. They'd have to feed him baby food through a spoon.

Stop. Stop. Stop.

He couldn't move his arms, so he started smaller. Fingers. He tried to wiggle his fingers. Again, at first there was nothing. But then, faintly, he felt the scratch of his nails against his own chest through the thin fabric of his t-shirt. It was one of his old Pokemon shirts, just a yellow shirt with Pikachu's face. Kind of small on him but he'd put it on this morning because Mom hadn't done the laundry yet and he couldn't find any of his newer shirts. It was comforting to think that just a few hours ago, the most troubling thing he'd had to worry about was finding a clean shirt to wear.

Moving his fingers loosened things, just slightly. Enough so that he could move his wrists now, a little. He rotated them, back and forth, until he felt his arms begin to free up.

"Quit yer figitin', Monkey!" the deputy driving the car yelled.

He's not the deputy anymore, Ben thought. *He's the Snowman now.*

Ben's arms were crossed across his chest, pressed tightly together. He began to move them in a scissoring motion.

"Don't make me come back there! I'll pull this carriage over and whup yer little ass!"

Ben tried to remember all the things his father had said about this sickness. He'd said that it made people weaker, so they couldn't fight off spirits and things. So the man driving the car wasn't crazy or evil, he was just being controlled by something bad. But maybe the good, normal person was still there, underneath.

Ben recognized the deputy. He'd often seen him around town. Once when Ben and his mom were walking downtown, he'd tripped, skinning his knee on the sidewalk and scraping up his hand. The deputy had been coming out of the diner and saw it happen. He had a first aid kit in his police car (*this* police car, Ben realized.) He'd cleaned Ben's cuts and bandaged him up, and then gave him a Snickers bar to make him feel better. He was a nice man.

Ben tried to remember the deputy's name. At first he wasn't sure if he even knew it, but then he remembered. Bandaging Ben's knee, the deputy had asked him his name and then he'd said: "Mine's Bryant. Like Bryan, except with a 't' stuck on the end. Which is funny, because tea's my favorite thing to drink." Ben had thought that was kind of a dorky thing to say, but he'd laughed because it had made him feel better.

"Bryant," Ben said. Moving his arms had loosened the tarp enough now that Ben could move his shoulders. He shrugged them up and down and felt the whole thing begin to loosen.

"Shut up, ya fuckin' Monkey!" the Snowman hissed.

"I'm not a Monkey," Ben said calmly, still working his arms. "I'm a boy. My name is Ben. You helped me one time when I hurt my knee and my hand. You gave me a Snickers bar."

"I'll help ya into a fuckin' hole in the ground."

"I'm not talking to you," Ben said. Now he could get his arms all the way down to his sides. He bent slightly at the waist, a sort of half-sit-up. "I'm talking to Deputy Bryant. I know he can hear me."

"He can't hear shit. I got him stuffed down so deep he ain't never gonna see the sun."

"Bryant," Ben called, louder, twisting at the hip. The tarp was loose enough now that he could start to move his legs. "I know you're in there. You can fight the Snowman. Don't let him hurt me, please. When the time comes, hold him back. Just for a few seconds, so I can run."

"Shut up, Monkey!" the Snowman roared. "And quit yer wrigglin'! I'm gonna kill you so fuckin' dead!"

He didn't stop the car, though. Didn't pull over to subdue Ben and wrap him up again. Ben somehow knew that this meant that they were getting close to wherever they were headed. Ben raised his arms and pushed out. The tarp split open, as if he was emerging from a cocoon. He made himself ready.

CHAPTER 18

"WE HAVE TO check the grave," Jess had said. "We have to make sure it worked."

Twenty years ago, on the first day of November. The morning after the night they had buried the Black Monkey down by the creek. Mark and Jess had hiked back out there in the cold morning. They'd found the Monkey's grave empty. The Monkey had risen. It had done what Jess had summoned it to do.

Then it came back.

Mark remembered this all now. He remembered it clearly. The memory had always been there, behind a door in his mind that he usually kept shut tight and locked, but which was now flung wide open.

And now they were returning to the very spot.

Missy reached the end of Park Avenue and slowed the car as they approached the entrance to the walled-in fortress that was the Lawndale Manor Master Planned Community. The barrier arm was lowered, as always. More ominously, a heavy metal gate that looked like it could withstand a tank attack had been slid shut as well. Mark had never seen that closed before.

He recognized the attendant inside the little guard house booth beside the gate. His name was Rodney, an eternally cranky older man with an extravagant mustache that hadn't been stylish even when he'd first grown it in 1973. In another worrisome portent, Rodney's bushy white 'stache was concealed beneath a blue plastic respirator.

Mark rolled down his window as Missy pulled up to the gate. In the front seat, Lana slid the gun down to her side.

"Rodney, hi," Mark called, forcing an easy smile.

Rodney's mask did not cover his eyes. They darted and jittered around, seemingly independent of one another. He had the sickness. Of course, this called the effectiveness of the respirators into serious question.

"I'm Mark Davies," Mark pressed on regardless of the man's infection. "Gillian Hudson is my mother. I was just here for a visit at Christmas."

"I know who you are," Rodney said. "You're the boy from the lemonhead church."

"Yep." Mark had by now learned to that it was best to play along. "That's me. Hey, can we get inside? I really need to talk to my mother."

"No visitors. We're in lockdown. Noah nin. Noah nout."

"Okay, then could you contact my mother and let her know I'm here? Like I say, I really need to talk to her and of course the phones are down."

Rodney's eyes steadied for a moment. "Your mother gave very explicit directions that you are not to be admitted."

"Me, specifically? Her son, Mark?"

"Yes sir. She's watching us right now. She's got flies in the sky."

"What did you say?"

"It's an emergency," Lana said, as if addressing a sane person. "Our son's been abducted and we have reason to believe he's been taken to your golf course."

"The flies see everything," said Rodney. He leaned back and pointed at the computer monitor in his booth. The screen displayed the feed from multiple video cameras, mostly scenes of the quiet neighborhood streets. One appeared to be a view of the golf course. Mark strained to see, but he could not tell if the tiny image showed his son or his son's kidnapper. "They even see the memories inside our dreams."

"Did a county deputy come through here?" Missy asked. "He would have had a little boy in the car with him."

"The flies showed me how I murdered my wife. It's funny, I forgot all about that until they put it on the TV right there so anyone can see. I found out she was fucking a black guy, see. So I stabbed the *shit* out of that bitch." He chuckled, amused. "I told the cops that the other fella did it. The *black* fella. Of course, they took my words over his words. The guy's on death row to this. *very. day.*" He tapped the glass to emphasize each word and then he shook his head. "I really thought he did it, too. But then the spies showed me what I forgot."

"All right, thanks for nothing," Missy said. "Asshole."

She slammed the car into reverse and pulled to a stop half a block away from the gate.

"Well, that was pointless," Lana said. "But Morris would have had to go through him, too. How sure are you about the golf course, Chelle?"

"I'm positive. They're in there right now."

"So what do we do? Do we," she lifted the gun up, "*make* him open the gate?"

"No." Michelle shook her head. She closed her eyes. A moment later, she opened them again. "There's another way in."

The stone wall barrier extended a few blocks east of the entrance gate. Beyond that was a cornfield, the rows planted right up to the neighborhood's eastern wall. Missy, steely determination in her eyes, floored the gas.

"What are you doing?" Mark screamed. He braced his arms against the front seat as they flew into the wall of corn.

The car jumped the ditch and barreled into the field, bouncing wildly over the rutted earth as the green tasseled stalks flew into the windshield.

"Now what the fuck is *this*?" Bates called.

He stepped into the yard, gun in hand, just in time to see Bill forcing Mara back into the storm cellar with a goddamn pool skimmer. The teacher was naked as a mole rat, his flabby old man buttocks flapping obscenely.

Bill's dog snarled at Nate when he walked through the gate. The animal took two running steps in his direction. Nate put a bullet in its head.

Potter gave a mighty flinch at the thunderclap sound, like he'd been the one shot. He spun around and saw the black dog bleeding its brains out all over the ground. The shocked heartbreak on the old man's face was so sweet, so gratifying.

"You shot my dog," Potter cried.

"Yeah, well, you fucked my wife. So that still don't make us even in my book."

"Are you going to shoot me, too?"

"I haven't decided."

"Will you at least let me put my pants on first?"

"Hell, Bill, I insist on it. Nobody wants to see your shriveled prunes."

Bill pulled his trunks on and slipped a t-shirt on over his head, Nate keeping a bead on him the whole time. He wiped his nose, which was bleeding slightly, and then stood before Nate with calm defiance.

"So, tell me," Nate said. "How long have you and that faithless bitch been carrying on?"

"It's not her fault," Bill said. "She's sick. She's got this sleepwalking thing."

"Really?" Nate hadn't considered that.

"She's inside of a dream."

"You knew that and you fucked her anyway? That's the same as her being blackout drunk. She couldn't give any kind of consent. So you didn't just fuck my wife. You raped her."

"No," Bill said. "It's not like that."

"Really? What's it like, then? Because now that you mention it, it kind of looks like she put up a fight. Was that a bite I saw on your shoulder?"

"Yep, she bit him," said Calvin Barber, stepping into the yard with his brother. "They were going at it right in the water there. The dog even jumped in and got in on the action."

"And you didn't think to come in here to help her?" Bates addressed Calvin without taking his eyes off Potter.

"You told us to hang back until you got here," Calvin said. "We were just doing what you told us to."

Bates shook his head. Goddamn morons.

"You can go ahead and shoot him, sheriff." Jesse Barber's grin was loathsome. "We'll back you up. We'll say he was rapin' Mrs. Bates and you came in and stopped him."

"Oh, so I got your permission to do that, Jesse?" Bates said. "'Cuz you know I don't make a move unless I get your say-so first."

"It's cool," Jesse said. "I'm just sayin'."

"Hell, let's vote on it. What do *you* want me to do, Bill?"

"I want you to rot in the deepest pit in hell."

Bates had to chuckle at that. "*Now* you grow a pair? You know, you always made it real easy for me, being the second husband. You set a mighty low bar. All I had to do was keep from comin' home smelling like pussy or letting one of her kids die because I was too stoned to keep him from playing in the road."

Bates was trying to goad Bill into doing something stupid, just to make this easier. And for a second, Potter's jaw clenched and he looked like he might try to grab for the gun. But then his shoulders slumped and a look of defeat washed over him. He glanced over at the cellar door.

"Just take care of her, okay?" Bill said. "She needs help. Will you promise me that you'll get her help?"

Nate sighed. So he was going to have to do this cold-blooded then. God knows when he was going to get another opportunity like this.

Nate raised his weapon.

Bill Potter closed his eyes.

"Sheriff Bates, thank God!"

Tim Black, who owned the motel just north of town, stepped into the yard. He stopped short when he saw the gun in Nate's hand.

"Whoa," Black said. "What's going on here?"

"Nothing." Nate lowered his weapon, with regret. "Just a misunderstanding. What can I do for you, Mr. Black?"

"I was just out checking up on my motel," Black said. "Charise Lovejoy was dancing around her room, stark naked. Curtains wide open, putting on a show like anybody'd want to see *that*. She had about a hundred candles lit in there. Then she started knocking them over. On purpose, I think. My motel is burning and the fire department's tied up with some craziness downtown. There's people running wild in the streets there. Everybody's lost their damn minds!"

Bates nodded, giving Potter a wry grin.

"You gotta come down there, sheriff. My business is going up in flames."

For a moment, just a moment, Nate considered shooting Black, too. Maybe Calvin and Jesse while he was at it. But, no. The opportunity had passed.

"Bill Potter," he said, holstering his gun. "You are one lucky son of a bitch."

Lana held on tight to the grab handle with her right hand, her left gripping the Glock. Her finger was off the trigger, though. She was afraid the gun would go off with how the car was bouncing. They flew blindly through the cornfield, stalks hammering the windshield with hard, unripe ears and turning to mulch beneath the undercarriage. Thousands of dollars in crop damage, easily. Chelle kept it steady, though. Foot to the floor, steering wheel locked forward, eyes straight ahead as if she was somehow seeing through the corn.

In the back seat, Mark howled with a stoned man's pure terror. Though Lana wished he would shut the hell up, she had to admit that she knew how he felt.

Then, by pure miracle, they punched through the other side. Chelle's little Honda was airborne for a heart-stopping second, jumping the ditch like a Hollywood stunt car before coming to rest on a little dirt road between the fields. The road led to a small gate built into the brick Lawndale wall. Some kind of maintenance access. The gate was gently swaying, Lana saw, and the metal bars were bent. As if someone had driven right through it moments before.

"That's how he got in," Chelle said.

Lana looked over at her wife with awe. If she spent the rest of her life with the woman, as she fully intended to, she would never get used to Chelle knowing things she had no way of really knowing. Lana was amazed every time it happened. In a way, it was terrifying.

"Are you guys ready?" Chelle asked.

"I'm ready," Lana said, taking a deep breath, hoping that was true.

"Go," said Mark, sounding steadier than Lana felt. He was kind of an idiot, bless his heart, but Lana knew he loved his son as fiercely as either she or Michelle did.

Chelle hit the gas. The car peeled out in the dirt. She threaded the accelerating vehicle through the narrow gate. Beyond the barrier, the rough road gave way to smooth green grass. Chelle drove straight across the greens with pure confidence, following fresh tire tracks gouged from the immaculate grass.

Hail Mary, full of grace, our Lord is with thee.

The words were only in her head, but Lana's lips moved slightly as if speaking them with her breath. She slipped her finger onto the trigger of the gun. When the time came, would she be able to do it?

Blessed art thou among women, and blessed is the fruit of thy womb, Jesus.

Lana knew what a bullet does when it pierces a man's body. She had witnessed her mother shooting her father when she was six years old.

Holy Mary, Mother of God, pray for us sinners.

Lana remembered her father as steady and hard-working. A bit dull and humorless perhaps, he had expressed his love for his children mainly by providing for them. Lana couldn't remember ever hugging the man, but even as a little girl she'd known that he took his responsibilities towards them with the utmost seriousness.

That is, when he was sober.

Now and at the hour of our death. Amen.

Thomas Blair had been a mean black-out drunk, though. Lana's mother took the brunt of his violence. She tolerated his abuse towards herself, and even towards Lana's two older brothers. But when he hit little Lana, she reached her limit.

Hail Mary, full of grace, our Lord is with thee.

Lana, standing on a kitchen chair to get a drinking glass down from the cabinet, had slipped. She'd blindly grabbed out at the shelf and inadvertently brought a whole stack of dinner plates down with her. She wasn't hurt, just a little dazed by the destruction she'd wrought. At the tremendous clatter, her father came running from the living room, where he'd been drinking all afternoon. He took one look at his daughter standing over the mound of broken dishes, and then punched her in the face with a closed fist.

Blessed art thou among women, and blessed is the fruit of thy womb, Jesus.

Lana was knocked out cold. She came to with her mother standing above her, asking her what had happened. Lana said one word: "Daddy."

Holy Mary, Mother of God, pray for us sinners.

Lana's mother nodded. She went into her bedroom and pulled the gun down from the closet shelf. Lana's father was flopped down on the living room couch. He might have been passed out. Lana's mother stood over her husband and fired one shot, right into his forehead.

Now and at the hour of our death. Amen.

While Lana's mother went into the other room to call the police and tell them what she'd done and why, Lana went over to her father. She looked closely at the bloody black hole right above his left eye. She saw white stuff that might have been pieces of skull or brain. To this day, she wasn't sure which.

Hail Mary, full of grace.

Because the act had been in cold blood, because her husband had been lying defenseless on the couch, because she theoretically could have called the police or taken her children to a shelter, Lana's mother was arrested. Because she was black (though that was never explicitly stated, of course,) she was sentenced to twenty years in prison.

Our Lord is with thee.

Lana, along with her two brothers and her sister, were sent from Chicago to live with their Aunt Roxy in Denver. Her mother served twelve years of her sentence and was released just before Lana graduated from high school. She was unrepentant. Proud, even, of what she'd sacrificed to protect her children.

Blessed art thou among women.

Could Lana do the same? She had no illusions about the likely consequences of a black woman shooting a white deputy in a town like this, no matter what the circumstances were.

Blessed is the fruit of thy womb, Jesus.

She knew she couldn't hand the gun off to Mark or to Michelle, though they were Ben's biological parents. Mark was too soft-hearted to pull the trigger, and so stoned he'd probably miss even if he tried. Chelle possessed the maternal grit to fire the gun, but if one of them was going to prison over this, Lana would rather it be her. Easier to wait on the inside with the satisfaction of knowing that she'd done what needed to be done than to wait on the outside with the guilt of knowing it should have been her.

Holy Mary, Mother of God.

The car crested a slight rolling hill and for one weightless second seemed to be suspended in the air. At the bottom of the little valley ahead, Lana saw the deputy's cruiser parked at an angle across a putting green. The back door was open. A small form dashed away from the car.

Pray for us sinners.

It was Ben. A boy Lana loved with an intensity she had never thought possible. A bright, funny, kind-hearted child. Her son. In terrible danger. A man took off after the boy, wishing to harm him. An anguished cry sounded out in the car, though Lana could not have said if it had come from her, Mark, Michelle or some combination of the three.

Now.

The car went into a skid, tearing an ugly dirt scar across the greens. Lana's door was open before the vehicle came to a full stop. She leapt out and hit the ground running, tearing down the hill faster than she'd ever run in her life. The gun was in her hand, safety removed.

And at the hour of our death.

The man caught Ben by the collar of his shirt, swinging him around and tossing him to the ground. For a second, he stood above the child. Lana fell to one knee, in a shooter's stance. She swung the gun up, bringing the man into her sights.

Amen.

Sam had almost forgotten that the whole world had gone to hell. His new best friend was out following his ex-wife's psychic hunch about the man who had abducted their son. The town was under quarantine, ravaged by some mystery illness, and Sam had been charged with babysitting an unconscious woman who believed herself to be a werewolf. In the midst of all this insanity, what was he doing? Playing "Super Smash Brothers" with a teenage cancer patient, stoned off his goddamn gourd.

She was kicking his ass, too. Sam tended to lose his concentration the higher he got, but the joint they'd sparked together seemed to give Alice increased focus and energy. He'd lost four battles in a row now.

Alice tried to pass the joint back to him, but Sam waved it away.

"Nah, you kill it, I'm good," he said.

Alice nodded, and took another deep drag. Truth told, he'd been good before they even lit up. Those amazing gummy bears were still working their rainbow magic in his bloodstream. But Alice had said she was feeling nauseous and asked him if he was holding anything. How could he say no when it was medical?

They were sitting on the loveseat, close together by necessity as Sam took up more than half the space by himself. The unconscious werewolf lady was on the couch across the room.

Alice exhaled and dropped the what little was left of the joint into an almost depleted can of Dr. Pepper that they'd been sharing, extinguishing it with a moist little sizzle.

"Hey, Sam," she said. "Do you maybe want to make out a little bit?"

"What?" Though he had no smoke in his lungs, he suffered a small coughing fit.

"Sorry," Alice said, once he'd recovered. "It's just, weed makes me horny when I smoke it. It's weird, the gummies don't really do that, but man, joints do."

"I'm twice your age!"

"Really? You're thirty-four?"

"No, twenty-six."

"Damn, Sam. You really think I'm thirteen?"

"No. I just...can't do math when I'm high. Anyway, that's not the..."

"Come on." Alice put her hand on his knee. "We can do anything you want. I've got this desperate fear of dying a virgin."

"Jesus." Sam pulled away. "You should...find a boy your own age."

Alice scoffed. "I'm a bald, one-eyed dying girl with no boobs. Boys my own age are *totally* into that."

"One-eyed?" Sam said.

"Yeah. You didn't notice?"

Sam looked into her big brown eyes. Soft and warm, like a tragic puppy.

"Which one is the, uh...?"

"You can't tell, really?"

Alice tapped her left eye. It made a little clacking sound under her fingernail.

"Oh, God." Sam recoiled. "Don't do that."

She rolled her eyes around in a way that reminded him of his grandmother. Her fake eye moved, though he saw now it wasn't quite in synch with the real one. It was just a little slower.

"It moves," Sam noted.

"It lays on top of an implant," Alice said. "Here, look."

She reached into her eyelid with her thumb and forefinger.

"Jesus, what are you doing?"

Alice popped her eye out.

"Holy shit, that's freaky."

She held the eye in her hand so it was peeking out of her closed fist. By moving her thumb, she made it wink at him.

"Hi, Sam," she said with a funny, high-pitched, side-of-the-mouth voice. "I'm a hand with an eyeball."

"Gyah, stop!" The winking fist was bad enough, but looking up at the smiling girl with the naked pink empty socket where her eye rightfully belonged was even worse.

Alice set the prosthetic down on the coffee table, right beside the Dr. Pepper can. The false eye wasn't round like a marble, as Sam had supposed it would be. It was shaped more like a really thick contact lens. Looking down at the very realistic eye looking back up at him filled Sam with dread. Removed from its owner's lid, the eye seemed to have an awareness and a consciousness of its own; an autonomous life that was both sad and sinister.

"It's staring at me!" Sam cried, aghast.

"Now I bet you *really* don't want to make out with me."

"Look, you're a sweet girl," Sam said. "You're smart and you're funny and you're really cool and I like you, but can you please put your eye back in your face? You're going to give me a panic attack."

Alice sighed. "Sorry, Sam." She picked the eye up from the table. Sam looked away as she replaced it in the socket.

When he looked back over at Alice, her real eye was watering slightly. She looked down, and then away.

"I'm sorry," Sam said. "Sorry I freaked. I know that's just part of your everyday life that you have to deal with. It's just, when I'm high, stuff like that...God, I'm an asshole."

"No, Sam. *I'm* sorry. I was deliberately fucking with you. Let's just... get back into the game, okay? Forget I even..."

Bang.

The loud noise made them both jump. They exchanged startled looks.

"Was that the front door?" Alice said.

Sam looked over at the door, and the sound came again. Twice, in rapid succession.

Bang. Bang.

At the same moment, Jen gave a start on the couch. Her legs kicked out and she made a growling, barking noise, though she did not open her eyes.

"Are you going to see who's out there?" Alice asked.

"Do you really think we should?" Sam whispered.

"No, Sam, I think we should just cower in here and hope they go away."

Bang.

"Well, why don't you answer the door, then?" Sam said.

"You're a big, scary biker-looking dude. I'm a scrawny little cancer girl."

"Right." Sam nodded, resolved. He stood up and crossed the room, though he was in no kind of hurry.

Jen let out a sharp yelp in her sleep, all four of her limbs twitching now.

Bang. Bang.

Sam took a deep breath and pulled the door open.

Ruby McCammon, the librarian, was on the doorstep, in a robe and nightgown, holding a hammer in her hand. She didn't seem to notice when Sam opened the door. Ruby lifted the hammer and pounded twice on the doorframe, though there was no nail that Sam could see.

Bang. Bang.

"What are you doing, Ms. McCammon?" Sam asked.

"Cracking walnuts," she stated, as if this was obvious.

"Um, I don't see any walnuts."

"They're not for *you*," Ruby replied testily. "They're for the people."

"What people?"

"The *little* people," she said, annoyed at being interrupted at her walnut cracking. She banged the hammer on the door frame again, three times.

Bang. Bang. Bang.

The sound had a weird echo to it this time. Sam realized that it was coming from somewhere else now, too. He leaned out the door and looked over towards the driveway. Jerry Walker, a nurse at the elder care facility, was whacking a big tree branch against the garage door.

Whack. Whack. Whack.

Ruby's hammering and Jerry's hitting the garage door were perfectly synchronized.

"Uh, Sam?" Alice called from inside the house.

Sam shut the front door and locked it. He turned to look. Jen was awake now, sitting up on the couch. She barked three times in quick succession.

"Arf! Arf! Arf!" she barked, in time with the banging sounds outside.

"What the hell's going on?" Alice said.

Someone else outside took up the rhythm. A dull thudding pound started up from the side of the house, exactly simultaneous to the banging and the whacking and the barking.

Thump. Thump. Thump.

Bang. Bang. Bang.

Whack. Whack. Whack.

"Arf. Arf. Arf."

All together, all at once.

With every repetition of the three percussive raps, someone else outside joined the refrain. Soon it was coming from every direction at once. There was even a light tapping from the roof that, in a more festive season, could have been taken for reindeer hooves.

Dave Cox, dressed in his bright orange hunting vest, stepped in front of the big bay window with a brick in his hand.

With the next round of banging, Dave pounded the brick against the glass. The window broke the first time he hit it, but Dave's arm was a slave to the beat. He brought the brick down two more times into empty air.

"What the hell is *happening*?" Alice screamed.

CHAPTER 19

BEN WAS READY. He lay flat on his back on the floor of the police cruiser, the tarp loose around him. They'd just been driving down a rough and rutted dirt road, and then there had been a screeching metal crash as they burst through a gate or a barrier of some kind. Now the ground was smooth beneath the wheels of the car, but hilly at the same time. The car rose and fell with altitude shifts that he felt in the pit of his belly.

"Bryant," he said again.

This time the deputy answered. *Yeah, kid.* It was strange, though. Ben couldn't tell if he was hearing the words with his ears or only in his head.

"Don't let the Snowman hurt me," Ben said.

I'm so sorry. I don't know if I can stop him. He's so strong. I got his flakes on my fingers and I touched them to my lips. That's how he got inside me.

"That was just a dream," Ben said. "You're dreaming, but you can wake up." He shouted it: "Wake up, Bryant!"

I ain't never gonna wake up again. This was a moaning lament, full of sorrow.

"Will ya both shut the *fuck* up?" This voice was loud and present, coming from the front seat, making it clear to Ben that the other voice had only been inside his head. "I can't hear myself fuckin' *think.*"

The man driving the car slammed on the brakes. The vehicle came to such an abrupt stop that Ben for a moment thought it was going to roll over onto its side. The man jumped out of the car. A second later, he opened the back door. Ben pushed the tarp all the way off.

Deputy Bryant's face was a quivering mess, all the muscles tremoring beneath his skin. His darting eyes dripped with tears. He clenched his teeth and brought his fists up to his reddened face, as if he was trying to tear off a mask.

"Kid," he said, in a guttural snarl. "Run. Run like hell."

The deputy stepped backwards, dragging the weight of the Snowman with him. Ben jumped to his feet and hit the ground running, his sneakers digging into the perfect green grass, the wind whipping past his ears. He ran faster than he had ever run in his life.

It wasn't fast enough, though. He knew it. The Snowman moved Bryant's longer legs faster than the old deputy could rightfully run, pushing him hard because the Snowman didn't care if he gave Bryant a heart attack. He just wanted to catch Ben, and kill him.

The Snowman grabbed Ben by the collar of his shirt and tossed him to the ground. Ben rolled to see the Snowman's hands reaching down to wrap around his throat.

"No!" Ben cried. "Bryant! Stop!"

By some miracle, Bryant heard him. He woke up. His eyes cleared and he got back to his feet, blinking in confusion for a second. A relieved smile flitted across his face.

Then his chest exploded outward, spraying Ben's face with hot, dark blood.

Ben tried to call out, but the blood dripped into his mouth, choking off his words.

Deputy Bryant looked down at the hole in his chest with utter confusion, as if he had no idea how such a thing might have happened. Then a second shot burst through his head, blowing the top of his skull off. Bryant fell to the side, the crimson puddle of his draining life turning the green grass black.

Missy and Lana were already more than halfway down the hill by the time Mark managed to get his stoned ass out of the car. He tripped and stumbled, then got to his feet and tore off after the women. It felt like he had to fight through a syrupy sluggishness just to make himself run, as if time was running slower for him.

He had thought that panic might scare him sober, but the fear if anything amplified his intoxication, whipping his blood into a cherry slushy. He could hear the pounding of his heart as it pumped this cold, fizzing concoction through his body, and feel the strange velvety sensation of the frozen foam flowing through his veins.

Everything was too vivid. Every blade of grass was sharply etched in his vision, too cartoon green to be anything produced by nature. The angry gray thunderheads distant on the horizon formed vast Rorschach configurations that brought to Mark's free-associating mind the impression of feminine curves; of massive goddess shapes in the sky. Mark had to pull his awareness by force of will back to earth, to where Ben was running across the greens, pursued by the deputy.

Ahead of him, down the hill, Lana dropped to one knee. She raised the gun up, her form perfect, like a lady assassin in some action movie. When she pulled the trigger, the sound was nowhere as loud as Mark had expected it would be. There was a flat concussive pop and a little puff of white smoke from the gun. Half a second later, a red bud bloomed on the deputy's back, stopping him in his tracks.

The deputy stood above Ben for another long moment. Lana fired again and the top of his head exploded. He finally fell to the ground.

Missy ran past Lana, and Mark was now close behind. They reached their son at the same moment, finding him lying motionless on the ground, covered with blood. They were too late.

Mark's heart stopped. There was a gaping, sucking void in his chest.

Missy fell to her knees and gathered Ben up in her arms, wiping the blood from his face. Mark knelt beside her. He felt helpless, impotent.

"Thank God," Missy said, "Oh, thank God."

Mark wondered why the hell she was thanking God when she should be raging to the heavens, but then he saw Ben hug Missy back. He saw as she wiped the blood away that Ben was unharmed. It was the deputy's blood all over him.

"I'm okay, Mom," Ben said, as though he did not understand what the fuss was about.

Though Mark did not believe in God, it seemed a waste to direct the surge of gratitude he felt out into the indifferent universe. Instead, he just spoke his son's name. "Ben. Oh, Ben."

Lana came up beside him. For a few moments the three adults passed the child between them, hugging him in turn.

"Is he dead?" Ben asked.

"Yes, baby," Missy soothed. Ben was in Lana's arms at this particular moment, but Missy reached over to ruffle his hair, which was still wet with blood. They were all covered with it now.

"But it wasn't his fault!" Ben protested. He wrenched free of Lana and got to his feet. "It wasn't him. It was the Snowman."

Ben tried to go to the dead man lying on the ground, but Mark pulled him back.

"Don't look, Benny," Mark said.

He pulled his son close. Ben buried his face in Mark's chest. Mark held him as he wept.

Mark looked down at the deputy's corpse, at the puddle of blood soaking into the grass. There was no way of knowing if this was the spot, but he was sure it was. This was same exact place where the Snowman had killed his prey, the same point where Jess had buried the Black Monkey. And now more blood had been shed here, soaking into the insatiable earth.

Mark looked up. A golf cart was speeding towards them, carrying two people wearing bright yellow, full-body hazmat suits. The driver raised a blue-gloved hand in greeting as he pulled the cart to a stop and stepped down from the driver's seat. His face was almost completely concealed beneath his tinted face-plate mask.

"Good afternoon," the man said. His voice broadcast through a speaker in the front of the mask, directly above the air filter intake. "This area is the private property of the Lawndale Country Club and Golf Course. Access is restricted to members in good standing and their registered guests. You are trespassing, and we must insist that you leave this area immediately."

"Trespassing?" Missy said. "Are you fucking kidding me? This man kidnapped our son!"

The man in the passenger seat, not quite as tall as the driver but otherwise indistinguishable in his identical suit, walked around to the back of the vehicle and removed what looked like a stretcher.

"We are aware of the circumstances," the tall driver said. "This is why we will not pursue criminal charges for your trespassing or for the considerable property damage your entry has caused. However, we again insist that you immediately vacate the premises. This community is under a quarantine internal to the broader quarantine that has sealed off the village of Bakersfield. Your presence here is considered a contamination, endangering the lives of the residents of this community."

"Look," Lana said. "I shot this man. I killed him. You have to report that to the authorities. There has to be an investigation."

"We will take charge of the remains," the man said. His buddy had set the stretcher down beside Deputy Bryant's body and was standing there patiently waiting for help in moving it. "In both the physical and legal sense of the word. Should there be a subsequent criminal inquiry, our lawyers will deal with the police. Your involvement need not be relevant."

"What?" Lana said.

"Wait," Mark said. "So that's it? We just leave?"

"Mark Davies," the man said. "Your mother would like to speak with you."

"My mother?"

The man tapped a button on the side of his mask. His faceplate lit up with a video image. For the second time today, Mark looked upon his mother's face on a video screen, in startlingly high definition. The other time, this morning at Shana's house, had been an illusion or a dream. Mark had been looking at his own face and only perceiving it as his mother's. Seeing her face addressing him from this man's hazmat mask was at least equally unnerving.

"Mark." Her voice emerged with perfect clarity, as if she was actually standing before him. "Is Ben all right?"

"Yeah," Mark said. "He's fine, but..."

"I'm very sorry this had to happen." She almost sounded sincere.

"You're saying it *had* to happen?"

"You need to get to a safe location."

"This is a safe location, right here," Mark said. "Isn't it? We're inside a goddamn walled fortress. Why can't we come over to your house?"

"I'm afraid that's not possible right now, Mark. You should go to the Hansard farmhouse. You'll be safe there. This will all be over in a day or two."

"How do you know that?"

"Oh, and Mark. Try not to ingest any more marijuana. You need to keep your wits about you, in order to protect your family."

"Wait, how could you possibly know about..."

Gillian Hudson's image disappeared. The man's faceplate became transparent again.

"Mom? Mom?"

"She has terminated the conversation," the man said.

"Yeah, I get that, buddy. Can you get her back?"

But the man turned away without another word. He went over to help his partner get Deputy Bryant's body loaded onto the stretcher.

Mark looked over at where Missy and Lana were holding Ben tight between them, all three looking bone-weary and blood-splattered.

"Come on," Missy said. "Let's go home."

"What the hell is *happening*?" Alice screamed.

The pounding stopped all at once. The man in the hunting vest dropped his brick and climbed through the broken window, not seeming to notice how the shattered pane cut his hand when he grabbed the frame to pull himself in.

At the same moment, Jen the werewolf lady leapt up from the couch and lunged after Sam. She jumped onto his back and went for his throat. Sam screamed. He spun around with the woman riding him, her flailing legs knocking stuff all over the floor. Sam reached his hand back, pressing against her forehead to keep her teeth away from his neck.

"Get her off me!" Sam cried.

Alice didn't know what to do. The other people who had been outside banging on the house were following the man in the orange vest through the open window, one by one. Alice realized that they had been collectively probing the house for weak spots and, once one of them found a way in, they all took advantage of it.

"Help!" Sam hollered, still struggling with the snarling woman clinging to his back.

Alice grabbed a *Time* magazine that had fallen to the floor, with Hillary Clinton's face on the cover. She rolled the magazine up and swatted the woman in the face with it. Jen let out a yelping bark and dropped off Sam.

A woman who had crawled in through the window grabbed Alice by the arm. Alice even recognized her. It was Diana Clayton, the realtor who had sold her dad the house they were living in. Alice happened to know she was on the village board of trustees. The respected local businesswoman and elected government official now looked like a homicidal street person. Greying hair wild and disheveled, white blouse torn to tatters, eyes wild and feral and darting, Diana Clayton yanked Alice's arm and reached up to grab her by the throat.

"You're the vandal who blew up my birdhouse!" Diana Clayton accused.

Sam pummeled Alice's attacker with all his considerable body weight. The slight woman was hurled to the floor, tripping up two more of the home invaders: the library lady who'd been knocking at the door with a hammer and Emma Holmes, a girl from school who Alice had hated for years. Emma was even wearing her stupid cheerleading uniform.

Sam grabbed Alice and half-carried her down the hall. They dove into the bathroom and Sam locked the door.

"Jesus," Alice cried. "What the hell?"

"This is crazy, I know," Sam said. "But we'll be safe in here."

"Safe? We can't just lock ourselves in the bathroom." The room was tiny and Sam took up more than half of it by himself. Just the thought of being trapped in here for any length of time gave Alice a breathless sense of claustrophobia. Besides, she could hear the people outside, knocking and scratching at the door. It wouldn't take them long to get in.

"It's the perfect place," Sam insisted. "We have water. And if one of us has to, you know, *go*, the other one can just turn around."

"No, Sam. Fuck that. We have to get out of this house."

"There's like half a dozen crazy people out there," Sam said. "How are we going to get past them?"

"There's got to be something in here we can use as a weapon."

"Weapon, yeah," Sam said. He opened the cabinet beneath the sink. "There's some toilet paper in here."

"Toilet paper? How is that a weapon?"

"I've got my lighter. We could use them as, like, fireballs."

"This isn't *Super fucking Mario Brothers*," Alice said. "You'll burn the house down!"

"How about this?" Sam tried to pull the towel rack off the wall, but it wouldn't budge.

"Sam." Alice picked up the wood-handled toilet plunger.

"Toilet plunger?" he said, looking at it doubtfully.

"It's the best thing we've got."

"All right," Sam said. "Give it to me."

"No. I'll take this. You should just run through these people."

"Run through them?"

"You're as big as a linebacker, Sam. Just plow them over. I'll be right behind you."

"Okay." He took a deep breath. "I think I can do that."

"I'll open the door. When I count to three, just run out there and knock 'em down."

"Got it."

Alice grabbed the doorknob. "One...two...three!"

She flung the door open. Sam let out an admirably loud cry, "Yahhh!" and ran out into the hallway with his elbows raised up to his sides.

There were three of them in the hall, crowding around the bathroom door. A dopey-looking guy in nursing scrubs, Emma the perky-ass cheerleader and Diana Clayton the birdhouse lady. Sam didn't knock them over so much as just force them backwards, pushing them out of the hall. They burst into the living room like a cork expelled from a bottle neck. Diana tripped and fell on her ass. The other two piled on top of her. Sam almost lost his balance, too, but managed to right himself.

Now they were in the more open space of the living room. Jen the werewolf girl made another snarling lunge for Sam's throat. Alice swung the toilet plunger with all her strength and caught the would-be lycanthrope right in the face. The rubber bulb wasn't the hardest edged weapon, but perhaps Jen's keen sense of smell made her recoil back.

For half a second, Alice and Sam had an open shot at the front door, but then the librarian with the hammer stepped in front of them.

"You stole my walnuts!" she accused. This offense apparently warranted a hammer to the face. She came at them wielding the tool, claw-end first.

Alice swung her plunger again, and managed to knock the hammer out of the librarian's hand. The tool went flying, and hit the guy in the hunting vest square in the back of the head. He had been sitting on the couch, cradling the brick in his arms like an infant. Getting hit in the head with a flying hammer enraged him, though. He stood up roaring and hurled the brick blindly back in the direction from which the hammer had come.

The brick missed Sam's head by inches, and shattered the big mirror hanging on the wall beside the front door.

Sam stood there frozen for a second, dazed by all the violence. Alice had to grab his hand and pull him out the door.

The bedlam inside the house seemed small in the face of what they found when they stepped outside. As soon as they stepped out of the door, sounds they had been hearing subliminally all along were now loud and undeniable. Sirens blared. People screamed. There was a distant popping sound that might have been fireworks, but which Alice was afraid was more likely gunshots. Alice saw people scuffling and fighting on their front lawns and, right across the street, a couple openly rutting beneath a lawn sprinkler.

"Fire!" Sam cried, pointing at a house just up the block with flames licking out of the upper floor windows, bellowing thick black smoke into the sky.

The siren screamed closer. For a moment it seemed to be the expected response to the house fire. But then the big ladder truck whipped around the bend at a dangerous speed. It actually went up on two tires for a few seconds before crashing headlong into a car parked off the street. As Sam and Alice watched, astonished, the firetruck burst into flames.

Riding back across town in the back seat of Missy's car, Mark held on tight to his son. Despite the heat, Ben had been shivering uncontrollably when they'd first set off from the golf course. He was still now. Mark thought that maybe he'd fallen asleep.

Mark was finally starting to come down. His teeming mind was gradually settling into something approaching rational thought; his simultaneously heightened and distorted senses slowly returning to the normal range of human perception. Mark was still high up in the stratosphere, but at least he was descending from orbit. The boy in his arms was the anchor pulling him back to earth.

Mark hadn't held his son like this since he was little. When Ben was a baby, Mark had sometimes held him for hours, the warm comforting weight of the infant laid on his chest while he watched television. Or, when he was just a bit older, Ben in his Blue's Clues jammies, snuggled in bed between Mark and Missy, in the days when the family was unbroken.

Ben sat up, pulling away from his father.

"Are you all right, Ben?" Mark asked.

"Yeah, Dad. I'm fine."

Ben replied with a weary, mature resignation, as if he'd left his childhood back there on the blood-soaked greens. He looked out the window and tilted his head curiously.

"Smoke," he said.

The cloudbanks gathering in the west had not spread to this side of the sky. The horizon out Ben's window was a soft, moist blue. The sky was cloudless save for the rising column of black smoke splitting it like a vertical charcoal smudge up the middle of a watercolor canvas.

"Mom," Ben said urgently. "Is that coming from our house?"

Missy looked out the window. "Shit," she said. "It's really close. Lana."

Lana didn't respond for a second. She seemed a little dazed, which Mark took to be a completely understandable response to having shot and killed a man fifteen minutes before. He doubted he would hold himself together nearly as well as she was under the circumstances.

"Lana," Missy repeated, louder. When Lana looked up at her, she pointed over at the column of smoke.

"Oh my God," Lana said. "Is that *us*?"

"I don't know."

Missy pulled into a squealing left turn onto Locust Street and punched the accelerator again. Her gas pedal foot was getting a real workout today. But their forward surge of speed didn't last. Missy had to almost immediately slow down to avoid colliding with a man on a riding mower, right in the middle of the street.

"Is that Virgil Jones?" Lana asked.

"Ew. I think so," Missy said.

Mr. Jones, notably, wore a John Deere cap to match his green-and-yellow mower, and nothing else. Virgil was a very large man. His flat, enormous buttocks hung out on both sides of the mower's seat. His entire bulbous body jiggled with the vibrations of the motor, like a bowl of Jello atop a washing machine.

Missy laid on the horn, but Virgil persisted in his slow, steady, jostling course up the center of the road. She even leaned her head out the window and screamed "Out of the way!" but he gave no indication that he had heard.

"What's that?" Ben leaned forward and pointed down at the bottom of the mower.

Something was caught in the outlet where the grass clippings were ejected from the blade. A slender, blood-streaked forearm dragged on the road behind the mower, bouncing along as the red-polished nails raked the asphalt.

"He ran somebody over!" Ben cried.

"Don't look, Benny," Mark said.

A diamond wedding ring glinted in the overhead sun. It was a woman's arm.

"But, Dad, he..."

"Don't look, sit down!"

Mark pulled Ben close again, pressing the boy's face close to his chest.

Missy pulled up onto the curb and sped past the fat man. Ben pulled away from Mark in time to get a look at Virgil Jones's face as they drove past.

"Why is he *smiling* like that, Dad?" Ben asked.

"I don't know, Ben. Just don't think about it, okay?"

But Mark knew he could never un-see the plastered-on grin old Virgil had been wearing. A look of pure clownish glee. He doubted his son would be able to, either.

Missy floored it again and left the murderous mower far behind. Within a minute, they were back in their subdivision.

As they got close, they saw that the smoke was not coming from Missy and Lana's house, but from another one up the block. Their relief was short-lived. Mayhem reigned all up and down their cozy shaded lane. The big firetruck was in flames, crashed into a car parked on the side of the road. People were running all over the place. Missy almost hit a young man dashing across the road. She slammed on the brakes just in time, and even so the man rolled up on the hood and hit the windshield with a huge thud. He barely slowed, though. He just jumped down from the hood and tore off towards whatever he was such a hell-bent hurry for.

Missy pulled up to her own curb. Sam and Alice were standing on the front lawn, looking a bit shell-shocked.

"The front window's broken," Ben noted.

Missy jumped out of the car and ran over to Sam. "What happened to my house?"

"Sorry," Sam said guiltily. "All these crazy people broke in. We had to get out of there."

"Where's my sister?"

Answering that question, Jen staggered out of the front door. She appeared to be winding down. She let out a yawning howl and sat down hard on the porch bench.

Lana got out of the car. Mark followed, keeping one hand on the back of Ben's neck. It seemed important not to break physical contact with his son.

Alice smiled when she saw Ben. "Thank God, you got him back." Then she seemed to notice the blood that was all over all of them. "What happened?"

"Later," Lana said. "First, I have to get these lunatics out of my house."

"They're not going to let you in there," Sam said.

"Yeah. We'll see about that," she said, lifting up her gun.

Sam raised his hands and stepped back by reflex at the sight of the gun. Lana rushed into the house, followed closely by Missy.

"Wait here," Mark said to Ben, and then he went into the house after them.

Inside, they found the strangest house party of all time. A pretty blonde teenager in a cheerleading uniform provided the music. She sat bouncing on the couch, clapping and singing at the top of her lungs. Though she was mangling the tune, Mark recognized the lyrics from the *Dora the Explorer* theme song. A man in an orange hunting vest and a middle-aged woman in a tweed skirt danced in time to the cheerleader's frenetic hooting and clapping, writhing against one another in a rhythmic grind that was little more than a standing dry hump. Meanwhile, a heavy, red-faced man in tight, greasy nursing scrubs sat on the couch. He pulled stuffing from a rip in the upholstery, eating it up like popcorn.

"Hey!" Lana called. "All you people! This is our house! You need to get on out of here right now!"

Nobody seemed to notice her. The cheerleader continued to riff about Swiper the fox. The dirty dancing couple ground even closer. The guy on the couch did pause for a moment in consuming his couch cushion hors d'ouevres, but perhaps he was just looking around for the dip.

"I'm not talking to hear myself talk, people!" Lana yelled in a voice she must have reserved to tame rowdy classrooms.

At that, a completely crazed-looking woman in a tattered white blouse ran screaming from the kitchen. Her eyes were bloodshot red and churning in their sockets. In her hand was a big carving knife.

Lana raised her gun and Mark braced himself for the shot. But Lana balked. She fell back instead. The three of them retreated out the front door, slamming it in the madwoman's face.

"I'm sorry," Lana said. "I can't shoot another person today. I just can't."

"It's all right, baby." Missy embraced her wife and gently took the gun from her hand. "It's all right. We'll just..."

She left this dangling.

"You know it kills me to say this," Mark said. "But maybe my mom was right. Maybe we should go out to the farmhouse."

Missy looked over at him. "Mark, that place is..."

"I know," he said. "But it's big enough for all of us and it's far enough out of town that maybe we'll be safe from all this." He waved his hand around at the mayhem that had consumed the once-quiet neighborhood.

"This is *our* house," Missy said. "We can't just leave it. Those people will..."

A huge explosion up the block made them all cower for a second. Flames had ignited the firetruck's big gas tank. A massive fireball erupted into the sky. The street was filled with thick black smoke.

A few moments later, the fat naked grinning Virgil Jones rolled his murder machine through the dark fog. Heading right towards them at a steady four miles per hour.

That seemed to make up Lana's mind, at least. She looked from the slowly approaching mower over to Mark. "You okay to drive my car, Stoney Man?"

"Yeah," Mark said.

"Well, the air bags have already deployed and the back end's smashed to hell," Lana said. "So I guess you can't fuck it up worse than it is. You take Sam and Alice. Ben and Jen will ride with me and Chelle."

"Wait," Sam said, rushing over to them. "You're not talking about going back to my Grandma's house, are you?"

"It's the safest place, Sam," Mark said. "It may be the *only* place."

"No way. Nuh-uh. Fuck that. You can drop me off at my apartment."

"Your apartment's right downtown," Mark said. "Who knows what kind of craziness is going on down there?"

"I don't care," said Sam. "I'd rather take my chances with that."

"Fine," Mark said. "We'll drop you off and meet everybody else up at the farmhouse. Let's get moving, though."

Mark helped Missy and Lana get the barely conscious Jen into the other car. Then he climbed with Sam and Alice into the battered Prius. In two cars, they retreated from the madness that had conquered the once-peaceful village street.

CHAPTER 20

THE OVERCAST BY now had consumed most of the sky with a chalky slate color, save for a jagged clear patch in the clouds through which a dazzling beam of sunlight shone. As if God was casting a spotlight on the wondrous, terrible pandemonium below.

Downtown Bakersfield was consumed with full-tilt, balls-out, wall-to-wall chaos. Mark drove past what looked like a full-scale orgy in progress on the square. A mass of naked, writhing flesh carpeted the green lawn over by the swing sets. Farmers and local business people and ethanol plant employees rolled together in the grass, uncountable as garter snakes in a mating ball, coupling in apparently random permutations without regard to notions such as age, gender, attractiveness, or social standing.

Competing with the orgy for sheer bizarre spectacle, a small herd of pigs frolicked upon the opposite corner of the square. Happy, smiling porkers mingled and danced in what appeared to a regular porcine soiree. Stranger still, the piggy festivities were joined by what Mark thought at first was a huge dog, but which on his second astonished glance turned out to be a black bear.

"Look out!" Sam cried.

Mark looked away from the bear just in time to swerve out of the path of the big RV barreling towards him. Lana's little car jumped up onto the sidewalk and knocked over a bright blue newspaper vending machine, scattering free real estate magazines into the rising wind.

The RV jumped the curb over on the other side of the street, took out a fire hydrant, rammed into the war memorial statue and was immediately beset on all sides. People ran in from every direction, including a few naked men and women who had abandoned the orgy to join the communal project of trying to tip the big camper over.

Meanwhile, the sheared-off hydrant released a skyward geyser. People and pigs danced together in the sudden rain while the gushing flood rapidly turned the lawn into a mud pit.

"Oh my God," Alice observed from the backseat as Mark pulled back out onto the street. "This is worse than the boat ride in *Willy Wonka.*"

Even above and beyond the anarchy all around them, what struck Mark as truly, overridingly strange was that all the movement; the humping and the thrashing of the orgiastic revelers, the rocking rhythm of the RV-tippers, the skyward pumping fists of the assorted rioters and even, God help him, the dancing pigs, conformed to an eerie synchronization. As if all were moving to the beat of pounding techno music only their sleeping ears could detect.

Mark was coming up on the front of the bank, and the doorway to Sam's apartment.

"You sure you don't want to come with us?" Mark said.

"Yeah, man. I'll be all right," said Sam.

"What's so bad about this house that you'd rather sit alone in your apartment, surrounded by all this crazy shit?" Alice asked.

"Trust me. You'll find out."

"Well, hell. Maybe I better stay with you."

"Whatever you want to do," Mark said, pulling to a stop. "But hurry up and...oh, what fresh fuck is this?"

Someone had driven a motorcycle through the bank's front glass window. The bike lay abandoned on its side, half in and half out of the storefront. A well-dressed middle-aged woman was crawling out of the bank window, over the motorcycle and the broken glass. She carried two fistfuls of cash in her bloody hands.

"That's Mary Roslin," Sam cried. "She's my landlady!"

A very large shirtless man with a massively hairy barrel chest stumbled out onto the sidewalk after Mary Roslin.

"That's Grizzly Gallatin," said Sam. "He's a guard at the bank. I know these people!"

The aptly-named Grizzly shoved a bill of some denomination into his mouth. Mary Roslin followed suit, stuffing several blood-stained bills into her mouth and chewing them greedily. Both Mary and Griz swallowed, consuming their currency, and then each helped themselves to a fresh mouthful of cash.

"What the hell are they doing?" Sam cried.

At the sound of his voice, both Mary and Grizzly turned towards the idling car. They rushed over, mouths open to show off their wadded clumps of half-chewed money.

"Uh, they're coming over here, Sam," Mark said, his foot itching to floor the gas pedal. "You still want to get out here?"

"I don't know, man."

"Well, make up your mind pretty goddamn quick."

On the other side of the car, a woman ran across the street towards them. It was Alyssa Wilson, looking frail and hollow-eyed. Her dark hair was tangled and she was naked to the waist. Alyssa's exposed breasts were covered with bloody bites and scratches. She'd somehow recaptured her squirrel baby, or perhaps it was another squirrel. In either case, she clutched the poor creature by the throat and banged on the back window with the half-alive rodent, leaving bloody smudges all over the glass.

"Okay, they're beating on the car with live squirrels now," Mark said. "That's my limit. Last chance, Sam. I'm going to go."

Sam nodded as if this caused his neck great pain. "Go," he said.

Gratefully, Mark peeled out back onto the street, leaving the money-eaters and the crazy squirrel lady behind. He accelerated south, putting precious blocks between them and the chaos of the town square.

Just past the elementary school, they came upon a man on horseback in the middle of the road. The man wore an old fashioned suit and cap, looking like he and his horse had just arrived via time machine from the late nineteenth century. Mark had to slam on the brakes to avoid colliding with the anachronistic man and beast.

"Go around him," Alice prodded.

Mark lurched the car forward, but the man turned his horse to block his path.

"He's not letting me past."

"Just...run him over," Sam said, anxious.

"You can't run over a horse with a *Prius*."

"Well, turn around or something, I think..."

Too late. The trap was sprung. Men with baseball bats fell upon the car from both sides, shattering the two side windows that weren't already busted out. Glass went flying everywhere and grasping hands reached into the car.

Lana finally breathed a little easier as Michelle cruised out towards the water tower, leaving the insanity of downtown Bakersfield behind for whatever insanity might lie ahead in this farmhouse that had everybody so freaked out. Her relief may have been premature.

"Dad?" Ben said anxiously in the back seat.

Lana turned around. Ben undid his seatbelt and sat up to look out the back window, very alert all of the sudden. Beside him, Jen started to stir, too. She let out a moaning whine, a sound a dreaming dog would make.

"What's wrong, Ben?" Lana said.

"I thought I heard..." Ben stopped and cocked his head to listen. "Dad just yelled, 'help!' Didn't you hear that?"

Lana and Chelle exchanged a look. "I don't hear anything, Ben," Michelle said. "Your dad's way back—"

"We have to turn around and help him!" Ben pleaded. "He's screaming!"

Michelle pulled over onto the shoulder. She gave the dashboard three even taps with her fingers in quick succession, an invocation of some sort, and then closed her eyes.

"He's right," she said. "I see...a horse. A man on a horse. There are people all around him. Mark's...he's trying to help Alice, but there are too many of them."

The weirdest damn thing was, Lana received mental flashes of the images as Michelle described them. She saw the horse. She saw the people crowding around her little car. She saw Mark lunging at a man who was attacking Alice. The brief glimmers broke apart before she could get a handle on any one of them, like a signal from a distant television station that came in with flickering bursts of clarity before fading into snowy static. Either the broadcast was strong enough now that Lana could receive it a little even with her lack of an antenna, or maybe it was just Lana's proximity to Michelle and Ben. Mother and son were both so strongly psychic that they boosted the signal to the point where even a normy like Lana could pick up on the second-hand telepathy.

"Damn it." Michelle said. She turned around to check the road in both directions.

"Are we going back to help him?" Ben cried.

"Yeah, Ben," Michelle said. "Put your seatbelt back on."

Michelle whipped back onto the road with a sharp U-turn. In the backseat, Jen gave a start. Her eyes fluttered and she let out a growl, then she slumped over again. She twitched in her restless sleep.

"Great. We need her waking up right now like we all need spare assholes," Lana said.

Alice had managed to pull off one of her boots. A tall, sad-faced man with a cigarette clenched between his teeth had leaned into her window, trying to grab her. She whacked him in the face with the heel, knocking the cigarette out of his mouth, and drove the man back from her window. Mark saw this and realized with dismay that Alice's footwear was the most effective weapon they had in the car.

A pudgy, balding guy in a rumpled suit, who looked like the world's meekest accountant, lunged through Mark's bashed-in driver's side window. The man snarled with rage, his face sweaty and red, eyes twitching with the sickness. Mark punched him in the jaw.

He had never punched anyone before, and was surprised at how much it hurt his hand. He felt every bone in the guy's face, and several teeth, hard and sharp against his knuckles. In movies, punching only hurt the guy who got punched, but in real life it seemed to be an even split. The accountant guy fell back briefly, but soon enough both he and the guy who'd grabbed for Alice had regrouped and were leaning back in for another try.

Alice screamed. Her attacker grabbed her by the shoulders and dragged her out through the broken window. Then the accountant guy returned Mark's punch, hard across the cheek. Mark had to concede that, yes, it did hurt more to be on the receiving end. Sam was having his own problems, with a husky woman who had grabbed him around the neck and was apparently trying to wrench his head off by the beard.

Mark shouldered his door open. The door hit the accountant in the midsection, knocking him to the ground. Mark leapt out of the car and went for the man who had grabbed Alice. Falling back on the most effective fighting move he knew, Mark kicked the guy in the nuts. That seemed to work all right. The guy let go of Alice and collapsed into a crumpled ball on the ground. This victory, though sweet, was only temporary, because Mark looked up to see at least half a dozen people descending upon the car with crazed eyes.

They were surrounded.

Lana held on tight as Michelle sped back into town. They came upon the other car about a half-mile back, out in front of the elementary school. It was just as Lana had seen it in her head. Mark stood beside her battered Prius, helping Alice to her feet as the people closed in around them. In the backseat, Sam was trying to fight off Pam Burke, the fat cafeteria lady from the high school. The guy on horseback stood above it all, shouting what may have been orders for the others, or perhaps just lunatic gibberish.

Michelle slammed the brakes and looked over at Lana.

"You ready for this?"

Lana looked down at the gun resting on her lap. It seemed to have grown much heavier. So heavy she didn't know if she could lift it. The sense memory of shooting Deputy Bryant was still with her. There was tension still in her trigger finger, the scent of burning powder still in her nostrils, the sight of the deputy's blood still fresh in her eyes.

"Sorry, Chelle," Lana said. "I meant it when I said I can't shoot anybody else today."

"Give it to me," Chelle said.

"You sure?"

"I got it, baby." She took the weapon and turned around to face Ben. "Stay in the car."

"Okay, Mom," he said, glancing sideways at his Aunt, who moaned and twitched in her shallow sleep.

The circle of aggressors had closed in tight around them. Mark made what he felt to be a valiant lunge, in an attempt to drive them back. This proved to be wholly ineffectual. The accountant guy he'd punched and a woman in a business suit grabbed him by each arm. They seemed to disagree, though, on who deserved the capture, because they began a tug-of-war over his body. It felt like they were trying to tear him in half.

Then there was a sudden gunshot. Both the people holding him let go of his arms and fell back at the sound. Mark looked up. Missy stood there, gun hand raised in the air, looking ethereally beautiful. A warrior goddess. An avenging angel.

"I am *so* glad to see you right now," he said to her.

Holding the gun before her, Michelle stepped into the midst of the people surrounding the car. She waved it back and forth, sweeping the small crowd.

"Everybody just back up," Michelle said.

Even if they were sleepwalking, the people seemed to recognize what the gun was. They backed away from its power, eyeing the weapon with an animal wariness.

Over on the passenger side, the big lady was still tangling with Sam. Michelle pointed the gun right at her face.

"Let him go, dump truck," she snarled.

The woman returned the snarl. She did back away from the car, though with a final ripping tear that yielded her a fistful of Sam's beard hair and a scream of pain from the big man.

"Get back into the car," Missy said to Mark.

"You bet."

Alice was still on the ground. Mark helped her to her feet and back into the car. He opened the driver's side door and was about to slide back in behind the wheel when a sound stopped him cold.

Over in the other car, Ben screamed.

Lana heard Ben cry out behind her. She turned and looked back into the car. He'd crawled into the front seat, to get away from Jen. She was awake, flailing her arms out, trying to grab him, but her seatbelt kept her pinned in the back.

"Help him!" Michelle called over to her. The people surrounding the Prius seemed to have lost their gun-shyness. They were closing in on Michelle and Mark again.

Ben opened the front door and climbed out of the car. Lana took a step towards him. Then a teenaged boy grabbed Ben by the arm.

Lana knew the kid. He was one of her worst students, in fact. It was Joe Foster, noted essayist, author of "Hunting Peasants with My Dad."

"Don't worry, kid," Joe said to Ben. "I got you."

There was a commotion over by the other car, a horse whinnying and human cries of alarm. For a second, Lana froze. She almost went back to help her wife, but she did not like the look on the face of the boy who had grabbed her son.

Luke Simmons appeared at Joe's side, which was not surprising in the least. It was rare to see one without the other. They were definitely of a pair, both members of the Future Redneck Hoodlums of America club.

"Oh, hey. It's Mrs. Blair-Delany," Luke grinned.

"This your kid?" Joe said. He grasped Ben's arm tight and chuckled. "He don't look much like you."

Lana glanced back. Michelle and Mark were both on the ground with a few other people. Chelle had lost the gun somehow, and they were all scrabbling for it. Still, Lana knew that Ben needed her more.

"Let him go," she said to Joe. She looked at his eyes, looked at Luke's. They were normal. These boys weren't asleep, weren't dreaming. They were just out here soaking in the anarchy for the sheer fun of it.

In the second Michelle was distracted by her son's cries, the rider spurred his horse over at her. The animal reared up. Its front hooves knocked the gun from Michelle's hand.

Michelle dove to the side, to avoid getting crushed by the horse. The horse's hoof stomped to earth a scant inch from Michelle's head, close enough that she saw the sparks of the metal shoe striking the pavement. She saw Mark lunge for the gun, but somebody kicked it away before he could grab it. It clattered across the asphalt, coming to rest underneath the car.

Michelle crawled towards the gun, flanked on both sides by men equally desperate to reach the weapon. Old Mr. Miller, who drove both a tow truck and a snow plow for the town when he was sober enough, elbowed her in the cheek just below her left eye. He reached for the gun, but Mark kicked him in the head and knocked him aside.

Her eye stinging and watering, Michelle lunged forward. She was halfway under the car now, the gun inches from her fingers. She stretched and reached, but a skinny teenage girl dressed in neo-hippie garb reached under from the other side of the car. She got to the gun first, snatching it triumphantly from Michelle's grasping fingertips.

Lana shut out what was happening back at the other car. Focused completely on her son and on the two young men before her.

"We were just talking about you with Jeff and Ray and them," Luke said. "You know, like locker room talk. Who's the hottest teacher at the school and all that. Those idiots actually said Ms. Winslow's hotter than you are. Believe that shit?"

"Winslow's got no titties," Joe said. "What's the point in that?" He had Ben by both arms now. Ben struggled a little and Joe grasped him tighter.

"We stood up for you, though," Luke assured her. "I said 'Blair-Delany all the way, motherfuckers.' Turns out they only like her better because she's white and they're a bunch of racist dickwads. To me, black or white don't matter if you're talking about a beautiful woman. What do you think, Joe?"

"Hell, yeah. I *like* black chicks. I think they're hot, and...ow, stop squirming, you little shit. I'm trying to talk to your Mammy here."

"Mammy," Luke laughed.

"Let him go," Lana said again.

"I will if you show us your tits," Joe said. His jaw had gone slack and he was staring intently at her chest. "I never seen a black lady's boobs in real life. Just in pornos and shit. How about you, Luke? You ever see a real-life black titty?"

"Just your mom's."

"Oh, hah hah. That's really fucking hilarious." Joe looked back up at Lana. "I'm *serious*, Ms. Delany. All we want is a peek, maybe a real quick squeeze for each of us, and I'll then let the kid go."

"Let him go first and I'll show you more than that." Lana tilted her head and gave the words what she hoped was a flirtatious tone, one that didn't betray her fear or her anger.

"Ho, *shit*," Luke laughed.

"Really?" There was sweat on Joe's brow.

"I promise."

"Is it..." Oddly, he looked nervous. Maybe a little scared. "Is the hair like really kinky? Can I touch it?"

"Let him go."

Grinning, Joe released Ben's arms.

"Get behind me, Ben," Lana said.

Ben ran over and slid behind her. Lana stood between her son and the two young men.

"All right," Joe said breathlessly. "Unzip your jeans a little. I wanna see what kind of panties you're wearing."

"Fuck you."

"Hey," Joe's face registered dull outrage. "We had a deal."

Luke stood close beside him. "A deal is a deal, Ms. Delany. Might as well give it up friendly, because we're going to take it anyway."

They took a step towards her. Lana stood tall, every part of her gone hard as steel.

Mark saw Missy lunge underneath the car, grabbing for the gun. He did his best to fight off the two men trying to get to it before she did. He kicked one of the guys in the head, which seemed to help, even though Mark only had his sneakers on.

It didn't matter, though, because a skinny shapeless girl with long blonde hair pulled over her face managed to grab the gun from the other side of the car.

"Thank God," the girl said, standing up. "I found my air hose. Now I can breathe!"

She put the gun into her mouth and drew a deep breath from the metal chamber.

"No!" Mark called. He tried to dive over the roof of the car, but didn't quite make the leap. His chest slammed against the vehicle, knocking the wind out of him.

Sam opened the rear door on the other side of the car, knocking it against the girl. The gun slid out of her mouth just as she pulled the trigger. The bullet that would have gone into her skull instead grazed a bloody diagonal line across her cheek.

The sudden pain seemed to wake the girl up. She let out a shocked cry and dropped the gun to the ground, beginning a new round of scrambling for the weapon.

Another shot rang out in the air. Lana didn't know who was shooting or who was getting shot or if Michelle was either of these parties, but she did not waver.

Joe and Luke both turned at the shot, and she took advantage of their brief distraction. All her rage coursing through her, she brought her foot up brutally between Joe Carter's legs. Hard enough to drive them to the roof of his mouth.

Joe made a satisfyingly comic "oof" sound and toppled sideways. Luke rounded on her, eyes blazing. Lana swung her fist hard into his stupid face.

It was like punching a wall. Luke staggered back on his heels for a second, but recovered quickly. He pounced at her, teeth clenched with anger. Lana stepped back and stumbled, falling on her ass. Luke was on her in an instant, pinning her to the ground. His eager fury prodded against her leg.

"Ah, God yeah," he grunted, thrusting against her, zealous enough perhaps to climax through both their layers of clothes.

Then, suddenly, he rolled off her, howling with pain.

Luke grasped his head in both hands. Ben was standing above him, a rock clutched in his fist. He wore a look of astonishment on his face, as if surprised at his own strength and fury.

"Thanks, Benny." Lana got to her feet. "Let me see that rock."

She stomped her heel into Luke's throat before he could recover from the blow to his head. He let out a choking gasp. Lana might or might not have crushed his trachea. She didn't really give a shit either way. She walked over to where Joe was still rocking back and forth on the ground, cradling his wounded jewels in his hand.

"Why'd you hafta kick me in the..."

Lana shut down his whining by cramming the egg-sized rock into the little punk-ass's mouth. She saw at least two of his teeth crack in half as she drove the stone in.

"You ever," she snarled, "*ever* disrespect me in front of my child again, I'll kill you. Understand, motherfucker?"

Joe's only response was a bloody, gurgling whimper, but she was pretty sure the motherfucker understood.

Sheriff Bates was badly shaken. Things, it seemed, had gone to shit with an alarming rapidity. He'd started following Tim Black out to the Bakersfield Inn, but halfway out to the burning motel, Black had veered his car off the road. He tore through the Casey's General parking lot, and missed taking out the gas pumps by a couple of feet. Then Tim punched his car right through the store's glass front door.

Bates pulled up over beside the wreck and got out of his truck. He peered through the shattered glass. Tim Black had leapt out of his car and run into the otherwise deserted store. The hotelier was over by the bakery case, his trousers torn open, sliding pink-frosted sprinkled donuts one by one over his impressively rigid erection. Like he had been possessed by a sudden yearning to fuck some donuts so irresistible that driving his vehicle right into the nearest convenience store to get at the objects of his desire was an entirely reasonable decision.

Bates watched, dumbfounded, as Mr. Black got six of the frosted pastries slid on over himself. Nate couldn't see if his eyes were twitching, but Black wore a look of religious ecstasy on his face. The sublime rapture only a man with a half-dozen donuts impaled upon his dick could possibly know.

Nate turned away from the display, forcing himself to chuckle. That should have been funny as hell, but the sight troubled Nate. Black had seemed fine when they'd left Potter's place ten minutes before. This thing was moving faster now.

The black column of smoke to the north that Nate assumed was the burning hotel was only one of many streaking the greying sky in every direction. Nate counted seven that he could see just from where he was standing. He'd already tried calling the cell numbers of every firefighter on his call list, but none of them had picked up. His town was burning down all around him.

He walked back to his truck. Mara was in the cab, wrists cuffed to the passenger side grab handle. All she had on was the silk kimono he'd bought her for Christmas last year. When Nate slid behind the wheel, she looked over at him with that unsettling eye tic.

"You dare to restrain me?" she said, in the same arrogant, condescending tone she'd been using since he'd dragged her out of her ex-husband's storm cellar. Like he was the one who'd done something he should be ashamed of.

Nate ignored his wife. He started the engine and pulled away from the general store, heading south back into town. Not that he had any real idea where he was going.

"Phone," he said to his truck. "Call JJ."

Three rings. "Hello?" came JJ's flat, indolent voice.

"John," Nate said. "How's your Mama?"

"Mama?" JJ came back. His voice was way, way off. "Is that you?"

"Oh, shit." Nate felt something inside him sink and drown. "Not you too, JJ."

"Mama, some angels came to the door," JJ said. Nate heard abject terror in his voice. "They said they were angels, but I didn't like the way they were looking at me. They saw everything I've ever done." He broke down into sobs. "I've done some bad things, Mama."

Nate terminated the call. He didn't need to hear any more of that crazy fucking talk. He'd heard enough to last him a lifetime.

But then Mara had to chime in. "I command you to release me, mortal," she said, pulling at her chains. "I must resume my hunt. With my arrows I have felled two boars."

"Shut up, Mara," Nate said. "I'm a little pissed off at you right now."

What the hell was happening? It was all falling apart. Not even an hour ago, Nate had felt completely on top of things. He'd just eliminated Pastor Tuttle and passed the torch onto Tom. His soldiers had seemed to have a good grip on the town. Things were sliding into place so that when all this was over, he'd be in a better position than he was before it had started.

But now it had all gone to shit. The town was burning and the people were running wild in the streets. He wasn't even sure if there was going to be a town left for him to inherit. What had gone wrong?

Then it hit him. It was his own damn fault.

Nate didn't believe in God. He didn't believe in fate. Didn't believe in karma or any of that mystical hippie-drippy third eye crystal-hugging bullshit, either. But he did believe that actions had consequences. Inaction had consequences as well.

Everything had been fine before he'd gone to Bill Potter's place. After that—hell time, man. And what had happened at Potter's house? Nate had failed to act. He'd had the one fucker he despised above all others standing right in front of him, hands raised. The gun was in Nate's hand, warmed up already from shooting that shithead's dog. And yet, Nate had backed down. He'd been handed an opportunity on a goddamn platter and he'd turned away from it. Not wanting to shoot the old teacher cold-blooded, not wanting to do it in front of witnesses, maybe even taking a measure of pity on the sad-sack fucker. Whatever the reasons, it boiled down to failure. His failure. And a rare opportunity like that was unlikely to be put in front of him again.

But then, as Bates drove past the churning sea of crazy that was downtown Bakersfield, a miracle. He pulled up behind a faded maroon Volvo, the tattered remains of a "Clinton/ Gore '96" bumper sticker still clinging to the back. Nate didn't recognize the vehicle at first, just wondered vaguely what kind of liberal douchebag didn't scrape off a bumper sticker twenty years after the goddamn election. Then he realized that he *knew* this liberal douchebag.

It was Bill Potter's car.

The opportunity was right in front of him again.

He pulled in close, just to be sure. Yep. He made out the schoolteacher's unmistakable silhouette behind the wheel, hair wild and crazy like he was too much of an intellectual to bother with petty things like barber shops or even a goddamn comb.

On the seat beside Nate, Mara leaned forward, looking out the windshield. Nate couldn't tell if she recognized the car that had once been hers, or if she was even really seeing anything at all of the real world through her corkscrew eyes. But he would make damn sure that she was watching before he blew her ex-husband away.

Nate stayed on Potter's ass as the Volvo cruised south. He considered giving the back bumper a little kiss, just to let Bill know he had some company. It would be fun to play some vehicular cat and mouse to get him good and scared before Nate finally ran the car off the road.

But then Bill did something unexpected. Coming up on the elementary school, a cluster of people had spilled out into the street. Two or three cars pulled over and even a guy on a horse. Some kind of commotion or disturbance.

Rather than slowing down at the blocked road, Bill Potter floored it as he came upon the little mob. Then, to Nate's astonishment, he veered off. Bill Potter drove right into a guy standing in the road, sending his body flying. Like a bowling ball picking up a one-pin spare.

Mark had lost track of the gun again. Sam and Missy and Lana were all lined up beside him along the side of the car. The four adults stood between the pressing crowd and Ben and Alice, who were huddled together within the dubious shelter of a Prius with all its windows busted out.

At least nine or ten people faced them now. It was hard to keep count. They kept moving in and out, new people arriving as others lost interest and left, their motives and plan of attack following some inscrutable dream logic.

Then a scrawny teenage kid with a bloody mouth shoved his way through. He'd found the gun and picked it up, was pointing it right at Lana's head.

"You broke my teeth, you bitch," the kid cried, with a miserable mush-mouthed sob. "I just wanted to look at it!"

Mark tried to lunge for the guy, but the woman in the business suit who had grabbed him before now clutched Mark's shirt in both her fists and tried to pull him in close. To kiss him or to chew his face off, either was equally likely given the hunger in her mad grinning eyes. Mark shoved her back into another man, the old guy he'd previously kicked in the head.

That guy staggered back, jostling the kid with the gun. The kid tried to keep steady, to hold Lana in his sights. He shouldered dreamers aside until he stood alone again. Then he twisted his arm sideways and racked the slide like he thought he was some kind of TV gangster. The muscles in the kid's arm went taut as he braced for the kick of the trigger. He was so close there was no way he could miss.

There, from nowhere and from everywhere at once, came an animal roar. Like an enraged tiger. Half a second later, a car slammed into the kid.

He went flying, flipping over the hood and over the roof of the car, tossed into the air, weightless as a ragdoll. The gun flew from his hand. Mark caught a glimpse of the weapon spinning through the air in silhouette and then lost sight of it again. The kid fell to earth with a splintering crack, landing in a bloody, twisted pile of shattered bones.

Their savior's car screeched to a halt and its driver emerged.

"Bill!" Mark cried.

Potter looked over at them. "You guys all right? I saw that guy pointing the gun at you and I just reacted. Who did I..." he looked back. "Who was that?"

"Joe Carter," Lana said.

"Oh," said Bill. He shrugged and nodded, apparently finding this an acceptable loss. "Get in my car. We'll get out of here."

A big truck pulled alongside Bill's car. Sheriff Bates, probably the last man on earth Mark wanted to see at that moment, swung down from the cab of the truck. He was grinning from ear to ear, gun already in hand.

Nate climbed out of his truck and was delighted to find not only Bill Potter standing there by the side of the road, but Mark Davies as well.

His two favorite shitheads in the world. And hey, look at that, fat-ass Sam Hansard, too. A three-for-one bonus. The only question was which of the fuckers he should ice first.

"Bill Potter," he answered for himself. Number one in his heart, of course. "A little vehicular homicide on top of the rape you already committed today?"

Bill didn't seem overly concerned at the gun pointed at his head. He looked over at Nate's truck instead.

"Is Mara all right?" he said.

"Shut the fuck up," Bates said. "God, I'm going to enjoy this. I just wish I could make it last longer."

So intent was Nate upon Bill Potter that he didn't really notice Mark Davies diving to the ground, except to wonder in kind of a subliminal way if the guy was really such a pussy-ass that he'd pass out cold from terror. But when Mark stood up again, he was holding a gun. And pointing it right at Nate.

"Fucking dumb-ass," Bates said, keeping his own weapon trained upon Bill Potter.

"Put the gun down, sheriff," Davies said, voice shaking almost as badly as his hand was.

"You want to think real hard about what you're doing there, son."

"Put it down."

"You really think you can shoot me before I shoot him?"

"No, but you'll be dead either way."

Bates had to laugh at that. "Pretty tough talk there. You sure you got the balls? You know your Mama's not here to wipe your ass when you shit your pants with fear."

"Put it down!"

Bates evaluated the situation at hand. He knew beyond any doubt that Mark didn't have it in him to shoot first. But if Nate shot Bill, Mark might pull the trigger in a panicked reaction. Close as he was, he might even score a hit. That made him dangerous. So Nate would have to shoot Mark first. He rehearsed the move mentally before he acted. A quick pivot on his heel, swinging his gun arm over, pulling the trigger before the quivering kid could react. Maybe distract him a little first.

"You ever fire a gun before?" Nate asked conversationally.

"No," Mark said. "But I've seen lots of movies."

"Well, then you should know that they work better when you take the safety off."

Just a momentary hesitation, the kid looking down at his weapon, trying to figure out where the hell the safety was located, but it was enough.

Nate swung around. He had the fucker dead to rights. But then, from out of nowhere, a woman jumped on Nate's back and sank her teeth into his neck.

"Jen!" Michelle screamed as her sister leapt on the sheriff's back and, with a vicious snarl, went right for his throat.

Bates fired his weapon, but the bullet went wild, into the air just above their heads. Lana grabbed Michelle and held her back.

The dreamers in the pressing mob didn't even flinch at the discharge of the gun. They were becoming inured to the sound. They had been wary, perhaps driven off by the car bowling down Joe Carter, but now they surged forward again.

Jen, rabid madness in her eyes, tore a chunk of flesh from Sheriff Bates's throat. She swallowed it with two chomping bites. Bates screamed as the blood poured down his neck. He raised up his gun hand, pointed it back over his shoulder at the crazed woman clinging to him.

Chelle grabbed Mark's arm. "Shoot him!" she screamed.

Mark lifted his gun, but hesitated. Bates spun around with Jen flailing on his back and Mark wasn't confident enough that he wouldn't hit her. He was shoved from the side by one of the crowding dreamers and lost whatever marginal shot he had.

Bates pressed his gun against Jen's cheekbone and pulled the trigger. The bullet punched a smoking black hole through her face.

"No!" Michelle screamed, pure anguish tearing through the air. Her cry of denial was echoed half a second later by Ben, from inside the car.

Jen dropped to the ground. Bates put another bullet into her head.

Lana held Michelle by both arms, restraining her. She was wild. Her desire to lunge at the sheriff was so clear that Lana felt it like a signal coursing through her muscles.

The sheriff turned, one hand pressed against his bleeding neck wound, the other grasping his pistol tight, eager to fire it again. But the dreamers, like sharks, went into a frenzy at the sight and the scent of his blood. They were on him in an instant, pulling him to the ground. Nate got off one blind shot as they piled on top of him. The bullet hit the man astride the horse in his shoulder, knocking him to the ground.

"Get the fuck offa me!" the sheriff bellowed from beneath the piling mass of bodies. "You know who I fuckin' am?"

"Let's go!" Mark screamed. He dove behind the wheel of Lana's Prius. Sam followed his lead, piling into the passenger seat. "Missy! Get in your car! Now!"

Chelle knelt by her sister's side, touching Jen's shattered face.

"I'm not going to leave her here," she sobbed. "I can't leave her here."

"I'll help you, baby," Lana said. She grabbed Jen by one arm and helped Chelle drag the body back over to the other car. Bill Potter appeared at their side and helped them lift Jen into the Honda's back seat.

The dreamers were still piled upon Sheriff Bates, who had descended into incoherent screams of rage.

"Follow us," Lana said to Bill. "We have a place we can go."

Bill looked back at the sheriff's truck. "Mara's in there."

"She'll be safe," Lana said. "They don't attack one another."

Bill gave a pained nod, but he did climb back into his own car.

They pulled out, with Mark in the lead. The caravan of three vehicles left the riot behind.

Mark drove out of town, quiet sobbing coming from the back seat that was either his son or Alice. He didn't turn around to see. Sam was in the passenger seat, dazed and bloodied. Mark himself felt numb and cold. He glanced in the rear view, just to be sure that the other two cars were still following. They were.

Driving past the water tower, Mark looked up and saw three dark forms up on the encircling platform. They'd defaced the tower with red spray paint, giving King Chip demonic eyes and bloody dripping fangs.

Words were painted above the name of the town, but before Mark could read what was written there, he was distracted by falling motion.

One of the people up on the tower jumped off the side. A moment later, another suicide followed. Mark looked away before he could see the bodies hit the ground or witness the third person on the tower diving to their death. He'd seen enough such things today and did not need to see more.

He drove past, leaving the tower behind, but could not resist a final look as it receded in the mirror, just to see what the people on the tower had chosen as their final statement. He grinned bitterly when he read it because the words seemed hideously apt. Two words had been painted in dripping red above the name of the town. Or, rather, the same word twice. The tower now declared this place to be BLOODY BLOODY BAKERSFIELD.

CHAPTER 21

THE TOWN WAS in Ben's blood. He knew it like he knew his body. He'd been down this road leading out of town a hundred times, but it had never looked like this before. The road was as black as the gathering storm clouds above. Black as a gangrenous leg about to fall off. Black, like the asphalt had melted back into tar that the car might sink into like a dying dinosaur. Ben had never noticed before how the black ribbon narrowed as it led out of town, as if being swallowed by the corn fields on either side.

The summer corn should have been green, capped with yellow tassels, but as they drove south, Ben saw that the stalks had all gone brown. The corn was withered and dead. He knew it was the house that had poisoned the crops. If he were to see the fields from the air, the dead corn would radiate out in a perfect brown circle, with the house right in the center.

Lana's Prius hardly made any sound as it hummed down the smooth black road squeezed between the dead standing rows. Dad was at the wheel, staring straight ahead as he drove. Dad's friend Sam sat in the passenger seat, looking pale and bloodless and afraid. In the back seat beside Ben was the girl named Alice, hugging herself and shivering. Nobody talked. There was nothing to be said. All four windows were broken. Ben heard the wind rushing past and the low drone of the tires on the road and another sound beneath both of these. It could have been the breeze rustling the dry dead stalks, but to Ben it sounded more like a man shoving his hurried way through the brittle corn. Running alongside them, as fast as the car and almost as quiet, rushing to meet them at the farmhouse that was his rightful home.

Dad had called him the Scarecrow, and that's how Ben pictured the man he imagined running behind the rows. A skinny thing in tattered denim stuffed with dry brown straw, his head a stuffed burlap sack with a smiling face painted on. Animated by some dark spell, clutching a scythe in his work glove hands. Eager to use the blade on human flesh again, to spill blood on the black soil as he had done many times in the past.

Ben knew that the Scarecrow was the same spirit as the Snowman who had infested the mind of the kind Deputy Bryant, but Ben couldn't help but think of them as distinct beings. They were one and many at the same time. And now Ben and everyone he cared about in the world were heading right to the heart of where one and all of them lived.

Ben knew that this was inevitable. He'd heard the word destiny before, but he wasn't sure if that was exactly right. The house did call to him, though. As if Ben had a made promise to it before he was even born and now that promise was coming due. Perhaps the sole purpose of his birth had been to drive out to *this* house on *this* day. It felt like he and the Scarecrow alike were returning to their true home.

They drove past the old barn painted with what looked like dried blood and turned off onto the dusty gravel road. Here the smell of the air changed. Ben caught a whiff of dry rot that reminded him of something very familiar he couldn't put his finger on. This was what people called déjà vu, but he knew it was just a memory of a dream that he'd had when he was very young. He'd forgotten the dream as soon as he woke up from it years ago, but the smell now brought it back to him in a fleeting, almost-but-not-quite-graspable way. He knew it was a bad dream, though. This was the place where bad dreams were born.

The house was in sight. Ben had never laid eyes on the big, yellow farmhouse before, but it was as familiar to him as the shadows he saw creeping up his bedroom wall at night.

He looked down at the floor of the car. The kit his dad got him for Christmas last year was still there. The Ecto-Spectrum Camera lay on the floor beside his feet where he'd dropped it when the Snowman had hit the car, but the EMF Detector and the EVP Recorder were still in the black carrying case with "Elsa West Digital Paranormal Investigation Kit" printed on the side.

Ben realized two things as he slipped the camera back into the case and gathered everything up. One was that it been no accident that he'd brought the kit with him in the car when he'd left the house an eternity ago, earlier that afternoon. He was meant to bring these tools to this place. The other thing he realized was that this house was nothing like the vaguely chilling, but harmless, frights on those TV shows. The shows seemed spooky while you were watching them, but were cheesy and fake if you thought about them long enough. This house was real, though, filled with things that wanted to hurt him. Ben could almost hear them whispering excitedly at their arrival.

Dad's Subaru was already parked in the drive. He pulled Lana's Prius in beside it and Mom's car pulled up beside theirs. The old teacher guy parked on the grass off to the side. Nobody wanted to block anyone else in. Ben didn't need to be told that this was in case they had to leave in a hurry.

Everybody got out of the cars. Mom looked bad; pale and sick and older somehow. Lana had to half-carry up the walk. Ben knew that Aunt Jen was lying on the back seat of his mom's car. Dead. No one Ben loved had ever died before and it seemed strange to him that he didn't know how that made him feel yet. The fact of his aunt's death had been swept to some back corner of his mind to be dealt with later, because there was so much else to worry about right here and right now. It seemed wrong, somehow, but Ben couldn't help the way he felt. He did go to his mother, though. He took her hand and she hugged him tight to herself, not wanting to let go of him even as they walked together towards the house.

"I don't know if I can do this, dude," Sam said. He glanced up at one of the upstairs windows, and then looked away quickly, shutting his eyes tight. He gulped and swallowed. There was a patch of his beard missing, the skin there red and irritated. Everywhere else, his face was deathly pale.

"It's all right, Sam," Dad said. "We're all here together."

There were seven of them, Ben realized. That was a good number. He just prayed there would still be seven of them left when this was over.

Ben's dad pulled out his keys. He slid the key into the door and tried to turn the knob.

"Stuck," he said. He grabbed the knob with his left hand and pressed hard against the key with his right thumb, grimacing with the effort. Then he cried out as it gave way all at once.

Dad pulled his hand away. Ben saw a red flash of blood before his dad brought his thumb to his mouth.

"What happened?" Ben said.

"The key *turned* in my hand," Dad, sucking at the wound. "Sliced my thumb."

"Are you all right?"

"Yeah. I think it's just the house's way of saying hello."

Clenching the wounded thumb in his fist, he pulled the door open with his other hand. Ben's father stepped into the house and, one by one, the rest of them followed.

Everyone stepped into the house until just Alice and Sam remained on the porch. Sam stared at the door for a few seconds, taking deep breaths. Alice patted his back.

"Come on, big guy," she said. "You can do it."

Then she wasn't patting him so much as leaning on him. Alice felt queasy and dizzy and strange. A combination, she suspected, of the weed wearing off and of all the violence she'd witnessed in the past hour or so. More than she'd seen in her whole life, easily. Maybe the house had something to with it, too. There was something creepy and awful about it, especially this close up. Whatever the cause, she felt suddenly weak.

Alice swooned on her feet. Sam caught her in his strong arms.

"Whoa," he said. "Are you all right?"

"Yeah. I just need to sit down. Can we go inside?"

Sam sighed heavily, but then he nodded. "Okay."

"Help me."

Surprising her, Sam swept Alice up in his arms. He carried her over the threshold.

"Does this mean we're married now?" Alice said.

Sam let out a weak chuckle and grasped her tighter. He was holding onto her like a scared little kid clutching his teddy bear.

The front door led to a short entryway, the kitchen just off to the left. Everybody was just settling in around the big table. Lana and Michelle sat close, holding tight to one another. Ben scooted a chair over beside his mom. Mr. Potter sat at the head of the table, looking down at his folded hands. The only one not sitting was Mark. He paced about the room, agitated.

Sam sat Alice down in a hard kitchen chair. She was suddenly shivering cold.

"Jesus," she said, looking up at Sam. "Is the air conditioning set to 'penguin house?'"

"There's no air conditioning," he said, his face wrinkling up with concern. "It's stifling in here. You're cold?"

"I'm freezing."

"You don't look well," Lana said. "Are you sick?"

"Yeah, but I usually don't get cold like this. It's cold as..."

"Cold as the grave," Ben said. "Right? Isn't that what people say? I feel it, too."

"It's the house," Michelle said. She was shivering as well. Her breath came out in a cloud. "It's not a physical cold. It's stealing heat from our souls."

"I can see your breath, Missy," Mark said with wonder. "It's ninety-some degrees in here and I can see your breath."

Then the cold was gone. Muggy heat penetrated Alice's skin with blessed relief.

"It's gone," Ben said.

"It was just showing us what it can do," Michelle said. "It's going to get worse."

"Some safe haven we have here," Lana said. "What are we going to do now?"

"I don't know," Mark said, resuming his pacing.

"We need to check out the basement," Michelle said. "That's what you really brought us up here for, right? To test your theory about the well down there being the source of all this?"

"You're making it sound like I have some master plan here," Mark said. "I'm just reacting to shit as it happens."

"That's your whole life, isn't it? Reacting to shit as it happens. Jen's dead because we were all following you out here to this fucking place."

"Oh God, Missy." Mark looked devastated. "I'm so, so sorry about Jen." He went over to where she was sitting, but she leapt from her seat rather than risk being touched by him.

"Stop it," Lana said sharply. "The last thing we need is to be at each other's throats. And you know it's not his fault, Chelle. There's only one person to blame for what happened to Jen. That bastard sheriff."

"Amen to that," Mr. Potter said.

"You're right." Michelle took a deep breath and sat down beside Lana again. She looked up at Mark. "I'm sorry."

"It's okay," Mark said. "But I think you're right. We do need to go down there."

"I'm know I'm coming in in the middle of this," said Mr. Potter. "But what's all this about a well in the basement?"

Mark went over it all again. How this was the Scarecrow House. How it was the source the disease. How it at all spread out from here. Hearing it all laid out on the table, Alice began to feel even sicker. She didn't know if it was the thought of being so close where it had all begun, or if it was just another cruel dip in the dismal roller coaster ride of living with her cancer, but she had to put her head down and close her eye. Behind her, Sam put his hand on her back. That helped a little.

"So," Mr. Potter said, once Mark was finished. "If I've got this straight, you're saying that the well in the basement has some kind of undiluted chemical or gas or something that, what, opens up a hole in your mind that lets evil spirits in? And once it's inside you, it becomes contagious, like a virus?"

"In a nutshell, yeah. You've got it," Mark said. "And believe me, I know how fucking insane that sounds."

"If you would have told me that yesterday, I would've laughed in your face," said Mr. Potter. "But that's more plausible than any explanation I've come up with. I have one question."

"What's that?"

"If you're right, isn't going down there unbelievably dangerous?"

"Probably." Mark shrugged. "But none of us are sick when it seems like almost everyone else in town is. Maybe we're immune."

"You're staking a hell of a lot on that maybe." Bill threw his hands up and laughed bitterly. "Hell with it, though. I've come to a point where I don't exactly have a lot to lose."

He stood up, and so did Lana and Michelle.

"Wait," Sam said. "No. Fuck that. I'm not going down there. And neither is Alice. She can barely stand up."

"That's fine, Sam," Mark said. "You guys stay up here. In fact, I want you to stay up here with them, Ben."

"But, Dad..."

"No, Ben. Bill's right. It's too dangerous."

"I'd rather be with you and Mom and Lana someplace dangerous than be apart from you someplace safe."

"Oh, Ben." Lana gave the kid a hug. "We'll be fine. We're not even going anywhere, just down into the basement. And trust me, at the first sign of anything freaky, I know my ass at least will running right the hell back up those steps."

Ben sighed. He put his head down for a second. "Where's your gun?" he asked.

"Your dad still has it."

"Give it back to her," Ben said to Mark. "She knows how to use it better than you do."

With a wry grin, Mark pulled the gun from his pocket and slid it across the table to Lana.

"Okay," Ben said. "Will you take this stuff with you, too?"

He unzipped the black canvas bag on the table.

"I know you think these are toys, but they really work. Right before Deputy Bryant took me, I saw something weird on the camera screen, floating above his car. It looked like a blurry balloon. So maybe they can see things that you can't, to help you be safe."

Lana took the camera. Michelle grabbed a little black box with a digital readout and red and green lights. Mark picked up a third device that looked like a microphone wired to an iPod and slipped the headphones on. Thus outfitted, Ben's three parents stepped back out into the entryway. Mr. Potter opened the cellar door for them and all four stepped down into the dark basement stairs.

Sam helped Alice into the living room, and laid her down on the love seat with the faded floral pattern that was in the exact same position it had occupied since he was a little kid. Very little in the room had changed, in fact. Gram might have added a few ceramic angel knick-knacks to her collection in the more than ten years since Sam had last been in the house, but some of the figurines on the shelf had probably not been moved more than an inch since before he was born.

Sam sat down on the chair opposite the love seat. The kid, Ben, did not sit down, but instead stood beside the doorway, his ear cocked for any sounds from downstairs. It obviously pained him to be separated from his folks.

This room was okay. When Sam had lived here, he had always considered it one of the "safe" spots. Nothing *too* weird had happened to him in here. At least not in the daytime.

Alice looked up at him and issued a queasy groan.

"You all right?" he asked.

"I don't suppose you could roll me another joint."

"I left all my stuff back at the other house," he said. "Sorry. We left in kind of a hurry."

"It's all right," she said. "Talk to me, though. Keep my mind off it."

"What do you want me to talk about?"

"You lived here growing up?"

"It's my grandma's house. I only lived here for a few years, after my folks died."

"And it's really haunted?"

"Really, *really* haunted."

"You've actually seen ghosts here?"

"I didn't see very many things. But I heard all kinds of stuff."

"Like what?"

Across the room, Ben was looking curiously up at him, too.

"Well, one thing that happened a lot was I would wake up in the middle of the night and hear a girl crying in the attic, right above my bedroom. I heard her almost every night. Most of the stuff that happened scared the shit out of me, but she just made me sad. The girl sounded so scared and lonely. I wanted to help her, but I didn't know how. I thought about going up there to look for her, but I was too scared. Even in the daytime." Sam shuddered.

"Sam." Alice tried to sit up, but this obviously made her feel worse, so she laid her head back down again. "Oh, God. That's…"

"What's wrong?"

"That was *me*," she said. "*I* was the girl in your attic."

"That doesn't make any sense."

"Listen to me. Ever since I found out I had cancer, or at least since I knew for sure I was going to die from it, I've had this dream. Like, recurring. In the dream, I'm already dead. I'm in a small, dark place. I can't see anything. I can't even move. I'm trapped there. I can't get out. All I can do is cry. When I wake up, sometimes my pillow is soaking wet with tears. I thought I was dreaming about being in a coffin, but I must have been dreaming about being up in your attic. It was *me* you were hearing."

"That happened when I was teenager," Sam said. "You would have been a little baby. How could you have been haunting my attic then?"

"It's like that movie," she said. "Did you ever see *The Shining*?"

"Yeah. Good movie."

"It scared the shit out me. Especially that very last shot, where they show the old picture of the party at the hotel. And Jack Nicholson's right in the middle of the picture even though it was taken, like, way back in the twenties."

Ben gave a little start, like he'd heard something from downstairs.

"I never really understood that," Sam said. "Was that like a time travel kind of thing?"

"You don't get it? He died there, and so the hotel *absorbed* him. He became part of the place, like he'd always been there." She looked around, desperately, as if coming to a terrible realization. "It's the same way in this house."

"Calm down, dude," Sam said. "You're freaking out."

"Don't let me die in here," she said. "Okay? If it...looks like I'm going to die, promise me that you'll get me out of here. Get me as far away as you can."

"You're not going to die."

"Promise me!"

"Okay, okay. I promise."

"It was me in the picture at the end. I'm the girl in the attic. I've always been up there."

Her good eye was twitching and rolling, the false one lagging just behind. She started crying, a low mournful weeping that Sam remembered all too well. He'd never forgotten it.

"I'm the girl in the picture," she sobbed. "You let me die here. You promised you wouldn't, but you let me die in this house and now I've always been in the picture!"

Sam looked up at Ben, appealing to him for any kind of help. The kid was distracted, though. Wild and agitated, pacing back and forth.

From the basement came the sound of gunfire.

Lana brought up the rear in the procession down the concrete stairs, thinking that there was a real difference between a country basement and a city basement. She remembered the downstairs laundry room in the Chicago apartment building where she'd lived when she was very young. The humid dryer vent smell of the place where she and her brothers and a few other kids from the building used to play hide and seek. Or the finished rec room in the basement of her Aunt Roxy's house in Denver, where Lana and her first real high school girlfriend Paquita had ignored dozens of DVD movies on the big screen TV. Those had been clean, living spaces. This here was a dead, dark place that smelled of dirt and organic decay.

On the far end of the space that appeared to run under the entire length of the house was a single dusty window pane, set close to the bare wooden boards of the ceiling that was really just the first story floor. The window cast a dim white glare, just enough light to blind them to the darkness of the rest of the room. Lana glanced down at Ben's camera in her hand. The little monitor screen showed a green night vision view, but Lana was afraid of what she might see if she peered too deeply into the ghostly monochrome. She was grateful for the weight of the gun in her jeans pocket.

Mark, walking point in their little formation, found a bare hanging bulb and pulled the chain to turn it on. The swinging yellow light did little to penetrate the gloom. It just cast skittering brown shadows into every corner. Big spiders or small rodents scurried to hide between the boxes stored along the walls. Or perhaps the shadows themselves were creeping sentient things.

"My kingdom for a flashlight," quipped Bill.

"On the floorplan, the well was right in the middle of the room," Mark said. He squinted down at the concrete floor, but it was difficult to see anything in the gloom.

Michelle swept Ben's EMF thing over the floor, though Lana suspected she was using it less for its intended purpose than for the scant light it provided. Then, suddenly, over one particular spot on the floor, the thing started beeping and flashing red. The illuminated LED display leapt from 2.3 up to 8.3. Whatever that meant. Michelle moved the device away from that spot and the reading dipped back down. She moved it back and the thing went crazy. 9.4.

"That's interesting," Mark said.

Bill Potter pulled his cellphone from his pocket and used it for about the only application it was good for now. The bright blue light of the screen lit up the dusty concrete. Mark cleared some of the dust away with his shoe, revealing wooden slats set into the floor.

"Bingo."

He knelt down and tried to pull the boards up, but they were set too close together for him to get his fingers in. Bill swept his phone light across the walls of the room and found an axe propped up in one corner. He grabbed it and knelt down to help Mark. Wedging the axe bit between the boards, Bill was able to pry one up. After that, the loose boards came up easily. Underneath, a stone-lined black hole led down into the earth.

The well's exposure seemed to change the quality of the air in the room. Not just more humid, as Lana might have expected. It was more like the gaping hole sucked away all the oxygen and made it harder for them to breathe.

"Oh, God." Michelle clutched her chest. "He threw them in there."

"Chelle?" Lana said.

"The Scarecrow," she moaned. "He threw the children down there. Some of them were dead, but others...Oh, God, he threw them in so they'd have to be in the groundwater with the dead ones." She threw her hands over her ears. "Can't you hear them *crying*?"

Mark, curiously, slipped the headphones over his ears and pointed the EVP microphone towards the hole.

"Fuck!" he cried a second later, tearing the headphones off and throwing them down to the ground. "Yeah, I hear them. I'm not fucking doing that again."

Michelle, damned to hear without the electronics, staggered back from the abyss. Helpless not to, Lana looked down at the green camera screen. Peering over the rim of the well, she stepped forward and pointed the camera straight down the shaft.

She saw it just for a second. Way down at the bottom. Two glowing points of light. A little boy's eyes, looking up at her. Desperate and afraid. Something else, too. Sluggish black shapes, crawling up the side of the well.

Lana stepped back, but did not take her eyes off the camera screen. The wriggling things emerged from the hole in the floor. Dozens of them. Fat black maggoty worms, as big as her foot. Lana could not see them on the dark floor with her naked eye, but they were clearly visible on the little monitor. The things crept towards her. One reared up and showed its face. Eyeless and blind but with a round toothy mouth. The thing grinned at her. Its tongue was a hard red jewel that glowed in a piercing contrast to the green light on the screen. It was hungry. It had been down the dark for a hundred years with nothing to gnaw on but the bones of dead children. Now it had fresh meat to consume.

Keeping the camera up so she could see them, Lana pulled the gun from her pocket and started blowing the things back to their watery hell.

CHAPTER 22

EVERY WINDOW IN the house was open. The air inside had the distinct scent and feel of an oncoming summer night storm. Charged and damp, the rising wind finally cooling things just a bit. Quick blue flashes of far-off electric light from the windows, the rumbling thunder peaceful at this distance. As Michelle went upstairs to check on the dreamers, she was reminded of a summer sleepover at her grandparent's house in the country when she was a little girl. Waking up thirsty in the middle of the night, scared to go to the kitchen alone in the not-quite-familiar house, she woke up Jen. The sisters ventured downstairs hand-in-hand in their nightgowns, tip-toeing through the quiet house to drink well water from a foggy glass pitcher in the fridge. The mineral taste of the water was so cold it had numbed their throats.

"Jesus, Jen." Michelle spoke aloud, and then pushed her sister from her mind. Later. She knew the longer she deferred that heartache, the more likely it would break her, but she had more urgent worries to deal with right now.

Lana and Alice Kiernan were tied down side-by-side on Linda Hansard's bed. The top sheet was wrapped tight around them, strapped down with ropes lashed and knotted to the bed frame. It strained the hairline fractures on Michelle's heart to look at them, but the restraints were for their own protection.

Lana had slipped into her dream while they were down in the basement. Michelle didn't know what her wife had seen with her rapidly darting eyes, but it had provoked her to empty her gun. She'd fired blindly, filling the dark room with bright flashes of muzzle fire and deafening echoes, the bullets ricocheting crazily about the concrete floor and walls. Flying shrapnel had nicked Bill Potter in the leg. They were lucky that was the only hit anybody suffered.

Once Lana had depleted her ammunition, Mark and Michelle had dragged her raving back up the stairs.

"There's one crawling up my leg!" Lana had screamed. She tore her jeans off and started beating at her bare legs. "Oh God, Chelle, it's going up inside me!"

She clawed at her own skin, trying to get at the things she imagined were crawling all over her. That's why they'd had to tie her down, so she wouldn't scratch herself bloody.

They'd tied up Alice Kiernan beside her as more of a precautionary measure. The girl just sobbed and moaned in her waking sleep, one of the most chilling sounds Michelle had ever heard in her life. She kept begging for them not to let her die in the house.

Both women were now calm. Lana's eyes were open, flitting around, and she was mouthing words in her sleep, a prayer perhaps, but she'd stopped fighting against her constraints. Alice still wept, but quietly now.

Michelle went into the room and wiped both their fevered brows with a dish cloth. Then she remembered something. She slid open the drawer in the nightstand beside Linda Hansard's bed. Inside, just where she'd known it would be, Michelle found a small pearl-handled pistol. She checked and saw that it was loaded. She took it back downstairs with her.

Crossing the living room, she checked in on Bill Potter and Sam Hansard. The two men were sitting across from each other, each having sworn a pact to keep the other awake. It didn't look like they were doing that great of a job at it, as both were on the nod.

"You guys doing okay?" Michelle asked.

They both bolted awake.

"I'm good," Sam insisted.

"How's your leg, Bill?" Michelle had patched the wound, a deep scratch, with a first-aid kit she'd found in the downstairs bathroom. Bill had been hobbling about ever since, using the axe he'd found in the basement as an improvised cane.

"Not bad," Bill said. "Though I should probably have a shot of whiskey for the pain."

"I'll get right on that," Michelle said, and then went into the kitchen.

Mark was sitting at the table. Ben was in the corner, asleep on a fold-away cot they'd found in one of the downstairs closets. Michelle went to her son and touched his shoulder lightly.

"There's no school today, Mom," he protested blearily.

Ben rolled over and fell back asleep. A normal sleep. At least Michelle prayed it was.

She scooted a chair out and sat down across from Mark at the table. He was munching on shredded wheat. The old-fashioned, unfrosted kind that came out of the box in huge biscuits that looked like little pillows.

"That stuff any good?" she asked.

"I suspect the box might be more flavorful than the cereal," he said. "And the milk in the fridge has turned to cottage cheese, so have to eat it dry. But I am getting my daily allowance of fiber. Want some?"

"Sure, hit me."

Mark reached into the box and handed her a huge clump. Michelle chewed off a corner, the strands of dry wheat so sharp they cut her tongue. She was just about ravenous enough to tolerate this, though.

"I realized I haven't had anything to eat today except two jelly donuts and a couple handfuls of pot-laced gummy bears," Mark said. "Unfortunately, we're stuck with the contents of an old lady's larder. I found some raisins, too, but I'm saving them for dessert."

Michelle smiled at her ex.

"How are you doing, Mark?" she asked him. "How are you coping with all this?"

He looked a little surprised that she would ask. "Actually, I feel kind of like Tippi Hedren in *The Birds*."

"You mean, psychologically abused and sexually harassed by Alfred Hitchcock?"

Mark laughed out loud at that, as she knew he would.

"You're good," he said. "No, you remember the crazy church lady in the diner? 'They say the whole thing started when you arrived! Evil!' I've been back home less than forty-eight hours and I managed to destroy the entire town."

"Oh my God," Michelle said. "Really? That is so typical of you."

"What, destroying a town by my mere presence?"

"No. Constantly believing that everything is about you."

"It's not?"

"Listen. This is going to sound really strange coming from me, but I'm glad you're here."

"You're right. That does sound really strange coming from you."

"I couldn't have got through this day without you. You climbed the water tower for James. You got me back into town when the quarantine went up. You talked me into finding Ben when he was taken. You even pulled a gun on the goddamn sheriff." She couldn't help but laugh at that, despite what had happened next. "Oh my God, you looked so scared when you did that."

"I only peed my pants a *little*."

Michelle sighed and blinked away tears. "My sister is dead in the back seat of my car in the driveway. My wife is tied to a bed upstairs, out of her mind. I know this is going to be the longest, most hellish night of my life. Please, just help me get through the rest of it, okay?"

Surprising them both, Michelle took his hand. She squeezed tightly for a second before letting go.

Mark looked down at his hand, astonished, as if the quick touch had left a lingering glow.

"Yeah," he said. "Of course."

Michelle, not wanting to meet his eye after that, stood up and went to the kitchen sink. She looked out the window. The darkness was shattered by cracks of electric purple, fissuring across the sky. The crash of thunder that followed rattled the entire house.

Bill nodded out for a second, but the tremendous crash snapped him back awake. He sat up in his chair, shaking his head. Had a sip of the by now warm water from the glass on the side table and poured what little was left over his head. He wished to Christ he had some coffee instead. Or something stronger. He hadn't snorted cocaine in a good thirty years, but a white line or two would be just the ticket right now. He could almost taste the drip in the back of his throat. The vivid sense memory was almost enough to perk him up on its own.

Across the room, Sam sat on the loveseat with the faded floral pattern. He was completely out, his head resting on his hand. Snoring, even.

"Sam," Bill said. Nothing.

"Sam," he said, louder. Sam snored on.

Bill stood up and crossed the room. He knocked Sam's arm away, so that his head fell to the side. Sam jerked awake.

"What the hell?" he said.

"You fell asleep."

"No, I didn't."

"Dammit, Sam. You were snoring. Now, come on. We had a deal. We were supposed to keep each other awake."

"Sorry." Sam drained his own water glass. "God, it's hot in here."

"It's beastly hot," Bill concurred.

Both men looked over at the open window. The rising breeze stirred the curtains and a quick double flash of brilliant light flared outside. A second later, this was followed by another tremendous crack of thunder.

Sam crossed the room and looked outside.

"The storm's getting close," he observed.

"Good," said Bill. "That'll cool things off."

Then, oddly, Sam seemed to be speaking to someone outside the window.

"Oh, hey there," he said. He took a couple steps backward and called: "Kit-kit-kit."

"What the hell are you doing, Sam?"

"Look."

A tiny kitten jumped up onto the window sill. Mostly white, with black and grey tiger stripes. The animal looked just like a cat Bill had once owned. When the kitten mewed, its voice was even the same. That other cat had been named Shredder, and it had even been about the same size and age as this one. But that was a long time ago.

"Sam," he said. "Do you see that cat?"

"Yeah," Sam said.

"So I'm not dreaming it? The cat's really there?"

"If you're dreaming it, then so am I. There is definitely a cat there on the window sill."

"Where the fuck did it come from?"

"It's a barn cat," Sam said. "Gram always keeps a few around to keep the mice down. They get pretty wild when they grow up, but the kittens are friendly."

Sam grabbed the little cat and carried it with him back to his seat.

"What are you doing?" Bill cried. "Don't bring it into the house!"

"Are you afraid of cats?" Sam asked, stroking the kitten.

"No."

"Allergic?"

"No, Sam. It's...I used to have a cat that looked just like that one. And I mean *exactly*."

Sam laughed. "What, you think this is a ghost cat?"

Bill shook his head. "Actually, it was my son's cat."

"Jack?"

"No, Donnie."

"I didn't know you had a son named Donnie," Sam said.

"He died when he was six."

"Jesus, Bill. I'm sorry."

"Donnie loved that little cat. And, actually...That was how he died. I was inside the house, but my neighbor saw it happen. She said Shredder ran out in the road and Donnie ran out after him. A car ran him down."

"That's terrible."

"I saw the cat in my yard when I came home from the hospital that night. Donnie was still alive then, just in a coma. He had swelling in his brain. The doctor said there was a chance he might come out of it, but I could tell from his face...So I came home from that to find Shredder crying to be let in the house, just wanting to be fed. And I just...hauled off and kicked the fucking thing. With everything I had. Sent it flying across the yard. Like it was the stupid cat's fault. I don't know if it crawled off somewhere to die or if it lived and just ran away, but I never saw it again."

"Holy shit," Sam said. He clutched the kitten protectively, bringing his body between the defenseless thing and the admitted feline murderer.

"It's the same cat," Bill said, convinced. "It's Shredder."

"That's crazy, Bill. How long ago did that happen?"

Once Bill could have answered that down to the hour, but the time had slipped away from him. "A good thirty years," he said.

"See? Cats live, what, ten years? Fifteen, tops. And this one's a kitten. Cats come in like four different colors. A lot of them look alike."

"It's the same one," Bill insisted. "This house does crazy things. You said so yourself."

"I have seen some crazy shit here," Sam conceded. "But not cats coming back years after they died."

"There's a way to be sure," Bill said. "Shredder had a black spot on his fur, right on the belly. Turn it over and look."

"I don't know if I should do that," Sam said.

"Please, Sam. Just look underneath the goddamn cat for me. I'm begging you. For the sake of my sanity."

Sam flipped the squirming kitten over onto its back. It playfully batted its little paws up at him and Sam, laughing, had to spread its hind limbs apart to get a look. When he did so, Bill saw his eyes go wide with surprise and bewilderment.

"It's there, isn't it?" Bill said. "The black spot."

"No," Sam said, still staring down with a puzzled frown. "There's no black spot."

"Don't lie to me."

"I'm not," Sam said. "There's something different."

"What? What is it?"

"I don't think I should show you, Bill."

Bill stood up. "Give me the cat."

"No."

"Give me the fucking cat, Sam!"

Bill grabbed the tiny creature out of Sam's hand and flipped it over. Right on its belly, right where Shredder's black spot had been, was a lump. A boil or a cyst or something, bright cherry red in color.

The frightened kitten twisted in Bill's hand and fell to the floor. It didn't run away, though, as he thought it would. Instead, it stalked across the room, low to the ground. It pounced on a spot on the wooden floor and started scratching at the floorboard.

"What's it doing?" Bill sat back down, hard in his seat.

The cat scratched frantically at the floor, gouging the wood, making a strange little screeching mewl that sounded like someone slowly opening a rusty hinge.

"Oh, God." Bill hated the sound. He put his hands over his ears, but the low grating yowl and the scritch scritch scritch of the kitten's claws against the wood penetrated through anyway. "What the hell is it doing?"

Sam shrugged. "Cats scratch shit up. It's what they do."

There was another tremendous clap of thunder and Bill sat bolt upright in his chair.

The sound had stopped, suddenly, and there was only the reverberating aftershocks of the thunder. Something else had changed, too. The quality of the light in the room was different, somehow. Bill looked over and the cat was gone.

"Where'd it go?" he said.

"Where'd what go?" said Sam.

"The *cat.*"

"What cat?"

"The barn cat you let in the window. It scratched up the floor, look."

Bill pointed over the gouges, still plainly visible on the hard wood floor.

"I did that," Sam said.

"No you didn't," said Bill. "There was a cat. I saw it. You saw it, too."

Sam was looking at him like he'd lost his shit. "I did that when I was twelve years old," he said. "I gouged the floor with a fork because I was pissed off at my Grandma."

Bill got up and looked closer. The scratches on the wood floor had the unmistakable aged, weathered look of an old wound.

"You all right, Bill?"

"No."

He saw quick motion in the corner of his eye. Something small, darting out of the room. Bill looked over and for a second he saw two glowing white points of light. Eyes, low to the ground, looking at him from around the corner of the hallway before backing away into the darkness. He saw them so quickly, he couldn't have said if they belonged to the cat or to a small boy on his hands and knees. But he definitely saw them.

"What are you doing, Bill?" Sam asked.

Bill grabbed the axe propped against the wall and ran into the hallway.

Another crash of thunder brought Sam awake again. He'd been drifting in and out. He and Bill were supposed to watch out for one another so they wouldn't fall asleep, but Bill was totally out in the chair across the room. Sam didn't bother trying to wake him. What were they going to do, never sleep again? He was totally exhausted. He'd never seen a day this crazy in all his life. A few hours of shut-eye on the couch would probably do him good. If he was sick with the sleepwalking thing, then trying to stay awake probably wouldn't do any good anyway.

So Sam grabbed one of Gram's little decorative pillows and tried to make himself as comfortable as he could on the little loveseat. Which wasn't very comfortable. Especially considering—though he had been trying to ignore this feeling for a while now—that he really, really had to pee. The competing drives for sleep and for urination had finally reached the tipping point where his bladder's urgency outweighed his drowsiness.

Goddamn it. This was a problem with a seemingly simple solution, but it wasn't as easy as just getting up and taking a leak. Not in this house it wasn't.

Some of the most terrifying moments of Sam's terrifying adolescence had happened on the occasions when he'd woken up in the middle of the night to use the bathroom. Whatever infested this house had delighted in tormenting him in those most vulnerable moments. It got so bad that he'd actually wet the bed a couple times as a teenager—which had of course caused Gram to fly into a rage. And here he was again, years after he'd thought he'd moved past all that, giving at least some consideration to just pissing his pants right here on the loveseat.

No. He was an adult.

Sam considered waking Bill up, to see if he'd come with him, but rejected that as being almost as pathetic as wetting himself. "Will you hold my hand so I can go potty?"

No. He was a man.

He sat there for a couple minutes, hoping maybe his courage would rise along with the ache in his bladder. But as he sat, he became aware of the weeping from upstairs. He'd been hearing it all along, but it now moved into the front of his consciousness. He knew it was just Alice, crying in her sleep, but this knowledge did little to soothe him. He liked Alice, liked her a lot, and the thought that it had been her up in his attic all along, so sad and lost and alone, gave his heart a chill.

Still, that did nothing to change the fact that he was on the verge of bursting. He stood up, the pressure down there manifesting now as a sharp pain.

"Cats scratch shit up," Bill mumbled in his sleep, distracting Sam for a second. "It's what they do."

"Whatever, Bill." Sam grimaced, bending over. Even having resolved to go relieve himself, there was still an important decision to make. Upstairs bathroom, or downstairs?

Upstairs was farther away and Sam would have the stairs to contend with. It would also take him past Gram's bedroom, closer than he wanted to get to Alice's sobbing. But the downstairs bathroom was, by far, the scene of way more freaky shit that had happened to him.

The downstairs bathroom had the claw-foot tub with the drain from which Sam had heard the screams of children. It had the mirror that reflected back the dark hallway behind you, in which Sam had once seen a tall standing shadow with glowing red eyes peering over his shoulder as he brushed his teeth. It had skittering sounds inside the walls and the wood grain pattern on the linen closet door that had the bad habit of twisting into the shapes of anguished faces if Sam looked at it too long. Moving shadows behind the shower curtain that always seemed to be pulled closed no matter how many times Sam had made sure it was open, blood backing up in the toilet bowl, moaning sounds from the floorboards.

Of course, the upstairs bathroom hadn't been free of incidents, either. Sam remembered helplessly taking a dump and watching his grandfather's can of shaving cream slowly sliding across the counter and then falling to the floor and exploding. That was also the room where he'd smelled the cloying scent of honeysuckle a few times, so powerful that it drove him out of the room gasping for air.

Sam had stood there deliberating for so long he'd begun to dance. At least now the choice had been made for him. The upstairs bathroom was no longer an option, he'd never make it in time. He'd have to use the more haunted, but closer by, downstairs toilet.

Walking with his legs pressed tight together, he peeked around the corner at the long dark hallway. He didn't see anything, so he bolted and ran into the bathroom. No time to close the door, but he did at least hit the light switch so he wouldn't have to do this in the dark.

Sam tore the front of his jeans open and whipped it out with one hand, lifting the toilet lid with the other. He let go, groaning with the relief that superseded his horror for at least a few exquisite seconds.

Sam knew he was in for a long haul. He'd always been a slow pisser, and was also congenitally unable to still the flow once it had started. Holding it in for so long meant he'd be standing there for at least two solid minutes. He just prayed nothing would happen for that length of time.

This prayer was refused.

Sam first noticed a chill, though he could not say if it was in the air or coming from inside him. He shivered, splattering a bit, and felt all the hairs on the back of his neck standing up. There was someone behind him.

Just your imagination, he told himself as his bladder continued its stubbornly slow, inexorable drain.

Then, no way to deny this, he heard running footsteps towards him down the hall.

Sam spun, in mid-stream, spraying a yellow arc about the room. Bill Potter was running towards him with an axe in his hand.

Bill raised the weapon and let out a yell, echoed a second later by Sam's cry of terror. He threw his hands up in a feeble defensive motion, still dispensing a mighty stream.

Bill, eyes lost to nightmare madness, ran into the little room. His shoes hit the urine puddle on the tiled floor and his feet slid out from underneath him. Potter fell to the side, dropping the axe. The heavy metal head cracked the tile when it fell to the floor.

Bellowing his head off, Sam jumped over his fallen friend and ran into the hall, leaving a dripping, streaming trail behind him.

Mark had almost given in. Missy was curled up on the little cot beside Ben, asleep beside their son. Mark's resolve to keep watch over them was faltering. So tired. He put his head down in his arms on the hard kitchen table and had just barely dozed off when the screams rang out from the back of the house.

He leapt to his feet. Missy and Ben both sat up, alarmed. At least two men were screaming. Bill and Sam, probably, though in this house there was no way to be sure of that.

Sam ran into the kitchen, face wild and crazed. Mark had to assume he was sleepwalking, a diagnosis only solidified in his mind when he saw that the big guy's dick was hanging out of his pants.

"Billtriedtokillmeinthebathroomwithanaxe!" he screamed, all one word.

Mark looked deeply into Sam's eyes. They showed obvious terror, but were not darting with the sickness. Mark glanced down to where Sam dangled.

He looked down at himself. "Oh, sorry." He stuffed himself back into his pants and zipped up.

"What happened?"

Sam looked back. There was a pounding sound now, like somebody trying to tear the place apart.

"Bill has an axe. He came right at me. He's totally out of it."

"Donnie!" they heard Bill call between splintering cracks. "I'm here! Where are you?"

"Stay here with Ben," Mark said to Sam.

Missy followed him out of the room. He saw that she had another gun in her hand. He didn't ask where she'd found it, he just hoped she wouldn't have to shoot his favorite teacher.

The lightning filled the hall with jittery strobe-light bursts of brilliant light as Mark and Missy ran back. The thunder was so loud Mark felt the reverberations in the floorboards beneath his feet. They came to the bathroom, which smelled strongly of fresh urine. Bill was hacking apart one wall with his axe. He turned towards them, his eyes rapidly darting.

"Help me," Bill cried. "My son is trapped inside the wall. Can't you hear him calling?"

He put the axe down and started tearing out the drywall with his bare hands.

Mark saw something there, behind the wall Bill had exposed. A tiny form. It might have been the mummified corpse of a small child, mounted inside the wall. He saw a twisted face and thin, dangling limbs. There were words, too, written on the bare wood beside the thing in what looked like long-dried blood. Before Mark could get a good look at either the figure nailed to the wall or the words beside it, the electricity went out. They were cast into absolute darkness.

Quick flashes of lightning clarified the details of the tableau one by one.

The thing was too small to be a child. The extremities were too skinny.

"That's not him," Bill lamented. "That's not Donnie."

The words read THY WILL BE DONE.

Mark stepped closer, and with the next strobing flash, saw that the thing was a doll. An ancient dusty rag doll, made from black stockings tattered with time and the predations of moths.

Another rapid burst of light etched the crimson writing into Mark's eyes. The last word had been crossed out and another written beneath it.

THY WILL BE ~~DONE~~ DEAD.

The flashes of lightning were coming so fast now they provided an almost steady illumination. Mark looked at the thing behind the wall. He saw red cloth lips and a beady black button eye. A skinny flopping tail.

It was a monkey doll.

They had found the Black Monkey.

SUNDAY

CHAPTER 23

THE POWER NEVER came back on, but Missy found a box of candles and a book of matches in one of the kitchen drawers. The country house was more prepared for the exigencies of an electricity failure than, say, their apartment back in Denver had been.

The Black Monkey doll lay on one of the kitchen counters. The candles all around it lent a shrine-like quality to the scene that was accidental and, to Mark's eye, repugnant. He had just wanted to examine it in the light, not venerate the fucking thing.

It wasn't Jess's Monkey. The effigy Mark's friend had constructed when they were children had pearl button eyes, stolen from Tammy Frank's funeral dress. One of this Monkey's button eyes was missing, but the one that remained was black, and looked like it was made of onyx. It was a fancy button, quite old-fashioned, perhaps torn from the suit a young boy had been buried in. Jess's Monkey's lips had been made from yarn torn from a sweater their friend Toby had worn the day before he died. This Monkey's mouth was a patch of red fabric with black thread stitched across the middle. This doll was longer and lanker, too, made from a girl's black stockings instead of the men's socks Jess had pulled from his brother's feet after he'd found him hanging in the garage.

This was the original Black Monkey, the one constructed by Jess's great-grandmother, the one which had killed the Scarecrow, Hans Klausen. It had been hidden behind that bathroom wall for almost a hundred years.

After uncovering the thing, Bill Potter had sunk into a brooding despair. There had been no need to restrain him as they'd done to Lana and Alice. He just sat in a chair in the living room, muttering about his son Donnie and someone or something called Shredder.

Sam had succumbed perhaps an hour later. He regressed to a little boy, speaking with childish dread about somebody named "Mr. Slinky-Bones" who was trying to make Sam eat his "skinny pie." Sam was quite agitated until Mark suggested to him that Mr. Slinky-Bones couldn't see him if he sat perfectly still, and couldn't force him to eat anything if he kept his mouth firmly shut. Taking to the suggestion, Sam sat back down on the loveseat opposite Bill, and had remained quiet and motionless since.

It was just the three of them now. Mark, Missy, and Ben, sitting quietly around the kitchen table, in the warm unsteady light of a dozen flickering candles. Outside, the thunder had subsided. The rain came in erratic waves, alternating between loud hammering downpours against the roof and periods of quiet black drizzle.

"What time do you think it is?" Mark asked.

"I don't know." Missy shrugged. "Sometime after midnight."

There was not a working timepiece in the entire house. The electrical clocks were of course all out. The old grandfather clock in the living room was frozen at a few minutes past nine, and perhaps had been so for decades. No one wore a watch, and every cell phone that had been brought to the house had either a dead battery or a bizarrely jumbled screen.

"Do you think it's anywhere close to dawn?"

Missy shrugged again. "Doesn't feel like it, does it?"

"No." In fact, Mark wondered if he would ever see the sun again.

"I don't think you should do it, dad," Ben said.

"I have to, Ben. I think it's the only way to bring everything back into balance."

"But you told me that when your friend Jess buried the Monkey, it came back and killed him," said Ben. "You said that was the price he had to pay to get it to do what he wanted."

"I don't think that's going to happen this time," Mark said, hoping that came out with more confidence than he felt.

"I think we should all go, then," Ben said. "Not just you."

"No," said Mark. "You and your mom need to stay here, to take care of Lana and Alice, and Sam and Bill. We can't leave them alone."

"It's not fair," Ben said. "Why does it have to be *you*?"

"Because there's no one else."

Ben nodded, more with resignation than acceptance. He turned away, but Mark hugged him anyway, pulling his son fiercely to himself. Then he stood up to gather his things.

He'd found a shovel on the back porch. He stuffed the monkey doll into the black canvas bag that had held Ben's ghosthunting kit, along with a flashlight. Missy had already given him the gun she'd found in Linda Hansard's bedroom drawer, insisting that he take it. The weapon was stuck into his belt like he was some kind of goddamn wild west gunslinger.

"Wait." Missy stopped him as he stepped towards the door. "Be careful, Mark."

"I thought you didn't believe in this."

"I don't know what I believe anymore."

She kissed him, quickly, on the lips. Mark remembered the first time Missy had ever kissed him. The first time, in fact, that he'd been kissed by any girl. It had been right before he and Jess had gone down to the creek to bury the Black Monkey.

Now, as then, there was little he could say. Mark stepped out into the rain, which had begun to pour again. He didn't want to run, because that would make this go faster, so he walked slowly to his car and got thoroughly drenched.

Missy's car was parked beside his, with Jennifer's corpse in the back seat. Mark didn't think about that. He pulled out of the drive and set off, back to Bakersfield.

Sheriff Bates stumbled through the rain in the dark, up some obscure country road, one hand covering the butterfly-stitched wound on his throat where that stupid fucking bitch had bit him. The bite itched like a syphilitic cunt, but scratching it hurt as if he was raking his neck with razor-sharp fork tines. The best he could do was apply slight pressure with his hand, which didn't really do shit for the pain or the itching. Bitch took a chunk of skin, but just missed tearing open the vein there. If she'd done that, Nate would've been a goner.

There'd been a moment, lying on the ground with all the crazy dreamers piling on top of him, when Nate had been truly scared. More scared than he'd been since the riot he got caught up in when he was a prison guard up at Stateville. Back then, some of the Aryan Brotherhood fuckers had held Nate hostage in a cell for a few hours. The white supremacist idiots had always hated Nate because he smuggled in drugs for black inmates and not for them. Nate seriously hadn't known if he was going to walk out of there alive, or if the skinhead sons of bitches were just going to fuck him and leave it at that, which would have been just as bad. These same thoughts ran through his head when the dreamy-eyed cocksuckers had him on the ground. And in this case, Nate didn't have anyone backing his ass up with tear gas and riot gear. He was going to have to make his own luck.

He stood up, roaring, lifting the weight of three or four of them with the adrenaline-fueled strength of his pure fury. He shook the shitheads off, punching and kicking his way free. His gun was gone, who knows where. Nate staggered over to his truck and saw that Mara was gone, too. She'd either snapped the grab handle right off the door herself or she'd been dragged out by one of the lunatics. At this point, Nate didn't give a shit. All he cared about was the first aid kid in the glovebox. He drove a few blocks, gushing blood, just to get away from the worst of the chaos in the streets. Then he'd applied the adhesive butterfly strips to the sides of the wound in his rear-view mirror, and stitched it closed with the thread. He was going to be all right. Meanwhile, the bitch who'd bit him was having to make do without brains in her goddamn head. Shows who got the best end of that situation.

Nate drove off again, not even sure where he was going until he got to Suzy Barber's place. He didn't know what he'd expected to find there, but what he did find was maybe the most horrifying thing he'd witnessed since this had all begun. It was even worse than Barry feeding his wife to the goddamn bear.

The front door was wide open when he'd pulled up. He stepped into the house to find Suzy naked right in the middle of the living room, getting spit-roasted by two of her sons. Chucky was getting head and JJ, the one Barber brother Nate would have put above such sick shit, was getting tail. The other four sons stood around watching, stroking themselves eagerly so they'd be good and ready when it came their turn to service Mama. John Barber was parked in his chair in the corner and, judging from the sheer horror in his non-twitching eyes, he was the one member of the family not afflicted by the sickness. For once, Nate actually felt bad for him.

"What in the unholy fuckin' name of Jesus whore-lickin' Christ are you motherfuckers doing?" Nate cried.

Calvin turned and smiled when Nate walked into the room, continuing to rub it without shame. "Oh, hey, Daddy," he said, his eyes spinning. "We been good boys, so Mama's treatin' us. You want her to treat you, too?"

Nate thought it couldn't possibly get any worse than that, but then it did. Because he saw that Chucky was looking away from him guiltily, refusing to meet his eye, which made Nate pretty sure that John wasn't the only Barber who wasn't dreaming this shit.

Nate staggered back out of the house and puked his guts out in the bushes. Then he got back into his truck and sped the fuck away from there.

He made it up to the Church of the Shepherd next. All those fuckers had gone batshit, too, but at least they weren't having incestuous gang bangs in the pews. Mainly they were just dancing around and spouting crazy bullshit gibberish, which wasn't all that different than an average Sunday at the Church of the Shepherd when Nate thought about it. Still, he had little tolerance at this point. He just wanted to check up on Tom Peters, on the remote fucking chance that there was one person from his side in this whole crazy-ass town who might still be sane.

No dice there. He found Tom out back, on the grassy lawn behind the main building. He was wearing a Halloween mask he'd found someplace. Tom Peters was disguised as Tom the cat, Jerry the mouse's eternal nemesis. Tom was taking the feline role very seriously, crawling around on all fours like he was stalking prey. Then Nate saw that Tom was actually stalking the parrot from the zoo. He'd released the beautiful red and blue bird from its cage and let it go on the lawn. He crept up behind it and pounced. The poor bird wings were clipped so it couldn't fly, and it looked like Tom had already broken one of its legs, too. He was toying with the thing, just like a real cat would do. Nate was on the verge of going over and rescuing the bird when Tom the cat tired of the game. He pinned the bird down with one paw, sank his fangs into the squirming parrot's neck, and bit its head clean off.

Tom carried the decapitated bird in his mouth, which dripped with blood and colorful feathers. He dropped the dead thing at Nate's feet, as an offering. Nate's capacity for horror had already been exceeded, though. He responded to this with little more than a dull disgust, kicking the dead bird away and turning to leave.

Unfortunately, he'd left his keys inside the truck. At least one of the Sheep Shackers had retained enough conscious awareness to drive it away, and now Nate was left without a vehicle. Perfect. He set off on foot, with no idea where the hell he was headed.

At this point, Nate might have disassociated a bit. He was a man who had always believed in taking what he wanted from the world, but in the space of hours it had all been taken back away from him. His wife, his town, his business, his authority. His gun, his truck. All that on top of the shit he'd seen in the past day and a half was enough to get any man down, even a tough son of a bitch as he'd always prided himself to be.

He walked south on Highway 54, through blazing, muggy heat. This would have eventually taken him back into town. After about only half a mile, though, he had to dive into the ditch to avoid getting run down by some clown driving a pick-up with four deer carcasses in the bed. No idea if the joker was a dreamer, or if he was just taking advantage of the situation to indulge in some unrestrained, off-season hunting. On any other day, driving a truck at Nathanial Bates like that would have ended up with Elmer Fudd getting his ass handed to him. But today, maybe for the first time in his life, Nate retreated. He slunk off the highway and cut across a dirt access road between two corn fields.

Half an hour later, maybe more, Nate emerged on the other side of the huge field. He was sunburned, seriously dehydrated and utterly exhausted in mind, body and spirit. He stumbled onto the high school football field and had a moment of reeling dislocation. The high school was way over on the east side of town, miles from where Nate thought he was.

Then he remembered. He was thinking of where the old high school had been, back when he'd been in school. They'd built the new school over on this end of town all of ten years ago. He didn't know how he could have forgotten such a thing. Thoroughly dispirited, Nate walked into the shade under the bleachers. There were some big blocking dummies stored under there and Nate leaned back against one, just to shut his eyes for a minute.

Nate awoke sometime later to a huge clap of thunder. He had no idea how long he'd been asleep, but it was nighttime now. Not only that, but the darkness was so absolute Nate would have thought himself blind had it not been for the flashes of lightning. The power must have gone out.

Nate was pretty disoriented, but he retained enough presence of mind to understand that hanging out under the metal bleachers during a lightning storm was not the best of ideas. So he lurched out into the darkness, not understanding for the longest time why his neck itched so badly, and why it hurt like hell to scratch it.

Then he remembered everything and wished to hell he could just go back to sleep. Nate longed for his bedroom as devoutly religious men long for the gates of paradise. He didn't even know where the hell he was, though, let alone how he could get home. He was completely turned around, in a part of town that seemed utterly unfamiliar to him, in almost complete darkness. And then, icing on the poison cake, the skies opened up and rained their fury upon his head.

The rain felt good at first, cool relief from the sticky heat. Nate leaned his head back and drank the slightly acidic-tasting water falling from the sky. But after about another half an hour of walking disoriented through the storm, Nate was shivering like a half-drowned rat. He was lost. Alone. Crying, not to put too fine a point on it.

Nate found himself walking down some muddy rutted road between two cornfields, not sure if he was in Bakersfield anymore. He wasn't even sure, truth be told, if he was alive or dead, awake or dreaming. Then he saw something curious up ahead. Hard to tell in the dark, with the pouring rain, but it looked like a metal gate built into a brick wall.

Nate got closer and peered through the gate. Even in the dark, he could tell how green the grass was on the other side. This had to be the Lawndale golf course, though Nate couldn't for the life of him say how he might have ended up here.

He barked laughter at the sight. Though not a particularly avid golfer, he was a member of the club. It was more of an honorary membership, he suspected, in deference to his prominent role in local law enforcement. He'd only taken advantage of it a few times, and on every occasion had felt out-of-place with those manicured douchebag executive types. Still, if he was a member, they had to let him in, right?

Of course, if anybody was immune to the sickness that had ravaged the town, it would be these Malovo fucks. They'd probably sealed up their gates tight as a schoolmarm's legs at the first sign of the disease. There would be normal, sane people in there. With towels. And coffee.

Nate looked down at the gate and noticed something curious. It looked like somebody had recently driven a car through the gate. The bars were all bent out of whack, and were only held closed by a chain wrapped around them. The metal was so twisted, though, that the gate wouldn't close completely. When Nate pushed hard enough against the gate, it gave way enough that he was just able to squeeze through.

He was in.

Nate noticed muddy ruts torn through the immaculate greens, as if the car that had burst through the gates had torn through here, doing all kinds of damage. He followed the gouging tracks with his eyes. There was a flash of lightning and, silhouetted for a second against the glowing sky, he saw a man up ahead. A man who, by his posture, seemed to be digging a grave.

Nate was dismayed for a moment. That shot to shit his idea about the immunity inside these gates, because digging a grave on a golf course seemed like just the sort of pointless shenanigans the dreamers got up to. But, and he couldn't have said why, there seemed to be something familiar about the man. He didn't know how he could recognize anybody based on a dark outline seen for a couple seconds during a flash of lightning, but the sense of familiarity was strong enough that Nate wanted to take a closer look.

He walked towards the man with the shovel and was just a few yards away when another flash of lightning revealed who it was. For a second, the sheriff wondered if perhaps *he* was the one dreaming, after all. Either that, or there was a God and he was offering Nate one last chance at redemption.

The man digging a hole in the earth just ahead was Mark fucking Davies. Nate clenched his fists and closed the gap between them with four running steps.

Bakersfield was completely dark. Mark had never seen a night so impenetrable. The rain was coming down heavily and he couldn't see more than a few yards in front of him even with the high-beams on. The wipers could scarcely move the water from the windshield fast enough. Mark felt like he was driving through the murky depths of a black water lake.

In contrast to the deadly riots they'd encountered on the way out of town that afternoon, Mark did not see a single human being out on the streets. Nor did he pass another car. It was too easy to imagine himself as the only person still alive in this town. He turned on the radio, just for the company of a living voice, but all he could pull in up or down either band was a low, stuttering electronic moan that sounded to him like the collective voices of the restless dead.

He almost got lost several times in the dark, and at a few points had to lean his head out into the deluge and point his flashlight up at the reflective green street signs just so he could figure out where the hell he was. Finally, he came to the Lawndale Manor main entrance. The big metal gate was still down, and the guardhouse was now unoccupied. Mark knew there had to be a way to drive around to the maintenance access road where they'd come in before, but he didn't trust himself to find it in the darkness. It was purely luck he'd found this entrance.

Besides, Missy had cleared out a pretty clear path for him through the corn. Mark considered driving through the field, but he was afraid his car would get stuck in the mud, considering how much it was raining. So he decided to walk. He grabbed the shovel and the canvas bag (doing his best not to consider what was inside of it) and then set off on foot through the trampled corn.

It did not take him long to decide that walking might have been a mistake. He lost one shoe to the squelching, sucking mud about ten paces in, and lost the other one before he was hallway through. At one point, he sank in all the way to his knees and had a bad moment where he was afraid he wouldn't be able to pull his legs back out. Even without the mud, walking through the corn in the ink-black night was scary as fuck. Rain fell on the green leafy stalks with a sound like a thousand whispering demons. His feeble flashlight cast more sinister shadows than it did actual illumination. The journey through the corn had taken less than a minute in Missy's car, but his squishing slog through the dark muddy rows seemed to take hours on foot.

Finally, he emerged on the other side and for a moment sank to his knees with physical exhaustion. Then he picked himself up and continued on shoeless, up the short gravel road that led to the maintenance entrance.

He had been hoping that the gate would still be smashed open, but unfortunately, Malovo security had fastened it shut with a padlocked chain. Bastards thought of everything. Mark tossed the shovel and the bag with the monkey over the gate and rolled the flashlight underneath it. He grabbed the top of the gate, easily six feet off the ground, and very awkwardly pulled himself up until he could get one muddy, sock-clad foot over the top. For a moment, he was balanced very precariously with one testicle on either side of the metal bar. From that point, it was a matter of creative imbalance to get down on the other side. Luckily, his left ankle broke the fall.

The gate swung as he dropped from it, and Mark saw that he could have easily pushed it open far enough to just squeeze through.

Mark picked up the shovel and the flashlight then wasted several minutes looking for the black canvas bag on the dark ground. Finally he found it. Balls aching, he limped into the golf course, following the rutted tire tracks. So far, everything was going swimmingly.

He reached the end of the path, at the approximate place where Deputy Morris had tried to kill his son, where Lana had shot him dead. He set the flashlight down and began to dig. The ground, at least, was very soft, though the mud was heavier to lift out of the hole than dry dirt would have been. Still, he managed to carve out a hole about four feet deep after fifteen minutes of digging. Good enough, he supposed.

He pulled the Black Monkey from the canvas bag and tossed it into the shallow grave.

There was ceremony involved, he knew, though he couldn't remember the words that needed to be spoken. It started out "monkey treats for monkey eats" or something stupid like that. It wasn't like they were written down anywhere.

More importantly than the incantation, though, was that there was a sacrifice that needed to be made. An offering. The gray monkey had accepted candy, while the Black Monkey had demanded more adult pleasures. Liquor and tobacco. Mark had none of these things.

(*the gun*)

Something had whispered that in his head.

"You want the gun?"

(*i like guns*)

Mark pulled the weapon from his belt and considered for just a moment before tossing it into the hole beside the Monkey. Then he began shoveling wet dirt back into the hole.

The burial had not progressed very far when Mark thought he heard something behind him. A sound like running footsteps on the wet grass. He stopped shoveling for a moment to listen and, just as he decided that it was a real thing he might want to consider turning around for, Mark was tackled about the waist by a few hundred pounds of muscular fury.

Mark hit the ground face-first, swallowing what felt like a lot of grass and dirt. He managed to roll over onto his back to face whatever force had toppled him.

"Oh shit," was all he could think to say. "It's you,"

Bates grabbed him one-handed and lifted him up off the ground. By the collar bone, from the feel of it.

"Are you awake or asleep?" the sheriff demanded.

"Would it make a difference either way?"

Bates smashed his fist across Mark's jaw. Prior to that moment, Mark had believed that he'd been punched earlier in the day, when the balding guy had taken a swing at him in the car. As it turned out, though, he'd been wrong. That wasn't a punch. *This* was a punch. Never had Mark been so acutely aware of the fragility of the human skull. He went flying, literally airborne, like Popeye taking a hit from Bluto. And there no fucking spinach to be had.

He landed on his back. Bates gave him gave him a kick to the ribs that at least took his mind off the blow to his head for a second.

Bates glanced back at the half-filled hole in the ground.

"What the fuck are you doing up here, anyway?"

"Digging out gopher holes," Mark gasped. "Those things'll tear the shit out of a course. You ever see *Caddyshack*?"

"You're making jokes? You do know I'm going to kill you with my bare hands now?"

"Yup," Mark groaned. He couldn't think of anything wittier than that, what with the internal bleeding and all.

"Killing your smart ass means at least one good thing's gonna come out of this misbegotten fucking day."

"All right, all right," Mark said. His mind latched onto a desperate, hopeless, last-ditch kind of idea. "Just promise me one fuckin' thing."

"I ain't going to promise you shit."

"No. Just...please." There was no way this was going to work. "Make sure I'm dead before you throw me in that hole. Don't bury me alive. I can't think of anything worse than that."

Bates stopped, looking down at him, thinking. He wasn't going to fall for it. If anybody was an Uncle Remus fan, it would be this goddamn cracker.

After an agonizingly long second, Bates laughed out loud, with what sounded like genuine good cheer. "You stupid little fucker. I never would've thought of that."

Bates grabbed him by the hair and dragged him over to the Monkey's grave, which was exactly as painful as it sounded.

"No!" Mark screamed. "Please! I've had that nightmare my whole life!"

"Looks like your dream's comin' true, champ."

Bates gave him a kick and toppled him into the grave. To the extent that he had any control, Mark managed to land face down. He dug around beneath him, feeling for the gun in the soft earth.

Above him, Bates had picked up the shovel. A clump of dirt landed on the back of Mark's head.

Mark grabbed hold of something, but it turned out to be the Black Monkey. Touching the thing, Mark realized how useless it really was. It was devoid of any power or magic. He wondered how he could have been so stupid as to think that burying the little doll in the ground could solve anything. All it had accomplished, in fact, was probably getting him killed.

Two more shovels of dirt. Mark inhaled it into his lungs. His choking cry of fear was not in any way an act. This really would be the worst possible way to die.

His desperate fingers found something hard. With his luck, it was probably a root or a rock or something.

Another shovel of dirt. Mark was completely covered with a thin layer.

He grabbed the hard thing, pulled it out. The smooth pearl handle slipped into his palm. His finger found the trigger.

Mark rolled over and was immediately blinded by a load of dirt hitting his face. He flung it from his eyes and raised the gun up.

Bates saw the weapon and staggered back, surprised.

Mark pulled the trigger.

There was sad, dry little click.

The thing was clogged with mud or maybe it was just shitty old lady's gun that hadn't worked for years. Whatever the reason, Mark was a little overwhelmed by the unfairness. That really should have fucking worked.

He tried to squeeze the trigger again, but Bates was too quick. The sheriff swung the shovel and knocked the gun from Mark's hand. Bates raised the shovel again, ready to bring it down for a final, stunning blow.

This was it, then. He was going to die.

Then Mark saw something floating in the air above Bates's head. It was black, the size of a large night bird, and it had a flashing red light on top. The hovering thing dipped down close, making a strange little whirring noise. Mark heard two quick pops of compressed air, and the thing shot what looked like twin darts into the sheriff's neck. With wires attached.

Bates looked up with awe-struck terror at the floating thing. He clutched at the wires stuck in his neck, but before he could pull them out, there were two sparks of light and a whiff of ozone. The sheriff's body went rigid and he fell convulsing to the ground.

Mark rose from the grave. He looked up at the drone. The single red light flashing on top made him seriously question if he was dreaming. Or maybe even dead. Either seemed equally plausible. This feeling was not lessened when the hovering machine spoke to him with his mother's voice:

"Are you all right, Mark?"

"Ah..." He wasn't quite sure if there was any way to honestly answer that question.

"Can you walk?"

"I think so."

"Follow me."

Though there were very few parts of his body that did not feel permanently damaged, Mark climbed from the grave and limped after the flashing red beacon atop the drone, leaving the fallen sheriff and the Black Monkey behind.

In the eastern sky, he saw the first pink wisps of dawn.

CHAPTER 24

MARK WAS FEELING pretty good. He had a concussion, two broken ribs, a badly sprained ankle, and nasty-looking scrapes and Technicolor contusions on pretty much every part of his body. And yet, his nerves vibrated with a velvety smoothness and he possessed a detached amusement about the bizarre horror-show his life had devolved into. That may have had something to do with the injection they'd given him when he first arrived here. He didn't know what was in the shot, but he'd taken morphine both medicinally and recreationally in the past, and that stuff was fuckin' garbage compared to whatever the hell this was. Yowza. It had even given him an embarrassingly acute erection, which had made the sponge bath the male nurse had given him downright awkward.

As for where "here" was, that was kind of an open question. He had followed the drone into a rear entrance of the Malovo ethanol plant, located just to the north of the golf course. Here an orderly had been waiting for him with a wheelchair. They'd descended in an elevator for what felt like a long time. In a basement exam room, a doctor took his vitals, and gave him that wonderful injection. After that, things were kind of fuzzy up to and including the sinister sponge bath.

The room he was in now could have a private room in any expensive private hospital. Soft lighting, comfortable bed, banks of sophisticated-looking diagnostic equipment. None of which immediately came to mind when one thought of ethanol production.

Mark was sitting there, amusing himself with the tones made in his head by opening and closing his mouth while humming, when his mother stepped into the room. She was flanked by two men, a tall, smiling Asian man and a stocky older white guy in a sweater vest.

The first thing his mother said to him was, "What the hell were you doing digging holes on our golf course at four in the morning?"

Mark opened his mouth, intending to say something like. "Thanks for your concern for my well-being, Mom. I'm glad to see you alive, too. But I have about a thousand goddamn questions I want to ask you first."

Instead, though, he said: "I was burying the Black Monkey to stop the Scarecrow from destroying the town."

Mark was surprised to hear that come out of his own mouth. This stuff was like heroin, Viagra and sodium pentothal rolled into one.

His mom and her two companions exchanged amused glances at his statement. The Asian guy took a little flashlight from his shirt pocket and shined it in Mark's eyes, examining his pupils closely.

"I thought you said he was immune," he said to Mark's mom.

"He is," Mom said. "He just has a very vivid imagination. Mark, this is Dr. Cheung, one of our Directors of Research. And this is Jerry Marsden, from our legal team."

"Terry," the lawyer said.

"I'm sorry?"

"My name's Terry."

"That's fine," said Mark's mom. "Can you just..."

"Oh, sure, sure. Sorry."

Marsden pulled a slip of paper from a folder he was carrying. He set it on the tray in front of Mark and handed him a pen. "I need you to sign this, Mr. Davies."

"Okay."

Enjoying the smooth, sensual way the pen laid the ink on the paper, Mark made his signature with a few more swirls and flourishes than usual.

"This is a really nice pen," he gushed. "Can I keep it?"

"No, Mark," his mother said. She plucked the pen from his hand and gave it back to Jerry or Gary or whatever his name was. The lawyer put the paper back into his folder and the pen back into his pocket, and then he left the room.

"What did I just sign?" Mark asked, wondering now if he should have asked that first.

"Standard non-disclosure agreement," Mom said. "We're going to share some sensitive information with you, and we need assurance that it's not going to leave this room."

"Oh," Mark said. "That's okay, then."

"Understand, Mark, that we're only sharing this with you because we know you've found some things out on your own. I believe you've drawn some rather...radical conclusions from the incomplete information you've gathered. So let's start with that. What do you think you know about what's happened in Bakersfield over the past few days?"

So Mark, blessed with verbal diarrhea induced by the drug, laid it all out for his mother and Dr. Cheung. He told them how seeing James's rapid eye movements atop the tower had reminded him of the effects of Neiro. How this had led him to Shana, from whom they'd stolen the porno files. How Alice had uncovered the hidden images, which had pointed them towards the Hansard farmhouse. He told them about how the Monkey and the Snowman had become imbalanced. About psychic immune systems and dreamers choosing their own masks for the spirits intruding upon their souls.

The whole time Mark was talking, and he talked for quite a while, his mother wore a half-smile of distracted bemusement. Dr. Cheung was more expressive. He smiled and laughed through the whole thing, shaking his head with disbelief and even clapping at certain points.

"That is a *great* story," he said when Mark finally finished. "That really makes me want to read this book your mother told me you've written. You have a *very* creative imagination. Unfortunately, you're almost completely wrong about all of it."

Mark glared at the guy. Perhaps the shot he'd been given was beginning to wear off a little. He was starting to feel alarmed twinges of pain from several parts of his body, and his mood was not entirely ebullient anymore.

"So what, then?" Mark said.

"Well, for starters, your friend Shana, aka Shaner Erikson, did work for us briefly more than ten years ago. We were forced to terminate his contract—and it is correct to say 'his,' as he was identifying as male at that point—when we learned that he had stolen a proprietary formula from a company laboratory. He made a few tweaks to it, and began selling it on the street as a recreational hallucinogen. We *hate* when people do that."

"Neiro," Mark said.

"That's what he called it. We identify it as Lot 472. Not quite as sexy a name, I'll admit, but then we're research, not marketing."

"And the formula was based on something you extracted from the well in the Hansard basement, right?" Mark said.

"No." Cheung chuckled. "I can't go into the source of the formula, but I can categorically deny that it was obtained from a haunted wishing well."

"So then why did Shana have the newspaper article and the floorplans from the house hidden in those files?"

"I hesitate to even speculate about that."

"But it did start at the house. Linda Hansard was the first one to get sick."

"That is correct. And here we're moving into a 'sensitive' area." Cheung put his palms together, as if praying for a moment. He looked to Mark's mother. "I'm not sure how much you want to..."

"This isn't just an ethanol production plant," she said.

"No shit," said Mark.

"The underground portion of the facility houses Malovo's 'next-gen' research labs. Much of the most cutting edge work being done in the fields of chemistry, genetics, nanotechnology, pharmaceuticals and agriculture is happening right here. We employ some of the most brilliant scientific minds in the entire world, including Dr. Cheung here."

Cheung actually blushed a little. "Thank you, Gillian. That's really kind of you to say."

"So," Mark said, annoyed by whatever was passing between this man and his mother, "Linda Hansard."

"Yes," Cheung said. "See, we weren't anywhere near close to the human trial stage for 472. We were testing it on pigs. One of our test subject boars escaped from his pen and mated with a sow owned by Linda Hansard. Mrs. Hansard assisted in the birth of the resultant litter of piglets, and she apparently had a cut on her hand while she was doing so. At that point in the organism's life cycle, it appeared to be blood-borne and so Mrs. Hansard..."

"Wait," Mark said. "Organism? I thought you said it was a chemical."

"Ah," Cheung laughed a little. "Here's where it gets interesting. We're not sure exactly what it is. 472 behaves like a virus in many respects, but its effects are similar to those of an extremely powerful psychedelic drug. It induces completely immersive hallucinations and a total loss of inhibition. What you described as 'intruding spirits' are in fact nothing more than deeply buried unconscious urges coming to the surface. Freud would have loved this stuff."

"How can you not be sure what it is? You created this thing."

"'Discovered' may be more of an apt word than 'created.' We have learned how to reproduce the substance under laboratory conditions, but even to say that we 'produce' it would be a stretch. More like we facilitate its growth." Cheung frowned. "Or at least that's how I would have characterized things until about a week ago."

"It didn't look like it needed any help facilitating its growth once it got out," said Mark.

"Precisely. None of us were prepared for the speed with which it spread once it was introduced into a human population. It exceeded all of our projections exponentially. It *evolved*. The incubation period dropped from a few days to a matter of minutes. It started out as blood-borne, as I said, but then it seemed to become airborne when Linda Hansard passed it on to James Delany and he spread it to a few other people. *Then* the rate of transmission jumped so rapidly that we're not even sure how it spreads anymore. It might be, and believe me I am hesitant to use this word, a *psychic* transmission. A *telepathically* borne contagion."

"Now who's talking crazy?" Mark said.

"Oh, believe me, I know how that sounds. I suspect we'll be trying to figure that one out for years to come. It's remarkable. The population reached a one hundred percent infection rate in less than forty-eight hours."

"It wasn't one hundred percent," Mark said. "I didn't catch it. Neither did Missy or Ben. Or Sheriff Bates, either."

"The sheriff was inoculated. I did that myself. And you were inoculated, too."

"When?"

"I bet you can figure that one out."

Mark closed his eyes, just for a second. "When I took Neiro."

"Yes. Worked just like a vaccine."

"But Missy never tripped on Neiro. And Ben sure as hell never did."

"That's one of the most remarkable things about this substance. It causes *genetic* changes. Slight mutations. You sexually transmitted your resistance to your wife, and then your son inherited the immunity. I can't wait to examine your blood and semen samples."

"My semen..." Mark shook an image from his head that he'd previously assumed he'd imagined. That had been no ordinary sponge bath.

This was way too much at once. "Let me get this straight. You inoculated *Sheriff Bates*?"

"I thought it was necessary to have someone on the inside who could maintain order."

"He's an evil fucker!"

"In retrospect, that may have been a mistake on my part."

"One of fucking many! The entire town is destroyed because you couldn't this fucking thing in your pants!"

"Calm down, Mark," his mother chided, in a tone he had not heard from her since he was a teenager. "You're being melodramatic. The town is *not* destroyed. There has been considerable damage, but Malovo already has deals in place with every insurance agency that anyone in town has a policy with. We're going to make sure that every claim is paid in full, in a timely manner. At *our* expense."

"What good will that do if everyone in town is completely insane?"

Cheung fielded that one. "Right now, as we speak, our engineers are pumping the cure into Bakersfield's water supply."

"There's a cure? And you're just now getting around to giving it out?"

"It took us this long to produce enough to create effective levels in the reservoir and enough for the cloud seeding project," Cheung said.

"Cloud seeding?"

"Yes. We put it into the rain to distribute it to more of the population in a timely..."

"*You control the fucking weather?*"

"Dr. Cheung," Mark's mom cautioned.

"Sorry," said Cheung. "I may have said too much there."

"Jesus," said Mark. "So you used the whole town as your guinea pigs?"

"Not at all," Cheung protested. "The release was purely accidental. However, once it was out, we would be remiss if we didn't study the effects. We have collected more relevant data in the past two days than we have in more than ten years of working with this thing."

"With your goddamn drones, right?"

"Unmanned surveillance aircraft have been very effective in collecting observational data," Cheung said, sounding a bit defensive now. "And considering that one of those goddamn drones saved your life, I'd be a bit more tolerant of their presence if I were you."

"So what is this thing, really? A biological weapon?"

"I won't deny that's one potential application," Cheung said. "A non-lethal substance capable of subduing the population of an entire town in that short of a time frame? That's invaluable from a military standout. But that's just the tip of the iceberg. In its advanced stages, we saw this substance stimulate verifiable telepathic synchronization!"

"Dr. Cheung," Mark's mom warned.

"Sorry," he said again.

Mark looked at his mother. "Ben was abducted because of this thing. He was nearly killed. Jennifer Delany *was* killed, as was Deputy Morris, and who knows how many other people. *I* was almost killed."

"You don't know how much anguish that causes me, Mark."

"Yeah, well, there's a lot of things *you* don't know. You're talking about opening people's minds up to telepathic whatever, *here*? In *this* town? I'm not making this shit up. I've *seen* the things that live beneath this town. I've been *touched* by them. And you, collecting your goddamn observational data, woke the fucking things up!"

"Mark." Gillian Hudson now spoke with a cold, hard impatience. Mark had the sense that he had provoked her into saying something she had not been prepared to divulge. "Do you think it's an accident that Malovo chose to build this facility here, in Bakersfield?"

He looked curiously up at his mother.

"These things that you've experienced," she said. "The Monkey, the Snowman. Those are childish names, but they are very real. Malovo has been interested in them ever since you and your friend Jess uncovered them twenty years ago."

"You knew?"

"Of course. Malovo has made a tremendous investment in Bakersfield. We want to study these phenomena, with the goal of harnessing and controlling them."

"What?" Mark gasped. This was insanity. "They're evil spirits."

"No," Cheung put in. "That's a regressive, superstitious term applied simply because people don't understand these forces. We prefer to think of them as potential energy sources."

"*Energy sources?* You're crazy!"

Cheung chuckled. "No. Quite sane, thank you. See, Mark, what people refer to as 'supernatural' is really just a part of nature that's not understood yet. Malovo wants to pioneer this field, just as we've done with genetics and nanotechnology. And we'd like you to help us."

"Help?" Mark saw a look pass between Cheung and his mother that he could not decipher.

"We understand that you have no scientific background," Cheung said. "No real education to speak of, in fact. But you have come into contact with these energy sources twice now, and seem to have an intuitive understanding of them. We could use someone like you in the field. A guide, as it were."

"You want me to work for *Malovo?*"

"I'm sure you'd find it more profitable and rewarding than the restaurant or retail work you'd otherwise be qualified for."

Mark's jaw dropped. He was almost too outraged to speak.

"I called these things evil, but all they do is possess and murder people. You're trying to *monetize* that. That's *fucking* evil. You want me to work for you? I'd rather starve!"

"I can see you're upset, Mark," his mother said, patting his leg under the blanket as she might have done when he was just a child. "We'll leave you alone now. Dr. Edward will come back in a few minutes to have another look at you, then we'll see about getting you home."

Mark could only shake his head in utter disbelief. All the pain and horror of the past two days, of the past *twenty years*, came over him all at once. He turned his back on his mother and her lunatic friend, burying his face in the thin hospital pillow.

Home? he thought. *What the fuck does that even mean?*

FRIDAY

CHAPTER 25

THIRTY-FIVE PEOPLE LOST their lives in the incident that would forever be referred to, when the people of Bakersfield deigned to mention it at all, as "the Sickness." Thirty-five deaths, hundreds of injuries, and property damage that easily ranged in the millions of dollars.

In that first week after the Sickness, the survivors regarded one another with the bleary mistrust of blackout drunks who had awoken in the same bed together via circumstances neither could quite recall. People's memories of the weekend were fragmented and the bits they could recall were either so disjointed as to be nonsensical or too disturbing to credit. It was generally agreed, by unspoken collective consent, not to closely examine one's own actions, or those of one's neighbors, during the forty-eight hours or so the Sickness had held sway over the town. It was better not to know.

This was an informal agreement, but it applied in a legal sense as well. No criminal investigations were pursued for crimes committed by citizens while under the influence of the Sickness. A blanket defense of temporary insanity covered all incidents of violence, sexual assault, and property damage perpetrated during the period in question. Insurance adjusters likewise paid out all claims made, with an uncharacteristic lack of inquiry. Unburdened of all liability or recollection, the townsfolk set about the business of burying their dead and rebuilding their town. For that week, the smell of sawdust surpassed that of mown grass as the signature scent of early summer.

The Malovo ethanol plant shut down production for the entire week, granting its employees full pay. The elementary, middle, and high schools cancelled the last week of classes. Graduation was postponed in favor of the more somber ceremonies of public memorial services and private funerals.

The village's official memorial was held on Wednesday night, on the freshly re-sodded town square. It was a multi-faith event, with addresses made by local government and business leaders, as well as representatives from all eight of the town's churches. These included stirring speeches by Father Bentley of St. Joseph's Catholic Church, just released from the hospital for injuries sustained diving down Bill Potter's chimney, and Tom Peters, the newly appointed pastor of the Church of the Shepherd. Pastor Peters also led his band, The Young Lions, in a newly written song called "Wild Faith," dedicated to the late Pastor Barry Tuttle. The heartfelt performance left hardly a dry eye on the square.

Conspicuously absent during this service were Logan County Sheriff Nathanial Bates and Bakersfield Mayor Buck Sager. The whereabouts of both men were unknown.

The service celebrating the life of Jennifer Delany was a much more modest private affair. There was a closed-casket wake at Newman's Funeral Home, which Mark remembered as the sight of many similar services twenty years before. In that same building, he'd personally attended the memorials for his good friends Toby and Jess, as well as both Jess's sister and his brother. Both funeral homes in town were booked solid for the entire week. The only open slot for Jen's viewing was early on Friday morning, and the mourners had to clear out by ten for Joe Carter's service, which would have made for something of an awkward overlap.

The wake was followed by a brief graveside service and burial, and then friends and family convened at the deceased's sister's house for an informal gathering.

Mark, to make himself useful, stationed himself by the front door, to greet visitors as they arrived and to thank them for coming. Most were far-flung relatives from both sides of Jen and Missy's family tree, some of them so old and out-of-touch that they weren't aware that Mark and Missy weren't married anymore. He didn't have the heart to break the news at this late juncture.

It wasn't until Bill Potter arrived, that Mark saw anybody he actually wanted to talk to. Mark's former teacher walked up the drive, something small and black cradled in his arm.

"Bill," Mark said, greeting him with a smile and a firm handshake. He hadn't seen him much since their time together up at the farmhouse.

Bill seemed to be avoiding most of the public and private functions. "How are you?"

"Mr. Davies, I am doing better than I have in years."

Mark finally noticed what it was that Bill held tight against his body. A squirming black lab puppy.

"Who's this?" he said.

"This is Ramone. He's my handy excuse for not staying too long."

"Why didn't I think of that?" Mark petted the little ball of fuzz. The pup went crazy with delight at the contact and thanked Mark with a little needle-toothed nip to his finger.

"I just dropped by to pay my respects, and to see how you're doing."

"Me? I'm good. Still kind of sore, especially the ribs, but definitely on the mend."

"I didn't necessarily mean physically."

"Oh," Mark laughed a little. "That. I guess you could say I'm on the mend that way, too."

"Nightmares?"

"Yeah." There was no need to elaborate. "You want to come inside, Bill? Have a drink?"

"Drink," Bill said. "God, yes."

A few minutes later, after Bill had expressed his sincere condolences to Missy and to her parents, he and Mark sat on the couch, glasses of whiskey in hand. Ben had shyly asked Bill if he could take the puppy outside to play, and had tried to suppress his smile at the obvious joy holding the little dog brought him. Ben felt guilty at having fun on such a somber occasion. That saddened Mark a little. His son felt things more deeply than he ever had. Grief and joy, both.

"So I went on a date last night," Bill said, sipping his drink. "With a lovely lady."

"Really? Good for you. Anybody I know?"

"Yeah. Mara."

"Oh." Mark took a big gulp himself.

"Don't worry. It wasn't like that. We're just...re-connecting. Becoming friends again."

"Has she heard from her husband?"

"Nope," Bill seemed very pleased to report. "She hasn't talked to him at all since. She has no clue where he is or when or if he's coming back."

"I hope wherever he is, he's suffering tremendously."

"I'll drink to that."

They clinked glasses and each drained their whiskey.

"Well," Bill said, standing up. "I'm going to retrieve my dog and get out of your hair."

"You don't have to go, Bill. I could stand the company."

"I know, but I have some work to do."

"What kind of work?"

"I didn't tell you? I've started a novel. The as-yet-untitled follow-up to *Graveyard Grove*. Long awaited by no one, but overdue all the same."

"That's great, Bill. I can't wait to read it."

"You need to get back into it too, Mark. You and I have been cursed with a rare gift."

"I don't even know if I can do that anymore," Mark said. "It's been so long."

Bill dismissed that with a scoff. "That's like saying you forgot how to be right handed," he said. "That's not just something you do. It's who you are. Anyway, I'm heading out. Don't be a stranger. I'll say it again. I'm glad you're home, Mark. And I'm not the only one."

They shook hands again and Bill left out the back door. Mark went back inside and fixed himself another drink. A tall one.

Alice and Sam staggered back inside through the sliding glass door, hurriedly putting their post-funeral faces back on. The dispensary was carrying freezer items now and Alice had picked up a box of Jen & Barry's brand Nice Dream sandwiches, mint chocolate cookie flavor. She and Sam had just had eaten one each in the back yard behind Lana and Missy's tool shed. The shit was creamy brilliance, but took a while to kick in, so they'd taken a couple puffs from Sam's one-hitter to tide them over.

They were both fuckin' lit.

Alice felt good. Better than she had in months. Maybe the sleep sickness had shoved the cancer aside for the moment. Or maybe, because she'd already dreamed her death, it didn't really have a hold on her anymore. Either way, the pain and the nausea both had eased back for the time being. She could enjoy just being truly and righteously stoned for the sheer hell of it.

Of course, she wouldn't live to see Christmas, but fuck it. She'd worry about that later.

Sam was right there with her. Before the wake and the graveside service today, she hadn't really seen the big guy since the long day of the quarantine. It didn't seem appropriate to invite a huge biker dude over to her house with her dad acting all super-protective to make up for abandoning her during the craziest weekend in Bloody Bakersfield history. It was good to see Sam again, though. There was nobody in the world she'd rather share pot-laced ice cream sandwiches with.

"Dude, they've got a cheese platter," Sam exclaimed with wonder as they passed through the kitchen.

He made a complete circle of the food table, piling a plate high with cheese and fruit and veggies, rolled up meats and a variety of dips. Sam and Alice staked out a corner of the living room and blissfully tore into these goodies with pure munchy delight. It felt so good to be ravenous, Alice thought, when so often she couldn't even bring herself to eat. She dipped a grape into the cream cheese sauce and it burst in her mouth with sweet juicy flavor. The pleasure this provoked was damn near sexual.

That was another consequence of her new lease on life, or whatever it was. An almost constant sensual awareness. She'd learned how to do some fun things with her own body, but her bucket list at this point was mainly composed of things she'd like to try with someone else's. And just recently, her generally indiscriminate curiosity had gained a new focus.

She'd seen James Delany around school before, but she'd never really noticed him. She sure as hell noticed him now. She liked how his hair was so blond it was almost white, and how his eyes were so blue they were almost clear, and how he was always impeccably groomed. There was a softness about him that appealed to her greatly, too, a shyness and a quietness. He seemed like the type who would let her take charge and she liked that. She could not envision a relationship with someone who thought they could tell her what to do.

Of course, he knew sadness as well. A boy who had fallen asleep and had awoken two days later to find his mother dead. That alone set him apart from most of the boys at her school, who had no inkling of the real meaning of life and death. Not the way Alice did.

"Sam," she said. "What would you say is the socially appropriate length of time to wait after someone loses a parent before you can start seriously hitting on them?"

Sam, about to toss a cheese cube in his mouth, paused and gave her a look. Then, following her intent gaze, he glanced across the room. "James?"

"Let's just say I'm paying him some attention."

"Dude, that's awesome." Sam barked laughter. "He's a good kid, man. You guys would be so great."

James looked up at the inappropriate sound and Alice had to look away.

"Shh," she said. "Keep it down."

"Sorry," Sam whispered. "I'm going to make this happen for you, seriously."

"I don't really need any help."

"No, trust me. I'm good at this," he said. "They used to call me Captain Wingman."

"I thought you were Captain Chill."

"I'm a Captain of many..." This was lost in laughter. "Oh, shit. I think your ice cream's starting to kick in."

She looked back over at James, who was staring straight ahead, lost in his own troubles. She wondered how much of her interest in him had to with the fact that he was Mark, Lana, and Michelle's nephew. Ben's cousin. Did she want to date him just so she could stay part of this family? She'd never really had an extended family of her own. It had just been her and Dad for so long, and with Dad the way he was, too often that meant it was just her by herself.

Last weekend had been horrifying and terrible in so many ways, but through the nightmare Alice had truly connected with some people she really liked. That was hard for her to do when times were normal. Was she just afraid of losing that? Would that be fair to James, to hook up with him solely based on who he was related to?

As a test, she imagined herself kissing him. She imagined it very clearly, and the swoony fluttering feeling this provoked was enough to convince her that she wanted this boy because she wanted him. That was good enough for her.

"I'd like to have just one nice, bittersweet John Green romance," she said. "My last hurrah before I shuffle off this mortal coil."

Sam's face fell. "Don't say that."

"Why not?"

"I don't like to hear about you shuffling off anything."

"It's going to happen, Sam. Sooner rather than later. I'm a gone girl. And I know it's not fair. I've got the easy part. All I have to do is die. You have to live the rest of your life in Bakersfield, Illinois."

The house was full of people. Mourners and consolers, family and friends. One and all offering love and support and healing prayers. Still, Lana longed to have their house back to themselves. She knew the real healing would begin tomorrow, when everyone was gone.

She lost track of Chelle for a while in the crowd. Lana finally saw her wife emerge from the bathroom, looking a bit wobbly in her black funeral dress and heels. With this one glance, she knew that Chelle had snuck a tall glass of white wine into the bathroom, where she could guzzle it down free from the disapproving gaze of her parents.

Lana met Chelle in the hallway and kissed her, deeply, just to taste the wine on her breath. It was more intoxicating for her in this way than drinking it herself. Michelle pulled her close for a second, into the hungry curvature of her body.

"God, I wish all these people weren't in our house," she said.

"How drunk are you right now?" Lana asked.

"Not nearly fucking drunk enough," Chelle said, and then laughed at how slurry her words came out.

Her laughter was loud in the somber quiet of the house, and she covered her mouth to stifle it. In that moment, she looked very young. Like a teenager. This always seemed to happen whenever Michelle spent more than a couple of hours under the same roof as her mom and dad.

For the first time since she had known them, Lana felt a measure of warmth towards her in-laws. Mitch and Lois Delany had attempted to raise their two daughters with the same stolid Midwestern conservatism that ruled their own upbringing. But then Jen had become pregnant while still in high school, and had brazenly raised her son without the benefit of a father. Not to be outdone, Michelle had turned out to be a bisexual divorcee who remarried a black woman. Mitch and Lois had always seemed to feel it was important to express their disappointment and sense of personal failure at the unfathomable lifestyle choices of their daughters. But on this visit, their typical passive aggressive disapproval had been gravely tempered by their grief. They just seemed sad and weary and very old.

"A mother should never have to bury her daughter," Lois had said to Lana at the graveside service, and the comment had contained none of the implied recrimination that she usually wielded so skillfully. She'd even accepted Lana's sympathetic embrace without her typical stiffening flinch.

Still, their very presence brought out a streak of the rebellious teen Michelle must have been. Sneaking drinks of wine in the bathroom as she probably did when she was sixteen. Lana had to be grateful for this. She found it almost unbearably sexy.

Their nights together had been long and strange. Sleep was shallow for both of them, plagued with vivid nightmares of being back on the golf course, arriving too late this time to save Ben. Or of being on the side of the road, where Jen was shot. Or of being back in that terrible house. In the basement, with the worms. It was worse, perhaps, for Lana, because she recalled the creeping confusion of the sleepwalking sickness, of dreams and reality bleeding together so fully there had been no line between the two. Almost a week had passed since she had taken the cure, and she still had moments of doubt. Dreaming, she wasn't sure she wasn't really awake, and waking, she wasn't sure she wasn't living a dream. Lana wondered if she would ever again fully trust herself to know the difference.

There was this, though: Lana and Michelle slept naked and entwined, and upon waking from shuddering terror, each found succor in the other's body. Terrible nightmares bled into sweet, fervent, half-conscious lovemaking. Gradually, they had begun to dream of the lovemaking, too. These sweet dreams were slowly beginning to supplant the bad ones. In this way, they would heal.

And then, last night, something new. Lana had forgotten the dream in all the funeral preparations, but it came back to her now, vividly. She couldn't believe now that she'd forgotten.

"Did I tell you about the dream I had last night?" Lana asked.

"I don't think so."

"It's funny, I remember telling you about it, but I think that was a dream, too. I had the dream, and then I had another dream where I woke up and told you about the first one."

"Was it a nightmare?"

"No," said Lana. "It was...the most beautiful dream I've ever had in my life." Tears came to her eyes as she recalled it.

"What was it?"

"You and I were standing together on a hill, looking down on a house in the country. Our house. It was around here, close by. And it must have just finished raining, because there was a rainbow in the sky. Really vivid and bright and..."

"Wait," Michelle laughed. "Shut up."

"What?"

"That was *my* dream," Chelle said. "I had that dream. I woke up and told *you* about it."

"No." Lana laughed, though the tears were coursing down her cheeks now. "I remember it so clearly."

"Oh yeah?" Chelle challenged. She was crying now, too. "What about the other part, then? The important part?"

"The important part," Lana said. "Was that Ben was there, too. And he was..." Lana couldn't stop the tears. It was like a floodgate had opened.

"He was playing with a little girl," said Chelle. "The most beautiful little girl."

"His baby sister," Lana nodded. "He was picking her up and spinning her around and she was laughing. The sweetest little baby laugh."

"She had brown skin. She was your daughter."

"*Our* daughter."

"Yes," Chelle said. "Our daughter. Yours and mine."

They kissed again, the taste of both of their tears mingling on each other's lips.

"We've talked about it before," Michelle said. She touched Lana lightly, just below the navel, in the place where this dream would become real. "Maybe this means it's time."

"It's definitely time."

"We can..." Chelle was sobbing now. "Please say we can name her Jennifer. Okay?"

"What the hell else would we name her?" Lana said. "Duh."

Chelle laughed again. She sniffed and wiped her eyes.

"Go get me some wine," Lana said. "I want to get at least half as drunk as you are. Then we can talk about where we're going to score some sperm."

Mark walked out of the kitchen, carrying his plate of food. He saw James sitting by himself on the couch, staring at the television screen though the set was turned off. He went to his nephew and sat down beside him.

James looked over at him. "Oh, hey, Uncle Mark."

"Hi, James." Mark set his plate down on the coffee table. "I know this is a stupid question, but how are you doing?"

"Well, terrible, of course. But, I'm okay, really. I'm just thinking. Actually, I wanted to talk to you about something. Something important."

"What is it?"

"I was wondering..." James gulped and nodded, misting up a little. "Okay, I don't turn eighteen until September, so I can't live on my own yet. I need a guardian, just for a few months. I was wondering...if that could maybe be you."

Mark was a little surprised. He hadn't been expecting that. "I thought you were going to stay with your grandparents."

"They want me to, but I only have one more year of high school left and I don't want to have to start over at some new school in Florida." He gave a little laugh. "Actually, I don't want to go to Florida at all. But it's more than that. It's..."

"What, James?"

"I want to tell you something, okay? And this is something I've never told anybody. Not even Mom. I wanted to tell her. I wanted to tell her for a long time, but it just never seemed right. And now I'll never get to…"

James broke down a little. Mark put his arm around the boy's shoulders and held him close for a few moments.

James pulled away, sniffling. "I'm gay."

Mark nodded. "Yeah."

"You don't seem surprised."

"It doesn't come as a *great* shock," Mark said. "I've always kind of wondered."

"Always?"

"Yeah."

"How did you know? It took me forever to figure that out."

"I don't know, James. It's not like it's something to be ashamed of."

"I know that." James nodded. "So it's not a big deal for you?"

"Of course not."

"See, that's why I want to stay with you instead of with Grandma and Grandpa. Because it *would* be a big deal for them."

"Give your grandparents some credit. They've come a long way. It was *apocalyptic* for them when your Aunt Michelle came out. She broke the ice for you there, big time. They've come to accept it. They've actually invited Lana to Thanksgiving for a few years in a row now."

"I know," James said. "I can tell you exactly what it's going to be like. They'll buy books about how to cope when your loved one's gay. They'll join a support group at their church for parents of gay children. They'll love me and support me and accept me, but it will be a *massive* deal for them. I don't want it to be a massive deal. I want it to be normal. With you, it'd be normal. And not in Florida."

"James," Mark said. "I'm…"

"I know, it's too much to ask. A huge responsibility to lay on you. Just forget I even…"

"James," Mark said again. "Listen. I am so…flattered that you would choose me for this…*honor*. I mean it." Mark felt himself misting up, too. "But since Sam's grandma got out of the hospital and moved back into her place, I'm basically homeless and unemployed. I'm staying in Missy and

Lana's guest bedroom, which is...let's just say it's not ideal. Right now, I couldn't provide any kind of home for you."

James brightened a little. "I was thinking about that, actually. Mom left me everything in her will, including our house. If you lived with me there, I wouldn't have to move. And she had life insurance and some savings, so there's a little bit of money. You wouldn't even have to work. Maybe you..." A thought seemed to hit him. "Maybe you could start writing again."

Mark smiled. Everybody seemed to think that was a good idea except him.

"I couldn't let you support me," he said. "I'll get a job."

"But you'll move into the house? Be my guardian?"

Mark saw Ben walking out of the kitchen, carrying some food.

"Ben, come over here. I want to ask you something."

"What is it, Dad?" He sat down beside Mark and James.

"How would you feel if I moved into James's house with him, so on our half of the week, you'd stay there with us too?"

Ben's eyes went wide. "James wouldn't have to move to Florida?" His face lit up. "You would take care of him?"

"Well, it's an open question of who's taking care of who, but basically, yes."

"That is so awesome. You have to do it, Dad."

"I guess it's decided, then."

"Wow," Ben said to James. "So we'd be like brothers?"

James smiled through his tears. "We are brothers, Ben."

There was kind of an awkward moment then, the emotions of all three of them right there on the surface, with no words that could really be said. Ben set his plate down on the table and walked across the room, over to the broken front window. Plastic sheeting had been taped over the gap for the time being, but Ben gazed out for a few long moments, as if it was clear glass.

"They're still out there, you know," he said.

"Who's still out there?" Mark asked.

"The spirits," said Ben. "The good ones and the bad ones. The sickness let them come out in the open, but now they're...underground, or underwater or under...something." Ben shook his head, words failing him.

"They liked being out, though. It made them stronger. And they want to come out again. They're not going to go back to sleep."

"Does that scare you, Ben?" Mark asked.

"Yes," he said. He turned and looked his father right in the eye. "We can never leave Bakersfield, can we?"

Mark sighed. "I don't know, Ben. I tried leaving once. You see how that worked out."

"It's because it's our responsibility, right? We see what this town really is, when other people can't. That means we have to stay here and stand up against the things that live underneath it. Nobody else is going to do that. It has to be us."

"You might be right, Benny," Mark said. "But I want you to let me worry about that. Me and your mom and Lana and the other adults. I want you to just be a kid."

Ben shook his head. "You can't just be a kid in this town. Not for very long."

Ben spoke with a maturity that no ten-year-old living in a just world should ever have to bear. Mark felt a crushing sadness. He had always sworn to protect his son from all the things, worldly and otherworldly, that had destroyed his own childhood. In this he had failed, utterly.

"We're not all alone," Ben said. "There are other people who will help us. Sam and Alice and Mr. Potter. Maybe a few others from town. But mostly it's us. Our family."

Ben looked right at James. "I'm so happy you'll be staying here, James," he said. "But I'm scared for you, too. Because we're going to need all the help we can get."

The room was empty, and vast. The walls rose up farther than Nate could see, as if he was at the bottom of an enormous underground silo. Pale white sunlight filtered into the space from an unseen skylight far overhead.

The very impossibility of the place reassured him. He doubted that they (not that he could recall precisely who *they* were) had constructed such a massive prison in which to hold him, a solitary prisoner.

Hallucination, he thought. *Something they put in my head. Or maybe one of those, whattaya call it, virtual reality deals.*

He reached his hands up to touch his face, to see if he was wearing any of that fancy headgear over his eyes. Strange thing, though. He could see his hands before his eyes, but when he touched himself, he could feel neither his face under his fingers, nor his hands upon his face. Like he had ghost arms. This was confusing and alarming at first, but he figured it out.

They got me in a straitjacket, but I can't see it. My arms are just pinned down at my side.

He was proud of himself for seeing through the deception. Testing out another theory, he slammed his head back against the wall. The silo walls he saw were metallic, but instead of a cold, hard, hollow echo, he felt and heard only a soft thud against the back of his skull.

Yep. Padded room.

They had him in some psych ward somewhere. Either dosed up on hallucinogens or wired into 3-D computer goggles. Maybe even both. Trying to fuck with him. He couldn't trust anything he saw or heard, only what he could feel. He still had his wits about him, though. They couldn't take that away.

You motherfuckers are going to have to try harder than that to get to me.

He tried to speak those words instead of just thinking them, but it seemed that he had no mouth with which to do so. That threw him off for a second, but he recovered quickly. That was just part of the same mind rape they were trying to lay on him. He wasn't having it, though. Let them do their worst. He wasn't fooled by their cheap tricks.

He didn't know how he'd come to be there, though. It was like a dream. He couldn't remember falling asleep, or how long he had been in this place. He tried, but could not recall the chain of events that had led to his captivity. Even trying to narrow down the last thing he could remember was a headache-inducing trial. It was all jumbled and blurry, his memories just shards and fragments. But he couldn't put these strange, disturbing images into any kind of chronological order. Couldn't, in fact, be sure how much of them had really happened.

Then, in a flash of lucid clarity, he remembered Mark Davies. That little punk-ass had pulled a gun on him like he thought he was in some kind of movie western. Nate had been about to bury the motherfucker alive, but the guy must have sucker-punched him somehow. Maybe he'd just distracted Nate so his dyke bitch wife could sneak up behind. Nate remembered *something* hitting him. Then he'd gone down and everything went black and he'd ended up here.

So this was Mark Davie's fault. That made sense. Little pussy probably went crying to his mommy. Those Malovo fuckers could rig up a deal like this, easy. Nate was probably in a laboratory somewhere, with wires attached to his head and cameras watching him. White-coated doctors were at this moment observing him on a monitor, taking smug little notes on their clipboards. These were cold motherfuckers. They'd note the time and intensity of every brain-wave fluctuation or spike in his pulse rate. They'd probably make notations every time he farted. Marking time until they broke him, and then they'd write that down, too. "Subject suffered complete breakdown after nine hours, twenty minutes of artificial stimuli."

Yeah, well, that wasn't going to happen.

Back when Nate was a guard at Stateville, inmates who violated the rules were routinely sent to the Segregated Housing Unit. It was the only thing that scared them. A couple days in the SHU was enough to make the hardest, coldest gangbangers buggy, but Nate had seen men sent to the seg for weeks and even months. They'd emerge from their confinement hollowed out and broken for days after re-entering gen pop. Some never recovered. More than a few attempted, and even succeeded at, offing themselves in their cells. In fact, in the ten years he worked at the prison, Nate had only seen one man who was made harder and sharper by his time in solitary.

Jordan Nickels, the guy who sold the drugs Nate smuggled into the prison, once did a thirty-day stint in the hole. Another prisoner had made an anonymous report to one of Nate's fellow guards that he'd witnessed Jordan having sex with his cellmate. It was bullshit, just an attempt to get Jordan out of the way so this other prisoner could attempt to take over the narcotics operation. But the administrators were taking a hard line on prisoner sexual relations at that point, and both Jordan and his cellmate were sent up. There was an extra level of humiliation involved, too, as the "witness" reported that Jordan was the punk in the encounter, the one taking it in the ass.

Two days after Jordan got out, the supposedly anonymous snitch was found face down in a shit-filled toilet, his throat slashed from ear-to-ear. Jordan retook his position as the inside man with hardly a hitch. The only outward sign that he'd been in the SHU was that he'd dropped a few pounds and looked even leaner and tougher than he had before he went in.

Nate asked him about it later, how he'd managed to hold it together when so many others, just as bad-ass as him, went apeshit in there.

"Hate, man," was Jordan's reply. "Hate pulled me through."

He knew who'd set him up, and had spent every waking minute of every day he was in the hole planning his revenge to the smallest detail, rehearsing it over and over in his mind.

"It got to where that was all I even dreamed about," Jordan said. "Then it got to where I'd dreamed about it so many times I couldn't even be sure if I'd done it yet or not. So when I got out and it came time to cut that fucker for real, it was nothing to me anymore. It didn't even feel like killing because to my mind, motherfucker was already dead."

Like Jordan Nickels, Nate now had a focus for his hatred.

Mark Davies. When Nate got out of this place, that smug little asshole would pay. No matter how they tried to fuck Nate's mind, the hatred for Mark Davies he kept kindled in his heart would pull him through and keep him company in his isolation. As long as he kept his hate alive, he would remain unbroken and sane.

Nate saw something out of the corner of his eye and turned to look. For a second, his newfound resolve nearly faltered. Because something had been added to his lonely cell.

A shelf that had not been there a moment before now stood just a few feet from where Nate sat on the floor. It was lined with those fucking porcelain dolls from Suzy Barber's house, with their dead glassy eyes and vapid grinning faces all turned to face him. Jesus. How did they know? He hated those things more than anything in the world.

Except Mark Davies.

Yes. Hold on to that.

Closest to him was an antique Shirley Temple doll in a pretty blue dress. Her cheeks were scorched and melted, most of her curly hair singed away. One eye was a shattered, empty orb. The doll tilted her head at him in a piteous wordless appeal, like a deformed baby too hideous for a mother's love.

Hate Mark Davies.

Nate turned away from the Shirley Temple doll, but someone had set up a whole new shelf of them on his other side. These were even worse. A finely sculpted redheaded child with delicate features and the haunted eyes of a holocaust survivor. A buck-toothed boy doll with half his skull missing. A chubby China girl with a caved-in forehead like somebody had bashed her skull with a hammer. Nate knew, somehow he *knew*, that the souls of dead children were trapped in these dolls. They were victims of abuse and neglect and molestation, murdered or driven to childhood suicide and damned to possess these broken doll bodies forever. The dead children were deserving of pity, but inspired in him only horror and dread.

All your fault, Mark Davies.

Then the dolls, all of them, turned their heads as one to face Nate. Their mouths moved, their cracked and painted lips forming perfect little circles. A sound emerged. A shrill, off-key warble; a hellish whistling choir in imperfect unison, echoing about the circular walls.

The dolls were whistling the theme from *the Andy Griffith Show*.

That almost sent Nate over the edge. His skull throbbed with a scream that could not emerge from his throat because he had no mouth to release it. For a moment, he teetered on sanity's high cliff, ready to dash himself on the rocks far below if only it would end the torture. That song. That fucking tune. That goddamn fishing hole.

Nate almost lost it, but he pulled himself together. He clung to one consoling thought as the whistling swirled around him.

When I get out of here, Mark Davies is going to die.

About the Author

CHRISTIAN H. SMITH is a novelist and screenwriter living in the dark, corn-fed heart of the Midwest. *Bloody Bloody Bakersfield* is the sequel to his first novel, *The Black Monkey*. Book Three in the "Bloody Bakersfield" series, *New Salem*, is coming soon from Permuted Press. He is also co-writer of the upcoming feature-length horror film, *Witch Child*. http://witchchildmovie.com/

KING ARTHUR AND THE KNIGHTS OF THE ROUND TABLE HAVE BEEN REBORN TO SAVE THE WORLD FROM THE CLUTCHES OF MORGANA WHILE SHE PROPELS OUR MODERN WORLD INTO THE MIDDLE AGES.

EAN 9781618685018 $15.99   **EAN** 9781682611562 $15.99

Morgana's first attack came in a red fog that wiped out all modern technology. The entire planet was pushed back into the middle ages. The world descended into chaos.

But hope is not yet lost— King Arthur, Merlin, and the Knights of the Round Table have been reborn.

PERMUTED
PRESS

THE ULTIMATE PREPPER'S ADVENTURE.
THE JOURNEY BEGINS HERE!

EAN 9781682611654 $9.99   **EAN** 9781618687371 $9.99   **EAN** 9781618687395 $9.99

The long-predicted Coronal Mass Ejection
has finally hit the Earth, virtually destroying
civilization. Nathan Owens has been prepping
for a disaster like this for years, but now he's
a thousand miles away from his family and
his refuge. He'll have to employ all his hard-won
survivalist skills to save his current community,
before he begins his long journey through
doomsday to get back home.

PERMUTED
PRESS

THE MORNINGSTAR STRAIN HAS BEEN LET LOOSE—IS THERE ANY WAY TO STOP IT?

An industrial accident unleashes some of the Morningstar Strain. The

EAN 9781618686497 $16.00

doctor who discovered the strain and her assistant will have to fight their way through Sprinters and Shamblers to save themselves, the vaccine, and the base. Then they discover that it wasn't an accident at all—somebody inside the facility did it on purpose. The war with the RSA and the infected is far from over.

This is the fourth book in Z.A. Recht's The Morningstar Strain series, written by Brad Munson.

PERMUTED PRESS

GATHERED TOGETHER AT LAST, THREE TALES OF FANTASY CENTERING AROUND THE MYSTERIOUS CITY OF SHADOWS…ALSO KNOWN AS CHICAGO.

From *The New York Times* and *USA Today* bestselling author Richard A. Knaak comes three tales from Chicago, the City of Shadows. Enter the world of the Grey–the creatures that live at the edge of our imagination and seek to be real. Follow the quest of a wizard seeking escape from the centuries-long haunting of a gargoyle. Behold the coming of the end of the world as the Dutchman arrives.

Enter the City of Shadows.

PERMUTED
PRESS

WE CAN'T GUARANTEE THIS GUIDE WILL SAVE YOUR LIFE. BUT WE CAN GUARANTEE IT WILL KEEP YOU SMILING WHILE THE LIVING DEAD ARE CHOWING DOWN ON YOU.

EAN 9781618686695 $9.99

This is the only tool you need to survive the zombie apocalypse.

OK, that's not really true. But when the SHTF, you're going to want a survival guide that's not just geared toward day-to-day survival. You'll need one that addresses the essential skills for true nourishment of the human spirit. Living through the end of the world isn't worth a damn unless you can enjoy yourself in any way you want. (Except, of course, for anything having to do with abuse. We could never condone such things. At least the publisher's lawyers say we can't.)

www.ingramcontent.com/pod-product-compliance
Lightning Source LLC
Chambersburg PA
CBHW051230260626
47162CB00002B/349